SCENES FROM A LIFE

Scenes From A Life

Richard Abbott

ISBN: 978-0-9545535-9-3 (softcover)
ISBN: 978-0-9545535-7-9 (kindle format)
ISBN: 978-0-9545535-8-6 (epub format)

Matteh Publications

Contact:
Web: http://mattehpublications.datascenesdev.com/
Email: matteh@datascenesdev.com

For Roselyn, for family

Contents

Cover information

Cover artwork © Copyright Ian Grainger
    http://www.iangrainger.co.uk

Original Matteh Publications logo drawn by Jackie Morgan.

Original photographs taken in Egypt and Israel by the author.

Hieroglyphic texts produced by the author.
Front cover reads:
    Makty-Rasut, true of voice
    and his beloved Milashuniyet, true of voice.
Back cover reads:
    She is fairer than flowers,
    more lovely than birds.

MAPS

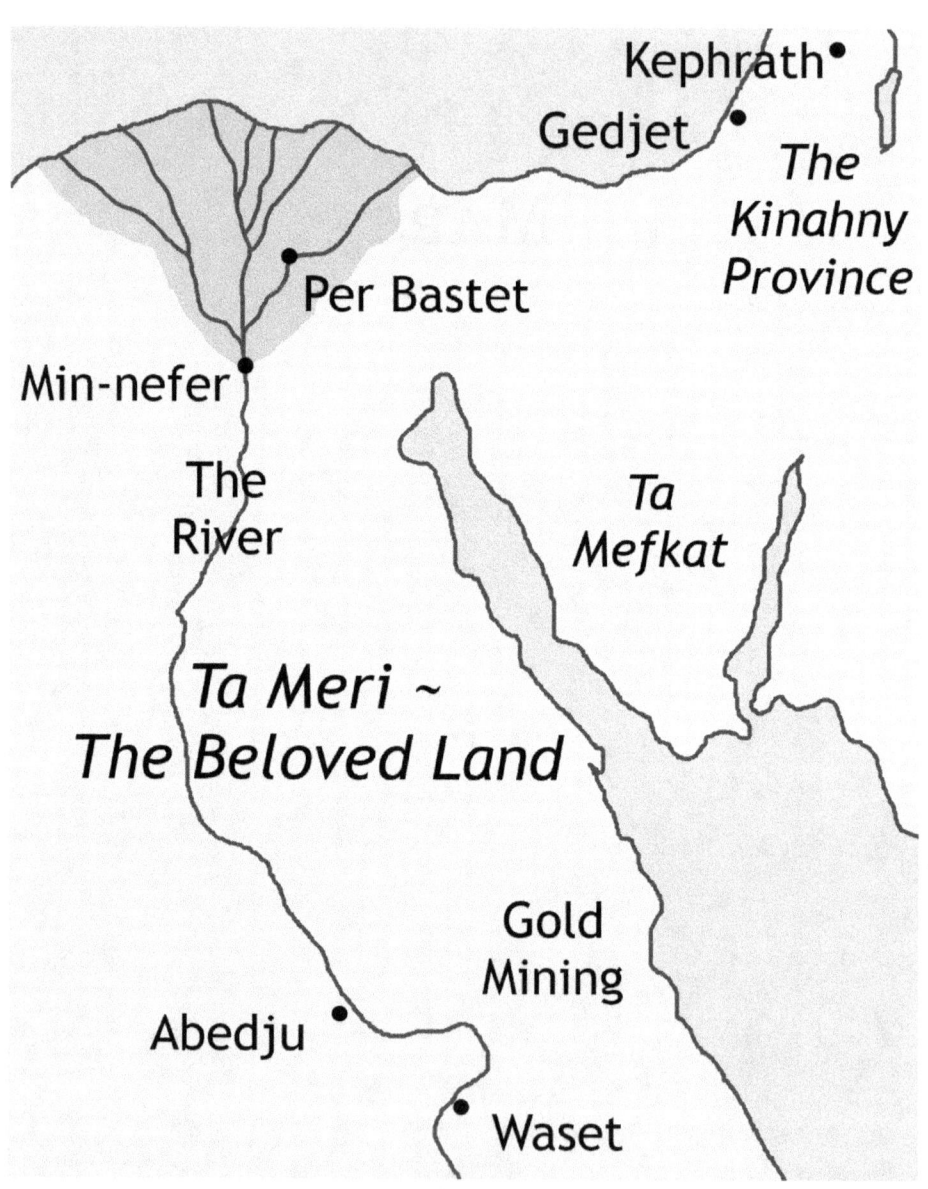

Kephrath

Gedjet

The
Kinahny
Province

Per Bastet

Min-nefer

The
River

Ta
Mefkat

Ta Meri ~
The Beloved Land

Gold
Mining

Abedju

Waset

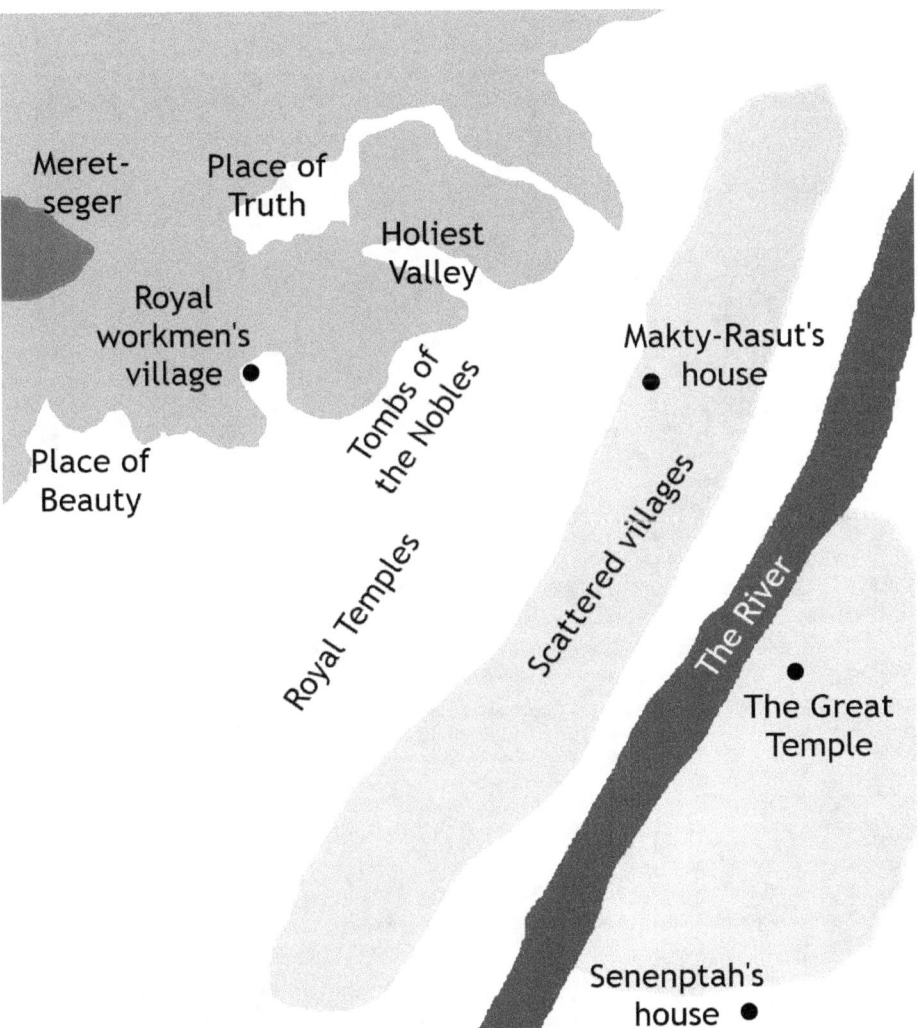

Meret-seger

Place of Truth

Holiest Valley

Royal workmen's village ●

Place of Beauty

Tombs of the Nobles

Royal Temples

Makty-Rasut's ● house

Scattered villages

The River

The Great Temple ●

Senenptah's house ●

1. Present – A Life

DREAMING EACH DAY of a sweetest sister,
    made like the best of all flowers –
Like the bud that unfolds,
    the tendril that grips,
        like the blossom that perfumes,
            the fruit that fulfils.

HOW SHOULD THE PATTERN BE FINISHED? Makty-Rasut leaned back against the tomb wall, rough and unsmoothed as yet, and nowhere near the full length it would extend out to. The courtyard designs were all complete, but the details for the transverse corridor had only been recently agreed with the senior priest whose eternal home it would be. Only a few of the key highlights of the main approach had been roughed out. In any case, these were just designs at this stage. They had not been called out of their potential to be created in sculpture and paint.

The man had insisted on one of the less common variations of the scene where his heart was being weighed. He had good reasons from his own religious experience, and Makty-Rasut had readily agreed once the request had been made. But in other things the old man was willing to be flexible. They had sat together while the priest told him something of his life's endeavours, and they worked together on the ideas that emerged.

Makty-Rasut marked two deep parallel lines on the pottery sherd he had brought, to represent the walls of the corridor. He had sent the rest of the team home early. It was a festival day tomorrow anyway, and he wanted the time to himself to think, alone in the tomb. It was easier. He wanted to have some ideas to show the priest when they next met, and he could not think clearly when the area was full of his team working and jibing.

Dreams had steered much of the old man's life. A dream had first sent him out, years ago now, into the provinces. Gedjet mainly, with a short spell up in Beth Shean at one point, and other brief sojourns elsewhere. Another dream had called him back to Waset. Other dreams, too, at different times, held less profound significance but were still vivid in the priest's memory. So dreams should figure prominently on the chamber walls. The journey out to Gedjet was a focal point. It could blend several traditional elements with some unique ones. That should please the old man, whose words often betrayed the same mix of past and future, convention and innovation.

He sat there for a while looking at the space available, working out in his mind where the main pictures and writing should go. Finally, happy that he had something definite to present to the priest at their next meeting, he added the ideas as rough notes scratched onto the sherd. He packed everything away. He would do a neat copy tonight, back at home with better tools and more light. For the time being he was content, and sat back again against the end wall.

He was very tired. There had been a series of long days. He had never worked with some of this team before, and he had wanted to be first in the workings every day and last out. It set a good example, and also gave him a good sense of the new men's attitudes. It was as usual: some good and some poor.

His second man, Sanedjem-Keni, was an old colleague, and Makty-Rasut had had no hesitation in choosing him. He had worked with him before, both recently here and also longer ago elsewhere in the land. For the first few weeks Sanedjem would lead the left side while he led the right himself. Then when the team came up to full strength he would move Sanedjem onto the right so as to be able to concentrate on the overall design and finishing.

He had no idea yet who would lead the team on the left. He was short of good draftsmen, who could take a plan and a blank wall and rough out the designs well enough to be ready for the painting. Several of the workers he had wanted on his team had moved up from working in the tombs of nobles to those of royalty.

Let them, he thought. The nobles' tombs were more interesting, and more diverse, than the eternal homes of those who were of higher rank. In them, the same religious motifs had to be portrayed in very much the same way, with very much the same words, over and over again. And they took so much longer. Years even. His work for the nobility suited him perfectly – a few weeks, or a few months, maybe a season or two, then the job was done and he could move on to the next one.

In fact, he thought as his eyes blinked shut, perhaps it was time to think about moving on from Waset altogether. It was considerably more than two years since he had come here, bored with the trips out into the eastern desert overseeing the gold mining. It had been a good couple of years, but perhaps it was getting to be time to move on again.

South to where the River turned turbulent, perhaps? That sounded very promising. He had no particular desire to head downstream again, back towards former homes, but there were enough places to ply his trade further up the River to keep him in work for a long time to come.

He caught himself falling asleep and sat up straight again. He would just wait a little longer in case some further inspiration came to him about the patterns. He really was extremely weary, though. His thoughts were flitting about like dragonflies, hovering here and there over the stream with constantly moving wings, unable to settle. For a little while he daydreamed about a woman he had seen briefly in the marketplace over at Waset last week, a junior singer at one of the temples from her dress. But she seemed very remote, separated from him by the width of the River as well as profession.

He sighed. He could not even remember her appearance well enough to conjure it in his mind's eye, and the daydream kept slipping back into an everyday fantasy, with nothing to distinguish her imagined body from that of any other woman. It was hardly different from reflecting on occasional nights spent at the houses of pleasure over on the east side of the River, although some part of his soul wanted the experience to have more meaning. The brief glimpse had not been enough to feed him with anything substantial.

He bundled the headscarf that he had needed in the cool of the morning behind his head, closed his eyes and leaned back against the wall, rough but solid and secure behind him. Perhaps he would think better like that. But in fact he must have fallen asleep, because all at once the dream came to him.

It was a familiar dream. He had had similar ones several

times before, each time with minor variations.

He was inside a darkened boat, somewhere below decks where the light of moon and stars would not reach. He was rocking in little waves, as though the boat was crossing gentle ripples as it drifted downstream. It was warm, and his body was cradled in a nest of soft fabric, dark and red all around him. The boat had eyes on the prow that watched out ahead, he knew, though he could not see them just now. The boat contained ample nourishment to satisfy him, though just now he did not need it. The boat had a wide beam that made her stable in the water. It was all deeply pleasant.

He looked down, still in the dream. He was wearing a pair of startlingly white sandals. The sandals were of a style and an extravagance that he would never think to wear in waking life, but here it was fine. More than fine: just right, in fact.

But then all at once the boat and the warmth, the eyes and the provisions were gone, and he was plunged in the cold water, tumbling in one of the River's turbulent places. The current pushed him away. He could not reach the banks of the River, could not see them in the windy mist that clung to him. He felt coldness everywhere, coldness throughout his body, clinging at him, and his mouth was filling up with water. He was still wearing the sandals, and they made it just about possible to remain at the surface.

He woke all in a rush, pushing away the scarf that had now tangled itself around him. He sat there for a while to allow his racing heart to return to a normal beat, trying to root himself back in this world. His oil lamp had long since gone out. Finally he got up, felt for his bag of tools, and walked slowly along the corridor from memory with his left hand trailing along the wall to guide him. Looking out from the courtyard, east towards the River, he found that the sky was starting to fill with stars, like jewels adorning the clothing of night. There was a sharp scent of a nearby herb, clinging to a crevice in the rock. No-one else was anywhere near him.

How long had he been asleep? The air breathing down the

hillside from his right, down from Meretseger's peak, was cool against his skin. He held on to the upright timber of the door-frame and steadied himself. Eventually he walked home, offered a pinch of incense and a brief prayer at the little shrine to Seshat that he kept, pulled at some bread and dried fish without really tasting either, and finally settled himself on top of his bedroll, tossing his unwanted clothes into a corner. He lay there for a while alone in the dark, feeling dislocated, and finally fell asleep again.

He woke in the early morning and lay drifting idly for some time. There was nothing really urgent to get up for. Finally he arose anyway, still much earlier than the rest of the village, which, with the day's festival at hand, was in no mood to rush. After his morning devotions to the Lady Seshat, the goddess mostly concerned with the scribal profession, he made himself some porridge with crushed grain from the storage pot and sat near the window to eat it.

Makty-Rasut was a scribe, but with the particular skill of being able to work with people's hopes and wishes for their tomb – the eternal home for their mortal parts. The true life within them would go to and fro as it pleased without constraint, enjoying the delights and duties of the light-land forever. However, it needed a real place to return to, an anchor point that would be recognisable and memorable.

The cycle of life in the light-land was like breathing, he had been taught. There were times of expansion, when the soul would go out into the day in order to experience more of that land, past the affirmations of an earthly life lived well. And there were times of contraction, when the soul would withdraw with the night to absorb and integrate what had been learned, recognising and passing by those same scenes again.

Makty's job, and his talent, was to create such a liminal place for these people out of chiselled rock, charcoal and coloured paints. He had the technical skills of laying out artwork and writing, of carving and brushwork. Most scribes could do that. But it turned out that he also had the ability to engage deeply with his employers in order to identify their needs, and here he parted company with many of the colleagues he had learned alongside.

Some of those others showed aptitude for accounting work, or estimating the effort and resources needed for buildings, or the exactness needed for recording laws, religion or spells. He could do those things, of course, but they were not his main strength. Even the women at the holy house where he had been a boy had recognised this. They had chosen his first master, Tety-Seneb, because he would draw out this faculty, and he had pushed Makty towards this line of work throughout his apprenticeship.

The nobles that he worked for certainly liked what he did, and appreciated the way he converted moments and fleeting events from their lives into everlasting statements in stone and ink. They liked the thought that their eternal self would pass endlessly by these beautiful scenes from their earthly lives, especially as they had been fashioned so as to highlight their pivotal significance. They commended his work to each other, and so far he had had no shortage of work to occupy his days.

He had found good fortune on first arriving in Waset those couple of years ago, able to take over a task that another scribe had failed to accomplish. The woman who had taken the risk with him had been sceptical at first, but had gradually been won over, and finally had become one of his most enthusiastic promoters. With her backing, and the genuine pleasure she had expressed about his artwork and insight, he had had no difficulty moving on from job to job with no gaps or interruptions. He knew that if he wanted to stay here near Waset he would find it easy to do so.

Perhaps, though, he should set himself the goal of working in each of the main towns along the River. To be sure there was nothing upstream, further south, to compare with the importance, and the wealth, here in Waset, but he was also aware that he was competing against a considerable number of other scribes and craftsmen living nearby. So far his abundance had come from making the most of his talents, and having a good measure of fortune as well.

Twice now, he was sure, he had been offered work simply because he had just finished a task and could begin straight away. Other men, perhaps equally skilled and certainly better known in this region, had been part way through a job and so not able to bid. So with one thing and another his reputation had risen high, like the River in flood, and he enjoyed the benefits of that. He had plenty of resources set aside for times of need, and no lack of men eager to work with him and share in his success.

It was a good time to be a scribe in Waset. With the fierce competition between the nobles to secure scribal work, rates of reward were considerable. Every worker received a daily allowance, usually of grain or other foodstuffs. Sometimes, though, it might be given in assets that were less tangible, such as the use of donkeys or other livestock, or the temporary loan of slaves and servants. The items could either be used or bartered. The more experienced and skilled the scribe, the greater the daily allowance. For some years now, with a modest lifestyle and no family to support, Makty's daily allowance had exceeded his actual needs.

At the end of a job, it was normal to receive an additional reward in recognition of a job well done. These gratitude gifts, unlike the daily allowance, depended entirely on the whim and pleasure of the giver regarding the final result. They might take the form of consumable supplies, but more commonly included gold and precious stones, or fashioned artefacts. Once Makty had received a papyrus scroll with an old text copied onto it, and had been able to trade that at one of the temples for the use of a house for a year.

Many of his friends and colleagues were spending both their

surplus daily allowances and their gratitude gifts on visible signs of wealth such as statues or amulets. One day these would go into their own eternal home, but for the time being they adorned spare corners of houses and were endlessly shown around and talked about in after-work evenings when household beer flowed liberally. Just three nights ago he had sat in a friend's house to celebrate his acquisition of a particularly splendid gold and lapis representation of Iset and Nebet-Het together. It had cost him all his accumulated gratitude gifts for over a year, and he clearly had no regrets.

But perhaps this time of excess would come to an end. There were stories that the tribes out in the western desert were becoming more aggressive again. That would mean raids and subsequent unsettlement in Waset until the great king heard, and was able to send army units out to the oases and encampments to renew old lessons. Or a few poor harvests in a row could take the edge off the present flush of work called for by the nobility and the priesthood. He, and others like him, could easily find themselves challenging each other for a shrinking pool of work. He knew that some of his fellow workers saw Waset as a permanent home. Even if times became difficult and work became short, some, like Sanedjem, would never willingly leave this place again.

Waset held no special ties for Makty. If he moved, he would certainly miss some of the excitement and pace of working here. However, the change to a new town, the chance to ply his trade with new colleagues and new clients held its own fascination. Some inner urge that he could never quite articulate had prodded him to move on from everywhere that he had lived after about three years. He became restless, dissatisfied, and eventually succumbed to the desire to change.

He was already starting to feel the internal pressure to leave. He knew from past experience that this would continue to build, and before too much longer it would become intolerable to stay here. It was as though somewhere in his soul there was a current every bit as powerful as the River, but flowing in the opposite direction. Each move he made was upstream, towards the unknown origins of the waters that gave life to the Beloved Land. Each move was away from the temple that was the first house he remembered, and that retained the secret of his own origins.

Perhaps one day he would even travel south as far as the borders of the Land. The big, dark-skinned man Hobniy who was part of his team at the moment, who he had worked with a few times before, had been a young child in the far south, beyond the borders. But his clan had moved north under the protection of the great king in order to avoid some kind of feud while Hobniy was very young. His speech and way of life were entirely naturalised now, and it was easy to forget he was actually a foreigner by birth. Makty liked him, and respected his work, and was more than happy to overlook his origins. Perhaps as he moved further south, there would be other men like Hobniy who he could work with. So long as he stayed within the borders of the land he was sure he could find a place to live and work safely.

He shook his head, trying to clear out the random thoughts that dipped like wading birds into the lake of his soul. Unless the great king took his armies far to the south and brought both peace and settled culture to the lands and tribes living down towards the head waters of the River, he would eventually run out of places to move upstream. What then? Would he finally settle into a life of homeliness somewhere, as Sanedjem had done with his wife Weret-Ib? The prospect seemed remote. He would face that when the time came, and there were still good places to move to for the next few years.

The house he lived in at present was quite small, and situated on the fringes of one of the little villages that were strung along the west bank, over the River from the main town of Waset. He had negotiated the use of it until the next inundation from one of the larger families, in exchange for a modest sum. It was also rather empty, as he only really used one of the rooms to any great extent.

1. Present – A Life

He had thrown away, or left behind, most of the things that he had used in previous places that he had lived. A few essentials, like his set of scribal tools, and the little statue of Seshat which was the focus of his twice-daily religious service, were carefully carried from place to place. Almost everything else though, all the bits and pieces that he might need for everyday life, could be discarded and collected again wherever he lived next. The houses he lived in were, like this one, negotiated from local families or other workers on a temporary basis.

As a result of this frugality, he was steadily building up an excess against difficult days in the future. His own extravagance this year had been to replace his old, half-worn collection of chisels with a new set, obtained from a local toolmaker with a good reputation.

He was not acquiring extra land, livestock, or prestige goods. Instead, the surplus was added to his longer-term store of wealth, by routinely leaving deposits at the nearest holy house of Djehuti. Even after supplying his team members with oil and wicks for lighting, and art materials that met his high standards, he had very good credit. Carefully bundled with his pack of tools was a sheaf of promises from these temples up and down the Beloved Land, which one day he would reclaim.

He was never entirely sure when or how he might redeem these pledges, but since he had never yet found a place that called to him sufficiently powerfully to settle down, the point was moot. Life was easier now than it used to be, to be sure. There had been times when he had lived in very ramshackle huts, or convenient caves, or even on odd occasions in one or other of the tombs he had been making and decorating for their wealthy owners. Even now he still lived modestly. He found enormous pleasure of soul in his occupation, and knew that he could do it well. Nothing else gave him such all-embracing satisfaction.

The land was brightening with the day. The dream that had come over him while he dozed in the tomb last night still pushed at him. He remembered having had similar dreams before, though none of them had seemed to fill him with anything like the same sense of reality and urgency that had gripped him last night. Surely it was trying to convey something of importance to him. But who had sent it to him, and why?

He sighed, pushing the empty bowl away, and fetched the rough drawing of the tomb he had made last night. It was light enough to work on now, over here by the window. He looked at it for a while, remembering all the reasons why he had sketched it out just so. Then he picked out a suitably sized slice of limestone and began marking out the neat copy he intended to show the priest. It was absorbing work, and as he put detail into the outline, he could easily imagine how the next few months would go. The work would take him well past the growing season, and the River would be perfect for a departure by boat, upstream or downstream, wherever he chose.

One episode from the old man's life caught him today. It was the journey he had made out to Beth Shean, where he had then spent just over a year before returning to Gedjet. It was a time of rivalry and conflict. Some of the tribes on the other side of the nearby river had refused to pay the regular tribute, considering themselves outside the borders of the province. There was a real threat that they would rise up in rebellion. It had happened before, at least twice, and each time had needed a sizable body of troops to restore order. Not only that, but one of the senior officials had sent a letter at the same time to the regional governor denouncing the conduct of another, alleging that he was in league with the rebels.

The priest had entered the town with a small retinue. He was charged with the double task of investigating the truth of the accusation, and also seeking to re-establish good relations with the restive tribes. Troops were not available in sufficient number to enforce obedience just now, so negotiation was called for. Makty paused to consider, remembering the old man's half closed eyes and expression of pride as he had told him the story. Counting back in years, this had certainly happened before Makty had been born, but the events were clear in the priest's mind even as they quavered in his mouth.

So there were two choices. Should he depict the arbitration between the two officials, with its intellectual challenge, its courtroom drama, and the painted magnificence of the official rooms in the town? Or should it be the making of the treaty with the Asiatic clans, which would call for wild landscapes, foreigners, and the personal bravery of the priest walking into their camp, protected only by the reputation of the Beloved Land?

Surely it had to be the latter. There were already enough scenes of splendid interiors along the walls here, and provincial Beth Shean could hold nothing really that could match other places that would be shown. But a scene with the lone figure of the tall priest approaching the gang of Asiatics and their pitiful huts would add something truly unique. He worked away at a rough draft of the idea for a while, seeing with inner vision what had to be drawn, thinking through how it fitted alongside other images.

He stopped his work and looked critically at the result. Perhaps by now, with this new addition, the walls were a little too crowded. He had seen a few places that friends had worked on where the pictures had been pressed hard up against each other, with barely any breathing room. He did not like the style – he wanted space and freedom for his tomb designs as much as for himself. This layout was becoming too busy. The old priest deserved to have his eternal home laid out in such a way that his deathless being could relax and enjoy the going out and the coming in, without having to thread his way among crowded rows of occupants. It needed thinning down. He would not use every one of these ideas, but would agree with the priest which were the most important.

The street had become noisy with adults and children as he worked, and at that point there came a cheery call and a bang on the window frame. He looked up, already knowing perfectly well that it was Sanedjem, come to persuade him to go out to the festival. Stalls and entertainers would be starting to gather in the open area beside the riverside path by now. Sanedjem's broad cheery face peered in at him.

"Makty, that looks like work. Have you no respect for the traditions of the feast?"

Makty-Rasut grinned at him.

"So all of a sudden you like to remember the traditions?"

"These ones – for sure. Why not? Now look, Weret and I, and the little one, we're all going down to the festival soon. I was going to ignore you but Weret made me come up here to see if you would join us."

He wrapped the diagram carefully in a spare rag, stowed it in his work bag, and stood up.

"Alright, I'll come along with you. But only because Weret asked me, you understand."

Sanedjem laughed, walked from the window round the outside of the house to the door and pushed it open while Makty-Rasut found some sandals. They were plain leather, not at all white, and quite serviceable. Sanedjem glanced around inside from the doorway.

"On your own, then?"

Makty-Rasut nodded as the two set off along the street.

"But I thought Merniyt was going to be the one for you?"

"Apparently she thought differently. As if it's your business."

"You made it my business when you went on about her all that time you were chasing her. Don't you remember how you used to go on? 'Oh, Sanedjem, I must have Merniyt. Oh, Sanedjem, Merniyt's so perfect. Oh, Sanedjem, I can't

be without Merniyt.' Quite put me off the writing on that
tomb we were working on at the time. That's why they ended
up with the wrong name for that daughter of theirs on the
wall. We only just got away with that by getting Hobniy to
stand in front of it when they inspected the whole thing. Do
you remember, he kept distracting them with those ridiculous
pictures of his of bees and honey-making."

They laughed.

"Well, she was fun to chase. And I really did think she was
good enough. Truly. But then when I caught her there wasn't
so much fun after all. She wanted more time out of me than
I wanted to give. Made me wonder who caught whom. I like
what I do, Sanedjem, and I wasn't going to stop doing it just
for her. In the end she got bored. Small loss, I reckon."

"But you never gave her enough time, did you. All that
time chasing. Couldn't you give her more than a few nights?
You barely gave her enough time to get herself through the
door and then you let her go straight out again. Pushed her
out again, most likely. Unless you just forgot she was there
and she got weary waiting for you to notice. And before her
there was that girl from all the way upriver. What was her
name? Djedet, wasn't it? Others before her who you never
told me about, I dare say. Not to mention those odd evenings
you spend over the River. You won't stay with anyone long
enough to enjoy the fullness of it. Running away again as
soon as you've made the catch won't help you in the long run."

"What can I say, Sanedjem? It's the chase and the capture
that I like. Well, the capture mostly, I suppose. But you and
Weret can do the long drag of living together for me."

He paused, since they were outside Sanedjem's house, but
his friend continued without stopping.

"Weret and the lad will be down by the River already. I
said we would meet them there. In truth, I thought I'd have
to spend longer getting you out of the house."

They walked along the open track, between fields of growing stuff. Not long ago, the waters of the inundation had cov-

ered this land.

"Talking of not staying in one place, I'm starting to think about how much longer I'll be here in Waset. I'll stay for this job, of course. Maybe another. Maybe even two. But then somewhere else, upriver again most likely. By this time next year maybe I'll have gone."

Sanedjem nodded, not very surprised.

"But what will we do without you?"

"Come on, Sanedjem, you could lead a team yourself easily enough. It's only me being here that keeps you back. Or you could come with me? Plenty of work for us both."

Sanedjem shook his head.

"I don't want to lead a team, Makty. Why would I want that? I'd have to put in all that extra time myself that you do just now. I'm quite happy being a second and then going home to Weret and the family at the end of the day. Let some other character with nothing better to do take your place. And I'm not up for leaving here. Plenty of work for me here without having to go looking. And Weret wouldn't want to leave. I know she wouldn't, not when there's no need. It might be different if there was hunger around here. She won't see any need to go. I won't ask her."

"I thought not."

They were almost down to the large stretch of land where the festival was being held. The centrepiece was a large area provided by the mayor of the west side for sports of different kinds. A number of casual wrestling matches were going on, each surrounded by a ring of shouting people. Another great group of men and women, singles, couples and families, was clustered around a roped area set aside by the great temple on the east side. Fortunes were being predicted, minor acts of magic performed, blessings and curses enacted. On every side, entertainments, noise, and the competing odours of food and drink drifted across the field. The festival had attracted people from both sides of the River, and from other villages up and down stream for a considerable distance.

Sanedjem turned to him. "Anything special you want to get up to?"

Makty shook his head. "I'll not stay long, Sanedjem, just enough to do one trip all round and see what's new."

"There, look, there's Weret now. And Ramose. Come on."

They started across to where Sanedjem was pointing.

"So you're only staying a while. Don't tell me you're going back to do some more work?"

"Actually, no. There's a few things I want to look at in some of the older tombs up around the ridge north of here. Some very nice old work I have a mind to imitate if I can. Bring it up to date. I'll be able to see it properly today with everyone along here, even most of the priests and all. But the best thing is over in the Place of Truth. All that lot are here too, they're not working either. And I persuaded one of the guards there to let me in to look at what they're preparing just now in the latest tomb. For the great king when his time comes to move on from this world."

"I thought you scorned all that stuff. Always said how working for the nobles was better."

"And so it is. Much better. I would never change. But the skill they have is real enough, and they get to hear about all the new ideas before we do. It's just they end up having to do the same old things time after time. But we can take some of their ideas and put them into the tombs of the people we work for. That way we'll keep getting work for as long as we want it. We have to keep up."

"Fine, you go off and do that, let me know what you find out up there and we'll work on it together. You can show me whatever you like that would be good to copy, But tomorrow, Makty. Tomorrow."

He kissed Weret, saying, "See, he did come," hugged his son, and then turned to Makty. "So will you stay with us or make your own way?"

"Hello, Weret. Yes, he did persuade me. And no, I think I'll make my own way round from here."

They parted, and Makty threaded his way around and between the crowds, gradually working his way north as he did
so. But he was genuinely interested in some of the stalls, so
his journey was extremely slow. He stopped beside the temple
area for a long time, watching the people go up to the priest
attendants. Their reactions were very diverse as they came
away again. He had half a mind to go and pay the token fee
to find out what they would say about his dream, and stayed
there, watching, considering.

But the priests were clearly in no mood just to say what
people wanted to hear. So far as he could tell from this distance, they simply spoke out as they felt moved to. He saw one
young couple step away, wreathed in smiles and with arms
wrapped around each other, but another couple stepped back
clutching at each other in disappointment. His caution got the
better of him. He would not mind hearing a word spoken to
him if he knew he would be sent away happy, but the prospect
of being crushed at the outcome was too much. News from the
other world might bring healing or harm, joy or anguish, and
just for now he did not want to take the risk.

He turned away and continued north, out of the festival
field and away from the River, angling uphill towards the rows
of older tombs on the hillside there. As soon as he had first
arrived in Waset he had cultivated friendships with the tomb
guardians in the region. Since then, judicious use of some of
his surplus wealth gave him occasional access into the older
houses for the dead, and the opportunity to see, and learn
from, former masters of his craft. One particular place caught
his eye this time, and swallowed up a good part of the day.

He felt a kinship across the years with the unnamed scribe
who had worked on this place, as they shared a desire to
stir new patterns into the traditional forms. The standard
scenes were there – an offering table, a banquet, a hunt in the
marshes, the annual count of cattle and other produce, and
so on – but each enlivened by a breath of novelty. Whoever
the man was, his eye for the movements of nature was excep-

tional. Within the herds of cattle and geese being processed past the tomb owner, each creature had some flair of uniqueness. But this artistry reached new heights around the little punt drifting through the reeds, where butterflies and water birds rose up and took flight pursued by a hunting cat, and scaled fish filled the water beneath the boat.

The man's son and daughter breathed individuality, though portrayed strictly according to tradition. The man's wife, Hatshepsut according to the blessing caption beside her, was delightfully feminine and lovely. At the feast, servants, dancing girls and musicians wove among the seated guests at the feast, with one of the musicians even looking out from the tableau as though catching the gaze of the onlooker. Had the scribe once taken her as a lover, he wondered, and in this tomb found a way to preserve her womanhood through all the ages to come? Makty had done this too, and the faces of women he had known adorned several tombs up and down the River.

The whole experience had been both gratifying and instructive. As the sun slipped past its zenith into the afternoon sky, he considered which of these features he would imitate next. Here, he thought as he walked by way of the hill track over to the Place of Truth, here was the immortality of the scribe. This man was separated from him by a gulf of time, perhaps six or seven generations at a guess. But his work survived, and spoke just as vividly now as ever. The man's name was gone, but his work lived on, and its silent inspiration would bear remote offspring in the places Makty himself would fashion.

Over at the Place of Truth, he was able to see some of the recent work that the royal teams worked on. He was forced to admit that it was elegantly produced, and that there was more variety than he had expected, but nevertheless, it was not for him. There was so little down here of the human stories that he took delight in, and was skilled at converting into art.

While he was in work, he was free to arrange the team's time and work as he pleased. To be sure there were the weekly reporting times to his employer of the moment, and the less regular times of inspection. But so long as his work gave satisfaction and peace of soul to one or other of the nobility, he was his own master.

The royal workers had priests beside them all the time, and were under constant supervision of all that they did. He knew that many of them had talent of their own, skills that he would love to imitate, but they were never given the creative space to work on it. No wonder so many of them decorated the houses and tombs of their own village so lavishly; they never had the chance during their everyday work.

He looked around, talked to the few people over in that valley who had not gone to the festival by the riverside, and finally left, climbing up the dry steep slopes onto the ridge. At the highest point of the track he sat in the shade of a rocky outcrop on the side of Meretseger's peak, ate some nuts and dried fruit he had obtained down on the festival field, and looked around. Little birds chittered amongst thorny bushes nearby.

Just ahead of him the path he was on joined another one running north and south. If he turned left he would be heading towards the Holiest Valley, with the path curling around the bay end and then down into the central well. If he turned right he would get to the workmen's village for the Place of Truth, located in a sheltered and rather barren valley. But he would only follow that track for a very short time, then branch off left and drop back down again to his own village. The village itself was hidden from his view by the swell of the ridge ahead, but he could see beyond that the vivid green and blue of the great River, and the fertile fields that bordered it.

On the other side of the River was the main town of Waset, with its several temples, the great market, and a sizeable population. It had swallowed up several nearby settlements, and the nearest villages were at least an hour up and down stream. Beyond that the ridges on the east side rose up, neither so high nor craggy as the place where he sat. He often had cause to visit that side to meet his employers, who uniformly lived on the east side, but he was always happy to return to one or other of the little houses on this side.

The west side had no great town, but rather a series of hamlets strung like beads of a necklace along the thread of the River. Really, there were two strands to the necklace – one for the living, set in or beside the fields, as close to the River as was prudent, and one for the dead, sprinkling the flanks of the limestone ridges that reared up beyond the flood plain. His work, and his life, moved constantly between the living and the dead.

He had finished his snack and had no reason to stay any longer. He took one more look at the vista, then got up and continued back to his home.

The next day, as he had expected, he was at the place of work much earlier than any of the other team members. In the cool of the morning, alone at the place of work, he was able to review how much progress they had made without distraction. The exterior courtyard was prepared, smoothed, skinned with plaster where it needed to be, but completely unadorned so far. The first part of the longitudinal tunnel had been rough-cut, a few paces past the transverse corridor but currently ending in the bluff wall against which he had fallen asleep last night.

The tunnel headed nominally westward, though because of the shape of the hill it actually angled slightly towards the north. It needed to be at least half as long again as at present, maybe a bit further. The two arms of the transverse corridor had been cut to their full extent but had had very little preparatory treatment yet. Then a short vertical drop into the actual burial place had to be cut down.

He frowned, counting weeks back since they had started, and estimating the amount of raw physical work remaining before they could begin artistry. It seemed about right, he thought. Progress was not bad at all, and there was nothing he needed to either confess to or conceal from the lord priest. Just as well, he thought; concealing anything from him was not an easy task, and the old eyes tended to see through attempts at evasion.

He found one place where a little trail of smoke from someone's oil lamp had smudged the wall. Easy enough to clean at this stage, but he should say to the whole team that this kind of accident was unacceptable. They should all know about adding salt to the oil. By the time that a clean skim of plaster had been added, and especially once there was colour on the wall, this kind of mistake would take much longer to correct. He would make sure no-one was working on anything too important today, in case fuddled heads made slips that then took time to be repaired. This early on in the work, it was not really a problem, but it was good to be careful.

While he was waiting for the others he worked his way along the transverse arms, levelling off the more overtly misshapen parts with one of his larger chisels. Most of the workmen straggled in eventually. One of the village children ran up the hill in the late morning to say that her father was ill today. Makty wrote all the details down in his log without comment. It was always this way; a day of festival cost another half day of lost time.

When they had all gathered together he also took the time to tell them what he had heard from the guards down at the Place of Truth. The desert raiders were becoming bolder again, after a couple of years of quiescence, and had been seen by one of the army scouts only a short distance out in the red land. The garrison for the royal tombs, though strengthened in numbers over the last two years, had no orders to watch over the graves of the nobles nearer the River. For protection, they would need to rely on the fact that they were relatively central. A raiding party that reached them would already have to have penetrated well into the watched area.

1. Present – A Life

Hobniy spoke up at this point, wondering if the lord priest would appoint his own guards to stand watch over them. There was a generally doubtful air, but then Khamu-Horiy said that down near Abedju the nobility had banded together and provided a shared protection group.

"Look now, it's their future more than ours. If they came together about this it'd be cheap for them all. Even just one armed lad would do it. You couldn't tell from a way off whether he knew weapons or not."

Makty nodded. The man was right, and he should raise it with the lord priest at the next weekly report, later that day. But in all honesty, he was not sure that he would get a response. Of course the great temple in Waset itself had its own militia, but they would not be ordered across the River in that way.

ᗯᗯ 🙰 ᗯᗯ 🙰 ᗯᗯ 🙰 ᗯᗯ

Just after the early afternoon break he left the men to their work, walked down the ridge to the fields and the River, and crossed over by ferry. From the eastern shore he ignored the main dock area, close to the smaller temple and the market place, and headed at an angle away from the River, off to his right and slightly uphill. The day was hot, but thin clouds like a skim of plaster took the edge off the direct sunlight. He stayed on the slightly more shaded side of the street until the town houses spread out, spaced further apart with the increasing status of their owners.

The lord priest's own dwelling place was almost alone. Far from being a single house, it consisted of a wide, sprawling cluster of buildings scattered around a central core. As well as rooms for refreshment and rest, there were numerous workshops for the preparation of pottery, clothing, or food nestling among orchards and vegetable gardens, along with shrines and pools of water. It was a little hamlet in its own right and, aside from bulk supplies of grain and the like, could remain

—23—

independent of the main town of Waset for some time if the need arose.

The population of this hamlet was almost entirely made up of household servants and slaves, and Makty had become accustomed to seeing them engaged in all kinds of duties around the house and gardens. So far as he could tell, there was a mixture of skilled and semi-skilled labour, of quite particular kinds. He knew there was an alabaster worker, and several small outhouses where papyrus was made and then filled with writing. There was a man who worked away at jewellery, ornaments and amulets, and several groups of women making clothes and household items. But there was no brick-maker, or metalworker, and from time to time he had seen even everyday items like baskets and lamps being brought in through the gates.

One part of the main building was set aside as a scribal school, and daily groups of youths were led there from the main gate, reed pens in hand. Clearly the lord priest did not teach all these youngsters himself, and Makty presumed that he called on members of the priestly hierarchy at the main temple to do this. In the day, it was a busy, active place, with all manner of people coming and going. But perhaps at night, the only free soul in the entire edifice was that of the priest himself.

He was shown through to a moderate-sized room with one side open to a colonnaded cloister facing west. Somewhere nearby two gardeners were talking in low voices. He already knew from previous visits that the tomb he was working on for the priest was not visible from this angle, but it was tempting to try once again to see it. A small table was off to one side, with several chairs nearby. A Senet gaming board had been casually left on one of them, with an unfinished game in progress.

Opposite this, a much larger table was partly covered with scrolls and writing materials, with more placed on shelves attached to the wall nearby. It was a considerable library, even if some of the scrolls belonged to the temple as a whole. Other than that the room was largely empty. The servant who had conducted him from the entrance to this room stayed in the corridor and closed the door behind him.

There was a foreign woman standing against one wall quite close to the table. Makty thought that she had been there on his previous visits, although at first he had not really taken any notice of her. She had the look of a girl from one of the eastern desert tribes out of Ta Mefkat, Maghariy probably, he thought.

It occurred to him that this was odd. Most of the servants that crossed his path in the lord priest's house were different every time, with nothing noteworthy to catch his eye about them as they fulfilled their duties. But here was the same woman present every time in this room. Thinking back he was sure of that. Now that he made the time to take notice of her, he realised that she was really quite striking. The different shades of her hair and eyes teased at him. She noticed that his eyes were on her, glanced briefly at him with a little smile on her desert lips, then settled into a neutral pose, looking at nothing. In the meantime the priest had turned from where he had been standing near the large table and was slowly making his way towards the chairs.

Makty bowed to the priest and stayed waiting near the door as the old man reached the chairs and sat down with a little sigh. He gestured to one of the other chairs, with some impatience, and Makty crossed over and joined him. The foreign girl poured some beer for both of them and then returned to the wall while Makty was unwrapping the limestone sherd with his design outlines cut into it. He placed the slice of stone carefully on the table and looked up at his employer.

Some time later the discussion of layout and design was over. Makty, hesitantly at first, broached the subject of armed protection for the work. The priest listened to the concerns that Makty's men had voiced about the tribal raiders, nodding from time to time. More than that, he took them seriously.

After Makty had finished, he stood up, stiffly, walked over to the open colonnade and looked across at the west side.

"These tribes are hot and hasty, and always have been. I despise their manner of living. It is contrary to the way of truth. There is no real dealing with them, ever, only vigilance and the occasional show of force. Your men are correct: you do need some protection across there."

Makty, trying not to sound surprised, came and stood beside him.

"Do you have armed men that you can post there, lord priest?"

"If you want men who truly know how to fight, I cannot help. We would need to approach the mayor of the west side for that. But if all you need is someone who can stand with a weapon and look the part, I can arrange that myself."

Makty nodded.

"That would be sufficient, lord, I think."

"Then I will see that there are always four men on guard there, night and day."

They sat down at the table again. The old man looked shrewdly at Makty.

"Of course, these men will need food. And there will be an interruption to their regular work."

Makty nodded, unsurprised.

"Perhaps as a gesture of good will, lord, we could ensure that they are fed out of the allowance you are generously providing for us all."

"Indeed. And I wonder if their absence on this side will mean I have to find other workers?"

Makty thought about it. If he was not careful, this issue of guards could become a considerable drain on his own share of the reward for the work.

"I wonder, lord priest, if my men have reacted too hastily to the news. Perhaps just two guards at a time would suffice, and only during the hours of labour. Your own work would not be held up then. I think that, if they serve us well, I would be happy to see personally that they were rewarded for their effort."

The priest nodded, pursed his lips. For a moment it looked as though he would continue the negotiations. Then a very weary look crossed his old features.

"I think in fact that we will divide their reward equally between us, you and I. They are common men: it will not amount to much."

Makty was surprised again. He had not thought to hear an offer made spontaneously like that. He leaned forward, concerned for the old man's well being.

"Are you feeling weary today, lord priest? We can talk about this another day if you prefer."

"No. Let the agreement stand. Your men need the reassurance. I am content with the arrangement. Today I am feeling old. Full of too many years."

"But, my lord, surely you have a good part of your life ahead of you, and great accomplishments still to achieve."

The old man shook his head.

"I think you will be writing on those walls that I have spent one hundred and ten years alongside the River?" Makty nodded. "I do not know the exact count. But sometimes I think that it is too long for a man to bear. Too long to be contending with the stream. There are days when I long to be allowed to cross the reeds into the land of light. You are an educated man: you have read the scribes. Remember what they say. The mouth cannot taste, nor the nose enjoy scent, the ear cannot hear the singer, nor the body respond to the dancer. My body is old. I cannot savour life as once I used to."

Makty was silent. He had no idea how to talk about this. After a pause the priest continued.

"It is a strange thing, to know all about that journey, its dangers and delights, and yet not to be permitted to walk that path yet. I know every footfall that must be taken, every phrase that must be spoken to pass safely, every key to unlock every gate. But I cannot go there yet. I feel that there must be some purpose here beside the River that I have not yet fulfilled, something that holds me back. If only I knew what it was. Then I could accomplish it and be released. But nothing, neither vision nor dream, neither word nor sign, nothing has revealed it to me."

He turned his head and stared out again towards the west. There was silence in the room for a while. Even the slaves in the garden had moved out of earshot. In the end the priest turned and met Makty's eyes once more.

"So it is agreed. I will provide the men and their weapons. You will feed them. We will divide equally the extra reward they receive at the end of the work."

They joined hands to acknowledge the agreement. While they were still touching, the priest looked towards the woman, who nodded to acknowledge her place as witness.

A little later he was walking beside her, back towards the outside world, along a sequence of rooms that he thought that he recognised amongst the perplexing network of halls that made up the house. They remained silent for the first few corridors, as though the old man's sombre mood had been contagious. Eventually Makty spoke, not wanting to lose the brief opportunity of female relationship.

"The lord priest was melancholy today."

She glanced briefly at him.

"Some days he is. I have not yet understood why it happens to him on this day but not that."

They walked a little further. She spoke again, her thoughts clearly still dwelling on the encounter.

"It disturbs you when he is like that?"

He nodded.

"I do not know how to speak with him about it. Why should this day be any different from the last time we met? The work has gone well. He is in good health for a man of his years. I had nothing difficult to report."

"And so you would rather he was cheerful? You would rather he suited himself to your mood?"

Makty stopped in the path and thought about what she had said.

"It sounds bad when you say it like that. You are meaning that I should accommodate myself to his mood and not the other way around? Presumably, by reason of his age and the fact that I work at his command and to meet his wishes?"

She looked at him, curious to see how he would resolve the matter. It occurred to him that he was starting to want her to accommodate herself to his mood, to shape herself around him in all the ways that a woman might. Perhaps some of his colleagues would deride her for her alien parentage, but he was willing to see past her birthplace.

This possibility was much more intoxicating than the question of the old priest's emotional state. And there was a real sense of excitement at the thought of pursuing the woman under the very nose of the lord priest. To that end, it was well worth yielding on the lesser matter. He nodded to her.

"You are right. He deserves better from me. Another week I shall remember that."

She looked mildly surprised at his response, but said nothing. They set out again along the path, side by side. At the gate he thanked her and went out into the hot street. It was just like a game of Senet, he reflected. It was better to give up an advance here, or allow a withdrawal there, in order to secure the overall aim of getting all your pieces home.

For a moment he wondered if they were both playing the same game, or were even on the same playing board. Then he laughed aloud in the glorious sunshine, uncaring of the curious looks around him, because the verbal foreplay with the woman had quite banished the melancholy of the priest, and he set off back towards the west side.

Richard Abbott

2. Past – Arrival

THEN I OBEYED the command of the god and settled near the great holy houses of Waset. I was diligent to carry out every task that was required of me. I adorned the eternal homes of the great ones of the land with every good thing that their hearts longed for, so that they were satisfied. Indeed, they were astonished at the work, and my name was honoured by the families of those who had gone ahead into the light-land.

THE LADY NEBET-TAWI IB-ISET sat in her chair, watching as the scribe approached. She had ordered the house-servants to place the chair in the shade of a sycomore fig, knowing that the craftsman would have to stand in the sun until she invited him to sit at the chairs beside the little table nearby.

It was part of the game she played with tradesmen, and a way of deciding which she wanted working for her and which not. She also knew that the setting flattered her vanity, as it imitated the several pictures she had seen where a goddess arose out of such a tree to bless others. Usually Iset, who she held in special devotion anyway. From the scribe's position, her body would seem to emerge in just this way from the tree behind her.

The man was brought in front of her by one of the servants, who withdrew silently without needing to be asked. She looked at him appraisingly. He stood on the edge of the sunlit area and returned her look. He was, perhaps, rather too bold for his age, and rather too confident of his own standing. In his favour, though, he did not burden her with unnecessary chatter, and waited where he had been placed without trying to wriggle into the shade. After a while she decided that he might be able to do the job; she had sometimes rejected potential workers just from the way they failed to wait properly.

"You are Makty-Rasut, and they tell me you can carry out artwork to a satisfactory standard."

He nodded.

"I can, lady, and the writing to go around the scene. And layout the whole design for you to approve before the work begins. May I ask what particular job it is you need doing? Your eternal home, perhaps?"

"No, I have provision for that. My husband went ahead of me into the light-land many years ago, and I shall dwell in the place he prepared for both of us. No, what I need is some work in the outer courtyard. He left most of that for me to finish as I saw fit."

The young man nodded.

"How big an area? And what is the surface?"

"You see that wall on the other side of the little pond? About twice that and a little more, half either side of the entrance. The stone is rough and apt to flake, but it is sheltered from above. It will need proper preparation. The place itself is across on the west side, of course. A prior attempt by another man will need removing. He was a disappointment. There are two scenes I require both left and right, arranged side-by-side with a narrow border above and below. I can show you some rough pictures shortly for what I have in mind. And I require it all to be finished before the barley harvest. Can you start tomorrow on this work?"

She watched as the man studied the wall, head on one side, and then lost himself in thought about the problem. After a little while he looked up again.

"I can do that for you. And yes, I can start tomorrow. I will need one other skilled man to work with me most of the time, and two others, just labourers of modest ability, to help for the first month while we prepare the surface and do the rough work. I can find these people if you want me to proceed. They may not be able to begin work for a few days, but at latest by next week. We will all need daily rations, of course. The others will need some additional gifts of appreciation at the usual value for their experience. For myself, I shall be happy to accept whatever comes from your hand, together with commendations of the work to your friends and associates."

She looked at him quizzically.

"What if I decide to give nothing?"

He shrugged.

"My risk. But from what I have heard, you give always in proportion to your level of satisfaction with a job. I intend to ensure you are satisfied. As I am sure you know, I have quite recently settled here in Waset, and need commendations from people of rank here in order to establish my name."

She laughed, deciding that she quite liked the young man.

However, there were other issues as well as liking that had to be reckoned. She considered for a short time.

"Your estimate for the first part of the job, the preparation, is very low. Too low, I think. This concerns me, since I want the work finished well with no more delays. You have not seen the wall yet, and I think you will find it less ready than you hope. I accept your offer to carry out the work, and will place at your disposal two young men of my own household for the first month, to work alongside these labourers you intend to recruit. They will be yours to order as you see fit during that time."

The young man looked dubious. "Do they have any experience?"

"Only of building and repairing around the house and the garden. Not of the work that you are doing." Seeing an objection arising in his face, she added. "I have seen this wall and you have not. I accept your estimate for the skilled work, and your ability to do it. But you must accept my decision concerning the unskilled work; you will need the extra pairs of hands at the start. Unless you would rather find another piece of work elsewhere?"

He shook his head, surrendering quite gracefully in the end, she thought. Deciding that she had carried on quite long enough the exercise of keeping him in the sun while she played at being the goddess emerging from the sycomore, she stood up and gestured that he should join her sitting at the curved table with her on the shade.

At the move, two of the servants brought in some beer and sweet cakes and then withdrew again out of sight. From under the table she brought out some sketches that she had drawn on the back of a papyrus sheet.

"Here, look at these."

He turned the sheet around, studied it in silence for a while. She watched him closely, fascinated by the way that his whole being was wrapped in concentration around the designs. The suggestion to use his services had been a good one, she thought, even though nobody nearby had heard of him. The commendation had come from an old friend downstream, whose opinion she trusted. Even if his estimate of the rough labour had been low – a sign probably that he wanted the work quite urgently – what she really needed was a craftsman of sensitivity who would be able to enact in plaster, stone and coloured ink the ideas that she had.

His hands traced out some of the patterns, smoothed out a crease that had started to form across the surface. Twice he started to say something and then stopped himself. Finally he looked up and met her eyes. He was very intense, she thought, and rather remote, as though in spirit he was already absorbed in the rock face.

"Now, I shall reward you as I see fit at the end of the work. For that, you will have to be patient. But since I do not want you to be distracted by the needs of everyday life while you are doing this work, I have set aside a small house at the end of the garden near the River. There is a gate beside it; you can come and go as you need to without troubling the household."

He began to speak then, to argue the point, but she held up her hand to stop him.

"This is not a matter for debate. While you are doing this I want to know I have your full attention. In the past I have taken on workers like you who remained in their own house while they were working. Their loyalty was divided, and in one case I found that the man was working on two other pieces of work besides my own. That is unacceptable. So you will be living on my estate until you finish the work. I think that we will both find that this way is better."

She waited for him to nod acceptance, then continued.

"To lighten your heart, and to ensure that the preparation of your food and the other necessities of life do not occupy your time, I am also providing one of my maid servants for you. She will live in the house with you, cook, run errands as you need her to, wash and mend your clothes herself or else at need take them to the laundrymen at the River and collect them again, and such like. For the duration of the work she will be yours."

This time when she paused he did not attempt to speak. Clearly he was a quick learner; this was another point in his favour.

"Now, you may order her as you see fit, so long as you always remember that she is my slave, and merely on loan to you for a season. But if she should fall pregnant during the time she is with you, then the child will still be part of my household, and I will hold you accountable for extra food rations for the mother through the rest of her term, and the first year of the child's life. This would represent a considerable dent in the reward you will earn for completing my work. Do we understand one another?"

He grinned and made a little bow. "Most thoroughly, lady. I do not intend to disappoint you. And with the rest of today, I should like to see this courtyard area, if you can spare a person to go over the River with me and show me. Then I must visit the men I have in mind for this project, and finally sit down with these plans of yours in the cool of the evening in the little house you are providing."

They talked a little more, practical things about inks and colours. It was a subject that fascinated the lady Nebet-Tawi, and there was genuine pleasure in finding someone who was prepared to talk at equal length on the subject. If the scribe was surprised at her levels of interest and knowledge in his trade, he hid it well. She was pleased that she had chosen him to do the work, but mistrusted her motives. She was genuinely thrilled to have made for herself a chance to plunge with another person deep into the subtleties of how colour and texture could be paired with surface and form. But from time to time, she wondered if she was indulging herself by simply taking advantage of him as a captive audience.

Truly it was a delight to be able to converse like this. If she had been a decade or two younger she would surely have taken the opportunity to take the relationship out of the garden and into other rooms, but the age gap seemed daunting. For the time being, the intercourse would have to remain verbal, and she would have to be satisfied with that. Sending the maid along was a poor substitute, really, a sort of surrogate interaction with his life. She sighed. Talking like this was not just pleasure for the heart, but always stimulated her into insights about herself which were not always comfortable. He misunderstood the action.

"Lady, am I wearying you? I do apologise for my enthusiasm about all this. The subject overtakes me, I fear, and I forget myself. In any case, I should be leaving to make sure I can get the help of the men I need."

She shook her head. "Not weary, no. Just regretful that it has been so long since I could share all this in conversation. It has been good for my heart." She sighed again, looking past him, past the orderly lush vegetation of her garden out to the rugged, bare beauty of the western ridge and Meretseger's peak. Pulling herself back into the garden with an effort, she stood up and looked directly at him. He hastily rose to his feet.

"You are correct. You should be away doing those things now. We will have other opportunities to talk together. I do not know what you are used to, but I will inspect the work once a week. If, as I hope, I am pleased, then perhaps you would gladden my heart by eating in my house from time to time so that we can talk."

She beckoned to one of the servants, who was working nearby in the garden. She spoke quietly to him for some time, with him nodding in acceptance at several points.

"So, Makty-Rasut, go with the lad here. He will show you the house where you will live, and then go with you on the ferry across to the place of work so you can inspect it for yourself. He will then come back here then for the rest of the day, but will report to you at the usual hour tomorrow morning along with another worker. I will send the girl down to the garden house so that she can make it comfortable for you."

The interview was at an end. He bowed to her, clearly very satisfied by the outcome of the meeting. The servant led him away through the garden towards the little house and the gate by the River.

Sanedjem-Keni was working on the finishing touches for an inscribed statuette. The piece was part of a complicated exchange of items he had agreed with another worker concerning a house on the edge of the village near the fields. After so many adjustments to the details of the exchange, so many compensating transfers of goods and obligations between the two men concerned, and a few close friends of both, it was almost impossible to work out who had got the better half of the deal. He was happy, since the acquisition of the house meant an end to months of never being quite sure where he would be living next. Judging from the other man's face after they had sworn oaths in front of the village elders, he was also convinced that the terms favoured him and his family. So that was good.

The house was small, barely more than a large hut on the outskirts of the village, certainly smaller than most of the tombs he had worked on. Sanedjem thought that it had perhaps started life as a guard post for some of the fruit orchards nearby. It was in serious need of some restorative work, but Sanedjem was content. It would give him a place of his own, and now that he had decided to settle in Waset for a few years at least, it was a valuable asset. He could enlarge it if he pleased, or trade up into somewhere bigger if the need arose.

He polished the surface of the little figurine with a piece of soft cloth to bring out the shine. It would do, and there was no need to spend much more time on it. There were voices outside, someone pointing out his house. He got up and was already half way to the door when there was a knock. He opened it, to see Makty-Rasut standing there.

"Sanedjem! They told me you were living here. Quite the domestic now, hey?"

Sanedjem embraced him, laughing.

"Better than sleeping in the tomb you're working on. Ah, Makty, do you remember that dreadful place near Min-Nefer? This has to be better."

Makty looked around.

"Well, it couldn't be called large. But it's alright. How much more does a man need? Not like you've got to share it with anyone."

"Not yet. But I have plans about that. There's a girl down the road, Weret-Ib. She's all right. But never mind that just now. I thought you were still on those mining trips out from Abedju? Someone told me they'd seen you here, but I thought it was just to get supplies, tools, whatever."

"No, I'm done with all that. I did another few trips out into the wadis after the ones we did together, but then I moved on. I could only work with all those slaves and military types for so long. Decent enough work for a while but I wanted to get back to tomb work full time, not just here and there in the gaps. That's where the real satisfaction is. And the real rewards."

"Took you long enough to realise that. I said the same thing to you a year or two ago. After that trip with all the fighting."

Makty laughed. "Fair enough. But look, we'll have plenty of time to catch up on all that. Can you help me on a job?"

"Maybe. Here or somewhere else? I've only just got this place so I'll not be wanting to move out just yet."

"No, no, it's here. Up on the hillside quite close by this very house, in fact."

He started explaining all about the job, his voice full of enthusiasm. Sanedjem smiled to himself, remembering other jobs with Makty starting in just the same way.

"And she wants us to start right away, so it's all finished by the time the barley comes in. About half a year all told. I'm starting tomorrow morning, but I only promised next week for you, just in case. But if you can do tomorrow, all the better."

"I'm not sure I can start that soon. Userhat has been asking me about joining him on a piece of work he's pitching for."

Makty barely hesitated.

"But he's not confirmed it with you yet? He's not got an agreement out of you?"

"Well, not in so many words, but he's quite persistent. He's sure he's going to get the work."

Makty-Rasut made a dismissive movement of his hands.

"You know he always sounds like that, Sanedjem. Remember that time at Abedju. He was sure about that one too, and nothing came of it. Left us all with nothing to do because we'd passed over other things. My offer, now, that's absolutely firm. Here on the table right now, sure as the inundation. I said you'd be on board next week, but if you could start earlier this lady would agree." Seeing his friend still hesitating, he rushed on. "Come on, look, it makes no sense to pass over a definite job, in your hand today if you want, for some scheme of Userhat's that might come to nothing. You haven't given your word to him have you?"

Sanedjem still wavered.

"Well, no, I haven't formally pledged, but it was a half-promise. I don't want to get a name for changing boats midstream."

"Tell me now, how big is the team already? When's the starting date?"

"He's still collecting. And there's nothing firm yet."

"Well, there you are. And there won't be anything better than that for weeks. Months even. You know what he's like. You want to impress this girl up the road? What was her name? Weret? Best way you can do that is to start work right now. Chances are you can finish this and still join Userhat." He paused, watching Sanedjem's face for the change of mood, and seizing the moment when it arrived. "You know I'm right. But look, while you're making up your mind, come up the hill and I'll show you what we'll be doing together. It can't do any harm just to look, can it? I could use some advice on one patch, anyway."

Sanedjem, grumbling a little, came up the ridge and then along the contours to Nebet-Tawi Ib-Iset's site. He was quite aware that Makty had already won the debate. They stopped just outside the rough area that was to be the decorated court-yard. Sanedjem was about to go in, but stopped short and looked at the tomb door.

"The main tomb looks finished already."

"It is. She says that her husband had that prepared a few years back. I suppose he knew he was dying and was moti-vated to get that part done. Our work will be the courtyard."

He walked around the area, sketching with his hands the desired layout. His decision made at the point he left the house, Sanedjem moved rapidly from polite attention, through professional interest, to active engagement with the plans. Before long, he knew that he was talking as though he was al-ready on the job. They walked back a different route, straight down the steep slope and then around the curve of the ridge through little strips of cultivated land back to the tiny house.

As they went in again, Sanedjem laughed. "It's just the same as always, we work in places ten times the size of the houses we live in."

Makty nodded and laughed with him. "It'll be different one day, you'll see, we'll all live somewhere fine." He paused. "So are you in with me then? Because if you are, there's a couple of others I want to see this afternoon to help with the first part. Just the rough labour."

Sanedjem sighed, formally yielding to the pressure. "All right, Makty. Count me in."

"Splendid. I knew you'd see the sense in it. Now, is Hobniy free?"

"No, not for another month or two. He's part of a big team working up the valley just now. But you don't need people with his talent anyway. Try Horiy's son, the other side of the village. He's looking for work just now. Horiy's off work since he twisted his guts moving a rock that was too big, so the family would be glad of the help. He might well know another lad that would do."

The two talked a little longer, but Makty wanted to be away, and before long they parted. Sanedjem looked down at the little statuette again. Just as well it was nearly done; he only had today to finish it.

Iunet, her baby Nakht held in a sling, finished grinding the day's flour and transferred it into a convenient vessel. It was getting dark, and the scribe she was supposed to be serving had not yet returned. Still, the mistress had said that he would keep his own time. At least it gave her longer to be with her son. The task she had been given was, in comparison with some of the work in the household, a very easy one. But time to herself was never easy really, and she missed the chatter and companionship of the other servants.

She looked out again into the gathering gloom and sighed. If she had known he would be this late, and with it being his first day, she would have slipped out at mealtime and joined the others. More company for her. As it was, she could not go now. If he came back to an empty house, who knew what he would do? Like as not he would tell the mistress, who could be severe in her discipline. Nor could she eat until he had had his fill, and she was very hungry. But then, so was little Nakht, and he would not wait for any scribe to get back from his work.

She closed the door again, settled herself on a stool, untied the sling, and started to feed him. His complaints turned to little noises of satisfaction, and she smiled down at his contentment. Their eyes met across her breast, and he gurgled happily at her. At least she still had one companion. Then the door opened all in a rush and a man came in, smelling of sweat, dust clinging to his clothes, hands and face. He was carrying a large bag of tools in one hand and a smaller one in the other. He was not at all like the scribes she sometimes saw speaking with the mistress. They were neat, precise, polished, but he had been exerting himself. He stopped as he saw her, clearly confused. Then his face cleared.

"Ah, I remember. You must be the maid that the lady Nebet-Tawi Ib-Iset talked about."

She nodded, trying to stand up to respect him properly, struggling with Nakht who wanted to turn around to see the newcomer, and wanted to complain as well, and having to mop with her untied clothes a little trickle of milk that was still dripping.

"I am, lord. I am here to serve you. And this is Nakht who does not know how to honour you rightly. For which I apologise to you."

He laughed, a little embarrassed. "No need. He has other things to attend to just now."

She giggled, watching how his eyes were still following her open shirt.

"This one holds honey for him, lord. The other contains beer but he has not got that far yet."

His gaze jumped up to her face. He looked confused again, perplexed. Surely, she thought, he had not taken her words seriously? Perhaps he was less experienced than he seemed, except presumably in matters of scribing. She sighed. Nakht was squirming back towards her again, but the scribe would also want feeding. She tied the strings on her shirt together again and stood up, resolutely trying to ignore the full pressure in one half of her body.

"Will you eat now, lord?"

He shook his head. "I can't yet. I have something I need to think about with the lamp here for a while. It became too dark outside."

"I can finish preparing the meal while you do that?"

He was already sitting on a stool, unpacking odd bits from the larger bag. He looked up, saw the baby trying to reach her, shook his head.

"Not yet." He took out one last item, then looked back at her, still standing uncertainly across the room. He laughed a little. "Look, why don't you give him his beer, then I can finish doing this and we'll both be happy."

She sat again, with some relief, and let Nakht finish feeding. The scribe ignored them as they did this. Before much longer, Nakht was drifting off to sleep, and she helped him by quietly humming one of the infant songs. Finally, she took him into the darkened bedroom and laid him down to sleep.

Back in the main room, she watched the scribe gradually work his way down an oblong piece of broken pottery, making little marks and scribbles as he did so, and, seeing his rate of progress, reheated the meal she had prepared earlier so that it was ready just as he started to pack his things away again. Then she carried the bowl over to him, placed it on the table, and stood behind his stool. His hair and smock were still very dusty. He took a mouthful of food, nodded and made an appreciative noise, then ate considerably more without speaking. Suddenly, he half-turned to see her standing.

"You ate your meal earlier?"

She had been looking over his shoulder at the markings he had been making on the pottery slab, looking at the quickly sketched diagrams and amusing herself by trying to guess what the writing marks might mean. Some made sense as pictures, but others were just squiggles. His question caught her by surprise.

"Oh no, lord, surely not. Why would you think such a thing? The mistress would not be pleased if she thought I had eaten in this house before you."

He looked down at the bowl, from which over half of the food had already disappeared.

"So what will you eat?"

"Whatever you leave, lord."

He put down the spoon.

"Fetch another bowl and we will divide this now."

"There is no other bowl, lord. Only yours."

He pushed the plate to the other side of the table. "There, I have had my fill. Now, do you like this bread?"

She nodded but made no move towards it. He shook his head, cut two rather ragged slices from it, took one bite out of each, and placed them on the plate. "I have had enough of those, too."

Watching him, she concealed a smile; he had quite quickly arrived at a scheme that would meet both his standards and hers. She stayed standing behind him, wondering what the next moves in their game would be. He turned to look at her properly.

"Why will you not eat with me?"

"It is not done like that in the house of the mistress."

"But you are in my house for the time being, not in that of the mistress. She gave this to me for the duration of the work. Her house is through the orchard and across the way."

She liked the response, and the way they were playing. If this had been a real game of chance being played by the men at the orchard hut, wagers would be starting to be made now. This scribe knew how to play by rules. On the other hand, she did not feel safe with him yet. Some masters that she had heard of would lead a servant on by trickery and then beat them for presumption.

"But lord, suppose you brought some honoured guests home with you, as the mistress does from time to time. You would not want to see me sitting among them. You would want me to stand and serve them until all were satisfied. How is this any different?"

"I have a serious lack of honoured guests that I might invite to such a feast. I think most nights in this house, there will just be me, you, and little Nakht who apparently just wants to sleep and to drink honey and beer from time to time. Should I call you an honoured guest so that you can sit and eat now?"

She grinned and surrendered this particular round of the game to him, sitting opposite and starting to eat what he had left. She was very hungry. He looked at her thin arms.

"Either you eat nothing every day, or he suckles all the food right out of you again."

She glanced fondly into the next room. "He's a greedy little crocodile. What I eat, he wants to take. I'm thin as a reed everywhere." She giggled again. "Except for the one part of me that he knows best. He and I will tussle over this body until he's weaned. A couple more years, I suppose."

"So you're his slave as well as mine?"

She nodded. "And I belong to the mistress too. It is not always plain for me to know what to do for everybody."

He leaned back and thought about it.

"I suppose that just for now, I belong to the mistress as well."

She put the spoon down and arched her eyebrows. "Well, she is a good mistress if you do all that she says. But I am very sorry to hear that she might have you beaten just the same as me if you made a wrong mark in one of her pictures, or forget to put one of those signs into the right place."

She gestured to the pottery slab with the rough outlines he had made earlier. He nodded ruefully, conceding the point just as she had done about eating together.

"Well, no, I would not get beaten for that. But if she was angry enough she could obliterate any name I have in this town so that I would need to move away in order to work again. I have already moved many times along the River, so another change would not be so bad. But the shame would be great, and I do hope to stay here for a while."

"If I may ask?" She looked at him, and he nodded. "Have you never had slaves of your own so you know what to expect of us?"

Again, he stopped to think about it. She liked that.

"Never in a household like this. Certainly not where there were great feasts held with honoured guests. I grew up in one of the holy houses far downstream from here, in the sedge lands, and of course there were labourers in the fields, builders, cooks and the like. But I was expected to eat with whoever else was in the refectory. Then I was an apprentice while I learned to be a scribe, and since I did get beaten a good many times I suppose that was a bit more like being a slave. Since I finished that I have lived on my own. But until just recently I was part of the gold mining trips out of Abedju, into the eastern desert and the wadis. I have been responsible for the well-being of nearly two hundred workers at a time, and always with an army officer and his men. The officer I worked with most often would always demand that everyone was fed together – scribe, soldier and slave alike. He used to say that out in the desert, a man was only a man whatever his station, and that death by thirst, scorpion or the weariness of heat could come upon any of us. Those afflictions pay no attention to rank or title. So while we are eating, I am used to setting aside such things."

He thought about it some more, then carried on. "Of course, when meal times were over, we all moved apart again. I did not dig the mines, the slaves did not hold the weapons, the soldiers did no writing, and so on. We took back our positions again."

There was a little crying noise from the other room. Iunet ignored it at first, but then it changed pitch. She felt her milk let down. She sighed and got up. He looked at her, seeing how the front of her shirt had become damp with milk.

"May I be excused for a few moments, lord?"

"Of course. Your master has need of you."

She nodded. "When he calls in just that way, my body answers before my heart does. But he is asleep really. I shall be back to clean before long."

When she came back in he had got some writing tools out again and was making some slight changes to the sketches. He had also set up in one corner of the room a little statue of a goddess figure, one that she did not recognise. The bowl was again on her side of the table, with several part-eaten pieces of fruit in it. Without commenting, she enjoyed them one by one. That done, she rinsed the bowl and spoon and set them to dry. He looked around.

"I realised while you were seeing to Nakht how much work you had done here while I was away. It is very different from when I last saw it."

"Well, I was here most of the day, and the mistress assigned one of the gardeners to bring all that I needed to look after you properly. She was most insistent." She came over and stood in front of him. "Lord, if I may, you still have the dust of today in your clothes and upon you, and I should clean all that for tomorrow."

"Surely that is not necessary. I have often slept in a worse state than this."

"But then you had no-one to look after you. Now you do. There is no need to lie unwashed in a bed as though you were a common labourer. The mistress would not want that to happen."

He stood up, obediently, and before he could stop her she had removed his smock and kilt.

"There, now sit in the warm evening air while all this is cleaned."

She rinsed out his outer garments while he sat, patiently, in his loincloth and worked a little more at his diagram. When the clothes were free of dust she hung them near the window and came back to the table.

"Lord, are you able to set that aside for a few moments?"

"Oh yes, I'm still thinking how all this should be set out. I'm sure I'll need to do several more revisions before I decide. This won't be the last. Why do you ask?"

"It is not just the clothes that have dust on them."

He glanced down at himself, looked at his hands, and rubbed his hair so that little trickles of rock dust scattered on the table. He pushed some of the grains together.

"Limestone. I don't think it has ever harmed anyone."

"If you will not let me clean it from your body now, I shall have to clean it from the bedding tomorrow."

Seeing the justice of her comment, he nodded. She brought over a fresh bowl of water and washed him. Unable to carry on working, he talked instead, about the day, the friend he would be working closely with, other workers, the ideas he had for the pictures for the mistress. She let the words wash over her as she cleaned his head and upper body, then squatted down to rinse his feet. The flow of words faltered briefly then, but she ignored that and simply continued. Finishing, she discarded the water on the vegetable patch outside and then barred the door for the night. He looked up at her.

"What now?"

"Whatever pleases your heart, lord. There are no more tasks that I need to do this evening to prepare for tomorrow."

"I think I am too tired to make sense of this design any longer. Perhaps it is time to sleep?"

She nodded. "Through here, then, lord."

He followed her with the oil lamp into the next room, glancing around at the changes she had made there too. Like the main room, it was altogether more welcoming. Nakht was asleep on a little bundle of cloths to one side of the bedroll, hands splayed out above his head. She pulled a thin covering over him where he had dislodged it.

"Lord, he will wake at least one time in the night and I must feed him. Maybe twice. But I will try not to let him cry long enough to waken you."

He shrugged.

"This is a much more comfortable place than many I have stayed in." Then he paused, and looked uncertainly at her. "Where will you and I both sleep?"

She glanced at him briefly.

"It would be better if I was the same side as Nakht, lord, but the choice is yours. I can always move him if you would prefer to change."

"That's not what I meant."

"Lord, the mistress said I was to gladden your heart in any way you chose. She was most explicit about that."

He looked around the room, awkwardly. She glanced at him again, curious about his reaction and realising that she enjoyed teasing him about the shared bed. She knelt down and pulled back the covers on the side closest to Nakht. "Shall I stay this side, lord?"

He nodded, still looking awkward, then apparently reached some sort of internal conclusion.

"Listen now, my friends well know that I can pursue very eagerly a thing that I desire. But I have never yet lain with a woman on the first day that I met her. Except for women in the houses of pleasure, and I was not expecting to meet them day after day. This is quite different."

He tried to laugh, unsuccessfully, and she smiled at him, trying to ease his mood with some warmth.

"But you do not mind if we share the bed? I can sleep on the floor in the other room if you will have it that way. And move Nakht. But it would be better here."

He shook his head, and hesitated a moment longer before continuing, still with a forced attempt at light heartedness. "Also, your mistress told me that you must not get pregnant while I am here. She was most explicit about that as well. She said that she will deduct the cost of food for you and the child for the first year from my payment if that happens. So you see, there is a risk for me if we lie together."

The smile froze on her face, and her expression went very distant. She looked away from him at Nakht. "Just as you say, lord scribe. A risk."

He knelt on his side of the bedroll and looked at her, puzzled at her withdrawal. "Have I said something to offend you?"

"You may say what you will, lord. It is not my place to take offence."

He shook his head. "That is no answer. If we are to live in this house together for a time, you must tell me. Tell me now."

This scribe seemed to be genuine in his perplexity, though one could never tell for sure. At the end of the day he was a master. She looked steadily at the wall ahead of her, trying to keep her voice neutral and appropriate to their relative station. Her anxiety about what he might do was being submerged by the strength of her reaction to his words.

"Lord, just a month ago a dear friend of mine died in the birthing of a child. We had played together as girls, and although we served in different houses, we met when we could, at the market or the riverbank. She became pregnant in her house while I was still carrying Nakht in my body, and her heart was full of delight when he was born. Now she is gone, lord."

She glanced briefly at him to gauge his reaction, then looked back at the wall. He was watching her, silent.

"Lord, you talked about this army officer who said that all men, scribe and slave alike, are the same in the desert, out in the red lands. Well, all women are alike in that very same way in the birthing house. Who can say which woman will live and which will die when she comes to term? Or which child? When I went in there because my time had come, lord, the mistress herself came down and let me hold her own magic ivory wands in the labour, so that the Two Ladies might look with favour on me. When I came through birth to the other side, with Nakht alive and placed on my body, she held me in her own arms and blessed me and thanked the Ladies. She knew as well as I that it can be a place of death as well as birth. She went in there three times herself, and although she came out alive again three times, only two children came out with her ever. So she knows that her high rank protects her no more than my low one. And then like your army man we went back to being mistress and servant."

He was still silent.

"So yes, lord, you do risk a few months of food if we lie together. But when I obey my mistress in this, as no doubt I will according to your desire, I will be taking a risk as well. Who can say which is the greater risk? Can you, lord?"

He pulled his gaze away from her and moved to sit upright

on the bed with his hands around his knees. There was a long pause in the room. She kept her own silence, wondering if the intensity of her heart had run away with itself, and if her words would be repeated to the mistress. Finally he spoke.

"I spoke in haste and without judgement, and you do right to tell me this. To correct me in my ignorance. And I am sorry to hear about your friend. If you can, please forget that those words of mine were ever spoken." He glanced at her, and she nodded, breathless.

"Look, I should be happy to share this bed with you, and I do not wish for you to be on the floor of the other room out there. Or your little boy. But I should like it better if we share this place, and this bed, just as companions for a time until we learn better how to fit each other's mood. That would please me more than if we were to rush headlong into arousing passion in each other tonight or tomorrow. I think tonight would be too soon. Will this bring you into disobedience with your mistress?"

She shook her head, not wanting to trust the steadiness of her voice. He relaxed a little, then looked across at Nakht, who had just started making little sucking noises in his sleep.

"It will be a strange thing for me, to live with a mother and child for a season. This is not a thing I have ever done before. You may find that you have to overlook several other things that I might say in ignorance."

She looked back at him, feeling relief flooding through her body and pushing away the earlier anxiety. Perhaps living with this scribe would not be a bad thing after all. She undressed and pulled the cover over her, knowing that his eyes were on her. She felt suddenly, acutely, aware of the thinness of her body compared to his well-fed limbs, and avoided his gaze as he lay down beside her.

She snuffed out the oil lamp and heard him sigh in the darkness. She settled back in the night, in a bed with a free man on one side and her son on the other, in a place they need not share with half a dozen others. Here, she could arrange the contents how she pleased. Here, she could make believe that she was mistress of a house herself. Smiling at the renegade thought, she reached to her left, found his hand and held it in her own as she fell asleep.

The lady Nebet-Tawi Ib-Iset walked over from her carrying-chair into the centre of the courtyard. Like every week on this day, she had travelled across the River to inspect the work. One of the men servants held a banner to shade her from the afternoon sun. Makty-Rasut bowed in greeting and carefully introduced his co-worker Sanedjem-Keni. He had done the same every week during the inspection, so she knew his name perfectly well by now. But the formality pleased her, and anyway this Sanedjem-Keni was obviously hoping that his name would be remembered to other people as well.

This was the first week that the proper creative work would start, and so the first week where her real interest was starting to be aroused. The preparation was all done, and her own servants had returned to their normal duties. In fact the work so far was a little ahead of schedule, which suited her in case this part ran late. This was the part she wanted to be done exactly right.

She listened politely as Makty-Rasut recited the accomplishments of the week, trying to restrain her eager eyes from scanning the rough outlines she could see off to one side. Eventually he was done.

"So, lady, would you like to see the layout that we have done since then?"

She nodded, and he led her over to the wall that she had been trying not to look at. He looked at her face, then wisely decided to give her time to look for herself without interruption. She stood back from the wall for a few heartbeats, taking in the broad divisions into vertical panels. The top and bottom borders were empty just now, with little chalk signs scribbled hastily here and there. But the panel immediately right of the tomb entrance, its borders marked out neatly, was starting to take shape. The pool and trees she had wanted were sketched out, with Iset emerging from the sycomore fig tree to one side. There were no other details yet, but there was space enough for everything.

She released her breath, realising as she did so how long she must have held it. How good it was that he had drawn Iset as soon as the position of the lake was settled. It might have seemed more natural to have worked on the trees that bordered the water, or perhaps the two figures of her and her husband. Perhaps he had seen through her little play-acting on that first day, and this was his way of acknowledging that.

Returning with an effort into the natural world of the court-yard and the hillside, she noticed that he was watching her closely.

"You are pleased with the progress on this panel then, lady?"

She nodded. "Very pleased. Show me the others now."

"Certainly, though there is little enough to look at as yet."

He was correct. The other three panels had been smoothed and skimmed with a first layer of plaster, but no more yet. She looked very closely at the surface for signs that he had taken short cuts, but if he had then he was better at concealing them than she at finding them. It seemed perfectly adequate, and she was impatient now to see how the artwork would be done. She nodded and walked back to her chair, shaded all the way by the careful servant.

"Here, look at this."

He came over to where she had pulled some papyrus out of the chair's pannier. She handed it to him, amused by the way he automatically felt the quality of the material. It was very good, she knew, having had it shipped up river from an old friend near the sedge lands, down near Min-Nefer. He studied the drawing she had made on it, then looked up at her.

"I imagine you want this on the third panel, lady, opposite

the sacred lake?"

"Exactly so."

He turned to look at the area of wall, scratched his head. He called out to his co-worker to bring over the earlier sketches. While the other man was finding them and coming over, he spoke again.

"If we keep everything else you asked for, will it not be rather full?"

"It would be. But we will not keep everything else. Here." She took the earlier pictures and pointed to several places. "I no longer want this, or this, and this section can be reduced."

He nodded in agreement, carried the papyrus over to the wall and measured the area roughly with his hands, then came back to her.

"Indeed, lady, that will work just as you say." He peered more closely at her writing. "And these words are for the top strip?"

She nodded. "I want it exactly as it says there. It must be exact."

She caught him watching her again, alert and curious, and felt herself reddening slightly with embarrassment. Foolish of her, she thought. He was just a workman. What did it matter what he thought?

"Of course. May I keep this sheet to be sure of it?"

"You may."

He gave it to the other man, who carefully stowed it away with the other design drawings. As he turned back towards her she spoke again.

"See now. Let us talk of that another time, perhaps. I am very pleased with all that you have done so far. Would you do me the further pleasure of eating in my house tonight?"

"The pleasure will be mine. I will be there after we have finished up here tonight."

"Have the girl clean you up first. I will send some suitable clothing along for you." He nodded again – he could do nothing else, really – and without thinking brushed at some of the rock dust on his tunic. "Is the girl adequate for your needs?"

"Oh yes, yes indeed. It is a luxury I am not used to, to be looked after in that way. I am most grateful, lady."

She turned to look once more at the courtyard space, especially the outline design of the pool. The arrangement was working well for her out here, and tonight she would be able to satisfy some of her longing for conversation. If she could loosen his tongue enough with some beer to discard some of the formality, the evening promised to be one of deep satisfaction.

Iunet walked down through the orchard back from the main house carrying some vegetables, a chicken, and a bundle of the scribe's clothes that had been cleaned properly by the laundrymen. It was rather over two months since he had started living in the little house. It had taken him just a week to decide, using his rather quaint phrasing, that it was right to arouse passion in each other.

The first few nights, like the first, she waited until they were lying side by side, and then reached out in the darkness to hold on to his hand. Then one night she had deliberately not done that, but waited to see his will. Sure enough, his hand had come across to her, encountering her waist and thigh instead of her hand, and it had taken no time at all for desire to ignite in them both. And since then, when the mood took them he was spark to her fire, and the little house sighed with their pleasure. Of course she told the mistress everything the next day, who right at the start had made it clear she must know all that happened between them.

What the scribe did not know, and in his ignorance had never asked, was where her body had been in its monthly cycle of fertility. She had not yet returned to a proper pattern since Nakht's birth, but simply counting by the moon she knew that the mistress had sent her down to the house at the time when she was at her most fertile, and that the week's delay had carried her past that. That little secret was part of her own game, threading her careful purposes between the clear will of the mistress and the rather confused wishes of the scribe.

The day after they lay together, he had brought back with him a second bowl and spoon, from his own house that waited empty in the village across the River. He insisted that they divide the food before starting to eat. Some of the thinness of her limbs and body was rounding out with food and the comparative ease of her work. Sometimes she wondered what would happen when the job was finished.

On this day, one of the older gardeners was working at the little vegetable patch outside the orchard hut. He straightened as she came up.

"Iunet, did you hear about those desert raiders that came in across the River?"

Anxiety clutched at her, and she held Nakht more tightly against her.

"No. Tell me, Hotep."

"I heard down at the market and by the riverbank. Some group of raiders were seen eyeing up the tombs and the houses over on the other side. A whole heap of them, from what I heard. No end of trouble. There'll have been fighting and all."

"Where? Which part?"

"Oh, I don't know. Somewhere over there to be sure. I don't know one name from another on that side. That's where your fancy scribe man spends his days, isn't it?"

She nodded, and quizzed him further, but he knew nothing more, and before long she went inside. If he had been able to tell her, the names would not have meant anything to her either. She had never been over to the west side. The small house seemed very empty, and she had little heart to carry on with the daily tasks. The time passed very slowly, and the day's light faded from the sky. She gave Nakht some little bits of solid food, then fed him in the bed she had shared with the scribe until he fell asleep. The food was prepared.

There was nothing to do except to wait. She sat blankly on her stool, unable to work away at everyday jobs. The noises of the garden work faded away. She was alone with Nakht in the empty house at the bottom of the garden. If he never came back, the mistress would reassign her before a day had passed, and all this would be gone again. It had only ever been an unexpected oasis on a desert journey, but her heart had thought that it was her life forever.

Finally she heard his step on the gravel outside, his hand on the door. He was inside the house, with time only for one glance at her drawn, tear-marked face before she had her arms around him and was holding him tightly. Her fierce embrace lasted for several long, trembling heartbeats before she stepped away again and composed herself.

"Lord, you are safe and well. My heart is very happy."

He shook his head.

"Why should I be otherwise?"

"There were raiders. I heard a long time ago in the afternoon. A big gang, a gardener told me. I thought that where you were working would have been pillaged, lord. Perhaps you were taken away into the red land as a hostage."

His face cleared in understanding.

"No, no, they came nowhere near us. And no fierce gang, only half a dozen or so scrappy men with no skill, just desperate men trying to seize something. They were seen near the Place of Truth, and again up near the valley where the royal workmen have their village. Not near me at all, nowhere near. But the mayors of both the west and the east sent out armed men to catch them. Their leader was beheaded, and his hands and manhood were cut off as trophies. They cut the right hand off the second in command, and branded him and all the others. Then they sent them back out again as a warning to their tribe not to do such a thing again. I saw the soldiers passing by with their spoils as they went back down again to their barracks. Not one of them was even scratched."

She relaxed.

"So it will not happen again?"

He shrugged.

"Well, I think that these raiders will become more bold in time, and that we will need soldiers out in guard posts. This will not be the last raid, and I dare say in time one of them will actually seize something of value. But not yet, not for a while yet." He paused and looked at her all over again, smoothed away a last tear. "I don't think I have ever had anyone that was concerned about me like this. Not since leaving the holy house as a boy when I went to be apprenticed."

She stepped away, feeling some embarrassment, and went back over to the fire to reheat their meal.

"Your food will be ready soon, lord."

He smiled a little, nodded in acceptance, sat in his usual place at the table and worked away at some sketches. In the other room, Nakht stirred, moved around, made little noises. She looked at the food and at the door, trying to gauge urgency. The scribe stood up.

"No matter, I will fetch him. I don't think it is hunger this time. I am learning the sounds he makes. This is just wakefulness, I think. Perhaps I can help with that."

She heard him go into the other room, greet Nakht as if he was another workman, and very soon after, he reappeared with the boy on his hip. He carried him over to the table, where Nakht tried unsuccessfully to reach some of the writing implements. She watched, intrigued, as he balanced her son on his lap and then made some marks on a tile.

"Here, Nakht, this is what your name looks like. Look, there's a long ripple of water, and a branch of a tree below it, two round marks like this, and finally a little child sign to finish the name off. What a lot of signs for a small boy. In a few years you can have a seated man instead, but you're not big enough for that yet."

Nakht put the old piece of pottery up to his mouth and sucked on it. Iunet brought the two bowls of food over and took the sherd with the little scratch marks on it so that she could look at it.

"Could you teach him to be a scribe, lord?"

He passed the boy over so he could sit on her lap.

"Well, not yet. He's a little too young just now. The earliest anyone would take him on would be six years of age. I was seven, or so I was told. Certainly he would have to be weaned, unless his master is happy with you coming in to feed him from time to time while he learns."

"But could it be done, lord? Could he learn enough to be able to work as you do?"

He looked at her for a long time, obviously realising that the request meant much more to her than he had expected. She kept her eyes down on the food. Eventually he spoke.

"If he has aptitude, there is no reason why not. Those who are apprenticed have started life in many different places. And they end up with many different tasks in the land, from the vizier who has the ear of the great king over all the land, who lives in prosperity and health, right down to those who are just responsible for, I don't know, for a granary perhaps, or a farm at one of the holy houses. My work is somewhere in the middle of all that. Listen though; it is not just to do with aptitude. There is a great deal of good fortune involved, to come to the attention of the right person at the right time. And them not having too many calls on their time from other things."

"But any of those tasks are better than just being a labourer serving in a household. Even the least of them."

He nodded. "Yes indeed. No question of that. But truly, it is too soon to tell. And there is a great deal of work. Not every person can do it." He paused, searching for good words to use. Perhaps, she thought, he regretted having spoken of the matter. "Look, if I was around at the time then I might be able to see if he has the beginnings of skill. But I could not teach him. I would be considered too young to do that, even by the time he has grown up a little. The most I could do for him would be to put in a good word with people I know. But tell me." Again he paused, trying to be careful. "Is it not true that the mistress would need to grant permission? From what you have told me, Nakht's life belongs to her just as yours does."

She nodded.

"It is true. After he is weaned, she may decide that she does not need a boy child around, and could give him or sell him to one of the other nobles. I know she will let him stay until then – she has done that faithfully with other women – but at that point it is her choice. No matter. Why should she choose that for him? Where is the benefit to her? It is just a day-dream that came upon me when I saw you showing him those signs."

Iunet, sitting on the floor, heard the door open behind her but did not turn round. She already knew that it was the scribe, and she wanted him to see this. As he came in, she called out to Nakht, who was standing upright holding on to one of the table legs.

"Nakht, Nakht, best of boys, come here."

He let go of the table and tottered unsteadily over to her to lurch into her arms. She turned her head then and looked with delight up at him.

"Did you see him, lord? Did you see him then?"

He squatted down beside her and tousled Nakht's dark hair.

"Truly, I did see him. What a magnificent triumph. Well worth writing on the wall of a courtyard so the world will remember it. When did he start?"

"Just today, lord. Of course you know he has been standing holding on to the table this last little while, and just this afternoon he let go of it and stood there upright, swaying a little, not holding on to anything. So I went near him and called him and he came to me."

He nodded and moved a short distance away. "Nakht, will you come to me?"

The boy turned to look into Iunet's face. "Yes, yes, dear one, go on, go to the lord scribe."

Nakht walked unsteadily the few short steps and half-fell into the scribe's outstretched arms. All three laughed at the result. They sat for a while opposite each other, in turn calling Nakht to move between them and catching him in his unsteady staggers. Suddenly she looked at the light still pouring in through the window, and jumped up.

"Lord, I have not prepared any of your food yet. You are home so early. What must you think of me?"

He shook his head. "I think you have been teaching little Nakht here to walk. But in any case, I am very early because the work is done. All of it finished. The lady Nebet-Tawi Ib-Iset, your mistress, came across the River today to inspect the work one last time, and she is content with what we have done. Well, not just content. Very happy, in fact. Delighted. And we have done the work for her on time, what with the barley harvest just now starting, and we have done everything that she wanted. Every single thing she asked. The work is over."

She stared at him, forgetting herself at the news, full of very mixed feelings. She had never thought to enquire how his work was advancing.

"So, you are finished here. Nothing left to do. My heart is happy for you, that you have come to a good place. But it is also a little sad. So you will move on again? Soon?"

He nodded eagerly, excited for himself and unaware of the conflicts in her.

"Yes, I have finished now. I am here for tonight, then tomorrow I move back into the little house across the River and see what work there is for me next. The mistress will praise my name so that others will hear. There will be other work. But not here, I think. Your mistress does not need me to do anything more for her. But because of what she will say to others, there will be other work for me somewhere nearby."

She nodded, letting her eyes fall again and holding on to Nakht as he swayed to and fro.

"So you will go back across the River, Nakht and I will go back into the main house, and this little place will fall empty again."

Her heart would be as empty as the house. But it was as she had thought before; this time was only a short stay beside a flowering pool in a garden, and another part of the journey was ahead. The scribe was clearly thrilled with the outcome. Perhaps she should take life from the overflow of his pleasure, and be content with that. In fact, she had always known that the work was due to be finished by the time of the barley harvest. She had been living from one day to the next, and had never given it thought. She put Nakht's hand in that of the scribe and went over towards the cooking area.

"Well, lord, at any rate I shall prepare food for you tonight." He shook his head.

"The mistress has instructed me that I shall eat with her tonight. And the other man who helped me, Sanedjem-Keni, we're both to eat up at the main house. But look, I can entertain your little crocodile while you make something for yourself." He saw her hesitate. "Please, I should enjoy that. He can help me finish off one last thing while you make food."

She used up the last of the beans and roots as she cooked. She had expected to replenish the larder tomorrow, but now there was no need. The grain would get carried back and absorbed into the main household resources, just as she would be herself. She took no notice of the scribe's chatter to her son, or his babbles in reply that were not quite words just yet. Finally she was done, and by habit carried the bowl of food over to the table, to her customary stool.

The scribe held something out to her. She took it, turned it over in her hand, looked at it. It was an oval piece of pottery, white on one side and smoothed around the edges. There was a little stylised picture of a mother and child down one side, and she used this to hold it the right way up. Beside the couple were some of his picture signs. She looked enquiringly at him. He pointed.

"Look, that is your name there. And that is Nakht's. And there at the bottom is a prayer to Seshat, the goddess who we call Mistress of the House of Books, that she will guide the footsteps of your lad so that he will come into her house one day."

She beamed, and her face lit up.

"What is the Lady Seshat like?"

"Well, you know how she looks from the little statue over there where I pray morning and evening. That's how we fashion her. But it is who she is that matters. She knows the limits of all kinds of things, the stars in the sky and the years of the great king. Anything. She can open the doors for us on the other side when we pass to the next life. But in particular she gives skill to the eyes, the hands and the hearts of those who write. Or those who want to do so."

She thought about what he had said for a long time, slowly eating her food and giving pieces to Nakht as it cooled down.

"You said it was a prayer, not a magic thing."

"And so it is. My training has not included much to do with magic. I had no real skill at that. You should ask a priest if that is your will. This writing here will not compel Nakht to do or say anything, nor those around him to accept him for something he is not. But perhaps it will be something that can reveal to him a path that he might follow, and perhaps it will be effective in opening the eyes of others around him. Who can say?"

They fell silent for a while. Eventually she stood up.

"If we don't get you ready for the mistress, there will be a mountain of trouble."

He let her wash him, take away his work clothes and prepare him for the evening with new ones the mistress had sent down before. As she finished, he took her hand in the little house.

"Hear me now before I go. You have been good to me these last few months. I had not expected this time to be so very full of kindness. It has been good for my heart, Iunet."

She looked into his eyes one last time, startled by his words. For a heartbeat she thought of denying that she had done anything for him beyond the work of any servant. But it would not have been quite true, and she had learned that he liked truth. She accepted the words quietly, making one last adjustment to his belt.

A little later he walked away, up the path to the great house to eat with the mistress. So here at the end of their time she had just washed him and dressed him for festival, then let him go out of the door without looking back. She waited, awake, for him to return, in case he would want them to lie with another one last time. To arouse passion, as he used to say.

But when he came back, in the depths of the night, he was very drunk and could scarcely find the bed they slept in, let alone the various parts of her body. She undressed him again, washed his face and hands so they would be clean in the morning, and pulled the covers over his nakedness. He did not respond at all as she did this, and seemed hardly aware of his surroundings. She left the oil lamp burning for a short time and sat looking at him. One day, perhaps, her son who had just walked today for the first time would be lying drunk like that, after successfully finishing a piece of work that had been placed in his trust.

Perhaps, after all, his incapacity tonight was for the best. She knew in herself that her body had at long last taken up its regular cycle, and was moving with the moon once again into fertility. She was becoming receptive and ready for seed just like the fields by the River after the inundation. He did not know that, would not have known the risk he was taking if they had satisfied one another tonight. She smiled to herself as though she had won a wager, picked up one limp hand and kissed it, then composed herself to sleep beside him.

The next day he was gone.

Richard Abbott

3. Present – Effort

WHEN WE KISS, her lips will open wide,
  willing for us to drink deep.
Now our time is at hand,
  the feast is made ready;
I draw near with joy
  to the place where she lies.

MAKTY-RASUT GATHERED THE MEN together in the courtyard, just outside the entrance. Inside, the walls had
now been properly smoothed as far as the transverse corridor, but were still rough beyond that. The main chamber at
the far end was only partly cut out of the limestone, and the
burial crypt below had only just been started. Today's daily
meeting, held like all the others some while after the hour of
work had passed, was a little different, as the remaining team
members were joining today.

All of them had arrived, except for the new leader on the
left, a man called Paneb-Re who Makty had not met before.
Sanedjem, who had been in that role, was moving across to
the right to take his own place there, and he was stepping out
of the teams in order to begin the real artwork. Hobniy was
also switching roles today, from leading the main dig back into
the hillside to starting work on the statues and standing stelae that would be placed in the main chamber. Two labourers had arrived to complete the cutting out work. The team
was at full strength now, and would stay at this number right
through until the job was nearly done.

At least, the team should be at full strength. Paneb-Re had
not yet arrived. He was very late. Makty looked again down
the track. Should he start anyway? He frowned. Lateness was
not just an annoyance for him personally, but showed a level
of disrespect for the whole team that he particularly disliked.
There was a scrambling noise from behind him, and he turned
to see a short man come into the courtyard from the uphill
side. Paneb-Re, he presumed.

"Ah, here you are. Sorry to be late but a boy down in the
village told me quite the wrong way. I would have been here
in time otherwise. You can't rely on the people round here,
you know. They're not like out in the sedge lands. You can
trust anything they say down there."

He took a place in the circle, nodding randomly to one or
two others. Makty caught a grin half-concealed on Sanedjem's face. His friend knew very well that Makty did not like

lateness, or excuses.

"Right, let us begin. Sanedjem, you start, please."

"Yesterday I finished off smoothing the left wall section down to the cross corridor. The wall flaked a little, nothing serious. Today I'm taking Makty's place on the right and starting on the first panel after the cross."

He looked at Setimose, standing beside him.

"Well, chief, yesterday I was working on the left as Sanedjem directed. I helped him on the flaking part he mentioned. Today I'll be working as Paneb-Re directs."

They went round the circle in the same way, with the new faces introducing themselves instead of describing their work. Eventually the circle was finished by Makty describing briefly the gist of his last meeting with the priest for whom they were all working. After that, he glanced briefly around.

"Right. Before we all start, just a few words. This is the full team now, so look around and get to know these people because you'll be working with them day after day for several months. Some of you will finish a few days before the job is completely done, but everyone here now will get a share of the reward at the end if the lord priest likes the work. I intend him to like the work: I am very committed to that. I expect you to be committed as well. We have a small amount of slack time in case anything is more tricky than I'm expecting, but not very much. So don't waste time. If something is not going right, if the wall starts flaking or the paint is not drying properly, if someone gets injured or sick, tell me at once so I can see what needs doing about it. I can change things around if I know soon enough. Anything else?"

Paneb-Re nodded and stepped forward slightly.

"I just wondered. Other places I've worked, the juniors on a small team have stood beside their leader, and the senior has spoken for all of them. It saves a bit of time, and you can easily see who is senior and who is junior. Maybe we should do that here. I think it's a better way to do it."

Makty thought about it very briefly.

"No, I don't think I like that. We'll keep doing it the same way."

Paneb-Re frowned.

"Well, it's your choice. But I think you would find that the other way is better if you tried it."

"You and I can talk about this another time. So far as I am concerned, for the time being we carry on the same way. I like to hear each man speak about his work in his own voice. But what I most want done differently is for everyone to turn up on time. Juniors and seniors."

There were several grins around the circle.

"Well, another time I won't need to rely on the locals to direct me here. And if you want to run the daily circles like this then that's your choice. I'm just saying that's what's happening in other places. Just takes longer to catch on this far up river, I suppose."

"If there's nothing else?" Makty looked around again, trying to ignore the amused expression on Sanedjem's face. "Then perhaps we could make a start for the day."

Makty soon became aware that Paneb-Re was extraordinarily slow. He kept a covert eye on the left side team over the next week or so, and became acutely aware that Sanedjem and his pair of helpers were steadily pulling ahead on the right. The drafting work on the right was more or less keeping pace with the work to smooth the rough-cut walls, but not so on the left.

Not only that, but although Paneb-Re clearly thought he was being precise and methodical, some of his work was actually not very good. Several times he found that outlines of figures that the man had laid out had to be redrawn, since they would obscure or crowd out parts of the scene that would be filled in later. The man had no real sense of the overall design, or how to plan early work so that it would fit into place as details were added later. When it came to completing the rough designs with colour, his skills became more obvious, but he seemed at a loss how to plan the stages leading up to that.

Makty worked late one evening to correct one such mistake. The design was clear enough; three small supplicants from different places in the Asiatic provinces were to be shown in front of the lord priest, and the text around it would describe his benevolence to all comers. But the way the priest's figure had been sketched left barely room for two others, let alone three. And the text would need to be drawn ridiculously small to fit. To correct this, the main figure had to be made smaller, and shifted right a little. He had worked for a while when there was the sound of footsteps in the corridor, and a shadow falling across him. He glanced up.

"Sanedjem, what are you doing back here?"

The other man looked at what he was doing, picked up another of the tools, and started correcting some of the misplaced lines in the area that Makty had not yet reached.

"Well, I went to your house, and you weren't there, so I guessed you'd be fixing this mess. It'll take half the time with two of us."

Makty grunted, and they worked in silence for a while. Eventually Sanedjem spoke again.

"How long will you let this go on? You can't keep doing both your job and his."

"Well, he might catch on. And anyway, I don't have to redo everything he does."

"No, it's the layout mostly. His colour work is not bad. But look at this now, there's no way this could ever have worked. Not with three figures to fit in there. What was he thinking?"

Makty squatted down to finish off erasing the lower section.

"Do you know what he said about this? He said that I had not been clear enough what I wanted him to do. That if I wanted it a particular way I should have told him. What could I say? The drawings were just there where they always are.

I'm not his wet-nurse. He should have checked. Then another time he tried to blame Horiy. You've heard him in the daily circles; there's always some reason why he couldn't do it in time. It's just the same when he talks to me directly, one excuse after another. I mean, does he want to be senior or not?"

Sanedjem listened as he grumbled on for a while.

"Well, I'm certainly glad you're not letting it frustrate you too much."

Makty looked up at him and shrugged.

"Look, if there was another choice I'd have gone for it. But there's nobody around just now. You know that. They're all either taken up on other jobs or out of town altogether. That priest caught us at a bad time for getting good workers. Even if this character only does half a job it's better than none at all. There, we're done now for tonight."

"Only because I came back to help out. You'd have been here twice the time otherwise. And it's showing; you're not getting enough rest."

Makty pulled a face.

"So now you're going to look after me as well as work for me? Look, if I wanted a wife I'd pick one out. Or a mother."

"Not me. But my Weret gets anxious about you. She made me come up looking for you. Said that when we were done here that you had to come down to our house and eat something. I'm not supposed to take no for an answer."

"I suppose you'd have let me starve."

"Absolutely. If you can't sort this out you deserve to starve. But maybe for today we could give you some food."

Much later Makty returned alone to his house. He had gone back with Sanedjem, eaten at his house amidst a life of domesticity he did not expect for himself, and heard in rather alarming detail about babies and early pregnancy. In the end he had left, reluctantly, well after dark. Sanedjem and Weret had kept the conversation resolutely away from matters to do with working life. It had been good. He had drunk more of Weret's excellent beer than he should have done, and was in a very mellow state as he settled himself for sleep. The night air was warm and balmy: surely Waset was a splendid place to live.

Sometime much later another of his vivid dreams came to him. He was walking alongside the river bank, chewing on some of last year's carob beans. On either side clumps of papyrus were growing; they were very far from full height yet, as the growing season was young. Little birds perched on plant stems near him or skimmed low over the water. He did not know the path, and the section of the river was unfamiliar. From behind him, upstream, a boat drifted around a bend on the river and came towards him. It was fully laden, carrying a granite statue down from the quarries, destined for one of the mortuary temples somewhere downstream. The river current brought it quite close to his bank as it passed him, but too far out to reach. She was drifting away on the stream, and he was suddenly possessed with the desperate urge to take hold of her.

The river was carrying her away, and he could not reach her. He ran as fast as he could along the path, but the water was flowing faster than he could run. The boat pulled away from him, started to disappear around the next bend. He ran faster, but she was gone. There was a great movement in the reeds beside him, and a crocodile was on the path there, great jaws clacking full of teeth. On the other side a mountain lion appeared, roaring. The head of a hippopotamus lifted out of the water, mouth agape. There was a scorpion on the path in front of him, tail raised high. He dared not slow down, but trod on it with his white sandals and ran at desperate speed to escape the other beasts. Fierceness raged both sides of the path and he doubled his pace again, sandals flashing white along the track. He rounded a corner, and there was a flat dish, empty on a low table in front of him.

He woke up in a sweat. The dream tugged away at him, still playing itself out in some recess of his heart. He got up, dipped a beaker in his water jar and drank it. He looked out of the window towards the cultivated fields and the distant River. Surely it was never as dangerous as that down there, not all at once. He sat on a stool for a while, slowly finishing the drink, and then settled himself back to sleep. The rest of the night was uneventful.

Makty walked up the last steps of the stony path to the chief priest's door. Wooden pillars and a leafy creeping plant that he did not recognise had shaded him since leaving the main street through Waset, but outside, on the way down from the community of the dead and on the little boat that had ferried him across the River, the direct heat of the sun had been very fierce. It was easy to forget while you were under the ground. He would have much preferred to complete the day's work first, and then made the trip down in the cool of the evening, but the priest thought otherwise, and always insisted on hearing a progress report once a week, in the middle of the third working day.

He knew how it would go – he would explain what progress had been made in which areas, and what was planned to be done during this week. It was just like the daily circles, but one level higher up. The priest would want to know why there had been a delay in cutting out the under-chamber, which should have been finished already. That was easy: they had reached a layer of much harder rock, which had blunted tools and slowed the pace of cutting.

More difficult, to Makty's mind, was the matter of the recent outline work done by Paneb-Re. He was seriously regretting selecting him as the draftsman of the left side, even though there had been no choice at the time. His work remained slow, and not very accurate when finished. The night when Sanedjem had come back to help him had not been an isolated episode. Makty had needed to redraw draft outlines or reposition guidelines for writing on several occasions.

3. Present – Effort

As he strode up to the door he debated with himself, as he did most weeks, whether he should continue to be keep silent about Paneb-Re, or simply recommend he be reassigned to some other task. Week by week, he was losing patience with him. The situation was very close to the point where the man's slow rate of production, and his indifferent quality of work, would start to impede their overall progress. All the team knew it, and it was already affecting their overall mood and respect. Before much longer, they would start to think less of him as overall leader for not tackling the matter face to face. To sum up, the man scarcely had enough experience to be part of the team, and certainly not to be directing the work on one side.

On the other hand, Makty had a feeling that Paneb-Re was well connected. If he was going to risk his own place of work over the issue, he wanted to be absolutely sure of his footing. As he came up to the door it was opened for him from the inside. One of the priest's attentive servants had seen his arrival, a heavily pregnant woman who had been sitting just inside on a stool watching the pathway. She called over a young lad and told him to conduct Makty through the house to see the priest. As he followed the youth he decided that – yet again – he would say nothing this week, and – yet again – he would carry the extra work himself.

He was led by a different route through some different corridors into the same room at the side of the large house. As usual, he looked out of the open side towards the River and the western city of the dead. Across the River, scattered here and there across the hillside in little clumps like thickets, were individual tombs. Lower down on the valley floor were the very much more substantial dedication temples for the dead kings. The priest was standing between two of the pillars, looking out at the view, and turned as the boy announced Makty's arrival and then ran off again.

Some beer and pieces of honey cake were on a nearby table, and as usual the priest gestured to the stool nearest the wall.

The cones and spools of the Senet board were packed away today, and Makty hoped that that meant they were not going to play. Having discovered that the priest was actually quite a poor player, he did not know whether to play to his own ability and win every time, or play badly to give the older man occasional victories.

The Maghariy woman was there again, and he felt his heart quicken slightly as he saw her. She poured them both some beer and then stood back, waiting on the priest as he crossed over from the portico. Makty was sure now that she would be there every time that he came to the house for these visits. While the priest made his slow way across the room he started speculating about her origins. If he was telling her story in stone and ink, how would that go? What scenes might be drawn from her life? Had she come willingly into the land, or was she taken captive in one of the great king's raids? How had she ended up as a servant in this house, albeit one who was apparently trusted with more personal tasks?

Pulling himself away from that line of thought, he made his weekly report as he had planned, careful to describe the difficulties with the vein of harder rock. The priest asked a few questions here and there but mostly listened in silence. Makty thought, as he often did, that the priest was a very silent man. When he had finished the weekly account there was a little pause. The priest got up again, walked over to a second table, picked up some sheets of papyrus, and then came back. Makty glanced at them, seeing that they had outline designs for a pair of matching stelae. Two suitably sized gaps had already been left in the designs for the eastern wall, at the far end of the corridor. The priest nodded.

"We will talk about that soon. But first, I notice that you have said very little about the corridor where the rough drafting is being done. Is there a difficulty with that?"

Makty hesitated. What should he say?

"Lord, we are making progress there. The scenes you asked for have been outlined. That is, the one where you first heard the divine word to travel into the Asiatic provinces, and also when you accompanied the new bride for the governor of Ged-jet from her home. They are both complete in rough form, and ready to have the base colours applied by my assistant."

"Excellent. I hope that I shall visit my everlasting house shortly, to see all this for myself. If only the weakness of this bodily frame will allow me." He looked up, rather intensely, at Makty. "But I cannot help but notice that both of those are on the right. You have said little about the left side."

"The left side lags a little, great lord, but I will see that it is done according to your plan."

The priest waited to see if he would add anything else to the bare statement, then shook his head.

"When you speak with me in this house, I would always prefer it if you said all that was in your heart. I am well able to decide for myself which things should go further and which should stay between us. There is a problem with the team on the left? As I recall, you have said nothing of real substance about it these last three weeks."

The old man's eyes were on him, insistent and piercing through his attempt to skirt the matter. Makty remembered all over again how many years of experience in priestly service the man had. He was, no doubt, well used to listening out for omissions or evasions in the words of others. He hesitated still. He had never been sure exactly how well connected Paneb-Re and his family were, and perhaps he was a relative of the priest sitting opposite him. He glanced across at the Maghariy girl, aware that there were other ears in the room that might report what they heard. The priest looked at her as well.

"Bring us some more of that beer and sweet bread, if you will, and then wait outside the door until I call you in again."

She nodded her head and left. The priest looked quizzically back at Makty.

"I do admire a man who keeps his peace about his fellow workers, but this has gone on for too long. Now that we are alone, tell me what you would not say before. You are not just a fellow worker with these other men, but you are leader of the group and I require you now to act like their leader. Even if it is not to your taste."

Makty nodded, and this time yielded to the demand. He talked at some length about Paneb-Re's modest abilities, his own anxieties and concerns, and the various ways in which the whole team had needed to work around the man's limited skills and impenetrable slowness.

"But lord priest, I think we can still keep to the plan we agreed. I do not think that the situation is beyond recovery."

The older man looked down, his eyes half closed as he absorbed the account. He rubbed the back of his bald head and then caught Makty's eyes again.

"Why wait so long to tell me this?"

Makty shook his head and looked out of the window.

"The man seems well-familied, sir. For all I know, he is the son of an important official. And the matter was not so far advanced as to be beyond recovery. But now it is starting to become a threat to the times and seasons that I agreed with you."

The priest laughed.

"He is not my son, if that is what you mean. To set your mind at rest, my only daughter is married and living out in the Asiatic provinces, in a city up the coast. I have no son of my body, and am looking to adopt a suitable man here in Waset to carry out the rites and duties of a son at my eternal house. Perhaps a junior priest: certainly someone who has scribal training."

He stood and looked across the River towards the clustering tombs.

"I can give you another draftsman in his place. I can move this man Paneb-Re to another task, here on this side of the River. What is he good at, seeing as how this task is beyond him?"

Makty thought for a while.

"He does not have a talent for laying out a design on the wall from a plan, lord. But I think he could execute the work if it had already been laid out in rough by someone else. And my sense is that he is better with brush than chisel. Certainly he is good with colour."

"Excellent. Then I have just the task here in the great temple. When you go back today, tell him that I require his skills on this side from the hour of work tomorrow. Now, about his replacement. I have a few men of suitable length of experience that I could send over to you. Let me think who would be best."

"Lord priest, I am accustomed to choosing men for my team myself. Who is it that you have in mind? I know most of the skilled workers who live nearby."

The priest nodded.

"Reasonable enough. I would say the same if someone offered me a priest to serve in the temple. Well, over here on this side I have these men."

He recited a list of names. Makty had indeed met most of them, and knew that they were not really suitable; that was why he had ended up with Paneb-Re in the first place. A name near the end, however, caught at him.

"Neb-Hotep, I think. I have not worked with him myself, but my second speaks well of him. If it would please you, could it be him who is transferred?"

"Certainly. He will be across with you on the other side at the hour of work tomorrow. See that he is well instructed in what must be done to catch up. I leave it to you to decide what you tell the other men."

He nodded with satisfaction, then called the desert girl back in to the room. She poured some more beer for them both and set a small plate of honey cakes between them, watching the scribe with eyes like ebony from behind the curtain of her hair. The two men drank together. Makty was profoundly relieved at the outcome of their time together, and allowed himself to relax, perhaps for the first time in the chief priest's house. They looked through the papyrus sheets and the priest's intentions for the stelae, and afterwards he found himself talking rather more extensively than he had intended. The priest was, seemingly, quite content just to listen.

"And then, lord, I have had the most vivid dreams recently. One last night that was different, but also I have had the same dream three times now, no, more than that." He stopped himself. "I apologise, great one, I am taking up your time, and I should be getting back to your everlasting house."

"No, no, not yet. Indulge me, if you will. I have an interest in dreams. A very keen interest. It was a dream that sent me out into the Kinahny lands, to Gedjet, and another dream that brought me back here to Waset. As you well know from what you are preparing across the River. They have been important to me at other times too. Will you speak of yours?"

Not sure whether the request was meant seriously, Makty leaned back against the wall.

"I do not remember it very well."

"But well enough to know you have had it at least three times? Come, with the change I have made to your team you will catch up on the left side within a short time. There is no rush. Stay a while longer and please me."

"Well, lord, I remember that each time I was resting inside the body of a great ship drifting with the stream, and that I was happy. Then each time it changes abruptly. Either the boat is gone, or water floods in and sweeps me away, or something of that nature. The last time I was suddenly flung into the River. And each time I know that I am wearing white sandals. Excessively fine ones of a kind I would not wear normally."

"Sandals? White ones? Then you will go on a journey. In the near future, too." He pulled a face and shook his head. "Not before the work is finished, I hope, but if this is truly out of the land of light we must all submit to it."

"Why a journey?"

The priest got up and walked over to a shelf that had a

number of rolled sheets of papyrus on it. He glanced briefly at several, and then brought one across, opening it out between them. There was a list made of several columns, with occasional words picked out in red.

"Here, look, read it for yourself. It is quite clear. 'If a man dreams of himself wearing white sandals: a long journey'. No doubt about it. I have used this manual for many years, and it has come down to me from the times of the ancestors. It is quite basic, but it has always proved itself to be most reliable as far as it goes."

Makty looked at the line the other man was pointing to, then let his eyes glide up and down the other lines in case a different situation seemed more to his liking. The priest had omitted to tell him that the interpretation had been marked as "bad". He shook his head.

"That does not look like a favourable outcome. But where will I journey to? And how soon?"

The old man was alive with excitement, more so than Makty had ever seen before.

"We do not know. Not yet. But we can work on this, you and I. The journey itself is obvious, trivial. The plunge into the river, now, that shows a good future for you. A very good future. Do not be alarmed by the shock of the water. The water offsets the sandals. It is a good outcome, not a fearful one. That is also quite straightforward. But the other details are more challenging, and that is where we must concentrate." He paused, trying without success to hide his anxiety. "You do want to find out?" As Makty nodded, he carried on. "Then each week you are here we will talk some more about it. It will be a good thing, yes?"

"Of course, lord, if that is your will. But I should not take up your time without reason."

"I must be the judge of that. I think you will find that each week we will see more of the divine plan being brought out into the light. We will start with this dream you have had several times, and then move on to the others. This is profoundly important for you, and will also enrich our own times together."

Makty nodded his head. He had known from the chief priest's descriptions of the scenes he wanted on the walls of his tomb that dreams were significant to him, but the revelation of exactly how important was new. He realised also that he was finding the intensity of the man's focus on the topic to be very unsettling. He looked out at the angle of the shadows in the garden.

"But lord priest, for today at least I must be getting back to the team."

The priest sighed, but nodded.

"How true. Especially since you have news to impart to this man Paneb-Re. Yes, indeed, you should start on your way back." He hesitated for a moment, then carried on. "Now look, Makty-Rasut. If we are to talk about these things together then I do not want to hear you calling me 'lord' or 'lord priest' all the time. From now on, when we are together like this, you must use my given name. Call me Senenptah from now on when we meet. Of course you must continue to use my title when your men are present. When I come to inspect the work for example, which I should like to start doing from time to time now, if my body permits. But here, just you and I together with this lady, it would please me to be called Senenptah."

Makty nodded in some surprise.

"I will try to remember, sir. You honour me."

Senenptah turned to the Maghariy girl.

"I wonder now, would you show Makty-Rasut back to the door for me?"

She nodded, turned to Makty and waited while he picked up his small pack, and then led him through the passageways of the house. After several visits, Makty thought he could find his way back to the main entrance, so long as he kept to the direct route. The house was still something of a confusing mystery. He was not, however, in the least surprised at the priest's gesture of courtesy in offering an escort.

What did surprise him was the priest's attitude towards the girl; normally with his servants he simply issued instructions rather than making requests. His attitude towards her was quite different. He was not sure how to understand this, and spent the time going from the interior room to the door to the outside pondering it. The pregnant woman was still by the door; Makty's guide stopped her rising to her feet and opened the door herself. Outside, the air was very hot, and the two went along the shaded aisle towards the gate onto the street. She opened that for him as well, and then stood back to one side.

"Thank you."

"My pleasure."

He started to go, then turned back to her. He could not bear the thought of parting from her today without enjoying more conversation. A sudden mood caught at his heart, and it seemed to him that he should not let these moments slip past.

"How long have you been serving in the master's household?"

She looked directly at him, in a way none of the other servants would do.

"Do you think I am just another of his slaves?"

"I don't know. I just thought you must be. Why else would you be here?"

"My mother was grateful to the lord priest for a kindness he once did for our family. I am fulfilling the debt of gratitude by being here in his household."

He spoke out his sudden thought without pausing to reflect.

"How did he come to know your mother? I did not realise that he had been out in Ta Mefkat for any great time? When in his life did that happen? Are you related to him? No, surely not?"

He looked back into her face, to realise that it had filled up with a remote disdain.

"Surely not what? Surely that he would not help my mother because she was not a River girl? Did you not realise that I am not a nice girl from Abedju or the sedge? I have been told this by other men. I had even realised for myself that I do not come from your River. Does it matter to you? Have you only just noticed?"

He shook his head, a little taken aback at the fierce response.

"No, no, that's not what I meant. Not at all. I said 'surely not', because I know most of his life story after talking with him so often, and sketching out so much of it for the walls of his eternal home. I would know if he had spent time in Ta Mefkat. I was not meaning anything about you not being born by the River. Or your mother."

She relaxed a little, but was still wary.

"Very well. Then perhaps another time we shall talk some more about it."

She closed the gate and turned to go back to the house, without looking at him again. He watched her through the open slats of the gate for a little while until she was out of sight, before setting off for the ferryboat. The rapport, with its developing possibilities, was increasingly exciting. But for the game to end the way he wanted, with her defences yielding to him, it was clear that he must move carefully when speaking of her origins.

Back across the River, and after a short walk through the hot village and up the little track onto the ridge, Makty approached the workplace. Hobniy was sitting outside, a little pack of food unwrapped in front of him. He waved casually as he saw Makty appear along the dusty track.

"Run out of work to be doing, Hobniy?"

A large grin spread across the big man's dark features.

"And it's a pleasure to be seeing you too, chief. Had a nice rest at the priest's house, have you? But in truth, I am a little stuck just now, until your man Paneb-Re can motivate himself to get the drawing right. I could do it better myself."

Makty nodded.

"Then leave that mess for a while and come inside with me. You'll want to hear this."

Hobniy raised his eyebrows, but closed up the food bag and followed Makty down the longitudinal passage. Paneb-Re was just under half way down along the left side, with one of the junior painters beside him holding some tools and an oil lamp. The other was standing off to one side watching, doing nothing. On the right, Sanedjem and his two helpers were considerably further down, all working together. Makty stopped by Paneb-Re and looked at the wall, then glanced to and fro along both walls. Paneb-Re turned towards him, then gestured at the rough area of stone and the partly outlined scene in front of him.

"This rock surface is really bad, you know. You just can't make real progress on it. And the tools you got us, I think they cheated you, they're just very poor quality. You should take them back. I did raise this as a problem at the daily circle three days ago now, and nothing has happened. And these wicks they gave us for the lamps, I'm sure they're short of the standard measure. No-one can get real work done with this kind of support."

Sanedjem and his team had stopped working when they heard the complaint. He started to come back down the corridor, mouth already opening to speak, but Makty looked at him, shook his head, and then turned back to Paneb-Re.

"From now on that is not your concern. I talked to the lord priest today. He and I have agreed that your particular skills are better suited to a project in the great temple on the east side. I think, and he agrees, that the work there will be better for you. And if you discover that the equipment there is not up to your standards, why then, you can tell the lord priest yourself. He wants you to report to him there at the hour of work tomorrow. As for this work here, I am giving you the rest of the day to yourself. Collect up whatever is yours and go home."

Paneb-Re looked around at the grinning faces of the team members. He was as aware as the rest that this was dismissal. He cleared his throat nervously.

"But this is not completed yet. Look here and here, I have work to finish on the wall first."

"No. You do not. Collect whatever is yours, go home for today, and report to the lord priest tomorrow at the great temple on the east side."

There was a short pause.

"Will I still get the gratitude gift at the end? You did say that we would all share, all of us who had worked together during this stage."

Makty stared at him, incredulous. Paneb-Re hesitated for a long moment, as though considering whether to argue further. He could see that Makty was entirely unmoving. He shrugged, picked up a couple of items and started towards the outside world. He stopped again.

"Whoever you get will have the same problems, you know. It's not just me. You'll find out. You'll find out I was right all along. You just never gave me a time to speak properly about it. You're the leader for all of us, you should have listened."

Then he hurried out into the sunlight before anyone could reply. There was a burst of chatter as he left, other workers asking who he had been able to find in place of Paneb-Re, different voices. He nodded to acknowledge the questions, turned to Sanedjem as his second.

"The lord priest is giving us Neb-Hotep to work on the team. He offered me several choices, and he seemed best. You've worked with him before, haven't you? Somewhere down river. I recognised his name when the priest told me."

Sanedjem was beaming.

"Yes, on a couple of jobs. He's alright. Quick, too, and we need that now. I'd have told you about him before, but he was already working on something else."

"Not any longer."

"Well, he's good with layout and colour, doesn't like statues and stelae but that doesn't matter on this job. Not with Hobniy here." He looked at the two juniors who had been under Paneb-Re's command. "You'll get on with him. He's a great one for doing it right first time, though, so make sure you don't make silly mistakes. He'll have you working all hours to get it right if you do."

There was an atmosphere of relief among the men. Makty took a deep breath. The priest was right: he should have done this a long time ago. It was not as if he owed Paneb-Re anything. The group was separating again. Sanedjem and his assistants were going back to the area they had been working on. Makty turned to Hobniy.

"Just for the rest of the day, leave what you were doing and direct these two, please. You can hand over to Neb-Hotep tomorrow and show him what's to do next."

Hobniy nodded, studied the wall, and picked up a couple of tools from the pile. Sanedjem looked back from his work.

"Hey, Hobniy, mind you don't take one of the cheap ones that don't work properly."

There was a great roar of laughter up and down the corridor. Makty was content: they would be back on schedule before long.

After his experience that day, Makty was not surprised to discover that the priest was quite determined to spend a little time each week talking about the dreams. Conversation about the tomb, its decoration, and its contents was kept as short as possible. In itself that was fair, as the work was at a stage where it had its own momentum and needed very little by way of direction or decision from Senenptah. All the choices had been made, and it was only necessary to enact them.

Makty had expected that the priest would want to inspect the work regularly, but every time he suggested it the old man shook his head. He was no longer able to make the journey over the River as often as he would wish, he said. He would come across to see it when the work was done, and until then he would trust the progress reports Makty gave him.

Indeed, the work on the tomb was progressing well, and there was no further need to try to hide things from the priest. As Sanedjem had promised, Neb-Hotep was a rapid worker, and although the left side never quite caught up with the right, it drew ever closer as the days and weeks went past. Makty had kept a discreet but close eye on the work for the first few days, and rapidly decided it was not necessary. The man had real talent, and could be trusted to do the work.

This left him free to do what he loved best, turning the rough designs he talked over with Senenptah, and the outline sketches done by his working teams on either side, into living works of art. They would gladden the heart of the old man for all time to come, whenever his roaming spirit would go to and fro along the passageways of his eternal home. Makty found himself unusually motivated to complete the job well. There was an urge in him to do well at this job beyond that of professional pride, responsibility, or the desire for his name to be made known to others. He already knew that the work was competent and good; he wanted it to be splendid.

Week after week the old priest would just listen to Makty's verbal report, and Makty could not persuade him to inspect in person. Perhaps the journey over the River and then up the hillside was indeed too much for him now. Makty found it very unsettling, though. He was used to being trusted in his work, but not at such a level that there were no visits at all. He felt as though he was dangling over the side of a tall monument on a rope, never quite sure that the strands would hold.

He was anxious in case the man did not like his eternal home when he finally saw it. Every week he would go to great lengths to describe what could be seen from different parts of the interior passages. He talked about the designs, the colours and shapes, the way in which the different parts made up the whole. Senenptah would sit listening with his eyes closed as Makty talked, applying his imagination to the words.

That done, the scrap of stone or pottery would be pushed to one side, and in its place some papyrus rolls of dream texts would come out for comparison. The Senet board was largely forgotten. Some weeks there was little enough to talk about, and his employer would visibly swallow his disappointment and reluctantly let him go back again across the River.

On other days some seemingly minor detail teased from Makty's memory would trigger a much longer study and discussion. On the whole, Senenptah did not suggest direct interpretations in the way that he had on the first occasion. Indeed there were times that he seemed perplexed by the accounts. On those days Makty felt more in control of the encounter. As the weeks rolled past, however, it often seemed that he was being carried along without volition in the matter.

But all of the difficulties he faced in relation to his dreams were more than compensated by the extra possibilities for relationship with the Maghariy girl. Each week she stood to one side of the table, listened to all that was said, served them with drinks and little delicacies from time to time, and remained enigmatically silent. Her foreign features and skin tone, while not so very different from someone born along the River, came to him to seem increasingly exotic and attractive. He started to long for the conclusion of his conversations in the priest's house, when she would walk with him back to the outside world and the outdoor heat, in between the colonnades and the shade of the climbing plants.

Each week, as they traced out the path away from the room where the men talked, back towards the road into Waset, he had a brief opportunity to converse with her and engage with her on a more personal level. During those times she sparred with him verbally, providing snippets of information about her past with the reticence of a Senet player yielding as little as possible of a strong position.

Slowly as time passed he found out a little more about her origins out in Ta Mefkat, and the family and personal commitment that called her to work in Senenptah's house for the time being. But he could never be sure he understood the basis of that commitment, and how far she was elevated above the regular household servants. Large parts of her self remained hidden from him, and he was never sure if this constituted a game or a test, and whether he was making progress or regress.

The experience was unlike anything he had known before when pursuing a woman, and he found himself entirely unsure how to navigate through the encounters. On some days it seemed an exciting game; on others, it was a frustrating and apparently fruitless way to seek satisfaction. He found himself unable to pull away from the challenge, and she began to play a regular, though enigmatic and always evasive role in his day-dreams.

He was quite certain that Senenptah was aware of the spark which was alight in him and which, he liked to persuade himself, was steadily being kindled in the woman as well. There were times between the progress reports, the rare games of Senet, and the regular discussions about his dreams, where he would catch the old priestly eyes flicking between the two of them, with something like a smile only just beneath the surface. The matter was never discussed openly between the three of them while they were together, but hovered like a bird of the reedy marshes around the borders of their conversation.

The first time that he tried to find out her name, she deftly avoided telling him and slipped the conversation into other channels. But the following week, when he persevered with the attempt, she yielded unexpectedly.

"In my own home I am called Milashuniyet. But it is a name your people struggle to say correctly. The first part of the name is difficult for you. Often I end up being called Desheret. You can choose."

He thought about it. 'Desheret' sounded too much as though it was a covert insult, and he knew that if he was intent on establishing closer relations with her, he must avoid saying things that sounded like slurs on her heritage. He would avoid that name. But the name Milashuniyet was indeed hard for him. He tried it three times silently inside his head, and none of them sounded like the way he remembered her saying it. He paused, searching for a strategy. This is why, perhaps, she had told him the name so quickly; it was itself part of the on-going game between them.

"Could I call you Shunaya? I'm sure I can say that right."

She laughed. "Close enough."

On balance he felt the exchange had been a success. The name Shunaya still sounded enticing and slightly foreign, and he was confident he would not stumble over it and cause offence. She nodded again, apparently turning things over in her own mind, then smiled at him in a way that disarmed all of his own preparations.

"Until next time then. I am sure you will be reporting to the lord priest at the same time next week."

Makty concluded another report to the lord priest. The work was drawing towards a conclusion. All of the heavy cutting work had been finished long since, and only a small portion of the detailed work remained. Makty had the more junior members of the crew working up and down the corridors and chambers checking everything against the original designs that had been agreed, and carefully removing the few remaining irregularities in the plaster work.

Meanwhile, he and Sanedjem crafted the final details of the main scenes. Neb-Hotep and Hobniy populated areas that had been deliberately left blank earlier with little clumps and thickets of written signs, enriching the pictures with descriptive text. Hobniy, with his usual flair for the unconventional, added in a few words from a labourers' harvest song above a group threshing in the fields. Senenptah had liked the idea, and had enjoyed several minutes in wheezy laughter at the thought.

"So, Makty-Rasut, when can I look forward to seeing the completed work?"

"Perhaps three more weeks, lord. Or perhaps four if we encounter problems with the final touches. I would rather spend an extra week now and ensure that everything is as you desire, than leave something incomplete for all eternity."

The old man nodded, then rose to his feet to look westwards, across the River. Makty looked at Shunaya. Were there really only three or four more of these sessions remaining? It seemed so little time in which to secure the possibility of seeing more of her. There would be no reason for him to visit the priest's house any more.

He had once played in a Senet tournament where each game could only be played until a wax candle had burned down, after which the game's result was awarded by the judges. Here too, there was a sense that the time he had thought so plentiful was burning away too quickly. How would this game be concluded? She looked back at him, her eyes holding his for a very long moment while Senenptah looked towards the descending sun.

"I am very pleased, Makty-Rasut. Scarcely any time now until I shall see the finished work."

He turned suddenly back into the room, and stood watching as Makty and Shunaya broke their mutual gaze to look at him. He nodded.

"Makty-Rasut, I want you to tell your men that after the work is done I should like them all to be my guests for the night at a feast and celebration. Here in this house. It will honour me to be their host, and I shall provide pleasure and entertainment for all of them. Some of my household servants shall be their companions for the night, if they wish for that."

Makty nodded.

"I shall tell them today, lord, as soon as I return across the River. They will be most grateful for your kindness. As am I."

A little later, he was walking with Shunaya back to the slatted gate. They were silent for most of the way. Then Makty, still gripped by the sense of time slipping like the River through his grasp, turned to her and touched her arm.

"Shunaya, will you be at the celebration that the lord priest talked about?"

She looked at his hand, then up into his face. "Would you like me to be there?"

He drew a long breath. "Yes. Yes, I would, very much."

She nodded in acceptance. "If the lord priest invites me, then most certainly I shall be there. But perhaps you would prefer that he ordered one of his household servants to be your companion? He has said that he will do that for you all."

He paused, feeling the delicacy of the moment. There was a thrill running through him, the kind that he felt when a competition hung in the balance, poised on the outcome of a single move.

"I would rather you were my companion."

She glanced towards the house, then back at him, and nodded. "I shall ask the lord priest if he would like me to be there. We shall both have to wait on his decision. But for my part, I shall be happy to be with you."

They walked together the remaining part of the way to the gate, with his hand not quite touching hers. Then he set off back towards the west side, filled with longing to find out what turn the game would take next.

4. Past – Mining

A ND I SERVED the will of His Majesty who lives in prosperity and health by finding great stores of pure gold in the red land. I brought it all safely back so that His Majesty who lives in prosperity and health would be delighted in his heart. Not even a single grain was lost to thieves or lawless men.

KHAEM-KAPERE WAS CHOOSING the squad of scribes he would take out into the eastern desert. There was also a unit of soldiers who would actually be setting up the camp and watching over the workers. They were already assembling in the open area at the start of the trail that went out though the network of wadis east from Abedju towards the ocean.

They were not really his concern, except that he had to be able to work with them and their commander from the moment that they formally came together. Informally he had already taken the time to visit the camp, where he had greeted the junior officer who was currently in charge. No surprises there – the young man seemed competent but had not been informed about his orders in detail. He had not yet seen the commander himself.

As usual, Khaem had been allotted barely enough literate men to record everything that was needed. And some of the characters who had turned up were scarcely worthy to be called scribes; their knowledge of the signs and all of the complex web of information that went along with that was so slight as to be almost laughable. With some of them he had been inclined to send them across to the group of labourers and see if they could dig for a living instead. He supposed the four people he had finally chosen would have to suffice, though one was very ill-looking, and another, Mut-Hotep, had a persistent cough that the desert sand would hardly improve.

He glanced again through the odd scraps of broken pottery he had used while talking with these people to remind himself of the bare details of each of them. That done, he put them away in the cloth bag that held his tools. There was a knock at the door. He opened it. A young man was standing outside, keen looking, with a well used pack over one shoulder. The man bowed his head briefly.

"Sir, my name is Makty-Rasut. They tell me you are looking for scribes for work out in the eastern desert."

"I have been. But I had finished. You are fortunate to find me still here."

"Fortunate indeed, then. See now, I have been working over on the west side for a little more than a year on the eternal houses there. Today I finished work with the draftsman Amenemose, and he told me to see you tonight, as soon as I could get here. He said to remind you that you have not found time for the Senet tournament you promised him, and he will expect it when you return from this trip."

"Did he now? I expect he said a few other things about that?"

"He did, sir. But I was not sure if they were to be repeated, seeing as this is our first meeting."

Khaem laughed.

"Tactful as well as skilled, then? If he said anything to suggest that I owed him still for a wager from the last time, he has less memory in his heart than skill in his hands."

He frowned at his bag, thinking again through the collection of roughly marked tiles. "Well, strictly speaking I have a full crew. But some of them are less good than I had hoped, and some look as though they may not survive the march out through the wadis, let alone a couple of months out in the red land. You'll do. Collect whatever you need to take and meet us after sunrise at the start of the eastern trail."

The younger man stood, a little taken aback at the quick response.

"Do you not want to see some of my work?"

"Not if Amenemose has had you in his team. He may be a poor loser at Senet, and have an appallingly bad memory, but I trust his judgement about who he works with. His commendation is enough for me."

They had been a week on the march out east, following a series of waymarks left by former similar expeditions. On one occasion they passed a stele raised by order of the great king Min-ma'at-Re Seti Mery-en-Ptah, describing where reliable water could be found nearby and celebrating the king's great wisdom and care for his workers.

For Khaem and his team it was much too late in the year for water to be a serious problem, but he knew that in high summer the casualty rates for such expeditions were often very high. The king had, naturally, taken credit for the water supply. Khaem had often wondered as he passed by this place, which nameless scribe or soldier had actually found the water, and what desperate circumstances had triggered the need to search for it.

They had started with two hundred workers, all looking quite under-fed at the start of the journey. The military officer, Penre Sa-Bunakhtef had decided the number needed, and it was the soldiers' concern to watch over them on the journey and at the mines. Khaem's only regular involvement with them was to oversee, and record, their food allowance each day, and to note in the formal expedition record the deaths as they happened. There were fifteen of these. Twelve were from exhaustion and ill health, but three of them were men who tried to take advantage of the confusion in a meal break to run.

Some soldiers were sent in swift pursuit and soon caught them. One died in the capture; the other two were brought back, pleading, and were first beaten thoroughly and then executed in front of the rest, their bodies being cast aside for carrion birds with no burial. Khaem watched silently as justice was carried out, and then later added another note to the record. A stupid act, he thought. The men would have had a better chance if they had waited until they all arrived at the mining area further along the wadis, where watchfulness would slip after a few days.

Khaem tried at first to become friendly with the commander Penre, but he proved to be a dour type who preferred the company of other soldiers and had no apparent interest in other ways of life. So, as he had expected from the start, his evenings were spent with the little group of scribes. He had been curious to see how the latecomer Makty-Rasut would settle with the others. It turned out that he already knew one of them from another job down the River, a slightly older man called Sanedjem-Keni.

Initially the others had been wary, as was only to be expected under the circumstances. That had worn off as Makty-Rasut conducted himself, on the whole, in a manner suitable for his youth. He joined in the little wagers that were gambled every evening and lost small amounts to most of the others.

Games of real skill, such as Senet, were banned by common agreement from the start. Khaem had seen, and served on, journeys where the competition had moved off the game board, into open hostility and the creation of vicious factions. He wanted none of that under his leadership, so only pure chance was allowed. He suspected as he watched the nightly action that Makty's losses were carefully planned in order to secure his place in the team. There was a calculating air about the size of all his bets.

Makty was friendly enough to the others in the group, but the same rather cold detachment that ruled him in games of chance also lurked in the background of all of his relationships. Khaem had the definite sense that they were held very lightly and could be swapped for something that seemed better at any time. This man was not used to permanence. His work, however, seemed excellent, though as yet there had been little chance to show it off.

Two days before their planned arrival at the mines, Mut-Hotep's persistent cough overcame him. During the late afternoon he had found the walking increasingly difficult, in the evening he started to cough quantities of blood, and in the morning he was found dead in his tent. There was nothing to be done, and no possibility that his body could be taken back to the River.

They spent a short time burying him in the sand some distance away from the trail, where animals would not disturb him, the wadi would not wash him out if it flooded, and his decay would not ruin any water supplies. They inscribed his name, home town, and status on a rocky outcrop above the grave, and all stood around it for a short time offering devotions each as they thought best. It was little enough, but all that could be done for him.

Khaem shared out those of his belongings that were held in common, and packed away the private goods for taking back to Abedju. So far as he could remember, Mut-Hotep had a brother who lived a short way downstream, and perhaps he would want the items back so they could be placed in an eternal home. Khaem had no idea at all if Mut-Hotep had already prepared one against an eventuality such as this. If not, then the little rock grave and the scanty inscription would have to suffice through all the ages to come. Then they marched on.

⁓⁓⁓ ◊ ⸺ ◊ ⸺ ◊ ⸺ ◊ ⁓⁓⁓

Abiyet, widow and mistress of her home, watched from the door of the winter house as the working party drew near. Of course they were here for the gold, as similar groups had been every season for a great many years. The mining area itself was just over a couple of ridges, in a little group of wadis north and south of the main track. In summer she travelled and lived in tents with the rest of her tribe, but in winter they settled here. The regular presence of groups like this from the River helped with food and wealth. It was a useful arrangement on both sides.

The tribal head had met their officer just outside the village perimeter, and the two men had exchanged the customary gifts and embraces. She knew the commander Penre well, as her husband Khepesh had served under him for ten years or so before being killed in an ambush. He would visit her to acknowledge old debts while he was here: he always did.

The workers and soldiers would be pitched in tents together beside the main wadi. The officers and scribes would be given places here among the village houses. She stood at the door of her house, her two children beside her in the steady east wind.

The headman led the elite group over to the houses, allocating a person here or two people there. He stopped at her door, looked at the men still remaining, and picked two of them. That was good. When the village was rewarded for their help she would get a double share. There was a younger man, nearly young enough to be her own son, and a rather older man who looked quite weary. She thought she recognised this one from a previous time, but had never taken him into her house.

The two separated from the main group and came across to the door. The older man handed his pack without a word to her daughter Nehomit and waited. His hands were trembling slightly, and his shoulders very clenched. She realised, now that he was beside her, that he was close to exhaustion. The last days of the march had evidently taken a heavy toll on him. The younger man, on the other hand, was in good health, but had no idea what to do next. Seti, her son, stepped forward, bowed to him, took the bag from him, and indicated the door. The rest of the group moved on. The commander caught her eye, nodded to her, and then passed on by to the next house. There would be another time for conversation.

She took them in, introduced herself and her children formally, showed them the room they would share, gave them bread and raisins as a welcome gift, and then left them alone in the room.

A little later the young man, who had called himself Makty-Rasut, came back out on his own. She gave him some mint tea, and he thanked her profusely.

"But, mistress, I fear that Akhmenu will not be joining us yet. The journey has been hard for him, and he is resting alone to recover. I can take him some of this tea if you have another."

"You have no need to do that, lord."

She glanced at Nehomit, who poured a small jug of tea and

went into the other room. Makty-Rasut glanced around, still very uncertain.

"Is there anything I need to do for you here?"

It was rude of him to think that she would need help in her own house, but his youth probably accounted for that, together with the incapacity of his colleague. So far as she could tell the offer was genuine in his part. Perhaps he was unused to being guest in a house like this.

"No, lord. Sit at the table there and we will serve you."

He sat, looking a little lost with nothing to do. She brought him food and drink, then busied herself around the room while he ate. The other man never appeared from his room that evening.

The days steadied into a pattern. The two scribes went out when it was light enough for them to tell one of their marks from another, and were gone all day until the evening. On their return, Makty would stay with her and the children in the main room, and the older man withdrew alone. Day after day he looked more drawn and weary, although for two weeks he was able to rise with the dawn.

Then a day came where Makty came out alone. He looked anxious, and in a low voice explained to Abiyet that Akhmenu had tried to arise and failed. It was no great surprise to her, having watched his steady decline. Soon after Makty left, the chief scribe Khaem-Kapere appeared. He went in to the sleeping room first, and then came out again to talk with her. Having taken some tea in to Akhmenu she had already formed the opinion that he was no longer fit for work. Khaem-Kapere agreed. He was clearly regretting choosing the man as part of his group, and now had to make the best of a difficult position.

"Mistress, if it would please you, I would prefer to move Akhmenu into a place on his own. This is your house, but I should like to put one of the other men in here with Makty."

She was content. She had no desire to nurse this man, nor watch him die if his weakness worsened. So four of the soldiers carried the ailing man and his belongings to Sheshan's house, who had some skill with healing. That evening Makty returned with a different scribe, Sanedjem-Keni, who settled into the room with a grateful acceptance that she liked. The two clearly knew each other well, and their conversation was full of men's jibing and boasting. It was a relief to her to have more life in the house after the rather solemn quietness that had prevailed while Akhmenu had been there.

One afternoon they got back much earlier than usual. She was gathering the day's washing when they came into sight over the brow of the sandy rise. She waited at the door, smiling to herself as Sanedjem saw her, waved, and beamed with pleasure. He took her hand and kissed it as they came up to her.

"Get along with you, Sanedjem. You think flattery will turn my eyes away from the hour of the day? Scarcely half a job done today, I'll wager."

He grinned.

"But we had the word of the chief scribe Khaem-Kapere himself to come home, mistress."

"He could no longer bear the sight of you at the workings?"

He sobered abruptly.

"In fact, mistress, the officer Penre himself sent all of us back to your village so we could protect each other. One of your village men came in with a report of wild men in a warband along the wadi eastwards, and his own scouts have confirmed it. So the day's work is over and we are all to huddle for safety."

She nodded, unsurprised but with fear starting to flood through her body. Such groups usually appeared around this time of the year, leaving a little trail of theft, rape and murder behind them. They were fortunate to have the soldiers here this time. Sanedjem was continuing.

"So the commander said he wanted to catch them in a snare

this time. He is planning to keep his own men hidden, and us all inside the houses, so that these others will think you are undefended. He expects to kill many, and enslave the rest. So we have been sent home early to be out of sight."

They went in. She trusted Penre, but his plan was gambling with the lives of her family and her tribe. She would have preferred a strong show of defence that would keep the band from coming anywhere close.

"Do you two have weapons?"

Makty and Sanedjem looked at each other.

"The commander gave us a spare knife each. He told us strictly that we must keep the door closed and protect you and your family, and not try to interfere with whatever we hear outside."

"He does not think we would use them well, mistress."

She laughed. "No indeed. Let us all hope you are not put to the test with them."

A long time passed while the sky darkened. They had put out the hearth fire long since, and made a brief cold meal in the gloom. Finally there came the sound of shouting from the south, a wild, aggressive noise that chilled the nerve and deadened the will. Abiyet had heard it before, and hated it. The raiding party was approaching the outskirts of the village from an odd angle, having presumably circled around a quarter circle from the wadi.

She pushed Nehomit back into the main sleeping room and stood in front of her, facing the entrance door. Seti was ahead of her, and the two scribes stood either side of him. In her hand was her husband's long hunting knife, out of its sheath now for the first time in several years. She had not had to use it in anger since the commander Penre had brought it back to her with the news of his death.

There was silence for a while, then that horrible shout, much closer. Her house was near the western edge of the encampment, and so far as she could tell the invaders were nearly in among the houses. Her daughter started to say something and then stopped. There was only the sound of breathing in the little house.

Off in the distance came another shout, then the sound of splintering wood. One of the sheds being broken into, she thought. Some animals gone, perhaps some tools as well, unless the commander's plan proved to be successful. The shouting started up again. She swallowed her anxiety. The band had split into several different groups and were scattering around the village.

Some would come this way. Looking at Sanedjem's face in profile, she saw that he had realised the same thing. He glanced around at the little group and gripped the hilt of his knife tighter. If the raiders got this far she would not wager on their chances. A knife was not easy to use in close quarters, and the attackers would be much more experienced than her son and the two scribes.

There was another, more solid sound of metal against wood. They were trying the strength of one of the house doors. Further away there was another outburst of shouts, a sense of exultation, a woman's scream. Then, finally, there was some response. A dash of feet, distant voices of her own people and the army men, the sound of weapons clashing. She started to relax.

Then there was a thud against her own door, wood against wood, trying for weakness. At the same time the wooden screen over the window in the room behind her gave way. Nehomit clutched at her, gasping, and as she turned she saw a big man in a sandy tunic pulling her away, pulling at her clothes. Abiyet shouted, outraged at the intrusion. Seti and Makty ran into the room beside her.

The big man, one arm tight around her daughter's body, looked at them and laughed. Makty circled round to one side so that the man's weapon followed him. Thinking he saw an opening, Seti tried to dodge around the other way, but the intruder pushed Nehomit to the ground and, with a great backhand swing, knocked Seti against the wall. He shook his head, stunned by the impact, blood coming from a graze across his face. The man moved slowly, steadily towards Makty, knife circling this way and that. Makty shuffled back towards the wall, step by step, drawing the man back into the room. Finally he could go no further, but stood in a half crouch, borrowed knife trembling at chest level. The other man laughed again.

"Little scribe should stay by his river."

Makty said nothing, but watched him as he closed in, keeping his eyes fixed on the other man's hands. Another step closer, and the big man opened his mouth to taunt again. But the words died on his lips as her husband's knife slipped under his ribs. She had used Makty's distraction to come up behind him. He half turned toward her, and she slashed the knife across his throat. He slumped down onto the floor.

"That's for touching my children." She looked at Makty, her eyes still furious. He was shivering with fright, staring at the body. "No different to gutting a gazelle, really."

He closed his eyes, drew a deep breath, then looked back at her.

"We cannot stay in this room, mistress. Not with two ways in."

She nodded. The battering at the main door was getting fiercer, and the timber would not last much longer. Nehomit was up off the floor again, and was wiping at Seti's face. They were both still here, both still with her.

"Where are the soldiers?"

Makty shook his head.

"Not at your house, at any rate."

She pushed the two children back into the main chamber, where Sanedjem was watching the weakening door, and from there into the other sleeping room. Makty looked around.

"Sanedjem, go and find the commander Penre. Tell him that the mistress needs his men to come at once. No delays."

Sanedjem looked at the door.

"How will I get through?"

"The window in that other room. No-one is out there just now. They won't see you. He'll be across on the east side. You'll find him."

Sanedjem looked around at the others.

"Are you sure? Seems wrong to leave you with so few."

"Neither of us are much use at this game. We need someone who can really fight here. Just go now and come back with him quickly."

Sanedjem nodded, ran across to the window and, after looking quickly around, scrambled through it and disappeared into the darkness. The others bundled into the last little room. Makty and Seti jammed the door closed as best they could with wedges of wood and rolls of bedding. Any delay was better than none.

There was a short, anxious pause, and then with a crash the outer door gave way. There were footsteps pounding in the main room, the noise of her few possessions being rummaged. Someone found the dead body in the next room and there was more shouting. Then someone pushed at their door from the other side, found it would not open, called out to the others.

Makty and Seti moved a little closer, knives ready. Abiyet made sure Nehomit was behind her and waited. The door rattled again, bulged a little where one of the raiders leaned on it. A heavier push forced back the slight barricade holding it closed, and a hand reached through the gap, trying to find the blockage. Seti stabbed at it, and there were curses from the other side of the door as it was pulled back. Makty grimaced and looked back at the two women. Now the invaders were sure that the house was occupied.

There were voices outside the door, perhaps five or six of them. Too many for the little group of defenders to manage when they finally burst in. The door heaved again as someone tried their weight against it. The bundle of wooden bits and bedding slid back leaving a thin strip of open space to one side. Another heave, and the gap widened. They could see several of the attackers through the gap. Seti waved his knife at them, shouting something incoherent. They saw him and laughed, then noticed Abiyet and her daughter.

"Send those women out here, boy, and you can go free."

The group stayed silent. The same voice came from outside.

"We'll treat then nicely, now." One of the others laughed. "Yes we will, like they were our very own. Is that your sister in there, boy?"

Seti opened his mouth to reply, but Makty looked at him, shook his head.

"Tell you what, if it was you killed my lad Mish out here, I'd let you join my group. Could use someone that can look after themselves. Give you a man's job instead of looking after a couple of women. We'll look after them all right."

Seti ignored him, but Abiyet called out.

"I killed that animal when he laid a hand on my daughter."

There was another burst of laughter.

"Come out here, little lady, and we'll talk about it. Maybe I'll let you come along with us instead of the boy."

She said nothing. All this was using up time, and that had to be good. It meant time for the scribe Sanedjem to find Penre, time for him to arrive here with some of his troops. Outside she could hear noises of fighting in several directions. Would there be enough time? The man in the other room had lost interest in talking.

The door shifted once, twice, as heavy bodies pushed against it. Makty and Seti did their best to replace the blockage, and to cut at arms and shoulders as they came briefly visible, but it was a battle they were sure to lose, and little by little the gap was widening. It was only her son's wild slashing that was stopping anyone now pushing through at them. The man who had taunted them, the leader, grinned at her and her daughter as he easily avoided the blade.

"Reckon we'll have earned these two, lads."

Suddenly there was another noise from the door. There were voices from the great river, the sound of real weapons, men being struck down, Penre's voice raised over all the others. She took a deep breath, feeling tension and anxiety all over her body.

The noise of fighting stopped in the other room. Steps came over to her door. Makty and Seti looked at each other, but it was Penre that called out to them. Makty closed his eyes, loosened his grip on the knife. Penre looked cautiously in, saw them all in the room, nodded in relief.

"We came in time, mistress Abiyet." He saw the long knife she still held, the blade marked with blood from the man she had killed. "I see that old blade of Khepesh came in useful. He will be proud of you."

She nodded, not quite sure of her voice. They came out into the main room. Two of the attackers were dead, the rest disarmed with their hands roughly tied behind them.

"Did any of them harm you, mistress?"

She shook her head. "I killed the one who tried to take my Nehomit." She pointed. "He would have done wicked things to us if he could."

The commander nodded, turned to the man she had pointed to, and plunged his sharp, slightly curved sword into the man's heart. He staggered and then collapsed. Penre looked along the remaining line.

"You others will work night and day to make good the damage you have done here. When that is done I will decide your fate, depending how well and how willingly you labour."

"Is the scribe Sanedjem with you?"

"He stayed back with the others. He reached us as quickly as he could, but he could not help with the work here. He is safe, though I think he had not realised before how fast a man can run if he needs to."

"And the rest?"

"I lost three men. All the raiders are dead or captured, save a couple who tried to escape. I have men on their heels: they will not get far."

He looked with distaste at the bodies on the floor, and the living prisoners lined up against a wall. "I will see to it that your house is repaired. But perhaps for tonight you would prefer to rest elsewhere. They will clean it again for you, but it is not a place where you will be comfortable until tomorrow."

She nodded. Reaction from the intrusion and the aggression of the men was starting to affect her. Her hands were trembling, and she felt as though she would not be able to stand up much longer. How close had they come to being violated, after all?

"I can stay with the children at my brother's house tonight." She turned to Makty. "I thank you. But how can I thank you? You and your friend Sanedjem have done more for my household than any guest should have to do. I shall understand if you would rather seek lodging with another household."

He looked slightly embarrassed, and to cover it made a little ceremony of handing the borrowed knife back to Penre. Then he looked round at the chaos in the house, the two children, and finally Abiyet herself. "If it would please you, I should like to remain with you now that this is over."

Several days had passed. Abiyet was sitting with Makty and Sanedjem in the restored main room of her house. Nehomit was preparing food, Seti was off with a group of the soldiers. When one of them had called at the house earlier, and Seti had gone with him, a great wave of remembered sorrow had filled up her soul. So had Khepesh been filled with fervour all those years ago. The time with him had been good, and fruitful in so many ways, but it seemed to her it would have been better to have shared old age with him. Would Seti one day leave behind a wife and fatherless family in the same way that she had been left?

She realised that Sanedjem was looking at her as she pulled herself back into the present day. Slightly embarrassed at not attending to her guests, she looked around the house. The commander Penre had been true to his word, and the new captives had been made to repair the rooms. It was better now than it had been for several years. Her household had fended off the assault, and the scars of that day were being mended. She realised that Sanedjem was repeating something he had already said once.

"So I think we will only be with you for a few more days, mistress. The commander has been able to finish the quota ahead of time seeing that he was able to add all those extra pairs of hands to the work crews."

She nodded. She had heard this from her neighbours already. She had made a point of not looking at any of the captives who had come to spoil their village, but she had heard that most of the survivors were proving to be hard workers once brought under the right yoke. For the moment at least they were stronger than the crew who had been marched out from the great river. The work had gone swiftly.

The few remaining scribes were worn thin, though. Akhmenu who had been in her house at first had not survived that night. Nobody knew how he had died, but when the conflict had passed by he was found lifeless, though unwounded. Perhaps the aggression of the attack had been too much for his feeble frame. Another of the group of scribes had died of wounds received while he was trying to defend the household where he had been staying. How close had they come to that in her own house? So Khaem-Kapere, Makty and Sanedjem had shared all of the scribes' work between them. They had ended up working longer hours even than the mine workers, in order to account for everything that was dug out, and to make a permanent record for the great king.

"You will go back to the great river, then?"

"To the River, yes, to Abedju first of all. Back west along the wadi, then the commander will leave us just outside the town. Our responsibility stops there, and Khaem will pay us off back in the town."

"What then?"

Sanedjem shook his head.

"No more of these trips for me. Too chancy by half. I'm going up river to Waset, to work for the nobles there on their eternal houses. I had a message from an old friend saying he thinks there's an opening for me there."

"Will you go with him, Makty-Rasut?"

There was a pause. Sanedjem looked at his friend.

"You should come, Makty. Plenty of work for both of us up there."

Makty frowned.

"I don't think I'm ready to move on just yet. I'll do a few more of these trips. It's reward for the job straight away. This trip will have been well worth it, even with all the hazard. I'll build up a bit more wealth here before I risk going somewhere that no-one knows me."

Sanedjem shook his head. "It's a waste of what you can do." He turned to Abiyet. "You haven't seen his work, mistress. He's very talented. It's foolish for him just to be writing down how much rubble was moved by how many workers, and how many of them died doing it."

Makty made an impatient movement of his hand. They had clearly had similar conversations before.

"Plenty of time to get back to that. These trips fill in the gaps. I can do the work one day and get silver in my hand the next. And if I do this a few more times my name will be better known. That has to be good. And I still am doing tomb work in between."

Abiyet was curious. She had no idea what a scribe might do other than record the work that was done in a day.

"Tell me, if it pleases you, about your real skill. What would you do in Waset?"

Makty still did not reply, so Sanedjem continued.

"Well, mistress, the noble men and women in the great towns want their eternal houses to be prepared well. They want their stories told on the walls and statues so that every-one will know, this world and the other, what it is they have done. What they should be remembered for. Makty here has a very great talent for that. I mean, I can do the work, the cutting, the painting, the writing and so on, but he'll talk to the people for as long as it takes, and decide what it is we'll show on the walls. The layout. The design."

"And this happens in Waset?"

"It happens everywhere up and down the River, but there's more of it happens at Waset than most places. That's why it's a good place for a man of talent."

"Alright, Sanedjem, alright. I know these mining trips are not what I do best. But right now it serves a need. My name will get heard more often if I do this a bit longer. Plenty of time to move on up to Waset. You know me, I'll get weary of Abedju before too long. When I move there, it would be better if I went with some sort of recommendation."

Sanedjem shrugged. "You'll get all the reputation you want when they see what you can do."

Makty looked down at the floor at his feet. "We've said all this before. Let it rest, please. Look, instead of this, why not tell the mistress what you're looking for in Waset?"

Sanedjem looked at him. There was a little silence. After a while Sanedjem met her eyes again and spoke.

"Well, I don't mind saying it. I have a mind to find myself a wife. You see, my father and mother live near Waset, just a little way upstream, and I want to be near them. So that they can see that their seed will carry on. I think I should like a family now. I can give them a good life now, I think."

She laughed at his earnest tone, but the laugh, as always, had an ache of loneliness gaping underneath it.

"If it's a wife you're looking for, I have not yet arranged a marriage for my Nehomit here."

Sanedjem looked startled, and his eyes jumped to the young woman at the cooking stove, just now completing the meal. She looked back at him in a measuring way, as though weighing up the possibility. She did not seem perturbed by the thought that the marriage might be arranged then and there. Makty laughed, apparently at some private knowledge of his friend.

Sanedjem looked back at Abiyet, trying to gauge whether she was serious. She kept her face very straight, already knowing that most men from the great river would never consider marriage into the red lands, even to a family like themselves who had been in alliance with them for generations. Perhaps it was cruel of her to tease him like this.

Finally Sanedjem spoke. "I think that my father and mother will want a say in the arrangement of my marriage. I am not really free to just choose any woman. Even a brave and honourable one."

Makty looked at him quizzically. Abiyet already knew that the words were a lie, but she also knew that the scribe had lied in order to spare her feelings, and those of her daughter. Better to accept his words at face value. In any case she had forced him into this place with her desire to tease. She sighed.

"Well now, when you tell your parents all about your journey, and this my household, perhaps they will want to visit us out here to make the arrangements."

She laughed as she said it, so that he would know it was not intended to bind his future. He joined her in laughing, and they left the subject to talk of other things. But from time to time she caught Nehomit's speculating eyes on the scribe.

That night she lay awake in the sleeping room. Seti and Nehomit were already asleep off to one side, but her thoughts were too anxious to let her rest, too much like a flurry of sand dancing across the desert rocks, stirred up by the restless wind. Would she ever feel safe in this room again? The wooden shutter had been replaced, stronger than before, but the memory of her house being invaded could not be so easily made good.

If the wild men came back one day when the commander Penre was not there with his men, what would happen? Horrible pictures came through her mind of a struggling Nehomit pinned down by a group of violent men, with Seti dead on the floor and herself already brutalised and discarded off to one side. She shivered, tried to form a prayer in her heart, then got up to fetch herself some water.

The two scribes were still talking in low voices, and did not hear her as she moved silently in the familiar space. The room they were in had been her last refuge on that day. Perhaps when her guests had gone again she should move her bed there and feel safer. But that would mean leaving the room where she had shared everything of herself with Khepesh, and she did not feel ready to do that. She would try to keep remembering that it was also a room of fulfilment, conception and birth, no matter what had happened since.

She drifted noiselessly across the floor towards the little room, so that the men's voices could be made out.

"And Sanedjem, what was all that about needing your parents to sort out a marriage for you?"

"I wanted to find something to say that would not hurt either mother or daughter. They deserved that."

"I think the mistress guessed."

"Of course she did. I know she saw through my words. She's not stupid. Not at all. But better to say what I said, than something that could only sound cruel. You know I'd never settle with a girl that wasn't born by the River. But I couldn't say that to them."

"But why not with her, Sanedjem? What's wrong with her? So far as anyone can tell under that baggy dress she wears, she's just the same shape as any other woman. I'm sure she has all the same bits and pieces as a girl from the sedge lands. Or anywhere else for that matter."

"That wouldn't change who she is inside, Makty."

"I saw how she was looking at you tonight. If you want, I'll give you some space to take the conversation just a little bit further. You might find something that you can like about her."

"Under her mother's roof? And after all of the trials we've faced together? Don't be ridiculous. Anyway, I feel like she's family now. Would you lie like that with your sister?"

Abiyet held on to the doorpost, leaned a little closer to the words.

"Well, whether she's your wife or your sister, the best thing you could do would be to get her wearing some clothes that would give the rest of us some enjoyment. Something more pleasing to the eye than those sacks. Especially if you did get to marry her."

"Makty, leave it alone, will you? I'm not going to marry her. She will never be River-born, no matter what she wears. Or doesn't wear. And I'm not going to lead her on under false pretences."

"But these people have been in alliance with us for generations. What's the difference between them and someone, I don't know, someone like Hobniy from all the way upstream?"

"I'm not planning to lie with Hobniy. Or live with him. He's only a colleague, even if a very good one that I'll gladly work beside all day. It's different. I don't know why you can't see it."

There was a little pause, and Abiyet scarcely dared breathe in the silence.

"Well, Sanedjem. You know who your parents are. Maybe that's why you feel it so strongly. I don't know whose body I came out of, and whose seed took root in her to shape me. Who knows what my ancestry is like?"

"But look at you. Anyone can see that whoever those people were, they came from along the River, didn't they? Didn't you tell me once that your mother was one of the women of Hekhet in one of their holy places?"

"Down in the sedge lands, where I was raised, yes. But actually the women there always said to me that I came from somewhere else. Some other house. For a lot of years I liked to think that my mother really was one of them, and it was a little pretence they made so as not to shame her vows. That's what I told you before. But in truth, I don't know. Perhaps what they told me really was the simple fact of the matter. Maybe Nehomit has better lineage than I do."

Sanedjem did not reply, though she could tell that he started to speak a couple of times without forming words. Eventually he replied, very quietly.

"It's just not what I want for my life. Don't you spoil what we have had here. It's been a good time, for all the difficulties. And don't you go chasing after her like she was your flower to pick, either. I know you've done that before in other houses too. You've told me about it. But if you did it here, the mistress would have that sharp little sword of hers at you soon as anything."

She smiled to herself, and supposed that Makty nodded, since when he spoke there was an air of finality about the words.

"But she's worth remembering, after all that. Good to look at, what you can see of her anyway. I tell you what. Next tomb I work on, I'll put her face onto one of the women I'm painting there. It's only you and I will know about it over there in Abedju, and she deserves to be remembered. But I'll dress her in something that flatters her more."

Sanedjem laughed.

"I'm thinking now that all the women you go with for a night or two end up in pictures like that. And all those who live in your day-dreams as well, I don't doubt. I've often wondered where you get the inspiration for all those faces. And why it is you insist on doing all the women yourself. But look, don't leave the others out. If you put Nehomit there, make sure Seti and the mistress Abiyet are somewhere alongside. It would be a misery for them to be in separate places and never meet up on the other side. And that husband she talks about, Khepesh. You know how she is about him, even if she hardly ever mentions his name."

"Of course I know. I'm not stupid either. Understanding what she is not saying is what I do all the time. Of course I'd have to guess what he looked like."

She could tell him everything there was to know, if he asked. Perhaps, though, he would make a truer picture by applying his imagination to all that she said, and all that she had left unsaid.

"Makty, swear to me that if one of them is there, then they all will be. Don't just paint the daughter."

"Alright, I will. All four of them somewhere on a wall in Abedju. Then whatever happens they'll be remembered forever." He paused. "We should sleep, I suppose. Khaem will want us up early again tomorrow."

Abiyet slipped away on bare feet in case they came out of the room, and lay down again on her bedding. Was it better for Makty to immortalise her family in art, than for Sanedjem to marry her daughter and give her children? Maybe that was how they thought about life down by the great river, but she found it hard to accept out here in the red lands.

Nehomit's arm had spilled out from under her covers, as though reaching out to her. She pulled a corner of the blanket back over it, and then kept hold of her hand afterwards. She would never see the pictures that Makty might make, and they would be veiled in darkness where only the dead could appreciate them. A grandchild could be held and celebrated in the light, but would have to suffer all the hurts of mortality, and could be lost again from one day to the next.

At least with Makty's pictures they would all be together through every generation to come, and her soul would be able to dance again with Khepesh.

5. Present – Completion

DELIGHT IN THE secret bower –

My lover's hair is the vine,
   her mouth the sycomore fig,
      her breasts the flowering lilies,
         her body the feast that delights.

SENENPTAH'S EVERLASTING HOUSE was complete. Today he had come over to the west side and carried out a thorough inspection, front to back. It was the only time he had seen the work. He had examined every scene, from the outer court down the main corridor, along each of the transverse arms, and all around the walls of the final resting chamber.

Makty-Rasut well knew that there were several imperfections – the wrong colour for a person's hand here, a person facing the wrong way there, a wrong sign in a few places hastily and imperfectly changed – but it was a very good piece of work. Senenptah graciously overlooked the minor flaws that he noticed, and seemed genuinely delighted.

After being shown everything, he sent all of the men out into the courtyard and stayed inside for quite a long time, at the far end of the corridor among the quiet scenes. Makty had glanced back just before stepping into the sunlight. Senenptah was standing with his back to the wall between the pair of stelae as if he was already a statue, and was contemplating how the view would look as the years rolled past.

Makty knew that from where he stood, on one side he would be looking at the scene of hunting among the flowering reeds. Makty had successfully incorporated a small flock of birds taking flight here, in conscious imitation of the much older tomb he had visited all those months ago.

On the other side was the time when the Lady of the Beautiful West opened up the doors of eternity to Senenptah and Tutuia. Both scenes pictured the long dead wife alongside the priest himself, and Makty wondered, not for the first time, what she must have been like to have exerted such a lasting influence. After her death Senenptah had never remarried, though Makty had gathered from chatter around his house that he was no celibate. Allegedly he called a woman to his bed when it suited him, but had never formed another permanent partnership. None of the numerous children that ran about and learned to help in the house were his.

As leader Makty was proud of the finished work, and of the

men in his team for accomplishing it. He was eagerly waiting now for the priest to announce to all of them what tangible form his gratitude for the completed work would take. The daily allowances had always been fair and supplied on time; nobody yet knew what to expect of the gratitude gifts.

The squad of men, from oldest to youngest, had been speculating quite openly on the matter, and knew from experience that it could be pitched at any level, from extravagantly generous right through to nothing at all. The lord priest, they collectively decided, would be moderately generous but not lavish. Most of them had been disappointed at some stage in the past, and they all knew that such benefits could never be relied upon. It did no harm to speculate.

The problems earlier in the work with Paneb-Re could be quietly overlooked now, pushed away to the silent place where things went that need not be talked about. Makty felt no particular need to expose the man's shortcomings publicly, but would be sure never to have him working in one of his teams again. That would be easy, unless some future employer insisted on his presence for reasons of family connection. But for now, especially if the forthcoming reward was erring on the generous side, he knew that he could choose his team however he pleased.

The next commission would most likely be another local priest of some rank, probably a friend or co-worker of Senenptah, but there was an off-chance that he would be invited to prepare an eternal house for some civilian official of real standing in and around Waset. The regional overseer, possibly. That would transform his reputation and future prospects from fair to absolutely certain. And the men he chose to work with him on such a project would rise high alongside him. It would serve him well in the remaining time he expected to stay here in Waset.

Senenptah was emerging into the light, taking in bodily form the route that his winged soul would take in every future age. He blinked and shaded his eyes against the sudden heat and brightness of the courtyard.

Makty was suddenly overcome with the poignancy of the moment. This area, with its own brief presentation of the priest's life and accomplishments, should properly be filled with the man's own family. They would gather here for delight and celebration on feast and festival days, gather especially today to congratulate him on the completion of his home for eternity.

That was how it should be. Instead there was only a gang of labourers, looking at him partly in respect for his rank, but mostly with expectancy for a reward. What was it he had said once? An only daughter somewhere in the provinces, no son of his own, and not yet even an adopted child to take up the duties.

He regarded the old man with a different perspective, as he came out of the tomb and looked around at the workers, nodding in eager pleasure at them and their work. This was, perhaps, the only family the old man would know during the remnant of his earthly life. No wonder the woman Tutuia featured so prominently in his chosen scenes; she at least could be pictured as eternally loving and tender towards him. He was speaking now, his voice faltering a little as he tried to pitch it loud enough for them all to hear. They clustered a little closer around him.

"Men, I want you all to hear that my heart is inexpressibly gladdened by what I have seen here today. This work has surpassed all my hopes. You all have a right to be proud of what you have done. Makty-Rasut has told me week after week of your efforts, and I know for sure today that he is a man of truth. Not one thing that he has promised is missing or out of place. My only regret is not having seen it before, but the pleasure of encountering it now whole, of walking around it in all its finished splendour, completely outweighs that trifle."

He paused to take breath in the dry heat. The men were grinning, pleased with the direction of the speech.

"Tonight you will be guests in my house, and you will lack

nothing. My heart will be glad to see you rest in pleasure with me, although my age will prevent me sharing all of those pleasures with you. Be welcome at my house as the sun sets tonight, and everything that pleases you will be ready. And in that house, in the cool of the evening, I shall reward you all in proportion to your efforts. None of you shall leave empty-handed, from the least to the greatest. And none of you will need to stagger away to find his home tonight in the darkness, for I shall provide rooms for your comfort and you can stay until the morning."

He paused, as though trying to remember if there was anything else he should have said, then nodded with satisfaction. There was a little cheer from the group, general noises of appreciation and approval, and then silence as they started to gather together tools and equipment.

Makty, looking to make sure he had Senenptah's permission, pulled the wooden door closed, locked it, and gave the key formally to Senenptah. They left the tomb, and its encapsulation of the old man's life, alone in the beauty of its shadows. It would be opened and entered again a few times, to fill the end chamber with the necessary things for eternity, and then would stand closed and waiting until the day of its occupation.

Senenptah had invited Makty to go back with him to his house directly, rather than going home first and then coming across the river later in the day. The old priest was very talkative, but bobbed unsteadily from one subject to another. He changed his mind several times as to which room they would sit in, and made some of the servants move tables, chairs, food and drink between each of them. They started a game of Senet but then abandoned it before they had been playing long enough for either to gain any clear advantage. He made Makty describe all over again some of his dreams and pulled out one or two papyrus sheets containing standard interpretations before putting them away again unread.

At one point he took Makty through the house to a guest room and waited in the adjoining chamber, talking all the time, while one of the servants helped Makty clean himself of the dust of the day and change into guest clothes laid out for him. Makty realised that the priest had been increasingly driven by a fear that he would die before the eternal house had been finished, and so perhaps might never have seen it with living eyes.

Now all those fears had proved groundless, and the relief was spilling out into every part of him. It was quite exhausting at first, until Makty learned how to drift over the surface of the conversation and simply allow himself to be carried along with the stream.

Shunaya had stayed with them for a while, until Senenptah went away with her a short time before sunset. Makty sat in the portico facing west, watching the sun drift down towards the horizon, wondering where they had gone. After all the weeks of verbal play between them as he had visited the lord priest's house, his intentions towards Shunaya were beyond any possibility of doubt. The completion of the tomb had brought the chance of relationship's end very close. He was sure that she felt the acuteness of this as much as he did.

Tonight, he had already decided, amongst all of the frivolity of the end of work party, tonight he would seek to consummate those intentions. But through all their brief times together she had slipped neatly through the net of his words, like a bird rising up from the whispering reeds into the empty sky. He still could not feel confident that his desire would be returned. After a while, the priest came back into the room alone. Seeing Makty's glance at the empty passageway behind him, he laughed a little.

"Don't be anxious, my friend. You will see the young lady again at the entertainment tonight. Just be patient for a while longer."

Makty laughed, sufficiently familiar with the priest's practiced insights into his habits of thought not to try to protest. They talked for a little longer, until the sun started to graze the top of the ridge across the river. At that point, Senenptah stood.

"Now, your men will be arriving shortly. Let us move from here across to the hall where the entertainment will be provided."

They went down some passageways that Makty had never used before, and came out on one side of a much larger room. There were several tables arranged at one end of the room, and Senenptah gestured towards the central one. There were only a few places set at this, with most of the seating arranged around the others.

"Here, Makty-Rasut. You and I will sit here, with the young lady from Ta Mefkat. Your second man Sanedjem-Keni will sit there, with whoever he is pleased to choose as his companion for the night."

The men started to arrive in ones and twos, ushered into place by some of the household maidservants, most of them naked for the party tonight, a few with little wisps of veil. Senenptah himself was gracious and welcoming as a host, greeting each of the workers by name as they were brought into the room and shown a place at the tables. Not long after Makty had arrived, Milashuniyet had come in through a different door and sat beside him.

She was wearing a patterned skirt in the Maghariy style low on her hips, an embroidered ribbon that held her hair up, and a necklace that was clearly too ornate and precious to be her own. Makty suspected that Senenptah had loaned it to her. A series of fragments of lapis lazuli were threaded onto a delicate gold chain, culminating in a larger stone that hung between her breasts, nestling in the pleats of a thin linen top.

Her skin, darker than that of any of the other women in the room, contrasted with the pale blue of the gemstones and the blue stitchwork patterns that decorated the skirt and ribbon.

The backs of her hands were speckled with henna, her eyes were outlined in kohl, and a fragrance of incense hung around her. She looked, to Makty's already persuaded heart, altogether desirable. It was as though she was more vividly alive than he could remember. She sat between him and Senenptah.

The party was going well. Makty had made sure that he was only mildly merry with the plentiful beer, but most of the men had become rapidly, happily, drunk. The serving girls brought the bounty of the feast to them, or sat with them for a while, giggling and alluring, swapping kisses and caresses for little gifts and promises.

Senenptah, who had eaten sparingly and drunk hardly at all, sat and surveyed the scene with satisfaction. At the start of the meal he had announced a range of gifts for the team, setting a tone of liberality from the start. Makty was very pleased with his own portion, and even more with the promise that the workmanship would be made known to the priest's friends and co-workers.

Sanedjem had leaned in towards him at that point, wanting to try to organise who would be doing what next time. They would need a bigger team – had he thought how many extras he would need, and which skills were in short supply? Makty had pushed him away, laughing, and told him not to mix work and pleasure. More work would certainly come their way, but tonight was not the time to talk of it. That was a long time ago now, and by now Sanedjem was not at all capable of such calculating thought.

There had been music off to one side, and other entertainments from time to time. Some dancers had performed just after a fish course, and Hobniy had tried to join them. The huge man whose great arms had such a wonderfully delicate touch while finishing image and script on a stele, leapt up out of his seat, inspired to join in after a particularly acrobatic move.

He cavorted about amongst the real entertainers, a slender girl from the villages of the sedge lands near the great sea balanced on his shoulders shrieking with excitement. The sight brought shouts of laughter from around the room as he dodged here and there around the tables. He flopped down again eventually, settling the girl more comfortably on his lap. The dancers continued for a while longer and then made an exit after bowing both to Senenptah and Hobniy.

Makty was only too pleased to be flirting with Shunaya. He no longer had any doubts as to where their liaison was headed tonight, nor whether her intention complemented his. He was aware that Senenptah was watching him off and on with mild amusement, and an unmistakable nostalgia, mingled with the air of a man whose plans were coming to fruition. Perhaps, he reflected, the priest could simply order her to do, or not do, whatever his guest pleased. He had still not entirely clarified in his heart how far she was able to act as she pleased. At any rate, Makty preferred to leave her with at least a semblance of choice.

On his other side, Sanedjem was watching the process with much less favour. He had his arm around another of the young women, whose accent showed that she came from only a short way down the River. Sanedjem's disapproval became more overt as he drank more, and eventually he prodded Makty's arm a couple of times.

"Makty, you know, you really really should stop this. Stop doing this right now."

"Oh yes?"

"Oh yes. You should be, you know you should be more patriotic tonight. More patriotic. Yes indeed. Stay on the River."

"Let it go, Sanedjem. Go dip yourself in a paint-pot while you think about it."

Sanedjem laughed and looked at the beaker of beer in his hand very carefully as though it might hold the paint he used every day at work. When he spoke again, he tried to articulate the words carefully, but they emerged very slurred.

"Not me who'll be dipping himself in a paint-pot tonight, is it? You'll end up all itchy with sand everywhere. I'm going to be drifting just a little way down the river and mooring myself at the dock in Abedju. Home-grown all the way for me. Along the River all the way. You can't say that. You can't."

Makty put his hand on his friend's arm.

"You can't say it very well yourself, can you? Listen to yourself. At least I won't be wondering tomorrow morning how to explain it to Weret."

"Oh, that's different. This is just a reward for work, just part of the reward. This is just part of the job. Doesn't mean anything. Weret will understand."

"Well, you'll find out tomorrow. Look, Sanedjem, you enjoy your lovely trip downstream and let me explore the world beyond the River however I want."

Sanedjem stared into his eyes for a long moment, unblinking, his breath full of beer, then gave up and turned away from him again to the Abedju girl, muttering something incoherent about sand everywhere. Makty turned back to Shunaya, who had heard every word of the exchange, and shook his head. Before he could say anything Senenptah reached over and grasped his hand.

"Makty-Rasut, there is a thing I must show you. Out there in the next room."

Makty got obediently to his feet but looked down at Shunaya who was still sitting. The old priest nodded urgently.

"Yes, yes, you come along as well. Both of you now, come along here and see this."

He led the two of them down a short corridor and off into a small chamber with a single window facing west. The sky was mostly dark now, except for a ribbon of gold along the rim of the western hills, but Senenptah had picked up a little hand-lamp as he had left the main dining hall.

The room they had entered was mostly bare, except for a table pushed against the wall with the window. On the table was a stone stele, complete with a carved scene filling the top third down from the curved rim, and an inscription below. It was a little dusty here and there, clearly not recently done, and not at all in Hobniy's style. Makty assumed that it held some family memory. In front of the stele stood half a dozen little miniature figures, as long as Makty's forearm. Makty nodded in understanding: here were some of the tomb contents. He had not seen them before, although he had carefully left the space agreed for them.

Senenptah watched him as he went over to the table. Five of the figurines were in conventional working postures. One man was sowing seed, another carried a hoe and scythe. A woman was grinding flour. They were servants who would be attentive to carry out after death whatever manual labour that Senenptah might be called upon to perform in the land of light.

Shunaya had come over beside him and had very carefully picked up a figure of a woman carrying a basket of food on her head and a jug of beer down by her side. Senenptah, an anxious look on his old features, stepped up beside her, hands raised a little as though ready to catch the figurine. As he approached, she put it down again slowly, as though it was made of eggshell and sunlight, in front of a man making bricks. Then she bowed a little to him, moved a little closer to Makty as though tucking herself under the wings of his protection, and spoke to the priest.

"Lord priest, is that figure made to be me?"

He shook his head and moved the figure fractionally back towards the others.

"No, no, she is not you. She is not any of the house servants either. Or rather, she is all of you rolled together to help me after I cross over. I suppose that a little of you is in her, and a little of all of the household workers as well. You see, I will still be looking out for your wellbeing in that land as well as this. As you all continue to serve me well, your names will be praised and remembered alongside my own. Yours and anyone who has worked in my house."

She bent down a little and looked at the column of signs down the woman's torso without touching the figure a second time.

"Is that my name there, lord?"

Makty had been looking at the writing on the stele set out below the seated figures of a man and woman in front of a generous offering table. They were identified as Senenptah and Tutuia, but were depicted, of course, as in the vigour of youth rather than old age. The man's picture looked nothing like the priest beside him. Hearing Shunaya's question, he glanced at the figure and shook his head.

"Nobody's name, Shunaya. It says that if the master calls in need, the servant will hear and attend."

He gestured to the single figurine standing off to one side, a tall woman with hair held back in a ring behind her shoulders, carrying a writing tablet and reed pen. She was not shaped to any design for these listening figures that he had ever seen before. To his surprise, she had already lost some of the newness of the ink and paint that had been applied only recently to the others.

"Lord Senenptah, if I may, what purpose does this one here serve?"

To his astonishment, Senenptah picked the woman up with great tenderness and started to cry. His left hand cradled the figure gently, while his right hand stroked the black wooden hair. His tears ran unheeded down his old face.

"She is my housekeeper. She will organise everything for me so that it is done well." He paused for a few heartbeats, nearly oblivious of the other two in the room. "I was very fond of her. She knew that, I think. I was very fond of her. I should have told her that. I hope she knew. She's gone ahead to arrange everything. She knows where everything is to be kept. She'll do that very well, I know she will. But I miss her here."

He suddenly put the woman back on the table in her place

to one side, overseeing the other five workers. He looked defiantly at Makty, who was struggling to understand what had happened, trying to adjust his perception of the servant figure.

"So lord, she is a real person, then? Someone who has actually lived?"

He looked at her again, touched her arm very gently, and then whispered so quietly they could barely hear him. "Yes. Yes, she is." He looked around, as though for a chair, but there was none in the room. He looked at Shunaya. "You never knew her. She was gone before ever you came into the household. You never knew her. But I did. She came with me up here to Waset from Gedjet in the Asiatic provinces, but she crossed over into the light-land just before you arrived. So soon after we moved here, so soon. Too soon."

He stared at the figure blankly for a while in the silent room, with his tears still struggling to emerge. The sounds of partying drifted down the corridor from the main hall. Eventually he shook his head.

"She'll be with me in the everlasting house, you know. She'll make sure everything is all right for me." He stopped himself, hesitated, and then continued. "For us both, I mean. Of course. Both of us." For a second he let himself cry again, but then sighed, rubbed his eyes with his long sleeve, and turned away. "I wanted you to see all these before they go into the house you made for me."

Makty looked at Shunaya in the hope that she knew how to manage the situation where he did not. She remained unmoving, standing in the waiting posture that seemed to govern so much of her life. Senenptah was also still, looking back at the housekeeper, lost somewhere in between memory and expectation. The surge of passion that had brought him to tears had ebbed away again, and he was quiet now, eyes moist. Makty took a deep breath, conscious of having witnessed something quite precious to the old man, and not sure how to fit it alongside what he had known of him so far.

Senenptah spoke again, suddenly, in a very different voice. "I don't have family here to carry on the rites, you know."

"Lord, you have spoken to me of your daughter, somewhere out in the Kinahny provinces."

He shrugged.

"My daughter Duat, yes. She married a man, an envoy in Djahy. Far enough away as it is, but then he was sent by his ruler even further north. Of course she went with him. Ikaret, when I last heard. I have not seen her since she moved there and I came back to Waset. I have had letters now and again. Short letters. Only ever short letters. She has twin boys, and a younger girl, but I think that I shall never see them. Such choices we make, all in a moment, and some of them can never be undone."

Makty looked again at the stele. Sure enough, there were three diminutive figures in a row behind a fractionally larger woman, placed below the seated couple, tucked underneath the two bench seats where the main figures sat. He was quite sure, though, that neither the daughter nor the grandchildren had been shown anywhere in the tomb. What, he wondered, had happened between them since the stele had been made?

"I told you before, didn't I, that I was looking to choose a man that I can adopt to be my son, to stand here beside me so I can depend on him to do all that is necessary for me. Several times I have thought I have found the right person, but always I have been let down."

He picked up the housekeeper again and held her gently, looking down at the painted features.

"She would have been able to help me choose. She would have seen much sooner than I did that I was about to make the wrong choice."

Still holding the figurine in the curve of his arm, he glanced briefly at Makty.

"What does your father think of you being here in Waset, then? What part of the land does he live in, waiting for news of his son? Waiting for letters that you do not write?"

"I cannot answer that, sir. I have never known who my father was. I have believed for some years that he was an important man from down the River somewhere, perhaps Min-Nefer or the sedge lands, but that is only a guess."

Senenptah nodded, all his attention focused on the figure he held as though waiting to hear an opinion. Shunaya looked up at him in surprise, touched his arm gently.

"And your mother?"

He shook his head again.

"Again, great lord, I cannot really say. There was a novice who mothered me in the holy house of Hekhet a little downstream from Per Bastet, where I grew up as a child. I always thought of her as my mother, but she told me many times that that was not really true. That she was only one among several. And indeed there were other women who passed me from one to another as I grew up there. Once I believed that this novice truly was my mother, but was not allowed to say so openly because of her vows. But I think now that that was the wishful thinking of youth. I really do not know the truth of the matter."

Senenptah nodded again, still focused on the housekeeper. He seemed lost in another world somewhere, listening to something that the other two could not hear.

"I do need a son, you know. I will need one in time to come. In all the times." Then he looked up sharply at Makty, abruptly back in the present moment. "You never told me that about your parents. Brought up in the house of Hekhet, you say? Why did you not tell me? You should have done so when we were talking about your dreams. Had I known that, it might have helped us considerably in the interpretation. And perhaps other things as well."

Makty looked at him, aware of possibilities opening up but reluctant to speak. If the old man was moving in the direction he thought, he wanted to do nothing that would put him off, and he was not at all certain of his ground in the charged atmosphere.

Senenptah held the statuette up to his face, touched his lips against the painted ones. It looked like a kiss. Makty thought about things he had heard from other priests, how this might be instead a way to breathe the breath of life into lifeless lips, to call something of eternity into a wooden heart. But then, looking at the old man holding the woman tightly against his frail body, perhaps after all it was a kiss.

Senenptah put her down again in her place and turned to the other two. All of the former vagueness and reverie had been pushed back again under the surface, and he was keenly alert.

"But I am keeping you here with me. I dare say that you would rather keep each other's company than humour me in this way. Come this way and gladden each other's heart."

He gave the lamp to Shunaya, then led them out of the chamber and further down the corridor, away from the boisterous noise of the celebration. He gestured to a door to one side, and then turned away from then to rejoin the others, his old figure fading into the shadows as he went.

Shunaya led Makty into the room. It was small and plain, with two chairs beside a small table, a single window covered by a cloth drape, and a single bedroll. She closed the door behind him, untied the bow of the ribbon and shook her hair free so that it fell like unfurled wings on either side of her face. She walked over to put the lamp and the ribbon on the table and turned away from him. He watched as she took off the necklace, the pleated top, and then the skirt, placing each of them carefully on one of the chairs. When she turned around again, she was entirely naked, her head poised at a slight angle as she watched him. She stood still, watching him for several heartbeats, her breasts rising and falling with her breath.

"So, Makty-Rasut, you don't mind being with this paint-pot?"

He grimaced at hearing Sanedjem's words echoing in her own mouth.

"Those were never my words. Take no notice of Sanedjem when he has had that much to drink. You may have better parentage than I, for all I know. You heard just now, I have no knowledge of father or mother. In any case, just now I am not so interested in your parents."

She grinned, rather impudently, and walked slowly over to him. The scent of her incense drifted around him as she came near. She turned a full circle in front of him, arms lifted up above her head.

"And see, there is no sand anywhere. Your friend need not be worried for you. The lord priest let me use his own chambers to wash in, so that I would feel ready. I think I am ready now, after all these months."

He shook his head, unable to find any words. He was certainly ready for this moment of intimacy. She untied his tunic and stood back while he discarded his other clothes, then stepped close again with a little sigh as he put his arms around her. The two of them joined together into a close embrace, body to body. They kissed for a long time, not feeling any hurry to complete their union but building satisfaction with every caress. Eventually they moved across to the bed and settled onto it.

After their lovemaking he lay awake for a while, as she fell asleep, tucked into his body within the curve of his arm. Eventually, when she turned away he got up to take one last look out of the window. The ridge of the mountain on the other side of the river, silhouetted against the stars, was deeply familiar to him, but was shadowed and veiled with the night. Truly, the goddess of the Peak was silent tonight. He turned his back on the outside world to look at Shunaya where she lay in the pool of lamplight. One hand lay delicately outside the sheet that covered her, the henna showing dark against her skin. His thoughts were very muddled about her.

Most of his encounters with women had followed a similar path, just as Sanedjem had pointed out with sharp, accurate humour not so long ago. If he was attracted, he had pursued them with determination and vigour, for a matter of weeks at most. If the pursuit was successful, he enjoyed the conquest for a few days, rapidly finding reasons why the match was less suitable than it had seemed before. Once captured, these women were inevitably less appealing, and more flawed, than they had seemed during the chase. They could not hold his interest, and he could not hold their affection.

He felt differently about Shunaya. His interest in her had grown more slowly, from a slow and uncertain beginning. He had persisted longer, with much less assurance of success, and with more interruptions and setbacks to his desires than he could ever remember. Perhaps even more surprisingly, he did not feel anywhere in himself the beginnings of disinterest in her that typically followed in the wake of sexual consummation. Was this something different? Was she different, or he, or was something about the combination of the two of them more alive with potential than other pairings he had known?

Finally, still feeling unanchored in his soul, he extinguished the oil lamp and joined her under the sleeping sheet. Her dark hair and her Maghariy skin leaned against him, warm with shared delight. After a while he fell asleep as well, feeling profoundly relaxed and at ease in his body, despite the doubts arising from within his heart.

He dreamed again. He was looking down from the mountain ridges below the peak of Meretseger down onto one of the royal mortuary temples. The columns and statues, bright with coloured paint in the sunshine, stood upright, bold but tiny below him. The river was at the height of its inundation, and a great barge was floating up a long arm of water leading from the swollen banks up to dock beside the temple. As before, little birds were flying low over the water or perching in the bushes nearby. Red and blue cloths covered the cargo, and thick ropes made sure it would not shift in wind, wave, or weather.

Curious, he leaned out to see it better. The mountain ridge was small now, no more than a dais at one end of a feasting hall, and the mortuary temple the size of a chicken coop. He leaned over and picked up the boat where it floated in the little runnel of water. It too was small now, only the size of an infant, and he marvelled at the intricate and loving detail that had gone into its shaping.

He turned around, finding himself in a large room with a table behind him. He placed the boat on the table beside a group of little listening doll figures like the ones Senenptah had shown him earlier. They were collecting carob beans into a single rounded jar from where they lay all scattered about. As he watched, the enigmatic housekeeper figure picked up one of the beans and placed it off to one side, where it sprouted leaves and a flower and seeds all of its own.

Ignoring that, he unwrapped the red and blue cloths that covered the boat. The hidden cargo was a statue, but unfinished. The arms had been outlined but not yet freed from the body. The legs were shaped but not finished. The head had been fashioned but no craftsman had yet chiselled features into the stone. A sceptre and throw-stick of foreign design lay beside it, but they had not been joined to either hand. The statue was not ready to be put into position in the temple: it never had been ready even while it was carried in the boat along the watercourse. It was unfinished.

He woke up at that point. The sky was still dark, but a waning moon peered in through the window and gave a little light. The house was quiet, with none of the noises of celebration that had drifted down the corridor earlier. Shunaya was fast asleep beside him, turned onto her back now with one shoulder showing. He looked at her with a sudden fondness, and touched her cheek very gently with one hand. She twitched slightly, and he smiled and lay back again. The mood of the dream stayed with him as he slipped back into sleep. If he dreamed any more that night, he had no memory of it.

They woke late the next morning, luxuriating in a day without work. As Makty surfaced, stray disconnected ideas and unformed plans came to him, but he let them idly pass by without taking any of them seriously. He had set aside a fair amount of the daily work ration he had received while working on Senenptah's tomb. Some of the perishable items had been passed on to others in exchange for material goods or future promises. What with that, and the gratitude gifts Senenptah had promised yesterday, he could easily afford not to rush in to the next job.

Perhaps he could just work on his own funerary equipment for a while. He had a part-finished stele listing his life's accomplishments to bring up to date, and if he purchased a small plot of land up on the hillside he could make a start on the outer courtyard. But that presupposed he was going to stay here in Waset, and it was hardly more than a few weeks since he had been definitely intending to move on up river. Had one night with Shunaya changed that? He looked across at her, noticing how she came from sleep into wakefulness. She stretched, looked towards the window to gauge the time, then laughed and curled herself around him.

"Most days I would have been down at the kitchens long before this, making sure that the lord priest's first meal was ready for him."

"So will he be going hungry now?"

"Oh no. He said to me before the party last night that I was not to get up as usual, and that he would make other arrangements. He would like to see us both in the western chamber when we arise. The room where you always met him each week. But there is no hurry."

They made a virtue of not hurrying, and considerably more time passed before they decided to get ready. Water had been left outside the room at some stage, and another change of

clothes for each of them. Eventually they left there, and Shunaya led him through an outdoor colonnade across to the familiar room. Senenptah was sitting at the table, poring over
an unrolled old papyrus sheet. Several other texts lay around
him, lying on both the table and the floor. He stood to greet
them, still holding the papyrus, and gestured to the stools beside the table. Shunaya started across to stand by the wall
where she had been, week after week, but he shook his head
and pointed again to the seats.

"No, no, not today. You must sit with us today." He waited
with some impatience until they had settled themselves. He
began with a rush of words, which presumably had been bot-
tled up for a long time while Shunaya and Makty had not
been hurrying. "Now look at this, Makty-Rasut. I cannot believe that all the while that we have been talking about your
dreams you made no mention of your unknown parentage.
That changes everything. So much more makes sense now.
Look at this passage that I have found. And these here."

He waved the old text in front of them and gestured at
some of the other ones nearby. Makty, taken by surprise at
the abrupt introduction to the subject, leaned back a little.

"Well, it's a thing I have lived with for a long time now. It
is not something new to me. How was I to know it would be
important to you?"

Senenptah stared at him as though he had made an ele-
mentary mistake in laying out a grid of squares on a wall.

"Of course it is important. Everything is important in understanding what comes to you in the night. Especially something like this." He shook his head as though in disbelief. "But
I forget myself. You are not trained as a priest. How could you
know all this? The fault is mine, I suppose, for never asking
this before."

Shunaya leaned forward.

"Lord priest, what exactly is it that you have found out?
Are the dreams sent by Makty's parents from the light-land?"

"Yes and no, I think. It is not as though one or the other

was speaking directly to him. Of course that can happen, but the signs are not present here." He paused, reflecting. "No, not at all, or I would have seen it long ago, even without being told. And perhaps they still live on this side of the reeds. Who can say? But nevertheless the dreams are full of the matter of Makty-Rasut's origins. Tell me, Makty-Rasut, have your dreams of late included little birds in flight, or a royal sceptre, or a throw-stick, or perhaps a large dish in a surprising place?"

Makty blinked in surprise.

"Well, yes. Three out of those four just last night, actually. How could you know? What do they mean?"

"Ha! I knew it!" The old man was positively exultant at the news. "You must go north to find out."

"North? Why? I don't want to go down river. If I was going anywhere it would be upstream, but actually," he faltered, looking at Shunaya, realising that he had not spoken with her about the future while they were not hurrying in the other room, "actually I was thinking of staying here."

They both looked at him, Shunaya with curiosity and Senenptah with some exasperation.

"I wish you had some priestly training in this. You must trust me. You must take my word for this. Three out of four signs is a matter of profound significance for you. You cannot just ignore it and go where you please."

Makty hesitated, then decided to carry on.

"Actually, I have seen a dish as well, not in this last dream but in an earlier one. You remember, the one with the wild beasts all around. There was a dish that I was running towards on the river bank while I was trying to get away."

"You see? It is all there." Seeing that Makty was still unpersuaded, he turned to Shunaya. "You must make him see how important this is." He leaned over the table to Makty and grasped his hand urgently. "Why did you not tell me about the dish?"

"I did not think it was important. In the dream I was

much more concerned to be getting away from the animals, the crocodile and all the others. Running away from them seemed more urgent than a dish lying ahead of me on the river bank. That seemed just a silly embroidery that my own heart might have made."

Senenptah gripped his arm harder and stared intensely into his eyes.

"It is this sort of detail that is most important, Makty-Rasut. The animals?" He made a dismissive gesture with his free hand. "Obvious. Trivial. Could have been any number of other things. Armed troops, perhaps. Or falling trees. It would not matter. But the dish was crucial. The little details are what matters most."

He leaned back and released Makty's arm, tapping his fingers on the table. Makty took a deep breath, trying to relax. Yet again, he was finding the priest's intensity unsettling. He looked at Shunaya, trying to find inspiration. Senenptah spoke again, in a more ordinary tone.

"Look now. I realise that you had planned to stay here, or perhaps go on upstream. But just for now, after finishing my house yesterday, you do not urgently need to work. Is that correct?"

Makty nodded.

"Then here is a plan. I need a statue delivered down river to Per Bastet. It is a nice piece, an inscribed seated official that I need to be put in the hands of one of the nobles who lives just outside the town there. It is valuable. I want it to travel accompanied by people I trust. This man knows the arrangement we have made regarding his gratitude. Will you take it to him for me, and witness the completion of our agreement when he has inspected it? I will tell you everything you need to know about him. During this time, you will still be working for me, and entitled to the daily allowance just as you have been. And there will be more for you by way of completion gifts. I will give you a letter that any temple in the Beloved Land will honour with the needful things of life. And another letter that you are not to open and read until this responsibility has been discharged. Take this statue down to Per Bastet, then spend some time there and see what comes to you. The boat for your journey down the River will arrive here from Yeba in a few days."

Makty looked perplexed.

"Spend some time doing what? Just walking around seeing if I can recognise someone?"

Shunaya touched his arm, rubbed at his shoulders where they had become very tense.

"Makty, look. We will go to the ladies of the house of Hekhet beside Per Bastet and see what we find. Who we find. That is, sir," and she looked at Senenptah, "that is if you consider that my family duty to you is best fulfilled in this way?"

"Definitely yes. Your family have honoured me and repaid me seven times over for the small service I was pleased to carry out. At this time now I feel most protective of this search, and I would like to be sure that it will be pursued. The best way to do that is for you to go with Makty-Rasut, and assist him as though he was one of my own family. As though he was my son."

She nodded, but Makty still felt rebellious at the prospect of being sent to and fro in the land in order, apparently, purely to satisfy the priest's obsession with his dreams. Senenptah looked at the stubborn set of his features and sighed.

"Look, Makty-Rasut, it is only a short break away from Waset for you. A matter of a few weeks, perhaps. Or maybe a few months. If you find nothing, you can return and carry on as before, knowing that you have at least looked. But truly, I do need someone to travel with this statue, and I need it to be a person who can read and write. If you do not go for me, I would have to find another scribe. That would be awkward as they are all occupied on other work just now. Your duties would be real, though very light, and after all of your effort on my eternal house it would do you no harm to have some easier days in company that you enjoy. Think of it as like an extended festival if you like."

Makty looked down at the table. The thought of spending the next few days and nights with Shunaya was appealing. So much of her was still mysterious to him, like an uncharted pool surrounded by fragrance and flowers. But part of his heart was questioning what would happen if he tired of her during the journey. Boat journeys down river to Per Bastet and then back again could easily take a couple of months at this season, even without any extra time spent going to deliver the statue, or visit the house of Hekhet. Could his interest in her last for that length of time? Would he in turn be willing to make an effort to remain appealing to her?

But if he was honest with himself – and at this stage there seemed little point being dishonest – other aspects of the journey were more unsettling still. He was more fearful of what he might find, or not find, among the ladies of the house of Hekhet. Up to this point he had moved successively further and further up river, away from that place.

The plans he had been vaguely making for going further on south, to Djebu, and then maybe Yeba beyond it, were all part of that flight away from his first home. How would it be, he wondered, to simply let the natural flow of the river take him back down there instead of always pushing against the current?

Shunaya's hand was still at his shoulders, easing the fierce tension that had knotted his body while he thought. It occurred to him that if he did not go on this journey, she would have no reason to stay with him. That was a thing he could not bear. He really wanted to carry on feeling the caress of her hand, the warmth of her body against his, the arresting presence of her soul provoking honesty out of him.

He sighed, looked up from the table first at Shunaya and then secondly at Senenptah.

"Yes. Yes, I will go. I will take this statue down to Per Bastet for you and see what else awaits me there. Perhaps then I will come back here, or carry on south if we think that a good scheme."

The old priest's eyes welled up with the same tears that he had shed while holding the little figurine of the housekeeper the previous night.

"I am sure you will not regret this choice in the end. And perhaps when you both return, you and I might think together whether this place might be a home for you for longer." He nodded to himself, several times, as though finding some kind of resolution or completion in the words that had been spoken, then stood up. "I must be about my duties in the temple. This house is your house for now, until the boat arrives. That will be some days away yet. We will talk tonight about the details of your journey down river."

As the two of them left him in the room, putting rolls of papyrus back on the shelf in their proper place, Makty realised that he would need to go to see Sanedjem and tell him about the journey he was about to make. So far as his friend knew, he would be spending a short time about his own affairs, but would then start looking to begin the next real project before too long. The news that there would be a minimum of a couple of months' gap before Makty would even begin to pitch for new jobs amongst the nobles of Waset would dismay him. He owed him as much prior warning as possible, and since the decision was now made, the visit should not be put off. He stopped as they crossed a hallway that he was sure they could follow towards the main entrance of the house.

"Look, I need to see Sanedjem and tell him that I will not be setting up a new team for a while yet. I don't want to get ready to leave without telling him first."

She nodded.

"What will he do?"

"If he had any sense, he'd set up his own team and lead it. He's got all the experience he needs to do that. But I expect if I'm not around and he needs the work, he'll go in with someone else and stay as second."

"Shall I come with you to see him?"

Makty shrugged, then looked at her in some surprise. He was not used to the idea that decisions like that might be made as another kind of united act.

"Just as you please. You don't know him, not really. And you did not see him at his best last night. I supposed you would not want to go with me."

She laughed.

"Life would be very difficult for me if I tried never to see every person that thought less of me for being born away from your river. And I have not often gone over to the west side. I should like to come, unless you do not want me there."

He shook his head, and before long they were crossing in the little ferry that Senenptah had provided out of his own wealth. They walked together between the small cultivated fields to the village where Sanedjem and most of the other team members lived. They stopped at his own house briefly to collect all the items he needed for the journey, including, most importantly, the little statue of Seshat and the few scribal tools he did not already have in his bundle.

As he gathered the few things together, she wandered between the three rooms, then came back and sat waiting for him in the main one. She had an odd expression on her face, but said nothing as he pushed a few more things into a carrying bag. He looked critically around, trying to think if there was anything else he would need.

"I'll take these last bits of food to Sanedjem and Weret, they'll not keep more than a few days. No point leaving anything that might spoil." He looked at her. "What is it?"

"Your house is very bleak. Very sparse. It does not show anything of what you can do."

He glanced around the familiar rooms.

"I suppose not. But what does that matter? Anyway, how do you know what I can do? You have never seen it."

"I have heard the lord priest speak about it. I have heard you describe it all so that he could see it with the eyes of his imagination, since he could not visit it. And I have seen the pictures you made for him while the two of you were planning it out. You put all of the beautiful things you make into other people's houses. None of it is in your own house."

He looked around again. The little house was perfectly serviceable for its needs.

"Well, I don't need that here. I don't ever bring people here that I'm doing work for." He laughed at the thought. "Can you see one of the nobles coming to visit this little place? You could fit the whole thing into one of the courtyards in Senenptah's house."

He looked around again, making an effort to see what she saw, and not really succeeding. It still looked straightforward and workmanlike to him, not sparse and bleak. "Come on, let's go down the road to Sanedjem's house."

Shortly afterwards they arrived there. Weret-Ib was outside shelling beans in the open air, her pregnancy well advanced now. A loose cloth awning shaded both her and her son Ramose, who was sitting beside her. She looked up as the couple approached, glancing briefly at Milashuniyet and smiling at Makty. She called back into the house, a cross edge in her voice.

"Sanedjem, get yourself out here, Makty is here to see you." She turned back to him. "He's not long been back from across the river. Middle of the morning. Ridiculous time. He says he doesn't remember much of last night. He was stinking like a hippopotamus when he got here too. He's still trying to wash off the smell of some slippery little mullet who was all over him last night. Nothing to her but a gabbing mouth and two legs that spread apart soon as look at you, I dare say. I've told him I don't want him near me until he's properly clean again. Or near my Ramose either. But he did bring home some gifts that your priest handed out. A bit more to come later on as well, he tells me. You'll not mind if I just get on with this?"

Makty shook his head. Weret was clearly in no mood to be sympathetic.

"Weret, that's fine, you carry on just as you need to. And yes, the lord priest is arranging for some extra goods to be shared out, things that were too bulky to be given last night. More will be coming your way for sure."

"Well, that's something. Good thing too with all the work you put in to his place." She turned her head again. "Sanedjem! These people are waiting for you."

Milashuniyet squatted down beside her.

"Can I help you with that, lady Weret?"

Weret glanced at her foreign skin briefly and shook her head.

"It's nearly done. Not as if I need a servant around the house. And you don't have to call me lady. But thank you all the same."

At that point Sanedjem appeared from inside, blinking and looking very rough.

"Hello, Makty. Good to see you." He looked at Shunaya, puzzled. "I don't think we have met?"

"I think you might have seen me at the lord priest's house."

Sanedjem nodded hesitantly.

"Ah, yes, you must be one of his foreign slaves. I remember there were a few of them." He turned back to Makty, clearly with no real memory of her. "So what brings you here today, my friend."

Makty glanced at Shunaya, who shook her head. He took her lead and ignored the matter for now.

"I came to tell you that I shall be away for a few weeks. Well, maybe a couple of months. So if you need work before I get back, then just go ahead without me. You should be putting your own team together, but I don't suppose you'll do that."

"No, I've told you, I'm happy being second. But where are you going?"

"The lord priest we just finished working for, he wants me

to deliver a statue all the way down river for him. Right down in the sedge lands. We'll be leaving in a few days."

Sanedjem looked mystified.

"Why did you take that on, Makty? Not your sort of job at all. Surely that only needs a guard or two and a servant he trusts? Hardly a scribe's job, is it?"

"Well, he needs the transaction properly witnessed."

"Even so. He could get one of his junior priests to do that. It certainly doesn't need someone who's got your talent. A scribe who leads his own teams as well? I don't understand this move of yours at all. You were all for going on further upstream. That made sense, even if I would never have come with you. Plenty of good work you can do up that way. But down river just to take a statue? That makes no sense."

Makty felt himself floundering under the torrent of Sanedjem's words, especially as they echoed so very closely his own doubts. He opened his mouth to speak but could not decide what to say in reply to his friend. Shunaya was watching him from her place sitting beside Weret. After a pause Sanedjem prompted him.

"Well? Nothing to say? Don't do it. You don't have to. Just tell him you've thought about it overnight and there's better work here. He won't mind, he'll still recommend us to his friends and colleagues and we'll be onto another job in no time. I know what happened, you were so relieved it had turned out alright in the end after the way Paneb-Re messed you around, you just agreed to whatever he said. But think about it. Do you really want to do this?" He glanced down at Shunaya. "Look, even this girl here would tell you that you have to take your chances when they come at you."

To his surprise, Shunaya replied.

"Actually, I think that Makty should fulfil this journey for the lord priest, and for himself as well. I think that this journey is a chance that has come at him."

Sanedjem looked at her, bemused.

"Why do you say that?"

Weret finished the last of the beans and tossed the last husk with the pile of others.

"I suppose she's just used to doing what she's told. She's not one of us. But you're right, there's no reason Makty should just agree without thinking."

Makty looked from one to the other, beginning to get frustrated.

"Well, I'm sorry, both of you. This is what is happening. I have thought about it and this is what I'm doing." He paused for breath, then saw Shunaya's face, remote and closed. "And Shunaya here is not a foreign slave. Her family is important in her own land and she has been working in the lord priest's house of her own will to honour a family obligation."

Weret looked her up and down, picked up the shelled beans and started to go inside, turning at the threshold to lift Ramose up onto her hip.

"So, there's a thing. What sort of job would the priest want of you, I wonder? But some of us have to get on and work in the daytime."

There was an awkward silence as she went inside and closed the door. Sanedjem cleared his throat and took a step towards them both.

"Well now. Can I offer either of you something to eat or drink? Let's sit down out here and talk about all this." He glanced into the house and added in a lower voice. "She's not usually like that, you know. She's angry with me after last night and you just happened to be in the way. On a normal day she'd be fine, she'd be the one offering you refreshment. You know that, don't you? She's a better person than I am about hospitality and all."

"It's alright. We caught you both on a bad day, I think. I did warn you last night. We'll just be on our way without troubling you more today."

Sanedjem scratched his head, apparently trying without success to remember what had been said.

"So you're determined to go ahead with this foolishness?"

"I am. You'll find work in another team easily enough if you won't set up your own. But I have to do this just now."

He passed over the bag of spare food items.

"Look, give this to Weret, will you, it won't keep. And you know where the house is, take whatever you need and make it up to me later on sometime. The house is negotiated through until the next inundation, so there's nothing more to settle there. Tell Weret I'm sorry to be leaving you like this. But you'll be all right."

He took a step back. Shunaya stood up and joined him. Sanedjem shook his head, suddenly looking profoundly upset.

"Will I ever see you again, Makty? I don't think I will, will I? Not now you're off like this. I don't think you'll ever come back here."

"Of course I'll be back to see you. It's only a few months. I'll be back to see how you're getting on. Of course you'll see me."

Sanedjem nodded, shrugged, smiled a little sadly.

"Yes. Of course. I'm sure you're right. But if not, it's been good to work with you. All those different places we've been to. Well, well. I hope your journeys are good for you now."

He turned away and went back inside the house without watching them walk away. Shunaya and Makty went down the street, down to the little ferry boat on the river, back to get themselves ready for the trip downstream.

6. Past – Apprenticeship

I WENT TO the house of apprentices to be taught the skills of the chisel and brush. I needed no instruction in the use of gold and silver, of true lapis, of fine wood and stone. My craftsmanship grew with my years, but even in my youth I was entrusted with beautiful works.

HIRARET-EN-SEKHMET LOOKED OUT of the window of the main room in the house. She was not expecting either her husband Tety-Seneb er-Djehuti or his apprentice until the evening, but it was always better to be sure. She turned back to face her two accomplices and stood up. They stopped their desultory chatter and looked at her. She liked it when they waited for instructions, and paused a little longer than she needed to.

"The former priest of Usar, then. Tomorrow night. Let's get this one finished quickly."

Nehesy grimaced. "Too bright a moon still tomorrow. We should wait until the night after, at least."

She frowned. Nehesy was normally the more timid of the two, but this time he might be right. Paser stirred.

"Besides, I don't think I can get the lads involved for tomorrow. Not with no warning."

"It's not like we have to rush it. That priest's not going anywhere in a hurry now."

Nehesy grinned at his own humour, looked hopefully at her. She sighed and sat down again.

"I don't want to miss this one like we did the chantress last year. Right fools we looked going to all that effort and finding we were not the first there. Nothing left of any value, and I still had to reward your lads for their time. There's no profit in being second."

"That'll not happen this time. Thanks to the discretion of your husband no-one else even knows about this place. For sure your Tety won't be doing anything about it himself. Too honourable for that. Just as well he tells you all this in private places where we're not allowed to go."

The two men laughed together, rather crudely. She kept quiet, ignoring the innuendo, thinking about the wider picture. She could always retaliate by cutting their share, and they had no real idea how much she would raise from the spoils. They were nearly as trusting as the dead whose eternal houses they would plunder. Ducks in a very small pond, just waiting for the fowler, she thought. But in this matter they were probably right: they could afford to wait another day. She opened her mouth to speak, when the door burst open.

Nehesy jumped up, startled. Paser stayed sitting, but a look of extreme guilt crossed his features. Fine conspirators, she thought, turning to look at the apprentice Makty-Rasut as he closed the door behind him. After this job it would be time to pay them off, and after a little while recruit some others who might have cooler nerves. She nodded to the apprentice as he stood, waiting for leave to speak. He had grown from anxious boy to impatient man in the ten years or so of apprenticeship to Tety, but she had never yet made the mistake of thinking of him as like a second son.

"Many apologies, lady. The master Tety-Seneb sent me back to fetch the spare colour mixer and his second-best set of brushes." He paused, looking curiously at the odd expressions worn by the two men. "And apologies indeed to you all. Have I interrupted something important?"

She shook her head. "Not at all. Just a business arrangement. You will find the tools in the hamper at the back of the house. Djoser-Akhet is out at the holy house training with the other acolytes, but Mahebeth can help you. You will find her in the back courtyard just now. You can go out of the gate by the stream when you have the things."

She watched with cold amusement as his face transformed from curiosity to eagerness. How easily he could be distracted, she thought, and how simple it was to divert his native intelligence by thoughts of a young woman. She and the two men waited, silently, as he went through the house to the back. They listened as his voice mingled with her daughter's, as the two of them laughed, as there were sounds of a swift search, and then finally as the river gate squeaked open and closed again. The men with her relaxed. In the meantime she had been thinking.

"Yes, I agree. The job need not be done tonight, or even

tomorrow night, But it must be the night after. No later. It
will be dark enough then, and you have time to recruit whoever you need. I will procure the key and leave it in the usual
place the day after tomorrow. When you are done, put it back
under the loose tile outside, and leave the goods packed in
boxes in the shed in my fields downstream. One of the field
workers will leave the door ajar. Make sure you pick the right
shed."

Nehesy nodded, turned towards the door. She held up her
hand.

"When this job is done we will break for a few months. Until next year perhaps. I want time to pass with nothing to
point back to us. You'll get your share of the wealth in a month
or two. Don't do anything stupid with the reward once it is in
your hands."

Paser shrugged. She looked at him. He would be cautious
and spend his portion slowly, or else set it aside somewhere
safe. But Nehesy would, without a doubt, squander much of
it in the first few weeks on gambling and in the houses of
pleasure. She supposed others would just assume he had had
a lucky win somewhere. He was looking sullen.

"Why can't we get the reward sooner than that?"

"You know perfectly well that I cannot sell the items here.
Anyone likely to buy here would recognise some of them at
least. It has to wait until I can make a trip up or down River
to another town. That won't happen for a few weeks yet. You
rely on me to move the goods, and I say it cannot be done for
at least a month. You just have to be patient. Cool tempered."

He scowled, but finally accepted her decision. The men left
not long after, still grumbling a little, and she was alone in
the room again. They would be happy enough when the reward came in. She turned and went through to the back of
the house where Mahebeth was supervising some of the house
servants dyeing some cloth, and put the planned robbery out
of her mind for a few hours.

Two nights later, she sat at the table to eat with her family. There was a certain secret satisfaction in knowing that, only a few hours from now, the former priest's tomb would be emptied of its movable wealth. He would still have the use of the wall decorations, stone statues, and anything else that was too heavy or insufficiently valuable to move. Those were simply not worth the effort. She supposed, thinking idly to herself as Mahebeth served out the food, that he would not be unduly distressed, and a little worldly impoverishment surely could not hurt him now. Presumably his eternal self would be able to focus better on the things that really mattered.

The apprentice Makty was sitting on a low stool off in a corner, waiting until last for his bowl of food. He had sat in the same place now for about ten years, and had not once joined them at the table. By the time he had accepted the bowl from Mahebeth, Tety-Seneb had almost finished his own helping and was asking Djoser-Akhet about his day at the holy house.

Suddenly Tety jumped up, a look of consternation on his face, and went over to his dusty bag of tools. He rummaged through it several times. The other family members ignored him at first, but as his search grew louder and more frustrated, one after another stopped and turned at him.

"What is it, husband?"

"I think I left my little set of balances at the place of work today. Yes, I'm sure of it. I can see it now, that new worker Ipuy asked me about getting more wicks for the lamps, and I put the whole set down in the back corner." He looked at Makty. "Just beside where we left that space for the offering plinth."

Makty nodded. Hiraret spoke before anyone else could.

"But they're fine there until the morning, surely? No need to be anxious."

Tety grimaced. "It's the thought of them being out there unguarded. That's a good set of balances. I'd miss them if they were gone. Took me ages to find a good set, and I'm not eager to lose them now."

"But still, they're at the back of the tomb. And it's locked, you always do that. Who would be looking there? Just leave them until the morning. You'll not be wanting to go out there at this time."

He frowned, shuffled through the contents of the bag one more time.

"It's not just the balance. There's a little bag of lapis besides. And the last leaf of that fine gold we use for picking out eyes in the best paintings. I can't leave all that just lying around."

She shook her head at him. "So why be so careless in the first place? Anyway, you know you don't like leaving the house once you've got home. Just leave it for tomorrow."

He started at her, speechless for a time. "You just don't understand the value of these things." He paused again, ignoring the look of disdain that despite her best efforts had crossed her face. "You're right, I don't want to go out again, not now. Makty will go for me, won't you, lad?"

Makty looked mildly annoyed, and looked down at his nearly full bowl of food, but years of apprenticeship brought him obediently to his feet. Tety gave him a key.

"You know where I mean?"

"I know exactly where you mean, master. I will be there and back in no time."

Hiraret opened her mouth to speak, but could not think of anything she could say that might stop him. He took the key and was gone.

While she was away she busied herself with the plates and bowls, piling a large extra portion for the apprentice in his absence. Tety continued talking with Djoser-Akhet, but as the time dragged out he started to look more frequently at the door. Eventually Makty was there again, a small bundle in his hands. He went straight over to Tety.

"Here, master. The balance, the lapis, and the gold leaf.

And also the smallest of the copper beakers we use."

Tety nodded in relief, opened the bundle quickly to check, and then nodded a second time.

"Good. That's that, then. But you were gone longer than we expected?"

"Oh yes." He paused, looking rather directly at Hiraret with an odd expression. She held his gaze unblinking, then gestured at the spare stool which she had moved up to the table.

"Sit at the table with us while you tell my husband. But remember that he is tired after the day's work and will not want to hear the full tale."

Both Tety and Makty looked surprised.

"I am hardly so old that a day at work wears me out, wife. I can still show you how much vigour I have at the end of the day."

Makty sat, and Hiraret pushed the full bowl of food to him. He looked at it with a curious expression for a few heartbeats, then turned to Tety.

"Well, master, I have often wondered whether the way along the river bank past the mayor's secretary's house was a little shorter, so I followed that track."

Tety shook his head. "I don't know what made you think that. Stupid path to take. It is quite obviously quicker to go up past the old shrine and along the ridgeway. No wonder you took so long. Waste of time. But your time, I suppose."

Makty nodded. "You are quite right, master. I am sure of that now. But it is important for me to find some things out for myself. I am sorry if the delay caused you anxiety."

He turned back to his food, glancing up at Hiraret with a rather knowing glint in his eyes. She frowned, well aware that she needed to find out what he had seen.

"Husband, you have been saying for a while now that you were going to show Djoser the scroll with the list of ancestors you found in your father's eternal home. Perhaps now is a good time for both of you?"

Tety nodded, evidently pleased at the reminder, and the

two left the room for the workshop at the back.

"Mahebeth, clear the table, apart from Makty-Rasut's bowl, and supervise the new maid as she cleans them. When all that is done, bring some fruit in here for the three of us."

Makty's gaze followed her as she left the room, jumping back to Hiraret as she sat opposite him.

"So in truth, what happened to delay you? I'm sure it never occurred to you to go by way of the river path."

He ate several more mouthfuls of food, obviously deciding how to choose his words.

"Well, lady, you're right. I did go by the usual route, but just up on the ridge by the stand of sycomore figs there was a man in the path. 'Turn around and go another route, lad, some of us are busy tonight', he says to me, and watches me while I go down past the fallen obelisk, sideways across the slope, and around the curve of the hill."

"So some men were working late."

He looked at her and shook his head.

"I thought that at first. But this man was the same one who was in your house the other day, the shorter one of the two."

"Hardly an odd thing. He works in the same trade. You saw him out in the city of the dead. I expect you see many of the same people both here and up on the western slopes."

Makty left a token account of food in the bowl and pushed it away from him.

"Not so many of them get to take things out of the eternal houses as put them in. And not so many get to open up tombs that have been locked for several years. On the way back I went round a bit on the uphill side in the shadows and watched them for a while. A lot of fair quality goods came out of that tomb. Then as I came back with the master's balances and all that, I was thinking how those two men got all nervous when I came in to the house all of a sudden the other day. They were both out there tonight, along with a little gang of others. And I was thinking too about how you were talking tonight, not wanting anyone to go out. Almost as though you knew something was on. So I doubled back around by the fields where you have a plot of land and some sheds."

She looked at him for a long time, silent. He waited. It was frustrating. Her intuition about the two men's carelessness had been right after all, and she herself had been foolish to keep with them for another job. For all his youth, the apprentice was perceptive. Tety had often said that the lad had a knack for hearing more in a word than was on the surface, and he was now exploiting the talent to the full.

"You understand Tety knows nothing of this?"

He nodded.

"And that you are only a matter of weeks from completing your apprenticeship? That this is not a time for having the taint of a bad name cast around you?"

He nodded again.

"I have spoken to you alone, lady. The master will not hear about it from me. But I saw what I saw, and I have a fair idea where those things will be kept for a day of sale. Your hut in the fields was not locked up as it usually is, and they were putting more than just some tools in it. But if we are talking about reputation, how would you stand with the master if he were to find out? I am sure that you have made arrangements to turn aside the eyes of the town judges, but how would your marriage survive this revelation, do you think?"

She frowned and looked down at the table. He was sitting, watching her, knowing he had the upper hand and seemingly quite content to wait and see how she would respond. From the kitchen, in the sudden quiet, they heard Mahebeth's voice as she explained something to the maid. He glanced towards the door, trying to catch her words. She tapped on the table to draw his attention back.

"If you speak out, it could go worse for you. Some of the men in the gang are violent by nature. And nobody would believe your word against mine. But you know all this."

"I do. Let the master do the honourable deed and make it

public, if he ever finds out. I will not speak of it, provided that we can come to a suitable agreement. But I think that there should be some sort of recognition owing to me for my silence."

She paused. His eyes were on her, but his heart was straying towards the kitchen. Mahebeth's voice could be heard from there again, a little louder, talking about dates and figs. It was becoming clear to her how he could be persuaded.

"I could share a portion of the proceeds with you. But I do not think that is what you want."

He shrugged. "That would be something, I suppose. But even with just my small share of the gratitude gifts that the master receives I am not in need at present."

Something that Mahebeth said had set the maid laughing. She leaned forward with urgency. Time was short.

"So what do you want, then?"

He sat up, pride squaring his shoulders.

"I want a name that is known in other places. I want you to make my name known. Up and down the River when you travel on your business. Your commendation will mean more to the nobles than that of the master. You are of their rank by birth, and he has simply climbed into it by ability and marriage. When I move on from here later this year, I want to find it easy to get work." He paused, then rushed on. "And I want to sit with you all at the table, and not squat in the corner as though I was still a boy. I will be treated as a man in this household now. Not a servant."

She smiled a little, though it was a cold and calculating smile, acknowledging something of the depths of the anger he usually kept concealed. The door from the kitchen started to open.

"You have my word. On both matters. And there is another thing we will speak of shortly. And I have your word? For silence?"

He nodded quickly. Mahebeth came over to the table and set down a mixed bowl of fruit. She looked at them both, quickly through her eyelashes at Makty and then more evenly at her mother.

"You both look very serious."

Hiraret nodded. "Makty-Rasut and I have been talking, my little petal. I think it is time that he joined us at the table when we eat, and that he took up a better place within the family. He will only be with us a little longer, and it is time we gave him more honour."

She looked again at Makty, openly this time, her brown eyes wide beneath the broad ribbon that kept her hair back.

"What will papa say?"

"When it comes to sitting around this table, he has no say. He can order Makty-Rasut's day as he pleases while they are at work, but this is my domain."

Mahebeth laughed and passed Makty one of the dates. Hiraret, watching the way his eyes followed her figure, and his fingers trailed across hers as he took the fruit, frowned to herself. There were limits to how far she was prepared to integrate him into the family, and he was all too close to those limits now.

"Daughter, I think we could share a little beer to mark the occasion."

Mahebeth got up and went again into the kitchen. Hiraret stood and looked stern.

"Have a care how far you think you can go in this house."

He looked up at her, a rather exaggerated look of innocence on his face.

"She has a better future than you ahead of her. If you ruin that future I shall not need the gang members to act for me in my fury. These two hands can do all they need to. There are other women nearby who can gratify you. This is the other part of your reward. I will arrange for you to have a girl once a week. Starting tonight. But my petal is not in your reach."

He nodded again, and took one of the little beakers of beer that Mahebeth brought in. They stood to drink together. Hiraret gestured to Makty to speak out the blessing. He held the beer in both hands for a very short time, eyes wrinkled in thought. When he spoke, it was with less confidence than usual, and he sounded as though he was repeating something he had heard elsewhere.

"May the gods watch over us. May the River's bounty fill this house and this household. May we who drink together now follow all the ways of blessing and delight."

Hiraret nodded, and they drank together. Mahebeth suddenly giggled.

"I just keep wondering what papa will say when he hears that his apprentice -" she hesitated, then rushed on, "- that Makty-Rasut now sits with us at the table and drinks beer with us."

Makty's expression suddenly opened up and he beamed. Hiraret glanced at her.

"I shall be the one to tell him. Later tonight, I think, when the house has settled and he is with me in our bed. For now, we all have other things to do."

Mahebeth picked up the empty beakers and jug, taking them back into the kitchen. Makty stood, reached out for the bowl of fruit, and started to follow her. Hiraret put out her arm to stop him.

"You have another house to visit just now. Just as we agreed. Leave these things here for us. I will not have you running after her all the time. Go on now, before Tety finishes with Djoser and thinks of another task for you."

The apprentice, his thoughts quite transparent in his head, looked briefly as though he would carry on with the fruit bowl. Instead he yielded to her implacability with a little sigh.

"Menhat's house, by the ferry boat and the upstream quay. Tell her I sent you, with this as token." She pushed a small clay name-trinket into his hand. "Return it to me tomorrow. Now go."

He turned, finally obedient, and went out into the evening light.

Several nights later, they were sitting around the table again, with Makty sitting in his new place beside Djoser-Akhet. Hiraret was perfectly aware that Tety was still unsure about the change, but he had accepted the version of events she had told him that night.

"Did you finish those last figures while I was away today, lad?"

"I did, master. The sacred lake is now complete. And I had time to look over the outline work done by your new paid helper."

Tety grunted.

"All finished, you say? And a day ahead of time as well." He paused and scratched his head, uncertain how to continue. Makty carried on quite smoothly.

"Of course you must inspect what I have done, to make sure it meets your standards. But I think you will be content." He paused, frowning. "The new man still uses the old proportions for figures. He executes them well, but they do not match the style you have taught me to follow. I was not sure what you would think."

Tety leaned back, eyes shut as he considered the tomb in his mind.

"He started at the back, around the corner, yes?" Makty nodded. "In that case nobody will see both sets of figures together. If he works near us, he must use the new sizes, but the old ones are acceptable back there. I will speak to him tomorrow."

There was a pause while Tety finished his food.

"But talking of old styles, see what I acquired upstream today. It is for the nobleman, to go on his offering table beside the end panel."

He pulled a package from his bag, cheerfully unwrapping what proved to be a little golden statue of an ibis. It was exquisite, and there were little appreciative murmurs around the table. Djoser-Akhet leaned over and carefully picked it up to look more closely, showing it to Makty beside him.

"Isn't it splendid? The man who made it, up River a little way past Min-Nefer, he makes a speciality of imitating older work."

Makty looked curiously at it.

"I see he even sprinkles old tomb dust on it."

Djoser nodded. "And puts a few little scratches on the legs and tail to help it look older."

Makty and Djoser-Akhet looked at each other, laughed together. Djoser inspected it once more, very closely.

"Father, you are sure this really is a new piece?"

"What else could it be? This man likes to imitate the old ways. He told me so. I don't hold with that for artwork, but metalwork is different."

"But you really think he made it new for you?"

Tety was starting to lose his temper.

"Not especially for me, but otherwise yes, new. Look, I can easily buff out those little scratch marks. They're nothing. Give it back here. You're making me sorry that I ever showed it to you."

Djoser passed it back, still looking sceptical.

"This is such a good imitation that you might even think it had been in someone's eternal house before."

Tety glared at Djoser. "What are you trying to say, boy?"

Djoser shook his head. "Nothing, father, nothing at all. I am sure it would make a fine addition to any tomb. Any tomb at all."

Hiraret kept quiet. She was quite aware that Makty was watching her intently, waiting to see if she would give away some knowledge of the piece. In fact she had never seen this one before, though little golden statues of about that size had often passed through her hands. She wondered offhand who her counterpart was upstream, and thought it best to redirect the conversation.

"Well I certainly think it is beautiful. And how unusual to cast a female ibis. But what makes you say it was in the old style?"

Tety and Djoser were still locked in each other's stare. Tety made a dismissive gesture with one hand. Makty glanced briefly at him and then turned to her.

"The way the head is poised like that. And the detail on the wing feathers. There are other things but those are the main two. On the other hand the way the bird's legs are set is more modern. Most older sculptors would have used quite a still posture, both legs together."

He paused, inviting her to comment. Mahebeth spoke while she was still thinking.

"But this one has her legs apart, as though the ibis was running forward eagerly?"

He nodded, all eager to run forward in his own way.

"Exactly. That's a newer style. It would be unusual for a really old piece to be poised like that."

Tety heard him, nodded vigorously.

"He's quite right. At least someone around this table can see it. Thank you for saying so. I think that the nobleman will be thrilled with this piece in his eternal house."

Djoser shrugged.

"Of course he will. It is a thing of beauty, and he has the chance to look on it throughout all the ages to come. I just hope he does not ask too closely where it comes from."

Tety snorted and started to pack the bird away. In the brief pause, Makty leaned forward and caught Djoser's attention.

"We can't be sure one way or the other, can we? It does have new features as well as old. Whoever made it, his work deserves to be seen."

Djoser-Akhet laughed, and some of the tension left the room.

"Or seen once again, you could say. But yes, I accept what you say, that the stance would be unusual if the piece really were old. Perhaps we should leave the matter in doubt."

Tety, now that the bird was securely wrapped again, relaxed a little and nodded at Makty. Hiraret leaned against the back of her chair. The apprentice had spoken out in support of both her and her husband, in a rather uncharacteristic gesture of generosity. She wondered, behind the unrevealing mask he wore, what had motivated him.

That night, as she lay beside Tety in their sleeping room, the thought still nagged her. She had listened patiently while Tety repeated all over again to her the reasons why it was actually a new piece of work. He added nothing, really, to what his apprentice had put in a few words, but he had had time to mull over the matter, and made the reasoning many times longer.

She herself was almost certain that it was an old piece, despite what he said, with the new stylistic additions simply the sign of innovative skill by the maker. The little golden bird had already seen the darkness of one tomb - perhaps more than one - and had been brought out again into the light by someone. It was hardly the virginal piece that Tety wanted to think.

She stirred a little, careful not to wake Tety again. She thought for a moment that she heard movement within the house, the slight scrape of a door, a low voice, a quick intake of breath. She raised herself on one arm, but then there was a clatter outside as a group of youths laughed down the street, setting all the dogs barking. She sighed and lay back again. It was nothing. It was just a noise outside. She relaxed, wondering how best to find out who Tety had bought the piece from. Perhaps she could speak with the man next time she went up the River.

―――⟨⟩ ▨▨▨ ⟨⟩ ▨▨▨ ⟨⟩ ▨▨▨ ⟨⟩―――

The following day Tety and his apprentice had left very early, at the same time as Djoser set off for the day's beginning at the holy house. They were talking all the way out of the door about the amount of work remaining. After the tension of the previous evening, and the day spent away from the workplace yesterday, Tety was positively bursting to get back to the painted walls.

6. Past – Apprenticeship

Makty-Rasut had an air of satisfaction about him, as though something had been fulfilled. Tety had made it clear that if this piece of work went well, it would mark the end of his apprenticeship. The work would get shown to the nobleman himself, as usual. But it would also be scrutinised by two other scribes with different skills, to confirm that the apprentice had absorbed the master's instruction correctly. Tety had no doubts about the outcome, and was already planning how best to receive the credit himself.

After they had turned the corner, Hiraret set off in the opposite direction, down to the house of one of the boat masters. She had a voyage up River to plan, and needed to know the vessel would have room for additional baggage. An amicable arrangement reached, she came home before the day grew too hot.

Curious about the noise she heard coming from the back room, she opened the door to find Mahebeth rubbing at some sheets. Her back was turned as she worked, and she jumped in surprise as Hiraret spoke.

"Whatever are you doing, petal?"

Her daughter turned, red with embarrassment.

"I thought you were out."

"Well, here I am back again. Why are you doing that?"

"I bled in the sheets last night."

Hiraret waved a hand.

"There are house servants who can do that. Or the washermen at the River if need be. Do you see me washing sheets ever?"

Mahebeth shook her head, eyes cast down, silent.

"I did not want them to see this. And they are busy with other tasks while I was not."

"I should hope they are busy. If not I will hear of it. They are kept in the house to be busy. Now leave that for one of the girls to clean and come with me."

Mahebeth left the wet sheets in a basin and went into the other room with her. As they sat down, Hiraret was suddenly struck by a thought.

"You are out of your usual time to be bleeding now?"

Mahebeth turned red again. "I am, mother, but sometimes it happens. You know that."

She shook her head. "Not for me any longer, hardly ever now." She shook her head, dismissing the thought. "But listen now, I have been thinking that next time I go up the River you should go with me. You shall become acquainted with some friends of mine. A day will soon come when I may trust you to meet them without me. It is time to introduce you to some of the work I do outside the house. Private work, which we do not discuss with others in the town here. Not even in the house."

Her eyes widened, then narrowed in calculation. "Just like Makty is doing his apprenticeship with papa?"

She laughed.

"Something like that, yes. You might say that our work depends on theirs, after a fashion. We will never speak of our work with them, but we need to listen carefully to all that they say."

Mahebeth thought about it.

"Like with that golden ibis? The one with the running legs? Papa thought you knew nothing about it. But you did, didn't you?"

"Not that particular statue. But that kind of statue, and how much it might be worth to a man, and where to find such a thing, then yes. Even if just now it was locked up in someone else's tomb and needed to be brought out again."

Mahebeth sat very still for a while at the table, considering.

"And papa knows nothing of all this?"

"Nothing. In all our married life he has suspected nothing. Better that way for all of us. He is my face of entire innocence. He works hard, he has talent, he is eager and obliging to the nobles who commission his work. But can you imagine him trying to keep a secret like this?"

Mahebeth shook her head. She was silent for a while longer.

"And you have been doing this a long time?"

She nodded. "Since before you were born. Just odd items at first, here and there. I was very fearful of being caught. You know what they might do to a person if they decided it was thieving."

Mahebeth shivered. "Down by the River?"

She nodded again. "So I was very careful; just little things here and there, with whole seasons in between each time at first. And I have a rule that I never sell within half a day's journey from here, up or down the River. And I never handle whatever another person has acquired nearby. So it has built up, little by little."

"So you have more now?"

"Oh yes. Now I have the wealth to buy myself out of an accusation, if need be. Come down with me to the shed in the fields and I will show you."

Mahebeth stood up, then looked back into the kitchen. Hiraret shook her head.

"Leave that."

As they left the house Hiraret summoned one of the garden servants.

"There is cleaning to be done in the kitchen. Have one of the girls see if she can do it, and if not take it to the laundrymen. Or get rid of it and find me a replacement if it cannot be remedied. By tonight."

The young man bowed in obedience, but she had already turned away from him and was going along the path to the fields.

"Djoser did not believe that the ibis was newly made. Nor Makty either, though he was careful to hide his opinion better. But papa believed it."

"He wanted to believe it, and that want closed his eyes to all that he might see. So it is with most people who buy from me. People so rarely see what is in front of them."

"Makty says that about some of the artwork they do. I mean, I know most of it is really good, but when something goes a bit wrong they know lots of ways to make their employer think that was what was planned in the first place."

They laughed together. "It is the same everywhere, then."

"And Makty says that when he is approved as a craftsman in his own right then he will watch over the juniors under his command more strictly. To make sure that the times they have to conceal things like that are very rare. And Makty says as well -" She stopped as Hiraret looked sharply at her.

"Do not be too familiar with him, child. He is still just an apprentice for now."

"Oh, but not for long. Makty says that when this piece of work is finished, papa will get some of the others in to look at his work. Then they will approve him to work on his own, under his own name."

"True enough. And from what I have heard he will have no trouble when the time comes. But for now he is just an apprentice, and I do not want you treating him with too much familiarity."

Mahebeth glanced briefly sideways, her cheeks slightly reddened.

"Of course not, mother. Just as you say."

A month had passed. Hiraret had taken her daughter to the shed in the fields another couple of times, and had talked with her about how things were organised. But so far she would not let her meet with any of the men she worked with, and had kept silent about when the next night raid might take place. There was, she thought, plenty of time for that yet, and she did not want youthful boasting to expose all that was done. She herself had felt her way into the trade little by little, and although she was happy to give her daughter the advantage of family privilege, Mahebeth needed to prove both competence and discretion.

So far there had been no disappointments, and Hiraret had

no cause to regret the choice. Since the day they had first spoken of it, after the night when the little golden ibis had been shown, Mahebeth had steadily grown in poise and confidence. There was a new vivacity, an almost unseemly boldness about the way she conducted herself around the house, the way she conversed with the rest of the family, and even with the apprentice.

Hiraret shook these thoughts off. After today, Makty would be an apprentice no longer. The work on the nobleman's eternal house was complete, and Makty's work had been scrutinised by two of the other master craftsmen. A few unimportant slips had been pointed out, as was traditional at these events, but the overall quality of work was excellent. Tety was to be commended for providing such excellent training.

Indeed, Tety had been conspicuously basking since then in the increase of his own reputation, rather than that of Makty. During most of the celebration party which still filled several of the rooms of her house he had sat in central position, receiving the compliments of his fellow scribes with great satisfaction. Makty had, for the most part, sat to one side and behind him, still in the junior place. Tety had given him a much larger share of the gratitude gifts than he had done before, and Makty had bought for himself a little statue of the scribal goddess Seshat. It was a small piece, but well executed and very shapely, and was admired by several of the guests. He had placed it beside him, on the stool that he had sat on in the house for many years. Seeing this, she wondered what fantasies had passed through his head when he had acquired it.

However, she had made time amongst all of the noise to take Makty to one side. She congratulated him for his patience, and also for his continued silence. She also gave him the names of three middle rank officials she had spoken to upstream. These men, and their families, would soon be needing some work done on their own tombs at low cost, and her introduction would get him a place on one of the teams. They were not people of real rank, but it was a good start, and it was up to him what he made of it. So far as she was concerned, their mutual debts were now cancelled. She would be, she continued, surprised if he ever needed to come back to the household once he left. He nodded quickly, but as always it was hard to tell what he was genuinely feeling behind the studied coolness of his face.

The household arose very late the next day, well after the normal hour of work. This day, at least, would be one of rest. Makty had few possessions, and after they had shared breakfast together he packed them in his travelling bag in hardly any time at all. Tety had passed on to him some old tools that were now his own rather than borrowed, and they were stored in amongst the clothing. The little goddess figure was by a considerable margin the most valuable item he was taking.

She supposed that the alcove where he had slept would be filled before long by another young boy. At the start, Makty had been small, frightened, and in need of frequent discipline to train him. Now he would be going away under his own name.

She watched as he spoke his farewell to Djoser-Akhet. There was a year or two difference between them, which had seemed so important in the early years but was now ignored. He turned to her then, bowed formally and waited for her to speak. She would say goodbye here, at the house. Then Tety would take him on the traditional journey to the quayside and pay a boat captain for a one way journey, upstream or downstream as the newly qualified craftsman chose. She was sure he would head up River. She blessed him and the journey ahead, speaking just this once as though in a mother's place for him.

He turned away when she had finished, looked at Mahebeth with a little smile. She returned it rather more enthusiastically than Hiraret thought suitable. Makty turned back to her.

"Lady, on this occasion do you think I might kiss your daughter at parting?"

Mahebeth was already moving forward, and Hiraret realised that she could not easily refuse and keep a good grace.
She nodded curtly, and watched as Makty put his arms around
her and kissed her first on one cheek and then the other. Mahebeth held on to him longer than she needed, and she saw
Makty whisper something in her ear and kiss her one last
time. With a sigh, she released him, held his gaze a little
longer before he crossed over to stand with Tety at the door.
Just as well he was going now, she thought, since he would
need watching all the more having left apprenticeship behind.

He left the house with Tety-Seneb, not looking back even
once. She heard their voices fading as they went down the
street towards the quayside. It was time to get on with the
activities of the day. She turned back, and saw to her surprise
that Mahebeth was crying, her face stricken with loss.

"What is it, petal?"

She shook her head and rubbed at her eyes.

"Mother, I just can't believe that he has gone now. And so
suddenly. One heartbeat he is here, and the next gone."

"Yes indeed. He'll be on the boat soon and away."

Mahebeth was calming down a little.

"Will he go up or down, do you think?"

"Up. Definitely. He will want the full length of the River
ahead of him, not just the little stretch between here and the
great green sea. He has ambition, and he will choose the way
that leads to greater possibilities. He'll be gone now, on board
the boat. Maybe casting off already. Your father will be in the
house again soon."

"Oh, but Makty will be back, I'm sure. I'm sure of it. For
me. Makty promised to come back for me one day."

She laughed.

"Not likely. We won't see him again. None of us. Especially
you. We have work to do, you and I, and not many months
before we plan a marriage for you. It must be someone who is
a suitable match for the discreet work that I am teaching you.
There is no place for an apprentice in your life now."

Mahebeth half turned away, then straightened herself and looked back haughtily.

"Of course you wouldn't understand. And he's not an apprentice any longer. He's a real craftsman, like papa, except one day he's going to be better even than him. He promised me he'd come back."

"So when did he make this great promise? You do realise that there is no place at all in you, or in this house, for a worthless promise that will never be fulfilled?"

"Just a few weeks ago. One night. It was when... it was..." She stopped, flustered. "Just recently. Not long ago. He did. He's said it more than once, too. And he whispered something like it again to me just now when we said goodbye. I'm sure he'll come back. I'm sure he meant it. He just has to get himself known first."

Hiraret started to say something, then stopped abruptly and looked at her daughter. She had suddenly realised that even within her own house there had been plots about which she was ignorant.

"What have you done? What have you both done?"

Mahebeth turned away, her face proud, if slightly flushed.

"I am not going to talk about it any more with you, mother. I just don't think you would understand any of it. You'll see when Makty comes back for me. In the meantime I am going out to the holy house to make an offering."

Hiraret waited until her daughter reached the door to the outside world, and had pushed down the latch.

"Next week, child, I am to visit the house of the priest of Djehuti. His younger son is of an age, and your father and I will consider if the match is suitable. We will each have our reasons, and they will be different. For my part, he could be a perfect source of information that we can use. If Tety and I are agreed, you could be married before the next inundation comes. Promises made between you and that apprentice count for nothing. They are breaths without life."

Watching the way her daughter's back stiffened, and listening to the slamming of the door, she allowed herself a small measure of triumph. Well before the time that Tety came puffing back into the house, she had laid out in her heart the speech that would persuade him that the planned marriage was ideal.

Richard Abbott

7. Present – Downstream

TWO BIRDS CIRCLE the reed beds,
  alight in the scented pools.
Time now to bathe in your beauty:
  come to me so our hearts can learn joy.

MAKTY-RASUT STEPPED ABOARD THE RIVER BOAT at the quayside at Waset, then turned to take the two travelling packs from Shunaya. She followed on behind him, pausing a moment to be sure of her balance on the gently rocking deck. The densely inscribed statue of the seated official was already on board, near the prow, and Makty went forward to assure himself it was properly secured, and that the protective linen wraps were still in place. The chief of the boat watched him, amused but not surprised at his diligence. It was not the first time he had carried cargoes like this. When Makty came back towards the stern he stepped over to meet him, pitching his greeting and attitude as that of equal to equal, skilled worker to skilled worker.

"The lord Senenptah has already told me all about the task he has entrusted to you, Makty-Rasut. Everything will be to your satisfaction, my friend. I am Mery-en-Hotep now, but call me Mentep, and tell me at once if there is anything you need."

Makty nodded absently and looked up and down the deck. There were only two other crewmen that he could see. It seemed a very small complement for the vessel, but he supposed that they would suffice since the boat would be going downstream with the current. The sail was not needed, and was already rolled up and stowed away for the return trip upstream. He hefted the two packs.

"Call me Makty. And tell me, Mentep, where should I stow these?"

The chief pointed to a short ladder descending into a square recess near the bows, quite close to the seated official. A cloth screen could be tied around the little well, but just now was pushed back to one side.

"Put them down in the cabin there, friend. That is where you will be sleeping as well." He glanced briefly at Shunaya. "And where will you expect the foreign lady to stay? We can set her a place on the top hamper just astern of you. Or further away. Wherever you please. My crew and I will be in the stern with the steering tackle at night when we moor up. But all through the day we will have one of the lads up there watching the lie of the River."

"She will be with me."

Mentep looked Shunaya up and down, then at Makty once again as though reappraising the situation. Makty went the few paces forward to the recessed area and leaned the bags under the wooden lip of the bow decking. They contained his tools, the little statue of Seshat, and their traveling gear. The letter for the nobleman buying the statue was wrapped up, carefully protected from moisture. At the last minute Senenptah had given him a second letter, with instructions not to break the seal and read it until the delivery was complete.

"How long a journey will it be?"

"If nothing untoward happens to the boat or to us, and allowing for a few stops here and there, then we'll be in Per Bastet about thirty days from now. Perhaps thirty-two. The longest I've ever taken downstream is forty-five, when the steering oar was dropped overboard, we stopped to give a tow back upstream to someone who got themselves into difficulties, and I had to make several extra stops to pick up parcels in Abedju and deliver them here and there. Downstream is always pretty regular. Upstream varies a bit more depending what the breeze is doing."

Makty nodded. The boat chief's practical estimate fitted very closely with what he had been taught about boat travel. He was glad to be on his way. The boat had not arrived at Waset until a day or two later than expected. Makty had been impatient to get away once the decision had been made, and had found the delay hard to bear. Senenptah had become distant and detached as the days passed, and had said no more about the possibility of adoption.

Mentep hovered nearby for a short time, but was anxious to get about the business of the boat, so Makty took Shunaya forward to the little well at the bow and kept out of his way.

He watched the small crew prepare for departure with some interest. He had hardly ever had cause to travel downstream on the water. Setting off was a much simpler affair than the long series of moves to rig the sail and make sure the vessel had enough steerage way to offset the current and move upstream. All they needed to do was push off, and fend themselves away from the cluster of other boats moored up against the dock.

The current of the River teased at them and, as the crewman leaned into the steering oar, propelled them northwards. Before long they were moving at a fast pace. The pillars and obelisks of the great temple of Waset, and the distant curves of the mortuary commemorations of former rulers slipped astern. The slope of the hillside where most of the nobles had their eternal houses stayed in sight for a little while, though Senenptah's new home was never visible from the boat. Somewhere at the base of that hillside was the village where he had lived – his house was there, Sanedjem's house, those of the other team members. He wondered, as Waset disappeared, if Sanedjem's rather sorrowful prediction was right. Would he ever see this place again, or his former workmates, or would the River take him away forever?

After the reaction they had encountered from Sanedjem and Weret, Makty had fully expected to have to defend Shunaya's alien origins every day on the boat. There was no need. It turned out that both crewmen were foreigners too, from different fishing towns a long way east and west of the sedge lands where the River joined the sea. Mentep himself had been brought in to the land among a group of migrants and adopted by a childless man. So in fact, Makty was the only native born one among them. From time to time the thought would come to him that their boat was a floating miniature of the world, with representatives of five different lands all travelling together.

They soon settled into a routine on the boat. Mentep really did not like to have to explain the choices he made as he ran the vessel. Makty could understand that, as he had always disliked having to break off work and explain a half-finished design to outsiders. So while the crew ignored them, they were free to spend the time together as they pleased, out on the decking or under the cloth awning that shielded them from the sun. The days blended into a single timeless experience, with no need to plan or account for the hours drifting by. They used the nights and the days to learn familiarity with one another, body and soul, and to his relief, Makty found that he need not lose interest in Shunaya.

In the early evenings they were all together, from the time that they moored and one of the crew members started to prepare food. Makty discovered almost at once that Mentep was a keen Senet player. From then on they played one or two games every night. Makty had not expected the other man to be skilled, and the casual strategy he chose for their first game was swiftly annihilated. Realising that he had been undone by his own prejudice, he switched to playing much more carefully. He should have realised, he told himself afterwards. The board they played on was a beautiful work of art in its own right, with little sacred images adorning each of the squares in turn, rather than just picking out the key turning points of the game.

In those first few games, Mentep played in a systematic defensive way, keeping all his pieces closely bunched together and slowly making combined progress. Then, just as Makty felt he had got used to that, he switched one evening to a wild attack, taking great risks with his moves and pushing the counters into isolated, exposed positions as though daring Makty to pursue them.

On balance they were well matched, and games were closely fought. They did not keep a score, though in the market places and temple courts, tournaments like this would be a focus of intense gambling by players and spectators alike. Makty knew that they were about even in victories, though he reckoned that he was usually slightly behind. He soon became much more intent on securing the next game than in counting the total.

After a long span of days in which the river banks floated by, finally the land began to change. Makty knew the area well: they were close to Min-Nefer. The broadening shape of the River valley, the way the little towns were clustering more densely together, the shapes of the tombs along the rising ground to their left, were all rooted deep in the memory of his youth. He found within himself a considerable store of ill-feeling about it all.

When Mentep suggested that they could stop off at the quayside in Min-Nefer and spend some time in the town, he shook his head fiercely and stared along the line of the River, as though refusing even to look at the town houses. The chief of the boat, who had been looking back upstream and had missed the gesture, asked again.

"Absolutely not. Do not even slow down opposite the quay."

Mentep looked surprised at his reaction. Makty glanced up at him, trying to soften the sudden tension in his face and body and the harshness of his words.

"I am sorry, chief. But there are people there I do not want to meet. Not even by chance."

They passed by Min-Nefer close to the further bank of the River, well away from the busy waterside.

That night they played a particularly long game of Senet in which neither could quite gain the upper hand, and the middle game saw frequent reversals of fortune. Finally Mentep, with one of his sudden changes of strategy, ignored Makty's plans completely and stormed his last pieces home to secure victory. Makty did not mind; to lose at the end of such a fine session was no shame. The evening group split up again. He and Shunaya withdrew inside the privacy of their awning to play a different game. Much later, while he was still curled around and inside Shunaya's body, content and replete with satisfied desire, she caressed his cheek and leaned back a little to look into his eyes.

"You always play the same way, dear heart."

Her eyes were like shaded pools in the night. Feeling himself floating on the open waters of her soul, and not understanding her comment, he was very slow to reply. She had seemed remote during the day, wrapped up in her own concerns. He had not known why, and had not asked, and simply wanted to take at face value her return to intimacy. She spoke again.

"The Senet games against the chief of the boat, Mentep. You always play the same way."

He nodded, pulling himself back with an effort into the everyday world of the River and the land. Little ripples rocked the boat where it was moored. The scent of river flowers near the river bank drifted past him. Somewhere nearby a heron called out across the lonely reeds as it flew home.

"Oh, I see. Well, I have studied about the game. I follow what is considered to be the soundest strategy. The best overall. A man called Reny-Seneb wrote about it long ago, many generations ago now, but his writing is still reckoned as a great classic. He wrote several texts on the game, some about the best way to play, some about the true acts of faith behind it."

"If it is the best strategy, why does the chief win at least half the games? I have watched him. He does not play the same way as you. He does not even play the same from one game to the next."

Makty shook his head, ruefully.

"No, he does not. He won that last game in a most unconventional way." They shifted on the bedding, to lie side by side, facing one another. He looked at her, pursuing her thought in his mind to its logical conclusion and suddenly struck with anxiety. "Shunaya, are we just talking about Senet here?"

She laughed, rolled on to her back and stretched sensuously. "Are you worried that I might get weary of you?"

He took a deep breath.

"No, of course not." But his voice quavered a little as he

said it, and she turned her head to look at him. "Why do you say that?"

"They say that you find it hard to keep an interest in women, and that you send them away quickly when you have had some pleasure with them. Perhaps you are anxious in case they tire of you first, so you do not give them the chance to show that."

"Who says that? Where did you hear that?"

She shrugged. "Is it true?"

He stared at her, swallowed, and decided that it was better to be honest.

"Before we left Waset, I thought that maybe several weeks with you the whole time, night and day, I thought that maybe that would be difficult. I was anxious what would happen if, well, if... I don't know."

"If you got bored of being with me."

His face froze into position, his hands clenched at his sides. He looked at her and nodded once.

"And?"

"And what?"

"Are you bored of being with me?"

He shook his head. He looked away briefly, then back into her eyes. He started to say something and then stopped before the words could be made out. She looked back, patient as the moonlight, and waited. Her silence finally pushed him into reluctant speech.

"Shunaya, are you weary of being with me?"

"No, not at all." She grinned provocatively at him. "At least, not yet. But I want to know you can be different with me than the way you have been with other women in the past."

"I can change the way I play Senet."

She laughed, cupped his cheek in her hand and kissed him.

"We shall see. Just now this is very important to me."

That night he dreamed again. He was in a small boat, paddling slowly along a section of the River that he did not know. Somewhere behind him, upstream, he could hear the tumult of water tumbling over stones and shingle. He had never seen any of the cataracts high up along the River, but stories that he had been told by travellers supplied images of rushing water, shallows, hazard all around. It was calm where he was, but the River was full of turns and twists, blocking his view. Little birds skimmed low across the water and flocked into tall reed beds to either side. A little way ahead the River forked.

He paused his idle paddling, letting the steady current of the River carry him towards the fork without volition. In his lap, he suddenly realised, was the barge he had seen so many times before. It was in its miniature form, which he had last seen on a table with other grave goods. He put the paddle down in front of him and picked the boat up to look at it. It was beautifully finished, better work than he was capable of. The long-lashed eyes on the bows looked at him, followed him as he turned the model in his careful hands to look at it, blinked at him.

He held the boat very gently against his heart for a long moment, feeling the soft crush of the red fabric on his skin, and then leaned out of his boat to place the barge back on the water. She started to drift ahead of him, and he picked up the paddle to follow. One after the other, the two boats were carried towards the fork in the River. Steadily, but unerringly, the barge turned towards the right, and he followed.

⁓⁓⁓ ⧠ 𝖄𝖄𝖄 ⧠ 𝖄𝖄𝖄 ⧠ 𝖄𝖄𝖄 ⧠ ⁓⁓⁓

The next night, after they had eaten, Mentep got out the Senet board again. The crew and Shunaya sat beside them, watching, waiting. Makty settled himself on the bench opposite and chose to play second, using the cones. His first few moves were entirely conventional, responding in obvious ways to his opponent's moves. Mentep had reverted to a strategy of keeping his spools in little self-protective blocks.

Makty knew the standard response – he should advance with caution, always moving whichever was his hind-most piece. Instead, at the first good score, he pushed his leading piece far ahead through the central region. The chief of the boat raised his eyebrows at the move but said nothing. Makty continued to depart from Reny-Seneb's text, ignoring obvious ways to bring other pieces up in support and rushing the single cone headlong on. When a lucky throw of the sticks moved it into the safe area near the end, scarcely any distance from home, he took a deep breath. The chief burst out in a great guffaw.

"Well, what would Reny-Seneb say about that, now?"

Makty laughed with him.

"I didn't know you had read him."

"Of course. A great work, a real classic. It was that one text that kept me persevering with learning the written forms. Now, I had to master some of the signs anyway to become chief of the boat, but I kept wanting more because of his writing. Didn't want to stop with just the essentials. A scribe read part of it to me years ago, and I decided then and there that I had to be able to read it for myself. But I don't agree with everything he said. Some things he got quite wrong, I think."

Makty leaned back on his stool, once again forced to re-evaluate what he thought of the man whose skill he relied on every day, but who, it turned out, he hardly knew.

"Well, I'm not sure he would have approved of what I just did."

"No, I'm sure he would not. But now it is my move, I think."

In fact Makty narrowly lost that game, more by bad luck when throwing the sticks than bad strategy. He was forced to retrace his steps at a crucial stage near the end of the game, and Mentep was just able to scramble his last piece to safety while that was happening. But Makty won the second game, using an equally unorthodox method, and felt vindicated.

Much later, he explained to Shunaya what he had done that was different, tracing out moves and counter-moves across the curves of her skin with his fingers past the houses of gods and mortals, past the shape of the sunrise over the mountains until all of his counters reached home and they fell asleep together. Five days later they tied up at the mooring place at Per Bastet and left behind them the boat, the captain Mery-en-hotep, and his crewmembers.

~~~~ ⌂ 〓 ⌂ 〓 ⌂ 〓 ⌂ ~~~~

They had delivered the inscribed statue of the seated official to its grateful new owner, Djehuti-Mose. He lived in a large house, nearly as large as Senenptah's residence in Waset, a short distance from the side entrance of the temple of Hathor. Just as Senenptah had been told, Djehuti-Mose owned large tracts of land at several widely scattered places along the River, and was paying for the work out of future crops. After carefully inspecting the statue on every side he passed to Makty a document promising half the yield that would be produced for three years by a large farm a short distance downstream of Waset.

Makty thought about the arrangement while he skimmed through the text. So far as he could estimate, it would mean a considerably larger sum than if silver had changed hands, but then Senenptah was making a wager that crops would remain good for a couple of years. For his part, Djehuti-Mose had no need to actually find the quantity of silver concerned, nor to worry about its safety on the journey upstream. On the whole it seemed fair, so far as he could tell. At any rate, simply as a formal document it was carefully and clearly executed, and he had no hesitation about accepting it on Senenptah's behalf.

Now, the document passed back into Mentep's safe keeping, they were back at the busy market of Per Bastet, acquiring a collection of food from various vendors. Makty, who remembered the town moderately well from his years nearby as a boy, led Shunaya down some side-streets to a grove of palm trees close to the River. They sat together in the shade to eat. After a while she turned to him.

"Where do we go now to find this temple that you spoke of?

The house of Hekhet?"

He pointed further downstream.

"About half an afternoon's walk that way, set back a little on a ridge to be above the waters of the inundation when
they come. But Shunaya, I don't know about it now. Perhaps
we should just go back to Waset with Mentep and the note of
promise. There's no rush for the other."

She shook her head.

"The lord priest thought you might say such a thing, and
he told me most strictly that it must not happen."

He looked at her in surprise. "He said that to you?"

"He did. I have already said to the chief of the boat that he
should expect to be taking that document but no passengers.
Those were the master's words to me to speak to him."

"No matter. There are other boats. And other places besides Waset. I had a thought of going further south anyway."

"And also he gave me words to speak to you in this case."

She paused, and closed her eyes to better recall the message. When she spoke, it was with something of Senenptah's
turn of phrase. Makty could easily imagine him delivering the
message in the room that faced west.

"If he then says he will return upstream, whether to Waset
or anywhere else, you are to give him these words which he
will hear as though from my own mouth. The dreams that
have been given to him can send either a blessing or a curse.
They will be a curse for him if he turns away from them, and
they will pursue him steadfastly and swallow him, just as
a crocodile pulls its prey beneath the water and tears it in
pieces. The food in his mouth will be dung and his drink will
be ashes. His religious devotions will be empty of meaning
and his heart empty of purpose. Wherever he goes, upstream
or down, the whole land will turn him away and his footsteps
will lead him in circles. He will have no safe place. But if
he listens to the dreams and obeys, if he floats his heart on
their waters and travels where they flow, he will find peace in
his soul and satisfaction with his life. He must not turn back

from the path that they make for him. This is the choice that stands before him like the double gates before the holy place. The choice cannot be avoided; it can only be delayed, and that for only a short time."

She stopped, and there was silence for a while. Then she added, in her normal voice and manner of speech, "He also said that if you make the better choice, he expects never to see you again. Your path and his will lead you away from each other, and he is simply glad to have spent this portion of the River's journey with you. In any case, his time in this land draws to a close at last, and he might not see you again even if you turned back now. Despite what he once hoped, he does not think that you will ever visit him in the eternal home you built for him, nor carry out the sacrifices and the prayers. But his inmost being that has life within it will go out from that house, will see what you do and be content." She paused again for reflection. "When you open the letter he sent with us, the one we were not to open until the statue was delivered, you will find it says much the same."

Makty stared for a while up and down the River, as though gauging its capacity to carry him along. He looked bewildered.

"What sort of word is that? I can accept that there is a need to follow this journey to its end. Before, I was pursuing the River towards its unknown source. Now I am pursuing the course of my own life back to its own origins. But why has he turned me away from his house like this? I believed that he saw a future there for me. In Waset, doing all those things that a son might do for his father. My life would have been secure at last. What has changed? This is very hard to bear."

Neither spoke for a while. Finally he frowned and turned away from the endless flow of the River to the ground at his feet before glancing briefly at Shunaya.

"Well, if we finish the journey swiftly we may yet get back to speak with him face to face, before he crosses over to the light-land. And what about you? What was his word for you?"

"He asked me to journey with you wherever you chose to

go, whether it be north or south in the valley of this river, or outside in the lands beyond. I am to travel with you so long as it seems good. He gave me no word about my future, though. Not like the one he gave you. I have no idea what he might have seen for me. I should have asked him, but I was too fearful."

"I could just order you to go back upstream, then do as I please."

She shook her head.

"I am a companion to you, not a servant to be ordered. He did not release me from my service to him, which in any case is as willing helper and not as slave. So I obey his instructions, not your wishes, if they are in conflict. And my own heart if it seems to me that neither of you is in the right. I think you will not find it so easy to send me away. I think you will find that the same part of his omen that said your footsteps would go in circles means that you will keep finding me at your side and in front of your face."

She looked directly at him and held his glance for a long moment, with the same look of amused impudence on her face that was all that she had worn just before they first lay together. "Would that be such a bad thing?"

He sighed and looked again upriver, gazing to where the water first appeared around a clump of shrubs. There were parts of the Beloved Land up there that he had never seen, that called to his imagination as possible futures. Beyond Waset there were towns he had never visited, places of work in which he had never plied his trade. He could simply go there and pick up his life and labour as though he had never met Senenptah. Or Milashuniyet.

But the prospect of food like dung and drink like ashes was not appealing, and he already knew something of the emptiness of soul that the old man had mentioned. Perhaps, after all, it was time for a larger change, for unmooring himself from the River's edge and seeing where the current would take him. After another pause to consider, he turned to Shunaya, already aware that he was yielding to the unknown path the old priest had anticipated for him.

"If we go this way, it may mean leaving the Beloved Land. At least for a while."

She shrugged.

"I was not born here. It has been home for a while, but it would be no great loss for me if I were to leave it again. What of you? Some of your people find it hard to leave the riverbank."

He stopped and thought about that. "I have never yet left the whole land behind me. But I have travelled many times out of this valley into the wadis of the red land. That is like another country, and I was able to face that. I think I would have no special difficulty if we have to go outside."

They stood up and walked for a few paces back towards the market area. He was still thinking about the journey ahead. She watched as little ripples of ideas crossed his face. "It's not as if we were going somewhere unknown. All the lands nearby are under the hand of the great king. Have been for a long time. I'm sure they can't be so fearful to visit."

She tried, unsuccessfully, to hide a smile. "You might find things a little less orderly than the peace and luxury you have been used to. But we do have our own particular flavour, once we get out of sight of your river."

He looked at her, startled, then caught the amusement on her face and nodded ruefully.

"It's a flavour I think I could grow to like. I find that I enjoy the taste of wild honey on my tongue. But see. Our path for the next little while follows the River very closely. Even the most fearful of my people could manage that."

He led her away from the centre of the town, away from the market and the building where the town governor held office. There were a few false trails where old memories proved unreliable, and once they had to retrace their steps out of a dead end. But soon the dense clusters of houses and town life thinned out. After that they walked for a while near the much larger houses of nobles and the elite, but by then their path was obvious. It ran parallel to the River and some distance from it.

The main track along the River bank itself was easy to see, but was too busy for comfort. It was in constant use by all manner of travellers including wagons, donkeys, and small flocks of animals. Every so often they would pass a village, where knots of local travellers would join or leave. The small path was much better suited to a pair on foot, and not many others were continuing on, past place after place, as they did.

On the far side of the main track they could see the flow of river traffic. Hoisted sails of boats heading upstream rose up above the animals and carts, as did the bare masts of those following the downstream current. It was a different world altogether from some of the almost empty stretches they had followed on board Mentep's boat.

They had set off from Per Bastet just before noon, and had rested a while under a tree during the hottest part of the day, so the late afternoon sun was leaning towards the horizon as they approached the walls. Makty recalled some parts of the terrain clearly, while other parts had been lost to his memory. But when the temple first came into sight, perched up on its ridge in conscious imitation of the first mound to be raised out of the primordial waters, a very strange sense of complete recognition came over him.

The way the gates stood up against the sky, and the tower on the north side leaned a little to one side, the way the flock of neat houses clustered around the mud-brick wall: all of these things stirred very deep memories and feelings within him. He stopped for a while, wondering what it was about the place that had the capacity to move him so deeply.

Shunaya stopped at his side and looked at it with him. For her, he imagined, it was just another place along the River. If she found any meaning in it, it was because of him, and because of the way they were becoming entwined. That thought was in its way even more troubling than his reaction to the building ahead of them. He had put considerable effort into avoiding entanglements over the years. What was he thinking, to be doing this journey at all? Surely it would have been better to have gone upstream as he had wanted?

He had no doubt that Shunaya had repeated the old man's words accurately, but he was not at all sure he believed that the substance of the words was true. Maybe now was the time to show his disbelief by simply making a different choice. He turned, and realised that Shunaya was standing in front of him. He smiled to himself, knowing that whatever his own views might be, she would adhere faithfully to the task she had been given, and had chosen. Surely she would indeed be standing in his way every time he turned to one side or the other. The entanglement had already changed him irrevocably.

She was still looking at the temple, seemingly oblivious to the debate that had been going on in his heart. She pointed to a short track leading from the River back up towards the temple wall.

"Is that the entrance?"

He nodded, feeling again the sense of being carried down the River without volition, watching places on the banks being brought alongside for a season and then swept away again.

"Yes it is. The main gate is there. The dock-gate for when the inundation is high is on the far side from us."

They began walking again. He led them diagonally across on tracks that meandered between some swampy reed beds to join the main track for the last part of the journey. All around the outside of the walls were little shrine booths, each below a large panel on the wall filled with writing and pictures of some agricultural activity. He pointed to one of them, a little way around the western wall from where they stood.

"Each village nearby provides something different to support the temple through the year, and the designs show what is to be given and when. My first piece of public work, before I was apprenticed out to Tety-Seneb, was to work on that panel there. Part of it had flaked off when a piece of the wall crumbled in a dry summer, and I was one of the crew that worked to make it good. And it was good, too. You could say that when I worked on that piece of wall, it set the pattern for my whole life so far."

They followed the edge of the walls around to the main door, which stood open in welcome. A junior acolyte sat in the shade to one side of the opening. She stood as they came through the arch and greeted them. Makty stepped forward and bowed to her.

"Lady, I wonder if we might speak to the chief chantress?"

She looked at them both, took in their appearance, hesitated a moment.

"My lord scribe, I can certainly ask the honoured lady if she will meet two travellers. Perhaps she already knows one or both of you? Is there a name I should give her in greeting? Or some particular purpose to your visit among us?"

"She will never have met my companion, the lady Milashuniyet, called Shunaya." He stumbled over her full name, as he always did, and his voice faltered for a moment before he continued. "But I grew up as a child in this place. I left here as a boy when I was made apprentice to the craftsman Tety-Seneb just outside Min-Nefer. If the honoured lady has been leading you for a long time, she may remember me. My name is Makty-Rasut."

She nodded and looked at him more closely. "She has served us for around ten years, so I think perhaps she will not know you. But please, come and wait in this room while I pass on your message."

She took them to a small chamber off to one side. It was built into the outer walls, and had a large open gap serving as a window facing in towards the courtyard. They watched the young woman cross the courtyard and disappear into a little door.

"They must have moved the place where the chantress has her rooms. They used to be up those stairs over there."

He pointed to a different corner of the open area, where a flight of steps curled out of sight, and an archway showed glimpses of a garden area beyond the first dividing wall. He paced up and down, restless. As the time drew out, he sat briefly at one of the several stools and then got up again. Time passed. Eventually the door-ward who had greeted them crossed the courtyard again, accompanied by the chantress, a considerably older woman who walked slowly with the help of a long stick, limping heavily as she came. Both her feet were turned in on themselves, and her gait was very awkward.

Makty realised that she had probably been one of the many crippled babies that were turned over to the temples by families or owners who did not want the burden of raising them. He watched her come towards them, proud in her difficulty. Suddenly struck with insight, he wondered if his heart limped in just the same way as it passed through life, if only one had eyes to discern the shapes of the inner world? What had Senenptah seen as he looked at him?

The lady came in to the room followed by the acolyte who had first met them. Moved by years of boyish habit, Makty moved across to her and knelt at her feet on the dusty floor. She put one hand on the crown of his head in blessing and he felt old memories of homeliness flood through his body from top to toe. He had been a very long time away from home, and he put his arms carefully around her crippled legs and clung on to her.

She whispered something he did not quite catch, probably a prayer to the Lady Hekhet, then bent down stiffly and kissed the top of his head. She straightened again and he reluctantly loosened his grip on her. She stepped a half pace back in order to look at him. He returned the look, breathing deeply as though he had passed through a deluge of rain and come out into sunshine again.

"Well, Makty-Rasut the scribe, it is easy to see that you grew up here in the holy house, and that you knew one of my predecessors. But you have been away a very long time. How can I help you now, after all these years?"

Makty tried to speak but failed. She waited, patiently, leaning on her staff as though it held all her years of service within it. Eventually she spoke again.

"Yes, it has been an extremely long time. You are not yet ready to speak about it." She looked across at Shunaya, who had taken up a pose standing against the wall as though she was back in Senenptah's house. "And who is your companion here?"

Makty, still kneeling, turned and tried to smile at Shunaya. It was a brave attempt, but not a very successful one. The three women waited for him to answer. Finally, after several deep breaths, he found a voice.

"This is the lady Milashuniyet, called Shunaya. She has respect among her own people, and has lived in the Beloved Land for many years. She has come with me all the way downstream from Waset and will, I am sure, go with me as far as this journey takes us. She has been more than a companion to me, and I hope..." He stopped for a few heartbeats. "I hope I have been more than just a companion to her as well." He turned back to the chantress and rushed on before anyone could say anything.

"I have come back after all this time to find out about my parents. Well, about my mother, at least. I was brought up in this house, and perhaps my mother still lives and serves here. I would like to meet her. I would like to see her again."

The chantress looked at him for a long moment.

"You do not know your mother's name?"

He shook his head.

"I was hoping that someone here would recognise me."

She nodded.

"Very well. You have come at a good hour. Most of the women are in the eating hall. I should warn you, though, that very few of them have been here longer than I. It is possible that none of them will know you. I can make no promise. If you are content with that, then walk with me and we shall see what we will find."

He stood up again and nodded to her. He was looking very anxious. The chantress turned to Shunaya.

"Will you come with us? The house of Hekhet is not closed to you. As she fills the River with life, and all the lands even to the very ends of the world, so we welcome all comers into her home."

"If Makty wishes it, I would be honoured to come into your house."

He nodded urgently. "Please come, please come with me."

The acolyte returned to the gatehouse while the other three of them set off through the little archway that Makty had pointed out earlier, into the gardens beyond. Little pools of water were scattered everywhere between grasses and flowering plants, and some of Hekhet's myriads of offspring could be seen and heard all around. Their progress was very slow, but they were heading unerringly towards the hall that Makty remembered.

Finally they went through another door into a large chamber where a group of women of all different ages were eating. The conversation slowed, but did not cease, as they walked in. The chantress picked up a juglet and tapped it on a nearby table to gather the room's attention.

"Ladies. This man here is called Makty-Rasut. He was raised here as a boy, he says, but it would have been several years before I joined you. He has asked if anyone here remembers the woman he called mother."

There was a pause. The older women looked at each other. Eventually one of them stood up.

"Lady, perhaps I remember this man? May I see him closer?"

The chantress nodded. "Of course, Ib-Anat."

The woman walked over to Makty. She was a little shorter than he, and looked up into his eyes, standing quite close to him. Then she turned to one of the younger girls.

"Shenty, fetch Iadet from the great pool in the water garden. She will want to see this man."

The young woman ran off. Makty watched her go, then turned back to Ib-Anat. He swallowed, started to speak, then stopped. There was a little silence, broken only by little whispers here and there. Before long the other woman was brought back by Shenty. Ib-Anat glanced across to them.

"Look who has come back to us. Iadet, see who it is."

The newcomer, Iadet, joined the other woman.

"Well, look, if it isn't Makty-Rasut? Ah, my best child! How many years must it be? You're looking well. Very well. You've made something of yourself, then."

Makty looked intensely, longingly, at the new lady who had arrived.

"Lady, are you my mother then?"

But she shook her head. He persisted.

"You just called me your child. And I remember calling someone 'mother' here. If it wasn't you, then who?"

"Well, none of us here. Oh, you called me mother, for sure, and you spent more time with me in those early days than any of the others. But this body of mine was never your first home. You never grew like an egg in me or any of the rest of us. I so wanted a child back then. All those years ago now. When you came, I thought you were the Lady Hekhet's gift just for me. But in truth there were several of us that you called mother. The chantress back then insisted. Six, I think there were at that time. Me, Ib-Anat here. Reneniyt joined a little later, she's upriver at Per Bastet just now, we're still here. The others, those who live, have moved on elsewhere now. We passed you around all of us, you and the other little ones in our care. Six of us, and, oh, at least twice that number of youngsters to care for between us. The younger women do that still, though not so many as in our day."

Makty blinked, taken aback, looking at each of the women in turn. As he remained silent, Iadet spoke again.

"Look, Makty, we raised you until it was time to be apprenticed out to a priest. Who was it, now?"

She turned to the other woman, who put her head on one

side to think. Makty replied. "It was Tety-Seneb, who worked in the city of the dead near Min-Nefer."

"Tety-Seneb, that's right. I remember. He was a strange little man. He took you off just before the inundation that year. Did he treat you well?"

"He taught me well. I stayed with him just long enough to learn my trade, and grow into manhood. Then I moved on." He took a deep breath. "So neither of you is my mother."

The two looked at each other and laughed. "Neither of us. Or both of us. All six of us, if you like. One or other of us would be holding you if you needed it, feeding and clothing you, making sure you were clean until you learned to do it yourself. Teaching you what was needful. But if you are wanting to find the woman who carried you inside herself, then she is not here."

"So where is she?"

There was a pause. Most of the women in the room had returned to their own conversation, or else were starting to move away having finished the evening meal. The chantress, the two women, Makty and Shunaya moved to an empty table and sat together at it.

"Makty, you have to understand. You were brought to us after you were weaned. Your mother was no longer allowed to keep you in the household where she was working. She was permitted to keep you until you were weaned, and then she was sent off one way and you another. You were brought here. We never met her. Whether she wanted you to be with her or not, I don't know, but most likely she was not given the choice. So you came here and we cared for you as though you were an orphan. When you were first brought to this house by slaves of that household, just as the inundation was starting, it was I who opened the door and first took you in."

"And where did she go?"

Iadet shook her head, but Ib-Anat sat thinking for a while. "She was moved to a house out in the Kinahny province. Was it in Gedjet? Yes, Gedjet for sure. The buyer was taking her out of the Land. He was a priest who was serving there. I got interested because it was not all that far from where I grew up as a girl, before I was sent down here. An important priest, called out there to service at the great holy house which stands in the middle of the town. She didn't mind about leaving the Beloved Land, or so we were told. So when the buyer wanted two slaves to go out there with him, the housekeeper she was serving under picked her as one of them. I don't remember any more. That was the last we heard of her, I think. No reason we would ever hear any more. Not our concern."

Makty sat silent for a long time, head down. The women looked at one another and waited. Finally Shunaya touched him on the arm.

"We can go out to Gedjet. It's not as far as the journey we have already made down from Waset. And surely the lord priest Senenptah always believed that you would have to go north outside the Beloved Land before ever you could come home."

Ib-Anat looked at her curiously.

"There's a thing. Senenptah was the name of the priest who was out in Gedjet. The one who had instructed the buyer, I mean. The household that this woman was going out to was his. I'm sure of it. Must be a common name upstream where you have come from."

Makty shivered suddenly, though the room was still warm. He shook his head.

"I have just finished crafting the eternal home of a priest called Senenptah who, when he was younger, spent years out in Gedjet. Shunaya here has been some time in his household, but the time we are speaking about was longer ago still. It has to be the same man." He looked at Shunaya. "He must have guessed. Why would he not tell me?"

She shook her head. "Perhaps he was uncertain. Perhaps he did not wish to raise your hopes on a falsehood. It would only have been a guess on his part; he could not possibly have known about the ladies here who raised you. You never told him about them, not until the very end."

"I should go back to Waset and ask him."

"He would not want that. His word to you said nothing of returning to ask questions, only of continuing until you find the root of all this. And perhaps he has nothing more he could tell you about the matter. Besides, the chief Mery-en-hotep and his boat have left to go upriver by now."

"There are other boats."

"Look now, that is a fruitless quest. If you went there, what answer could he give that would send you anywhere but back here to Per Bastet, and then out to Gedjet? Why make that journey twice over, when we are here now, and we can simply move on?"

He closed his eyes, bent his head down to rest it on his hands. Iadet reached out and smoothed his hair as, no doubt, she had done when he was little. He sighed and relaxed a little. The chantress looked at each in turn.

"There is a group leaving here for Gedjet in a week or two. A local merchant with some goods, a messenger for the governor, and an armed escort. They say that out there it is not like the Beloved Land; a person should not travel alone for fear of robbers. Especially a woman. I can introduce you to them so that you can travel together. You are welcome to stay here until then."

Shunaya nodded.

"That would be most kind, lady. How far is Gedjet?"

The chantress shook her head.

"I am sorry. I have no idea."

Makty straightened again. "But I do. A fully equipped and provisioned army would take ten days to go from Tjaru to Gedjet. A mixed group will travel slower, and we are a few days south and west of Tjaru. With a few days delay until we depart, I should say we will reach Gedjet about twenty days from now. At least that, perhaps a little longer. And maybe we will have to go beyond that again. So although you are right, Shunaya, when you say that Waset is much further away than Gedjet, yet nevertheless we are barely half way along the journey. The River speeds everything. We travel two or three times as fast in a boat as we do along a road."

⌇ 𓋹 𓏤𓏤𓏤 𓋹 𓏤𓏤𓏤 𓋹 𓏤𓏤𓏤 𓋹 ⌇

Makty was sitting with Shunaya and Iadet on a wooden bench beside the great pool. In the pool, around and amongst the water plants, Hekhet's children were playing, or resting half submerged on rocks and lily pads.

The caravan for Gedjet was leaving early the next morning, and Makty had wanted to spend the last afternoon in the gardens. He had already seen the chantress and been given prayers and a blessing by her. He had also insisted, to her amusement, on making a gift to the holy house out of the wealth he had stored up, and felt that he had discharged some small portion of unresolved debt. Now he was impatient, and only the ambience of the great pool was helping him to relax.

Iadet looked at him. "You want to be on your way again?"

"I do. This place is a haven for me, and I had never thought to stay here again. But I am restless now for the next part of the journey."

Shunaya watched as two of the orphans ran across the open space, sent on some errand by one of the ladies in the refectory.

"I thought last night how our journey is like one of your games of Senet."

He glanced at her.

"Great scribes and priests have written on that very subject."

"I'm sure they have. But I was meaning something much more ordinary. We are about to leave on our next stage, yes? This will be the third stage. The first was in Waset up to the night of the party after you finished working on Senenptah's tomb. When we first lay together. What is the name of that place in the middle row of the game board? On the chief Mentep's board it was particularly beautiful."

"The House of Life. It is the most important place on the board, except for reaching home."

"The House of Life." She repeated it several times, nodding to herself. "Well, I think that fits well. Then there is a gap until the next place where something important happens."

He grinned. "The House of Splendour. On the final straight, just before the Waters guarding the safe area near to home."

"Well, here we are at the House of Splendour."

Makty looked around at the gardens and the brimming pools, the mud brick walls and the wooden trimmings. It was homely and comfortable – not magnificent, but it satisfied his heart. Iadet laughed and clapped her hands.

"Isn't the holy place up at Waset a hundred times more grand than this little home?"

Makty shook his head.

"Only in wealth such as gold and lapis. This place seems more splendid to me."

He looked around again, nodded, and then touched Shunaya's arm.

"I'm still not convinced this a true way of seeing, but go on. What's next? The House of Waters. If we go there we cannot proceed, but must go back again to the House of Life. Is that Waset? Or a shared bed?"

Iadet laughed again. "That would not have occurred to you when you left here all those years ago."

"We are not going back to Waset without finishing this journey. I don't know how that place fits into this. But what comes next?"

"The houses of gods and mortals, then sunrise in the valley between the mountains, then home."

Iadet nodded. "The great holy place in Gedjet is a godly place."

"And Gedjet is a great town with many people, they say."

Makty looked from one to the other. "Lots of places are

great towns with many people." But he sounded hesitant, as though starting to see some merit in the idea. "And there are mountains for sure in the Asiatic lands. Not by Gedjet, I think. Further inland. Hills and valleys which we do not have in the Beloved Land. I was taught their names, and the way to travel from one to another, but have never seen them."

"So our journey will not stop in Gedjet after all."

He looked away from the women, into the great pool as it reflected the cloudless sky.

"I don't know. What if the House of Waters is all there is ahead of us, and we are forced to go back over the same route over and over again. Like the circles that Senenptah talked about in his word to me. Maybe the trip to Gedjet is a blind alley. I have already had my hopes trimmed once, when I found that my mother was not here, in this place."

"And she may not be in the next place either. If I am reading the game right, she is certainly not in Gedjet, but somewhere beyond. But look, Makty, every one of your games has come to an end sometime. Perhaps to go past this House of Waters, we must both travel away from your river."

Makty stood up and looked north, as though trying to see past the wall which rose up only a short distance away.

"I am afraid of all this, Shunaya. Some games you lose, even if you make all the right choices. But in any case I think we are committed to the journey now."

8. Past – Adoption

MAKING PRAISE BEFORE the Lady Hekhet and kissing the ground at her feet, because I was brought to one of her holy houses. There I was an obedient child, diligent to carry out every word that was spoken to me. Every day I was quick to do the will of the ladies who had charge over me, so that they blessed me and commended my name.

IADET-EN-TEFNUT FINISHED THE MORNING devotion at the holy place of Hekhet. The inundation had just started to come up. Today the water was lapping on the edge of the river track. Tomorrow it would be over the rough stones and partway across the stretch of open ground in front of the entrance gates.

A few days more, and the temple would be cut off on its little island for a time. The dock gate on the north side would be the only means in or out of the place until the water subsided again. While the river was in flood, the women devoted to Hekhet here would recreate, in word and dance, the time before time when the dry land first arose from the waters of creation.

It was a good time of year, when Iadet could feel the ancient roots of her womanhood gripping securely onto the foundations of the Beloved Land itself. The whole land was passing through its own colossal version of her monthly cycle, with the gush of water first overflowing its everyday bounds and then subsiding again to leave fertility in its wake. She sighed, feeling deep inside her again the tug of her own desires. Once again, she suspected, the fields on either side of the rising river would have to grow seed for her.

She left the shrine area, taking five steps backwards still facing towards the altar and its little oil lamp before turning away towards the refectory. She was hungry now, and quite ready to break her fast. As she crossed the pillared central court, she heard a voice calling out at the side gate. No-one else was nearby, so she went and opened the gate herself.

Two people were standing outside, slaves from one of the nearby households, she thought, with a very young boy standing between them, holding the woman's hand. The woman was carrying a small bundle of clothes, the rather older man held a small bag. She looked enquiringly at them. They both bowed, recognising her rank, then the man spoke.

"Honoured mistress, we come from the house of the honoured lord Unen-Nefer. He has sent us to come here with this child for your care. He wants us to also offer you this gift by way of meeting the costs of raising him."

The woman pushed the boy a little towards Iadet, not unkindly but quite firmly. He accepted the change passively, as though there had already been too many changes to manage. Meanwhile, the man pressed the bag into her hands; it was heavy, and she presumed without looking that it contained silver and a few other valuables. The two turned to go, leaving the boy standing there just in front of her. She took a step forward and stopped them.

"No, wait. You must tell me more. What is his name? Are you his mother?"

The woman stopped at the question, half turned, shook her head.

"No, honoured mistress. His mother has been given up to a greatly honoured priest going on a journey further up into the sedge lands, somewhere far away. He did not want the child, she was not allowed to take him. Our master had no use for him and ordered us to bring him here. He is called Makty-Rasut."

"Who acquired the mother?"

The two looked at each other. The man replied. "Forgive us, honoured mistress, but we were not told his name. It was his housekeeper who collected the woman."

Iadet looked down at the boy, who was still facing in towards the open door and the courtyard and seemed either unaware of or uncaring about the conversation. The man looked at her briefly.

"Honoured mistress, might we leave now? Our master told us to come straight back again to the household."

Iadet nodded. The man was clearly anxious that too long an absence might cause trouble and punishment for them both.

"Tell your master that we thank him for his gift and shall remember his name before the Lady Hekhet."

At her release, they went immediately, hurrying away into the morning, not looking back. She took the boy's hand. He looked up at her, clearly having no idea of who she was. She squatted down beside him so that she could talk directly to him on his level.

"So, Makty-Rasut, here we are. It seems that you will be living here at the holy place with me and with the other sisters. For a few years, at least, until we have taught you the beginnings of a trade, and found a man who will take you as apprentice. I think I will be one of the women you will call mother, but the lady chantress will decide that for sure."

At the word 'mother' he looked up into her face for a long moment, then looked puzzled and shook his head. She sighed, stood up, put an arm around him, and took him through the gate and into the colonnade.

"For sure you'll not lack brothers and sisters, nor mothers either in this place. But it's confusing for a soul to get accustomed to this all at once. Come in now and we'll find you some food and have you meet all your new family. Come along now."

She took Makty into the refectory. About half the women were still there, and the buzz of conversation halted as one little group after another saw the two of them. Here and there, dotted about amongst the women, were other children. The youngest were barely able to toddle. The oldest were about eight years of age or so, and likely to be apprenticed out when the water subsided. Some would be in the care of one or other temple for their whole life, where ill chance at their birth or accident afterwards had left them lame, speechless or confused. Iadet's close friend Ib-Anat called out from one of the further tables.

"Look now, our sweet Iadet has had a baby in the night. She's always wanted one and now look at her with him. Hasn't he grown quickly?"

There was answering humour from different parts of the room. Makty shrank back against Iadet at the attention. Neb-Khaty, the oldest woman and currently appointed chantress, stood and came over to her. One or two of the other orphans followed her, a few paces behind. Makty turned away and clung to Iadet's legs, burying his face in her skirt.

"And who is this, sister? How did you come by him?"

"Mother, the two slaves that left him said that he was called Makty-Rasut. From the household of the lord Unen-Nefer, the child of a woman who has been sold on to a priest travelling away. Neither the new owner nor the old wanted to take responsibility for the child, being so young, so he was given to us. And this was sent along with him."

She held out the bag of valuables that the man had given her. Makty was starting to look around a little but was still holding determinedly on to Iadet's legs. When one of the other orphans reached out and touched his shoulder, he looked very solemnly at the other boy but made no move away from Iadet. He still had not said anything.

"We will keep him and raise him, mother?"

The chantress nodded.

"Of course. Since he was brought to you, and apparently does not want to let you go just now, you will see that he has a place here. Get him settled in and keep him with you in your room until the inundation has passed, so long as the other sisters you share with are willing. After a time he must be placed with the other boys. See that he gets some new clothes after he has eaten, and make sure those are cleaned. Or even thrown away if needs must. Who knows what he has been living in just now?"

Iadet nodded, bobbed a little bow of obedience, then turned to Makty and knelt down in front of him to make sure she had his attention. She took his hands.

"Makty, for now I shall be your mother. You will be living here with me and the other sisters. Come now and get some food, then I'll show you where we live."

She stood again, still holding the boy's hand. The chantress was in front of her.

"And make sure that he knows that you are not his only mother. Make sure you share him with the other women. I'll not have you treat him as though he was yours alone. He must

learn that he has to share women, not have them to himself.
Teach him to say 'mother' to all the women in your room. Do
we know the birth mother?"

"No, lady. The slaves who left him did not tell me her name.
Only that she had been bought and taken away from here."

"Find out what you can, Iadet. And see if you can find out
in time what sort of aptitude he has. He won't be leaving us
for a few years yet, but we might as well get him started on
something productive as soon as we can. It would be better
for all of us if he had some natural talent we can work with."

Iadet took him over to the bench where a selection of food
still part-filled the serving bowls. The boy looked listlessly at
them, barely responding as she tried to interest him in one
thing or another. She sighed. It was remotely possible he
had already eaten something earlier in the day, but not likely.
The first month was always the worst for the new children,
and she knew to expect a series of difficult days and disturbed
nights.

⁓⁓ ♤ ☖☖ ♤ ☖☖ ♤ ☖☖ ♤ ⁓⁓

Ib-Anat was working in the garden with the great pool,
clearing away weeds and the accumulation of time from the
herb beds. She looked up, brushing sweaty hair back from her
forehead. As a child out in the Kinahny province, she remembered wearing a headscarf every day. That was before she had
been chosen from her village and sent down amongst the Mitsriy to serve in this holy house. A kef, everyone used to call it.
She had not worn one for many years now, but summer work
in the sun always brought the memory back, together with a
wish that the custom held sway here as well. Iadet was coming towards her, holding the new boy by the hand. The two
had been inseparable since he had arrived on that morning.
Her friend looked extremely cross.

"What is it, Iadet?"

"It is the chantress, and what she has just said to me."

"Yes?"

"She said that I must give my Makty up to another woman. And it has only been six months. Not even that. Scarcely more than a season. You remember, he came when the inundation was starting."

"But you always knew this would happen."

Iadet turned away for a moment, looking with some anxiety to where Makty was leaning over one of the smaller pools. She relaxed as he sat down on a nearby bench and started to push some twigs around.

"I did. But not now. It is so soon. Too soon. He should spend a year with me so that he can settle down into his new home. How can he find himself after all these changes?"

Ib-Anat looked carefully at her before answering.

"Are you sure it is the boy's best interest you have in mind, or your own?"

Iadet flushed a little.

"Of course I want this for me as well, but it's not just that. Truly, it is for his own good as well. I won't deny that I want a child."

She paused, blinking away the sudden tears that filled her eyes. Ib-Anat nodded and took her hand, squeezed it lovingly, then put her arms around Iadet and held her tightly while she shook with passion, like a cloudburst filling a dry wadi. Makty, feeling the emotion from where he sat nearby, started to sob his own tears. Iadet detached herself from her friend and ran over to him, scooping him up and holding him close. He dabbed at the tears which were still wet on her face. She laughed between her ragged breaths.

"My special boy. You know when I'm upset, don't you? But I'm not upset with you, it's nothing you've done."

Still holding him, she came back over to Ib-Anat and sat down again, keeping Makty on her lap.

"So who will be the lucky woman?"

"I don't know. I think the chantress was going to tell me but I stormed out of her room. I have not been back to see her yet." She glanced at Ib-Anat and shook her head. "Don't tell me I should not have done that. I know that already. I'm sure she will tell me herself and have some kind of penance arranged for me to do."

There was a long silence. Makty scrambled down and began to collect some stones together. They were all pale, and about the same size, and he was arranging them in a ring around her feet.

"It might be you, Ibby."

"It might. I expect I'll get a turn at some stage before long. You know how she likes to do things."

"If it is, you will let me share him with you? I can't bear the thought of him being with someone else to fall asleep. I mean, if it was you it would be different. But you would let me be with him, wouldn't you?"

Ib-Anat hugged her tightly, her fingers smoothing away the last tears from her cheeks.

"Of course I would. Now go back to the chantress, make your apologies, and listen to what she says. Better that you go back of your own accord than to wait until she summons you there. If you do that it'll be someone in our dormitory who gets him this time. If not, she might send him quite away from us to another house. Don't take Makty with you when you go. He's far too sensitive to your moods, and you'll just set each other off. Go on now, leave him with me."

She picked Makty-Rasut up and settled him on her lap. Iadet stood, stepped over the stone circle that Makty had made, and started off towards the main building. Makty stared after her, not realising the changes that her departure would mean to him. Ib-Anat turned him around so he could not see when she disappeared inside, and started to play one of the children's counting games on his fingers.

The sun was high, and the women of the holy house of

Hekhet were preparing the feast for the celebration of the longest day. The kitchen, and the main refectory, were the focus of intense activity. Outside, there were processions of slaves with gifts from one or other of the nearby great houses, or freewill offerings brought from individual families. There were queues at the gates where people were bringing baskets, or driving small animals or geese in unruly herds.

Inside, Makty-Rasut was furious, with all of the unbridled anger that a young child can muster when thwarted of a desired goal. His shouting could be heard all the way from the great pool, where one of the women was trying ineffectually to quieten him, to the kitchens and to the chamber of the chantress Neb-Khaty. As she came from one direction, Iadet appeared at a run from one of the other courtyards.

The chantress held up a hand, stopping Iadet some distance away, and strode up to Makty. He looked up at her, shouting something incoherent. She stood over him, stern and unyielding. Gradually silence fell again. He was looking over towards Iadet, but when he made a move to go to her the chantress stood in his way. For a brief moment a ferocious look crossed his face. He tried to peer around her to see Iadet but Neb-Khaty moved to prevent him again. He stared up at her. The courtyard was silent, so that the noise and bustle of incoming goods for the feast could be heard near the outer gate.

"What is this noise about, Makty-Rasut?"

"I want to be with my mother. With her. She's just there. Why won't you let me be with her. She wants me too. She told me."

Iadet took another step closer, and was stilled by a glance from the chantress.

"You have to share and be shared. You know that. You cannot have her to yourself, and she cannot have you to herself. You both know that this is the rule here."

"I want to be with her. She's better than everyone else."

Neb-Khaty took a deep breath. There was too much to do

today, with all of the preparations for the feast going on all around her. She had no time to spend on this. She frowned at him.

"If you make a noise like that once more I will make a rule that you will never see her again."

A look of intense pain crossed Makty's face. Behind her, Neb-Khaty heard Iadet gasp. "I do not think that you want this?"

He shook his head.

"Then listen to me, Makty-Rasut. If you shout and scream hot words like that any more today, I will make that rule, and I will send this woman to another holy house nearby. But if you are quiet and hold your peace, and if you work hard for me at the things that I say, you can be with her. Every time you work hard, your reward will be to spend time with Iadet. Every time you make noises like this, you will be taken away from her. Do you understand?"

The boy nodded, visibly swallowing what he had been going to say. She looked at him for a long moment, trying to assess his resolve.

"What must I do today, mistress?"

She thought about it. "They tell me you are good with colours and shapes?"

He nodded again.

"Then sister Iadet will take you to the lady Set-Rettawy, who is setting out the beautiful things in the entrance hall to the sacred place. Iadet will leave you there. You will help the lady Set-Rettawy lay things out properly so that they bring praise to the Lady Hekhet. Then if I hear good report of you at the end of the day, you shall be with Iadet in the evening, at the feast and afterwards. But if you are a trouble and a noisy nuisance, and you will not listen to Set-Rettawy when she instructs you, I swear today that you will go hungry tonight, and then tomorrow you will be separated from Iadet and never see her again. This is my word, and I will not alter it. If you understand, repeat back to me what you must do."

"I must go to the lady Set-Rettawy and help her with the beautiful things of this house so that they are set out right. I must listen to her and do what she says."

"Good." She turned to Iadet. "You have also heard my words. Be sure that I mean every single one of them. Now take the boy to Set-Rettawy and tell her what I have said. Then come away again and get on with your own work. I will not have you stand around idle when everyone else is busy."

Iadet came across, her hands shaking a little. "I understand, mistress." She paused, swallowed, then made her little bob of obedience. "And I want to thank you for your kindness, mistress. I will make sure Makty here understands what must be done."

She took Makty's hand and started leading him towards the central building. The chantress turned to go, then stopped and turned back to the pair of them.

"Makty-Rasut, remember this. If you work hard in this place you will be rewarded. For now, your reward will be to spend more time with Iadet here. Other things may come to you in time. Perhaps we will find a skilled man who will teach you as his apprentice. He will discipline you as he sees fit. But if you are lazy, or if you take other people away from their work with your noise, you will be punished, and your punishment for now will be to take you away from Iadet. Remember this, when the angry mood comes over you, and think of all the things that you will lose if I hear about it."

The boy turned and looked at her. "I will work hard for you, so I can be with her."

There was still a sullen tone to his voice, and she was quite certain that his eyes betrayed an unresolved layer of anger beneath the surface. For now it would have to do. There were too many other things going on today to spend more time on him.

Richard Abbott

9. Present – Meeting

THIS THAT SHE did to me, this sister,
   will I ever keep quiet about it?
She made me stand outside her house
   so she could slip back inside:
but no word to me, "Come in for delight",
   so frustration for me in the night.

MAKTY-RASUT AND SHUNAYA were following a well-used track up into the hill country. So far everything had been exactly in accordance with the directions they had been given in Gedjet. They had spent much more time than they had expected there, rather more than a month in fact by the time all was done. The temple in the centre of the town was easy enough to find. It had not taken long to follow directions to the house that Senenptah had lived in either, since the present senior priest was using the same building. But for a while the trail ran cold there, since no-one serving in the house now remembered those days.

They had persevered, though, using up more of the good will that Makty had accumulated, along with the letter of commendation from Senenptah himself. Finally they tracked down a man who had been a door-warden there. He was quite elderly, but his memory of those years was clear.

A village priest from the hill country had bought the woman, on the very same day that the lord priest's own daughter had left for the north to marry a man of Djahy. The man was called Damariel. He had come all the way from a town called Kephrath, though his motive was unfathomable. Were there no slaves closer at hand for him? But no, he could not tell them the woman's name. Nor how to travel to Kephrath. The soldiers would know that.

Makty had become anxious, irritable, as the fruitless days had rolled by, but had been suddenly restored with the fresh news. Shunaya had lost her appetite for food, and in the evenings in the temple refectory had picked unenthusiastically at the provisions. She had not been sleeping well, and Makty would wake to find her sitting up beside him, pale and preoccupied. In the mornings she often felt sick until the warmth of the day eased her, but the sickness never developed into anything more serious.

Finally they were on their way, with ample provisions and a clear set of directions to follow. They had gone along the Sea Road for some distance before branching off past a fair size town called Ayaluna, climbing steadily as they went. Makty remembered that town from the route lists he had been taught, but now they were following a way that he had never learned.

This track was considerably smaller than the Sea Road, but was clear enough, easy to follow, and seemed entirely safe for travellers. It was all quite different from the gloomy and dangerous region they had been told about in Per Bastet and along the way to Gedjet.

In Gedjet his dreams had been broken up, fragmentary, and he had not needed the priest to tell him that they reflected his outward confusion. This had changed as soon as they were on the path and had purpose again. Once he saw the little barge floating peacefully in a small pond. Another time he watched Senenptah's housekeeper as she tended a flowering seedling. The scenes were quick and fleeting, but peaceful, and left him feeling content.

It was early afternoon. Ahead of them the track zigzagged up a steeper stretch of land between small clumps of trees and scrub.

Before the climb, on their left, was a small village. Makty stopped, looking at it. Shunaya was slightly behind him, walking a little more slowly and wearily than he had expected. He turned to wait for her. The small cluster of buildings looked as though it had been abandoned some time ago, then resettled, and was still recovering from desertion. About half the houses were in use, and were well cared for, but the others were in various states of disrepair. Haphazard patches of low bushes and trees adjacent to the houses had been cleared of scrub for cultivation. Two stone pillars with a wooden lintel served as the town gate. A faint smell of wood smoke drifted in the air.

Attached to one of the pillars was a flat wooden sign, a little faded but quite well executed in the Kinahny signs that were being used out here in the province now. Makty glanced at it, thinking to himself that the workmanship indicated scribal training. However, it would take him longer to remember how to read the signs than simply to ask the man who was approaching them where they stood on the track.

He let Shunaya do the talking; although he could speak Kinahny, she was much more fluent than he, and less likely to make a mistake. The man stood under the lintel of the gate with the air of someone who controlled the right of entry. He was middle aged, with a shrewd air about him, and he waited for them to speak.

"Sir, we were directed along this track in order to find a town called Kephrath. Is this the town?"

Makty had puzzled out enough of the wooden sign to be almost certain it was not, so it was no surprise to him when the man shook his head.

"No indeed. This is Bayth Horon. But Kephrath is not far for you to go from here." He pointed up the hill. "Follow the track up that hill into the valley bowl at the top, then one more ridge and you will see the first houses. You will be there well before the afternoon is done." He paused, looking at the packs they carried and the well-worn state of their footwear. "Will you come in and accept the hospitality of the village?"

Shunaya looked at Makty, who shook his head in reply. The sense of expectation, of the possibility of resolution, which had started building in him at the holy house of Hekhet outside Per Bastet, was becoming overwhelming, and the idea of stopping at this point was unbearable. She turned back to the man under the gate.

"You are kind, sir, and generous, but we have travelled a long way to be here and would rather continue the journey."

The man nodded, not especially concerned whether they decided one way or the other. They turned to go, when Makty suddenly turned back.

"Look, sir, see, we were that told there was a man who lived there once, a priest there in Kephrath that was called Damariel. Is that true? Did he live there? Is he there now?"

The other looked curiously at him.

"Damariel, yes. He is the seer and priest up there. Has been for many years now, much longer than I have lived here.

Do you know him?"

Makty shook his head, gripped Shunaya's arm, thanked the man as best he could and then started up the track, leaving the half-built place behind. He walked very quickly up the path, stopping every now and again for Shunaya to catch up with his urgent paces. They came over the lip of the ridge to see a wide sweep of boggy land ahead of them.

The rains of recent weeks had brought the water to the surface, and little pools gleamed like silver between the reeds and tufty grasses. The path followed a narrow dry ridge between scrub and soggy ground before rising up again the other side into a smaller crest. They carried on along the path.

At the top of another steep section of path, just as the man had said, they could see a string of small houses around the crest of the next ridge. Neat terraces of cultivated ground and olive trees replaced the native woodland there. He stopped, looking at the place, then sat down on a nearby rock. Shunaya sat beside him. He was silent for a long time. Eventually she leaned in against him.

"Makty, my heart, it will not get any closer while we sit here."

He shook his head.

"Very true. But do I want it to get closer? Every other time we have thought that we were getting closer, our goal just moved further away again. What if we get into this Kephrath and find that the same thing has happened. The woman has been sold on again. Or this is not the right place and she never got here. Or this is the wrong woman from the start and the whole journey from Per Bastet has been fruitless. Those wretched words that Senenptah spoke to me through you will go on haunting me."

"Then we will carry on seeking elsewhere. You know yourself that eventually in your games of Senet all the pieces come home. Even if there are turns and unexpected setbacks along the way. But now that we have come so close, we should find out for sure."

He sat, irresolute.

"Perhaps it is better not to know. I have lived up until now without knowing one way or another. Will it make so much difference? You and I could go anywhere we wanted in the Beloved Land. What if Senenptah was simply wrong, and I do not have to face a lifetime of moving in circles. And all the other things he said. Ashes and dung and such like."

"But what if he is right, and this will simply grow ever larger in your heart, waking and sleeping? What will that mean for you and I, if you leave this thing unfinished? I do not think that I could bear that easily. It would not be good for us. We are so close now. Let us at least try this one place, and see what news awaits us. How could you ever go back to the lord priest and say that you had come within sight of the chance of an answer, and you turned back again without even asking?"

He grunted.

"Well, perhaps I have no intention of ever going back to him."

She stood up again, looked down at him where he sat still. She was in front of him. He sighed, put his head down in his hands for a long moment, then stood up beside her.

"All right. We will go. But I don't know if this place holds more of anticipation or fear for me. Which is better? That we are sent back again by the house of Waters to retrace our steps, or that this is truly the home place? At very least, let us follow the track around and go in through whatever passes for a town gate in this place, rather than scramble up between those terraces and poke about between their houses."

He shook his head, looked back down the hill again, although the village they had passed was hidden by the curve of the land.

"This is all so different from what I expected. These places, they are all so meagre. That last place now, half of it was in ruins, and the good half was tiny and poor. Pitiful, really. A few dozen people there. What will this place Kephrath be like?

I don't know which is worse, to find out that this woman is not here, or to find out that she is here but lives in some wretched hovel that a farm hand would turn down in the fields outside Waset."

He shook his head again, looked for a long moment back down the track that led to Ayaluna, Gedjet, the Beloved Land, the River, and finally Waset, then with an air of resignation set off walking uphill again. She caught up with him and took his hand.

"It is strange to you, I know. But my people live in settlements not so very different from this. Here in this land they have trees in profusion, where we have only the clean mountains, but perhaps the living is not so different. If ever you come to see the place where I was born, then you must be prepared to see little villages and communities like this. Not all of us live in the great towns that you know beside the river."

The track curved to their right around the base of a steep slope, crowned by olive trees whose silvery leaves caught the lowering sun. Somewhere off to their left they could hear the noise of children playing. They followed the path as it swung to and fro up the last climb.

Suddenly they were at the top. A short distance ahead of them, the way they had been following joined another path, running left and right along the ridge. To their left, mostly hidden now by a low swell of the hillside, was Kephrath. Just at the junction of the two ways a man was sitting on a rock, watching them, waiting for them.

As they came up towards him, he stood up. He was about twice Makty's age, and was wearing one of the headscarfs that the Kinahny seemed to favour, both the men and the women. They had started to see these in Gedjet, and then with increasing frequency as they climbed into the hill country. This man's scarf had a more elaborate pattern sewn into it than most they had seen, but Makty did not know how to interpret the design.

Looking at the two of them, he bowed slightly and greeted

them in their own language. Makty was surprised, and the look must have shown on his face. The older man grinned.

"I have had opportunity to practice the Mitsriy tongue over many years now. Your arrival seemed a good chance to use it again, since you, sir, have clearly come from there. But perhaps you, lady, are not from the Beloved Land?"

He looked keenly at Shunaya. Makty tried to collect his thoughts.

"Sir, yes, you are right." Shunaya paused, and then, seeing that Makty was still at something of a loss how to respond, continued. "This is Makty-Rasut, who has lived all his life at different places up and down the river. I am Milashuniyet, who is called Shunaya. I have lived in Makty's Beloved Land for some years now but am not native-born there."

He nodded, repeated "Milashuniyet" to himself a couple of times, frowned in concentration briefly, and then spoke out one of the morning greetings in her tongue. It was the wrong time of day, and the words were not well pronounced, but the attempt was enough to relax her body and reassure her heart. She gave the correct response, then added in Makty's language, which the man had called Mitsriy, "For your kindness I give thanks, sir, but Makty here speaks none of my language."

The other laughed. "And I speak little enough of it, as you have heard, and none of it well, I think." He looked at Makty again to check that he had gathered himself together again. He pointed along the track. "Now, Kephrath is that way along the path; you can see some of the houses already. Jarrar's town, which we also call Woodlands, is the other way, and beyond that is Shalem, an altogether better-known place that perhaps you are seeking?"

Makty drew a deep breath.

"Sir, in fact it is Kephrath we have been looking for."

The man looked a little surprised, but gestured towards the houses.

"Well, I am going there myself now. Let me take you there and make you welcome with some hospitality."

They began to walk together along the track.

"Do you live there, sir?"

"All my life. But has the fame of Kephrath grown so much that travellers seek us out from the Beloved Land?"

Shunaya glanced at Makty, but his gaze was fixed on the gradually expanding view of the village.

"Well, sir, we heard of Kephrath down in Gedjet, and we were directed there by the ladies of the house of Hekhet in Per Bastet. That was where Makty was a child, and we returned to them for guidance. But we began our journey together three months ago in Waset, where I was working in the house of the lord priest Senenptah."

The older man stopped and looked at her oddly. She caught her breath, wondering suddenly what the name meant to him, wondering what the strange look that crossed his features had meant. Makty, even more acutely sensitive to the atmosphere of the moment, closed his eyes and clenched his hands together.

"Sir, we were told to look for a man called Damariel here. Do you know him? Can you direct us to his house? Introduce us even?"

"Well, yes I can. Yes to all of those questions, in fact. I am Damariel son of Yeresheth, seer and priest of Kephrath and, for the time being at least, the most senior of the seers of the four towns. Kephrath and her three sister towns, that is. You will be most welcome in my house when we reach it."

He pointed ahead. The track curved around a bluff of rock. The ridge here extended in a tongue of land out westwards, and they could see houses in a loose row above terraces of crops and fruit trees. There were other roofs visible behind the first row, and they could not see how extensive the town was. From memory of seeing it from below, however, it could not be very large. There seemed to be splashes of colour outside many of the houses, but it was not possible at this distance to make them out clearly. Damariel looked at Makty.

"Should we sit and rest for a while before we go on? Perhaps you are finding this difficult?"

Makty looked about at the terrain, the little town ahead of him, the slope on his left dropping down towards the track he had climbed with Shunaya, and finally back at Damariel.

"No, sir, no, although the thought is kind. At this stage I would prefer to complete the journey we have made."

They walked closer, and it became clear that the coloured splashes outside each house were in fact flowering plants, established by design outside each of the little doors. Like the headscarfs, the purpose of the plants was obscure, as though they too were written in the script that he could not read properly.

They branched off the main ridgeway path onto a smaller track that curved around the rocky outcrop and ended at the town gate. Beyond that there stood a rough circle of standing stones. Makty presumed that this would be the religious focus of the community, though to his eyes it seemed unfinished because of the lack of smoothed columns and the absence of decorations.

A larger house stood off to one side, with an extensive vine draped around most of the lower storey. Two boys were coming out of the village towards them, driving some goats. Makty stopped again, a short distance outside the gate. The priest Damariel was watching him, had been watching all of his reactions as they had walked along the path, had been watching the way he carried his body and moved his limbs.

"The large house you see there by the high place is where I live with my wife. Your way has been long, all the way up to Kephrath. Do you need time to think before we go in among the houses?"

Makty shook his head, but was still unmoving.

"Then perhaps you can satisfy my curiosity as to how the name Damariel has become known down in Waset? And what Senenptah has to do with all this? He must be a very old man by now. And he still lives in Waset? Did he send you here? To Kephrath?"

Makty shook his head and walked on a few paces before turning suddenly to Damariel.

"Look, sir, do you know that the lord Senenptah has a special interest in dreams?" He waited while Damariel shook his head. "Well, he does. And as I was working on his eternal house he helped me to understand some dreams that came to me. All my life I have moved further on up river, against the current. He wanted me to turn back downstream again, to go all the way back to my origins. Shunaya has been my companion all the way, and has comforted and persuaded my heart when it faltered."

Damariel nodded.

"Back to your origins, you say. And yet you did not stop at Pcr Bastet, although Milashuniyet says you grew up among the ladies there. Instead, you came up here to this particular place. That must have not been easy."

Makty shrugged.

"I had become quite motivated by then."

The boys with the goats were nearby, and the older man bent down to one of them and said something quietly to him. The boy nodded, turned, and ran off down among the houses. Damariel led them through between the standing stones of the high place, towards the house, pointing off to one side.

"The first Mitsriy man I ever met talked to me as we sat together on that stone over there. He had come to count the tally of goods in our village. He gave me a flake of pottery with some writing, before ever I knew what my life's work was to be."

Makty glanced at the stone and then stopped, taking a deep breath.

"Sir, I must ask you. Did you once buy a woman slave from the lord Senenptah when he lived in Gedjet? A woman who had come from the Beloved Land even as I have done? Did you bring her up here after you had bought her? Where is she now? Is she alive or dead? Have you sold her on again?"

A look of understanding crossed Damariel's face, opening

his face like the light of dawn as it chases away the shadows of night. He reached out, placed a hand on Makty's shoulder.

"I think after all that we should go in now. Come in and be welcome in this house."

A young man of about the same age as Makty was inside, working away on a writing frame. He stood as the three of them came in through the door, trying not to look surprised at the presence of the two strangers.

"Yissi, I wonder if you could do me a great favour? Could you and Hephzibah give us a little time to ourselves for a while? Until the evening, perhaps? Tomorrow morning would be better still, if you can prevail on someone to let you rest in their house overnight."

The man nodded.

"Of course. Hephzi is down at Ayala's house just now. I will go down and tell her, and we will go on from there to stay with my mother for the night."

He left. Makty had turned away from the exchange and occupied himself looking at some musical instruments on a nearby table. After Yissi had left he came back, noting with professional interest that the wooden tablet that the young man had been crafting was of very reasonable quality, though he was using the Kinahny letter shapes and not proper signs or writing.

"Sir, I must ask you again about the slave woman."

"Be patient with me a little longer, if you please. I think my wife will want to be here to meet you and speak with you. She will only be a few moments. In the meantime, sit there and I will find something for us to eat and drink together."

Makty turned away again and began prowling around the room, restless. Shunaya sat at the little table.

"Was that your son, my lord priest?"

"My son? Oh no. But then, I suppose yes, if you mean in a spiritual sense. He and his wife are apprenticed to learn from my wife and I. We have a duty to raise up apprentices for the ministry, and it is often easier to think of them as sons and daughters. But we do have a son, a true son from our two bodies, I mean, Ankhy-hotep, who has married and now lives in his wife's mother's house."

"You chose a name for him from the Beloved Land, lord priest?"

"Yes." He smiled a little. "We chose a Mitsriy name, and perhaps the reasons will become clear shortly. But please, this is not Senenptah's house, and I would prefer you call me by my given name rather than by a grand title. My whole village is scarcely bigger than the household I expect that Senenptah lives in. And I dare say that by now the full count of all the people he serves as priest is many times greater than everybody in our four towns all put together."

Damariel sat with her at the table, watching Makty as he paced restlessly around the room. He stopped at the door into the next room, his attention clearly caught by a wooden rectangle hanging from a hook on the wall just inside it. The wood had been written on, mostly using the Kinahny letters but with some proper signs on it as well. He looked back at Damariel with a question on his face. Damariel nodded.

"By all means yes, take it down from the wall and bring it over here."

Makty carefully unhooked it and placed it on the table between them, sitting beside Shunaya as he did so. She looked at the writing, trying to puzzle out what was on it. There were two words written separately at the top, one each in letters and signs.

"Is that one of the goddess names?"

Makty looked at Damariel, but he was content to stay silent and see what would happen.

"Yes, it is the name of the Lady Tefnut. But I do not know this other writing well enough to read it properly."

Damariel nodded, glanced up at the door as though uncertain whether to continue, but then replied.

"That is the name of our Lady Taliy. She is very like your Tefnut, enough alike that we made a vow to both of them together."

He pointed to the bottom, where again two names were written side by side, one each in letters and signs.

"That is my name, Damariel son of Yeresheth. And that, as I am sure you can read, is the name Nepheret er-sefet Tefnut. We will talk of all this in a few moments. But now, if you will suffer me just a short while longer, tell me of Senenptah. He must be truly ancient by now. It is a surprise to hear that he still lives."

Makty, who had been staring at the writing on the wooden board, took a deep breath and tried to quash a sense of unreality. Were they really talking about his former employer, and the way in which he had instigated the journey from Waset to Kephrath?

"I have just completed work on his eternal house. Yes, he is very old. I do not know the exact number, but inside the tomb I wrote that it has been one hundred and ten years since he made entrance into this world. He still serves as senior priest in the temple at Waset, though he has others around him who now share that burden with him. Do you know him, sir?"

"We met only once. But the meeting was memorable, and what I brought away from it has shaped the rest of my life. I do not know if he would remember our encounter with the same intensity that I do. Perhaps for him it would have been less important. His daughter travelled north to marry on the same day that I left, and I suspect he will remember her departure much more than mine."

Makty shrugged.

"Perhaps not. I think that he has become estranged from his daughter now. He speaks of her rarely, and with a great deal of regret when he does so. He was looking for a man to adopt as son who would perform the rites and rituals for him after he had crossed into the light-land. I think he might have been considering me at one stage, but here we are on this journey now."

His voice had roughened. Shunaya placed her hand on his

arm, pushed the beaker of mint tea into his reach. Damariel smiled with memory.

"He once tried to get me to call him father as well. But I think that it was done as a way to tease a young man who he found entertaining, rather than as any kind of true gesture. I am sorry to hear that Duat is lost to him, though. They seemed very close, at the time."

Makty suddenly laughed and lifted his beaker as though to recognise a distant relationship that he might have shared.

"So you and I have both thought that we might be his son, in one way or another. The world is small, after all."

"Indeed it is. Very small. I think we are about to find that out all over again."

There was the sound of voices outside. Then the door opened and a woman of about Damariel's age came in. She was dressed in the Kinahny fashion, headscarf and all, but was quite clearly from the Beloved Land. Damariel was rising to his feet.

"This is Nepheret er-sefet Tefnut, whose name you read on that board there. She is my wife, and has been since very soon after she came up out of Gedjet with me from the priest Senenptah's house. Nepheret, this is Makty-Rasut, who has lived at many places up and down the river, who started a journey in Waset at the place where Senenptah now lives, and who has come to us from the ladies at the house of Hekhet at Per Bastet. Which is where he first remembers being a child. And with him is Milashuniyet called Shunaya, who is his companion. They have come all this very long way in search of a Mitsriy woman who was once a slave in Senenptah's house."

Nepheret had crossed part way towards them as he was speaking, when abruptly she stopped as his words caught at her. Her eyes opened wide and her hands went up to her mouth, trembling a little. A little gasp came out of her as she stared at Makty, taking in his age and appearance. Makty rose to his feet and took a step towards her.

"Lady Nepheret, if you truly were in the house of Senenptah, I would very much like to talk to you. About, well, about..."

He trailed off, as unable to speak as she was. She shivered.

"I must sit down, I think. Do you mind?"

Without waiting for an answer she sat on the bench beside Damariel, gripping his hand fiercely with her own, staring all the while at Makty with a mixture of fascination and anxiety. Suddenly she laughed, a slight, brittle sound in the room.

"So you are a scribe after all? That's good. That's very good."

He nodded, felt for the chair by Shunaya and sat in it without in any way altering the fixity of his gaze on Nepheret. The two stared at each other silently for a long time, trying to absorb the reality of the other. Eventually she sighed, and little tears ran down her face. She took her headscarf off and dried her eyes with it absently. Her hair, loosed from under the material, curved away from her face in the same way that his did. She twisted the fabric this way and that in her hands, then put the scarf on the table and took a deep breath.

"All these years of wearing the kef, and I still take it off when something sudden happens to overwhelm my thoughts." She looked very briefly away from Makty at Damariel, and her eyes flashed a little. "You could have given me more word of this."

He shook his head. "When I sent Eli to fetch you from Sosanneth's house, I had little more than a guess. Only sitting here did the guess become more certain, and by then you were on your way. What could I do?"

She sighed again, then reached out very tentatively towards Makty's hand where it rested on the table between them. She stopped short of touching him, waiting for a response. He was still silent.

"You know, all that time in Senenptah's house at Gedjet I would day-dream that my son who had been taken from me would become a scribe. Not a labourer, or a soldier, or anything of that kind. That he would suddenly come to the house one day and buy my freedom so that I could live in a great house near the River and have slaves of my own to care for me. Then Damariel came and brought me here, where I have no servants but have been made more glad in my heart than I thought possible."

She looked at the wooden board where it still rested on the table, touched it. "Though I mistrusted his motives at first and had to be reassured."

Damariel laughed a little. Makty, casting about for something to say, skirting the main issues, pushed at the board from the other side.

"What does it say?"

The village priest smiled and recited the words from memory, looking all the while at Nepheret.

"Listen, all you gods of the nations,
    in the divine assembly take note:
record the words of Damariel,
    the oath of the son of Yeresheth.
Taliy, I call to you to hear me,
    Tefnut, I kiss the ground at your feet.
Nepheret's freedom was bought for her pleasure,
    and for her own delight has she been released.

May I find blessing when I look out for her well-being, body and soul, and may I find a curse if I do anything to her, soul or body, against her will and invitation."

The room was silent for a little while. Makty nodded, moved his hand a little towards Nepheret but still made no contact.

"Tell me, why would a mother leave her son? What does the scribe say? That the mother has no abomination for the infant who she has suckled for three years?"

Nepheret wept a little again, dried her eyes again with the edge of her kef.

"But that was just it. You had already been at my breast for three years and you were weaned. The housekeeper for my master at the time knew this. The buyer for Senenptah guessed it. Neither of them wanted the extra mouth to feed. So I was sent away north and east into the sedge lands, and then straight away out to Gedjet and other places. My son was taken away. You were taken away. I was told nothing of what would happen to you. I was given no choice in the matter. All I could do was think of you every day and pray that you would find a vocation. I was not free to travel up and down the river. And when I did, finally, find freedom, where would I have looked for you? And, look, truly you have found something after all."

He nodded, very slowly, and looked at Shunaya, who had been silent all this time as though waiting for her heart to beat again. Hesitantly he stretched out his hand a little further, reached out to Nepheret's hand where it rested on the table, and let her touch his fingers, then take his whole hand in her own. She sighed, a long exhalation of breath that seemed to fill the room.

"My heart is so happy that they let you keep the name I chose. One of my fears was that they would give you a new name, and that even the little I had been able to give you would be taken away." She stopped, then added, all in a rush of extra words, "Are you happy to see me?"

He turned his hand over in her palm where she was touching the work calluses on his fingers.

"I don't know yet. This is all too sudden. This is not what I expected. None of it is. Ask me tomorrow, maybe."

Her expression crumpled a little. She swallowed, nervously, and looked at Damariel. He nodded.

"You must take time over this. Stay here in this house while you think about it. Stay as long as you want. The house is amply big enough for that." He paused, then continued with a little smile. "Though not, I think, as big as the houses that you know down in the Beloved Land."

〜〜〜◊ ﷽ ◊ ﷽ ◊ ﷽ ◊〜〜〜

Morning came. Makty and Shunaya had slept in a large upstairs room which seemed to be part of the roof. Makty had wanted to sleep early, pleading exhaustion. He had clung at first to Shunaya in the bed as though she was the only source of comfort in a turbulent world. She had willingly cradled him against her body, but he had fallen asleep almost at once, worn out by the experiences of the day.

Shunaya had lain awake beside him for a long time, listening to the hill country wind sighing around the walls and roof of the building, listening to the murmur of the priest and his wife talking quietly downstairs for some while before the house fell silent. She felt at peace here, and the stones of the village high place beside the house were similar enough to the holy places of her childhood to quieten her soul. Was there any real difference between life springing up here in this place, and life lived down alongside the river that flowed through the Beloved Land?

In the morning they woke together as the outside door of the house closed. A woman's song was drifting quietly up to them. Going down they found Nepheret on her own, sitting in a low stool by the fire, heating porridge. She looked up at them, apparently content but holding most of her emotions in check. She was as bare-headed as Shunaya this morning, and her headscarf was dangling from a peg in the wall.

"Damariel is outside there among the stones, performing the morning rites." She paused briefly, eyes scanning both of them with a thorough appraisal. She looked quizzically for a longer moment at Shunaya, and then spoke again.

"Makty-Rasut, I think Damari would appreciate it if you would join him. Milashuniyet can help me finish in here while you do that."

"He would not be offended?"

"Not at all. There is nothing about this observance which would be improper if you were to join him, and he would be glad of the company."

Makty went to the door, half-opened it, then looked back at Shunaya. She nodded. He continued out, saw the priest off to one side of the circle just rising from a prayer. Makty started to walk towards Damariel, but then, wondering if the central area was held sacred, carefully walked around the outside of the ring of stones to join him. The priest gripped his hand in greeting.

"One more prayer at each of the last two stones, then I am all done for the morning. Sit there a moment and I will join you."

Makty looked at the low flat stone he indicated. The action seemed slightly irreverent.

"Here?"

"Just here is fine."

Makty sat, slightly awkwardly, and waited while Damariel knelt beside each of the last two places of prayer. Then the priest came over and sat beside him.

"Morning blessings to you, Makty-Rasut."

"And to you and yours, sir." He paused, unsure of his ground. "What are your intentions for the day?"

"We have none. I went down early to see Yissi and Heph-zibah, to make sure that they were prepared to do by them-selves the things that we had planned yesterday. So, now that the morning prayers are done, Nepheret and I are entirely at your disposal. Whatever you want to talk about, whatever you would like to ask, anything is yours. We can even take you on the grand tour through all of Kephrath if you so wish."

Makty looked around at the stones, the nearby town gate, and the scattered houses nearby, then back at Damariel.

"I think I should like that. After coming all this way, I should not want to miss anything."

"It will not take long. I dare say that Senenptah's house is larger than our whole town."

Makty looked around again.

"Perhaps it is. But then, I never did succeed in finding my way through that without one of his servants. I think I could find your house again from anywhere in Kephrath."

Damariel laughed.

"Come up on that ridge with me for a short time. You can

see most of the village from there."

He led Makty diagonally across the ring of stones, then up a short steep scramble to the top of the rocky bluff that over-looked the high place. Seeing several large stones and some scattered offerings pushed up against the rock face, Makty guessed that the dead were laid to rest in caves here. Before turning to face the village, Damariel pointed east and a little south, where Makty could see a small track curving away in the morning sunshine.

"Our three sister towns are that way, only a short distance. And there," he gestured more generally south, "a little further away is Shalem, where I thought you might have been head-ing. The main ridgeway track is a little to the east of here. You will know the names of places along that from your training."

Makty nodded. "You mean Yanum, Darbon, Aphqar and so on. But I do not remember the name of Kephrath in among them."

"Indeed not. I think we have been left out of all of those lists. Perhaps our little town has not been here long enough."

They turned to face the village. Damariel said nothing about it, giving Makty the chance to absorb the scene. The whole area was, at a guess, actually a little larger than Senen-ptah's estate, but laid out completely differently. Around the edges little terraces with crops and fruit trees clung to the fringe of the housed area. The buildings themselves were clumped together, with tracks of varying sizes between, each with some kind of growing plant outside the door. Scattered here and there were shared resources such as cisterns or stor-age sheds.

"We will take the two of you around the town later. Just now it is time to break our fast."

⁓⌂☷⌂☷⌂☷⌂⁓

Inside, Shunaya had poured water to start heating in a pan. Nepheret pointed to a large bunch of mint leaves hanging below a shelf. Shunaya stood again with a little sigh, feeling abruptly faint at the move. Nepheret stood beside her, took her hand, cupped her cheek in a gesture of intimacy Shunaya had not expected.

"Will you have your baby here in Kephrath, or back in the Beloved Land?"

Shunaya caught her breath and looked at the door. The older woman nodded slowly.

"So Makty-Rasut does not know?"

"Not yet. I have not told him, nor has he guessed, I think. I can keep it from him for a little longer. He does not really know what to look for in a woman's changes."

Nepheret pulled the two pans away from the heat, keeping contact with Shunaya with her spare hand. They sat down, side by side on the bench by the table.

"Why not tell him?"

Shunaya was silent for a while, looking at the table. Eventually she looked up into Nepheret's face.

"Our life together so far has been simply one of undertaking his search. Down the river, across the lowlands, then up into your hill country. To find the end of the journey. To find you, I suppose. It has all been about his journey. I did not want to burden him with this as well."

Nepheret looked back at her, steadily, patiently.

"I think there is more. After all, this shared life you now carry is also part of his journey. It is hardly as though you fashioned it on your own."

Shunaya closed her eyes, which had welled up with an unexpected surge of emotion. Nepheret surrounded her with her arms, cradled her head on her shoulder, kissed the hair on the crown of her head.

"Ah, Milashuniyet, how far away your family must live."

"Just now, lady, you are all the family I have. All that either of us have." She fell silent again, feeling the breath ease in and out of her body. She felt Nepheret prepare to say something, and carried on before that could happen. "What was it like for you in the lord priest's house?"

She did not look up at the older woman, but felt her stir her head a little restlessly.

"I suppose that is an experience we have shared. Some years apart, though."

The sounds of village life drifted through the open window as she continued.

"The lord priest was very remote. I thought at the time that he was cruel, but looking back I think he was just lonely. There was some small pleasure for us slaves in the way that we shared in one other's lives, our small satisfactions and times of distress. But it was a narrow life. I was glad to leave it and come here. Even if Damariel had wanted me only for a few nights' journey, and not for life, I would have been glad to leave. What was there to go back for? As if I had the choice anyway."

After a short pause Shunaya spoke again. "It was different for me. He has become more kind, perhaps, in his old age. But we two, Makty and I, we have had so little time together. Barely a single season if we were still back there in Waset. But I am sure that this happened the first time we lay together. How else could I be this far along? In truth, I knew at the time what might happen."

"Some great things take hardly any time to accomplish."

Shunaya looked at her, then smiled and rubbed the curve of her body below her ribs. She could feel that she was already different there, and it surely would not be many weeks until Makty's exploring hands and eyes would notice too. She sighed.

"Lady, there is more. Makty has made a life for himself that means he can move on from a place whenever he wants. He has gone from one town to another every few years. He has no real home in Waset, and has arranged his life so that he has no debts to pay. He has never, so far as I know, stayed with the same woman even half the time he has spent with me. I have no idea what he will do when he knows."

Nepheret nodded. "Would you like me to talk with him?" She sounded suddenly fierce, like a lioness preparing to sprint for her prey.

Shunaya turned her head to look directly at her. "How would you talk to him, lady? As a friend? As a priest? As his mother? How will he hear any of those?"

They both looked at the door. Outside, Damariel was laughing at something Makty had said.

"If you know, does your husband know too?"

"Not yet. Not unless he has had some word of insight as he has performed the morning rites. That has happened before. But I only knew when I saw you standing there this morning."

Shunaya looked down at herself.

"We should finish making food before they come in." She made as if to stand up again, but then stopped. "If he does not want me like this, could I stay here? I would be ashamed to go back to the lord priest's house without him, and in any case I cannot make another journey like that now. Not even to Ta Mefkat. It would be too much for me. I have never farmed crops or herded flocks, but I can be a good house servant to someone, I think. Makty would easily find another place to live and work, anywhere he wanted, but I do not know where to go."

Nepheret held her tightly, fiercely, and then released her to stand up. "Up here we have no house servants. Only townspeople or captives of war. But there are other ways for you to live. What other skills do you have? Can you sew? Deliver babies? Mix herbs for medicine? Prepare amulets?"

"None of those things, lady." She paused, thinking. "But I can weave. I learned in Ta Mefkat, and then I used to help the weaving women in the lord priest's house."

"Good. Then you have a craft that we value, and you can live from that." She paused. "That is, if you choose to stay here in Kephrath. Will you do that, do you think? Or move on again?"

The men's voices could be heard outside, and the door began to swing open. Shunaya looked at Nepheret, shook her head, put a finger to her lips. Nepheret nodded and rattled the cooking pans.

"So I think that after we have eaten, and you are comfortable as guests, we should take you all around Kephrath and show you all that there is to see."

Much later that day, they returned to the house beside the circle of stones. They had remained in the house for much longer than they had expected that morning, while Makty and Shunaya had recounted all of the journey from Waset. In turn, they had heard about Damariel's journey down to Gedjet years ago, and how Nepheret had come up into the hill country in time for a great struggle against the former chief. The land sounded restless, constantly eager to push for change in its human occupants. Finally they had left the house and been taken all around the lanes and houses of the small village.

Now, Damariel held the door open under the prolific leaves of the vine which covered most of the front of the house. During the tour, Shunaya had soaked up the network of names and family relationships with apparent delight, while Makty had become increasingly confused. The people here identified themselves by means of interconnections between women, but he was used to thinking in terms of occupation.

For a while he had asked what the men in the households worked at, but most answers sounded the same to him. The men worked, it seemed, mostly at growing plants of various kinds, mainly food crops and trees, on little strips of land bordering the village. A number of them cared for small flocks and herds. From time to time he came across something more familiar – a potter here, or a wood-worker there – but for the most part there was a blur of sameness. He missed the diversity of individual jobs and skills that he was used to, and seriously doubted his ability to fit in to this place.

There were not many people in Kephrath with any kind of scribal talent, leaving aside the seer and his wife together with their apprentices. So far as he could remember only one other person had had any real training at all. A few others knew how to make the quick brush signs for the first few numbers, but no more. At one stage he day-dreamed about setting up a real school here. He would teach far more than the basics to every one of the children who ran about. Steadily, however, it dawned on him that the villagers had no need of it.

Even Damariel had none of the standard texts that he knew, and which were absolutely basic down in the Beloved Land. Of course papyrus would fade in no time in this climate, and he guessed that if left accidentally outside for even a single night in the rain it would split apart. The writings they did have – a few songs, some tales of their deities, and a handful of lists of various kinds – were either scratched on pieces of fired clay, or more often just pressed into wax coatings layered on wooden frames. He found it quite depressing.

They sat together in the large room, around the long trestle table. Some sort of herbal infusion together with flat barley cakes had appeared, seemingly out of nowhere. Shunaya was still talking excitedly with Nepheret, sorting out in her mind the intricacies of relationship among the houses of Kephrath. He watched both of them for a while, wondering how he could begin to think of the older woman as his mother. He suddenly realised that Damariel was talking to him. He mumbled something apologetic.

"I was just wondering what you think you might do next, Makty-Rasut? There is no need to hurry a decision, no need at all, but if we can help you in any way to choose then do not hesitate to ask." He paused to reflect. "There is a house where you can live for a while. I can help you speak with Tarpashai about that. Or you can remain here with us if that suits you better."

"I thank you for your kindness, sir. Just now I am not very sure about anything. Where to live, what to do, anything."

He hesitated, wondering whether the words he had in mind would sound discourteous, given his weak grasp of the Kinahny language. Damariel nodded, anticipated him.

"I fear that there must seem very little for you to do up here. It is hard to see how your talents could be used."

Makty nodded, with some relief that he had not had to say that himself.

"I thought that perhaps we should go back to the Beloved Land now that our quest is complete. Perhaps even all the way back to Waset and Senenptah."

The two women had stopped talking in order to hear what he said. They looked at each other.

"Makty, dear one, I am not going back to Waset just now. It is too great a journey for me."

"But we have made the journey once. And the return upstream will not take much longer at this time of year. The winds are favourable. What is different?"

Shunaya hesitated. Nepheret put her hand on her arm. In the pause Damariel spoke again.

"There is another choice: the town of Shalem. It is only a short journey along the ridgeway track, and you might find some work there. More like the kind you are used to, I think, though I cannot be sure. I can give you the names of some men who were scribes there a short time ago. Who knows if they still work at that now? But we can find out."

"I do not know, sir. Certainly you are right that there is no work for my hands here in Kephrath. But will there be anything at all anywhere in your hill country? Perhaps it is better just to go back to the Beloved Land." He searched around for a Kinahny word that fitted his mood, finally found it. "I feel very despondent."

Damariel leaned forward as though to say something, but Nepheret shook her head and he stopped. In the silence, a noise of goats passed by outside. Makty glanced around the room.

"I am sorry to cause trouble in this way. But what is there

for me to do here? I have never lived as someone who depends on the goodness of others without giving something in return. Perhaps it is best just to go back again. To the lowlands or the sedge lands at least, if not Waset." He looked at Shunaya. "Would you make just that little journey with me?"

She looked down at the table, picked up one of the flat cakes and put it down again, and finally shook her head.

"Why not? It is not far to go. Much less far than we have already gone. You are making this very difficult."

She was still silent. Nepheret squeezed her arm again. Makty shook his head, leaned back and looked at Damariel as though for support. Shunaya took a deep breath.

"Look, my love, I am pregnant. I am carrying our child. I will not make another journey of any length until I have seen this through."

He stared at her, astonished, speechless for a long time. Finally he broke her gaze and turned towards the window.

"But how can this be?"

He looked back again. The other three were watching, waiting. Damariel had a quizzical expression.

"No, I don't mean it like that. I mean, how long have you known? Why did you not tell me?"

"I have only just become sure. On the boat of the chief Mentep I missed my time, and wondered, but there were so many other changes that it did not seem strange. Then again just before we reached Gedjet. But by that time all that mattered was that we found our way up here. To the lady Nepheret, to Kephrath and all. I was not certain, and you were full of other thoughts. Also," and she paused for several heartbeats before hurrying on, "Also I did not know what you would say. I could not be sure. But now that we are here, at least I am certain of the changes in myself."

"You should have told me as soon as you first guessed. On the boat, even."

He stood up, paced around the room for a while, avoiding everybody's eyes.

"I just don't know about any of this. First there's nothing to do here. Now this news. I am a ship floundering at sea." He shook his head, still separating himself from the others. "Don't think I'm not grateful for all you have done while I have been here, but I do not know where to put myself now."

"You must take your time over this. Stay here in Kephrath, in this house or another, for as long as you need. After all these years, to know that you live in health and prosperity, to see you again is so good for my heart. There is no need to rush over your choice."

He turned to face Nepheret, a stubborn cast to his body. He started to speak twice and gave up each time, then turned away again.

"I think I should go back to Gedjet before I decide where to settle. I will redeem all my letters of promise and collect what I have from the holy house there. The trip will do me good."

"My heart, I cannot make the journey down to the sea coast and up here again just now."

"No, I do not think you should. I will go on my own."

Milashuniyet swallowed and looked anxious. He rushed on.

"It is an easy journey, is it not? I follow the track down past the half-built village to Ayaluna, and then join the Sea Road along to Gedjet. I will find my way without difficulty."

"I can ask somebody to guide you if you wish?"

"That will not be necessary. Your people are all busy. And I am right about the directions, I think?"

Damariel nodded. "Absolutely right. So long as you stay with the road the journey is easy. Some of us would take a direct route across, but you need to know the land well to do that."

"Then it is settled. I will go down to Gedjet for a time. Shunaya, you stay here and accept the hospitality of the town while I am away. Let us not talk of it any more." He sat again, with a forced enthusiasm on his features. "So I noticed in your village that some of the people use the quick brush signs for numbers. Can you not use the Kinahny letters for this? Are there not signs for numbers?"

Damariel and Nepheret looked at each other. She shrugged slightly. After a pause, Damariel answered, and the conversation turned to little things. Milashuniyet sat through it all, silent, brooding, with Nepheret's hand still resting lightly on her arm.

That night, when Makty and Milashuniyet settled for bed, she put her arms around him, but he turned away and faced in the other direction to fall asleep. She herself lay awake for a long time, her hand on her belly, listening to his steady breathing, her eyes wet with tears that she would not shed in case he woke up again.

In the morning he arose first, dressed and went into the kitchen area while she was still hardly awake. By the time she joined him he was already dressed and shod for travel. Nepheret had packed some food in a travelling bag. Damariel came in from his daily circuit of prayer at the stones of the high place. Makty looked around at the others.

"I will not be gone very long. I shall make my way there and back again with no difficulty."

He started towards the door, then as an afterthought came back and gave Milashuniyet a perfunctory kiss. The door opened and closed, and he was gone.

Milashuniyet stood staring at the door for a long time after he was gone. Nepheret sat her at one of the benches by the table.

"This is not at all what I dreamed of while we were on the road past Gedjet and up to here. I thought that we would walk along for a while and find Makty's mother somewhere. Then I could tell him about this and we would be happy together."

Nepheret took her hand. Damariel sat opposite and spoke very gently.

"Look now, these things do not always happen as we would wish. Here in Kephrath, babies are sometimes conceived by surprise to a woman, especially at a festival. But the news does not always draw a couple to one another. It might do the opposite. We must take thought of your own future with this child."

Milashuniyet sat listening silently, her head down, lost in thought. After a pause, Damariel continued.

"You would be very welcome to live here with us while he is gone, if you like?"

Milashuniyet looked up at him and shook her head.

"Thank you for the offer, sir, but I do not think it suitable that I live here with you. I lived in the lord priest's house in Waset, to be sure, but there I had a family obligation to fulfil, and a task to perform for him. And I was one among many others. Here, you have your own duties as priests to perform, and my presence in your house would hinder that. How would your own people in need come to speak with you? And where would your own apprentices stay? This house has been a good place to come to, but it is not right that I stay here. It is not right to carry on for more than a day or so like this."

"Then we will find somewhere else." He paused, and Nepheret spoke before he could continue further.

"I will not see Milashuniyet turned out as though she were homeless."

"Of course not, Nepheret. I went down to see Sannah before the time of prayer. She said that she is willing for Milashuniyet to live there. That might be a better plan. Of course, at the time I thought Makty-Rasut was going to be there as well." He took Milashuniyet's other hand. "Nepheret said that you could weave? My sister Sosanneth is the weaver here in Kephrath. She will give you a home and, when you are ready, you can work with her. When Makty-Rasut comes back we can think again."

Milashuniyet finally let herself weep and leaned on Nepheret as though she were herself a child. "I do not think he will come back here. I have a great fear that he will just stay there in Gedjet. Perhaps even go back to his Beloved Land without ever sending word to me."

Nobody spoke. After a while, Milashuniyet sat straight

again, dried her face with her sleeve, and took on a determined look. "Well, I have another life to carry now. Yes, I would be grateful and honoured to stay with your sister, sir. If I am to be alone in this then I must learn to live as one of you. I am sure your sister will be kind to me and teach me how to be one of your people. Can we go to her house now?"

She stood up and looked around the room as though fixing it in her mind, then looked enquiringly at the others. They went over to the door, opened it, and all left together.

They walked past the large cistern just below the high place and its stones, then followed some of the winding tracks between the houses. Damariel led them to the southern edge of the ridge, to a house where a mimosa bush spread leaves and bright flowers beside the door. An elderly woman opened the door when she heard their voices outside. Milashuniyet stopped and bobbed her head to her.

"Lady, I think you are the lord priest's mother? It is my honour to meet you again."

The woman peered at her. "You'll be here to see my Sannah, I expect, dear. Or Sophireth. One of them, I dare say. But Sophireth is not here just now, she's on auntie duty down at the stream with the little children. You're that new Mitsriy girl, aren't you? You could be Nepheret's daughter. Well, come in, silly to stand out here in the wind."

She looked past Milashuniyet to see Damariel and Nepheret standing there, and her old face crinkled in a smile. "Damari, you have come down to see me again, so soon. Are you coming in as well?"

"Not today, mother. We have just come today with Milashuniyet here. And she is not Mitsriy, she comes from the mountains in the wilderness far south of here, where the Mitsriy dig turquoise."

"Are you sure about that?" She looked uncertainly at Milashuniyet. "What do they call you?"

Sosanneth appeared at her mother's side. "Come along now, mother, let our guest come in. She will be living with us for a while. We can worry about where she comes from later on tonight, when we have made her comfortable."

She looked left and right. "I thought there were two of you?"

Milashuniyet looked down, unsure how to answer. Damariel shook his head. There was a little silence.

"Well, anyway, you'll be staying in the little room upstairs. Mother and I swept it out earlier. Damari, are you sure you won't come in for a while?"

Damariel shook his head. "Not just now, Sannah. Tomorrow, perhaps, when Milashuniyet here has had time to settle in to the house." He leaned in and kissed his mother on both cheeks. "We will come back tomorrow, mother, both of us together."

He turned away with Nepheret, and they were gone around a corner of the alleyway. The old lady watched them go with regret.

"He's very busy, you know. Doesn't ever stay long." She caught the edge of Sosanneth's expression. "My daughter, she thinks I am too slow about things. Come in now, come and meet my Tobiaz. That's him by the table there. What do they call you now?"

Sosanneth patted her on the arm. "Mother, why don't you and Tobiaz sort out some mint tea and raisins for our new guest. I will take her upstairs and settle her here, then we will come down again and be with you."

She took Milashuniyet up a narrow flight of stairs to a small room tucked off to one side. A window with an undrawn drape looked out southwards over the narrow terraces. There were two other small covered rooms beside this one. One side of the upper storey had been left open to the elements, to be cool in summer.

"It's only small, I'm afraid, but it will be quiet at night for you, and gives you a place of your own." Sosanneth looked briefly up and down Milashuniyet's body, an unconscious womanly glance. "I suppose the stairs won't be difficult for you yet?

They will get to be too steep. I remember staying downstairs all the time in the end. Couldn't manage them in my last month or so."

Milashuniyet shook her head.

"Good. Take your time, then come downstairs again when you're ready. My mother will have the tea all ready for you, but she won't remember your name or where you come from. I suppose from what Damari avoided saying, your man will not be with you for a while? Tell us whatever you want, whenever you want."

Sosanneth turned to go, but Milashuniyet stood up and took her hand.

"Thank you for this, lady."

Sosanneth laughed briefly and shrugged. "I'm getting another person in the house who can help out with the loom. I should thank you. Is there anything else you need?"

"There is just one more thing, lady. I should like to start wearing one of your people's headscarfs. Do you have a spare one at all? And could you show me how you tie it? I feel that I should learn to dress as you do in Kephrath now."

"A kef? Of course. I have several down below. I'll get mother to show you that when you come down. She'll be good at that. Just tell her you lost yours somewhere, it'll be easier for her to understand."

She closed the door, and Milashuniyet heard her footsteps going down the wooden stairs again. She looked around the room, put her little travelling bag on the bedroll that was curled up against one wall, then sat beside it after looking briefly out of the window. This room, and the weaving work with Sosanneth, would be her world for a time. She would dress herself with this world along with Sosanneth's kef, and learn to wait for the baby to arrive.

10. Past – Infancy

THE LADY OF the Scribes saw me in my mother's body and said, "Yours will be an excellent life, O scribe, for I have seen you and will watch over you through all your days."

Nepheret er-Sefet Tefnut listened to the sound of the other slaves getting dressed in the half-light around her. Her baby, Makty-Rasut, was starting to fidget, and she gathered him to her breast and let him feed before he fully woke up. One or two of the other women smiled at the noise of him suckling, touched mother or baby as they filed out to their day's labour. For a moment, his dark eyes opened wide and the two gazed at one another. Then they closed again while his little hands and mouth clung to her. Left alone in the room, the two wrapped themselves in each other and drifted back off into a warm slumber.

Some time later Nepheret woke again. The sun was much higher, and the opposite wall was bright with the light streaming in from the window above her. Makty had released her at some point, and was now lying on his back. She frowned. Although she knew the count of days perfectly well, she rehearsed them again. It had been nearly a month since his birth. Winter had passed into summer. It was her own last day before she too would be leaving the room with the others before the sun rose, leaving Makty on his own for periods of time. Almost a month had passed since her labour and his first breath, his first cries. It seemed all too quick.

The mistress, the chief wife of the honoured master himself, had come to see her that first day. At the time her body was still aching with the pain and effort of childbirth, and she was pale with loss of blood. The mistress had not stayed long, just long enough to ensure that both lived and thrived, and to offer the formal household prayers giving praise for safety and prayers for the future. Since then mother and infant had spent the time away from others, sequestered in the shared space which was full of a dozen other slaves at night, and empty in the day.

The door opened, and the housekeeper came in. She was an older woman reporting directly to the overseer who was responsible for the master's entire household. Nepheret scrambled hurriedly to her feet and pulled her crumpled shift into a semblance of order. Makty stirred but remained asleep. The housekeeper glanced at him and nodded.

"I see you both continue in good health."

"Yes, lady, by the grace of all the gods. And I give thanks both to you and to the honoured master for granting me the time to stay with him."

She nodded again and looked Nepheret up and down, appraising her appearance.

"You gave birth to him on the fifth day of the fourth month of winter. Tomorrow is the fifth day of the first month of summer. Is there any reason why you cannot resume your proper place in the household?"

Nepheret shook her head. "No, lady. I shall be ready at first light tomorrow. Is it right that I can come back to the room to see to his needs during the day?"

"It is, so long as you are not needed elsewhere by order of the mistress. That being so, for the next two months you may come back here four times in the day. After that we will consider again what is appropriate. Less often, though. You must make your own arrangements for his needs, so long as they do not conflict with the needs of the household."

Nepheret looked down to where Makty lay. Though not yet awake, he was becoming aware of her absence, reaching out to where she had been lying.

"Lady, if I might ask?" She waited for the other woman to nod assent. "I do know that it is a long time away yet. But if by the grace of the gods he continues to thrive, will you allow him to stay in the household when he is weaned? I am sure that he will be a benefit to the house."

"The master will decide when the time comes. If he is a quiet baby, he may look favourably on him. I cannot say. Every new mother asks me this, and only a handful see their wish granted. Work hard and well, and train him to be calm and quiet, and there is a better chance."

Nepheret swallowed, bobbed her head, then bowed more fully as the housekeeper left again. She had one last full day to spend with Makty before he would have to start learning to do without her.

_____ ⟨⟩ ▱▱▱ ⟨⟩ ▱▱▱ ⟨⟩ ▱▱▱ ⟨⟩ _____

Nepheret ran back to the long room she shared with the other slaves. She could hear Makty-Rasut crying, and one of the men trying to comfort him. The master's wife had kept her for a very long time cleaning the great room where the feast would be held tonight. Everyone had been too busy to help, and so she had simply had to leave Makty alone in the gloomy empty room with the door closed.

From the sounds he was making, it was clear that Makty had reached a high pitch of frustration, and the man was having little success with him. She burst in. One of the junior record-keepers was beside Makty, Samut-er-Tawi, who she saw only occasionally when their paths happened to cross.

Samut lived in quite a different part of the house. While not at all at the elevated level of the master's own family members, he was considerably above her in the household hierarchy. He shared a set of rooms with only two other scribes, and each even had their own chamber. It was tiny, of course, and she herself would not want to sleep in a room without companions alongside. Samut, however, saw it as a clear sign of his status, and quite often used to his advantage.

It was pure chance that he was anywhere near. On another occasion her son would have had to vent his anger alone. She took him into her arms, and he started to quieten at once. Samut sighed with relief.

"Ah, Nepheret, he's your child, then? Is that right? I am so glad you came. He was not interested in me at all."

She nodded, fussing over Makty. "There now, my little man, why all the noise? You know you need to be a quiet boy now. I always find you again, you know that." She looked up at Samut. "And many thanks for being here for him, sir."

He laughed, shrugged.

"I was passing along the hall and heard him. But there was little enough I could do. I think he wants food, and that is something I cannot give him."

She glanced down at the boy, gripping on to her.

"Nor I really, not like I used to in the summer. But, please sir, you mustn't say so to anyone. Certainly not the master."

"The lord Unen-Nefer? Why? What possible interest could he have in that?"

"If Makty is weaned, he can be separated from me according to the custom, taken away from me. So it is good if I can give him even just a little. But for real nourishment, Makty must wait for the mealtimes along with the rest of us. Just now all he can have is company, not food. But I have to leave him again in a few minutes. The mistress sent me on an errand, and this room was near enough that I could hear him. But I cannot stay with him."

He looked around, then out of the door, then moved back a little closer to her.

"Nor I. I must report to the overseer of the farm records shortly. But I could come along this way again in a while to see him again. I can make a reason to pass along this hall." He paused. "Can you not leave him something to do, so he does not just sit there and cry like that? He's old enough to be doing something useful with his time. It is a fearful waste."

She shook her head.

"I don't have anything to give him. If nobody is around to be with him, what can he do?"

"I might be able to get him some old colour dabs. They get worn, and then they're of no use to us. The chief scribe is very particular about quality. But they'd be fine for a lad that does not know how they should be. He'd make a mess of them, but better that than having nothing to do. Most of them just get thrown out anyway. And I could find a bit of limestone that's not good enough for real use."

"He'd hurt himself on stone, sir. He's not old enough."

"Some old rags then."

She looked up into his face. Makty, settled now, reached out a hand towards him.

"You would do that, sir? Is it allowed?"

He nodded, touched the boy's little fingers and then rubbed her shoulder.

"I would. And it is. But it might be difficult to say when. It depends what has been thought unfit for use. I could try. I'd be willing. It might possibly be quite soon, if you'd like. If you're willing."

There was an eagerness in his expression, a desire that mirrored the hunger Makty had voiced. She sighed to herself.

"Sir, look, I do not think the mistress requires me to attend the feast tonight. If she does not, I will come to you after we are given food. But if she does, then it must be some other night."

He nodded quickly, touched her hair, then hastened out of the room. She listened to his footsteps diminishing along the hallway, then kissed Makty.

"Ah, the things I do for you, Makty-Rasut. But now, see, I have to go and do what the mistress wants, not what you and I want at all. If not there will be all kinds of trouble."

She put him down again. He watched her, perplexed, as she moved away towards the door. As she moved into the hall, he wailed again, a despairing sound that tore at her soul. Out of his direct sight, she leaned back against the wall, her own hands clenched, tears running down her cheeks. He did not stop. She started to move away, counting heartbeats that the mistress might well count against her. He did not stop. The howls of abandonment kept coming from the room. She closed her eyes, unable to move, full of both his hurt and hers.

One of the kitchen slaves came towards her, an older woman, Nedjmit. She stopped beside Nepheret.

"I have to go, Nedjmit. I can't stay with him. The mistress will punish me if I don't get back to her soon. But it's like he's pulling me apart, one limb at a time. I don't know who is worse."

"I'll take him, Nepheret. There's always something I can do with a lad in the kitchens. Even one as little as he. There'll be something I can give him to do. He'll be useful. You go on so he doesn't see you now."

Nepheret took a deep breath, hugged Nedjmit, and set off again at a run down the hall. She had a lot of time to make up if the mistress was not to notice the delay.

⁓⁓ ◊ ▨▨ ◊ ▨▨ ◊ ▨▨ ◊ ⁓⁓

Nepheret walked with the other slaves who shared the same room towards the main courtyard. She had no idea why they had all been ordered outside: it was a most unusual interruption of their routine. She had left Makty with one of the pregnant women, whose condition had excused her from the general assembly. They walked in silence together, not caring to talk about the situation. The last time this had happened, it was to witness one of the men being beaten with wooden rods for impudence. He still walked with a limp, and one broken arm had never set correctly, but he said, loudly and often, that he considered himself lucky to be alive.

Once in the courtyard, she saw that some of the other slaves, from different rooms, had also been brought out and were standing in the sun. There were only women standing there, no men. The master was in the shade on the opposite side of the yard, with two of the scribes behind him. He had the air of a man whose duty requires him to complete a tiresome task as quickly as possible. To one side of him was the overseer of the household. Nepheret had often seen him at a distance but had never heard him speak.

On his other side stood a lady who Nepheret had never seen before. She wore her hair back, threaded through a copper ring, and had a serious expression. Her hair was already showing flecks of grey, though she could not be too many years older than Nepheret herself. She was clearly studying the women as they arrived, but gave no clue what she was looking for. As the last of the women filed in, the overseer turned to the master for permission and then stepped forward. His voice was quite high pitched, and carried easily in the still air.

"This lady is standing here with us today in the place of a most honoured lord priest, who has been pleased to accept the generous gift of two female workers granted by your honoured master. She is here to choose the two. From this day onwards the two who are chosen will pass into the household of the most honoured lord priest, and will be subject in every way to his wisdom and justice. This is the will of your honoured master."

In the silence that followed, the women exchanged little glances at one another. The priest's name had not been given, and if it had been they would have no idea how his household was organised. The change could be good or bad. Either way, it was unavoidable.

It was clear, however, from the way the overseer had spoken, that the unknown woman was a worker herself, and not a noble lady. She was here at the bidding of this priest, and was presumably some sort of housekeeper. She had a foreign look about her, and Nepheret guessed that she was not from the Beloved Land.

The woman moved forward and went up and down the rows of the household women, looking closely at each in turn, saying nothing. Nepheret felt her inspection as though it was a tangible weight moving across her shoulders. She avoided the stranger's gaze, keeping her eyes on the ground near her feet. This woman was clearly not going to be rushed by the presence of the master. Her own master's superior authority shielded her.

Eventually she looked across at the more junior of the two scribes, who moved to join her. The master ignored the whole process, talking instead in a low voice with the senior scribe. The woman pointed to one of the women from the group to the left and then at Nepheret. When she spoke, her foreign intonation was quite clear, even in just a few words.

"This one. And that one."

A little sigh ran around the others in the group. They were relieved not to have been chosen. Though they knew nothing about the priest's household, experience had taught them that change was usually for the worse, and stability for the better. Nepheret, however, felt a pang. She took a step towards the scribe, who was making marks on a broken piece of pottery.

"Lord scribe, sir. I have a son here in the household." She paused for a few heartbeats. "I am still feeding him."

The scribe frowned, looked at her, then turned to the woman.

"I do apologise most humbly, mistress. I thought we had selected only those who were suitable to go with you. We follow the customs here about weaning. Perhaps another woman would suffice, honoured lady? I can easily change the name I have written here. We can find another woman of about the same age and experience."

The woman straightened a little and came closer to the two of them.

"Not yet. This one seemed right to me. I will hear more about this. If I made a wrong choice I shall want to know why. Are you still feeding him?"

Nepheret swallowed. The master had glanced over towards the group at the delay, but clearly had no real interest in intervening.

"Yes, honoured lady."

The woman nodded slowly, looked into Nepheret's face, then studied her body up and down. Nepheret felt entirely exposed by the scrutiny.

"In truth now. You are sure you are feeding him? Real sustenance? Not just comfort to fall asleep?"

Nepheret flushed, and hesitated for a short time. The woman waited for her reply, her eyes steady on Nepheret's, her face patient but unyielding. A little wordless sound escaped from Nepheret before she was able to find her voice.

"In truth, not any longer, lady. I am dry now. You are correct."

The other woman looked at the scribe. "I will keep the same choice. Tell me when you have finished preparing the dockets." She turned back to Nepheret. "A good answer, and a hard one, and I am content with it. I cannot abide deception, and my master the lord priest is the same. Your answer is a credit to you."

"Honoured lady, pardon me, but might I be permitted to bring my son with me? I am sure that he will bring benefit into your household. He is only young yet, but one day he may be a blessing to the most honoured lord priest."

"That will not be possible. The lord priest cannot take the extra mouth out to Gedjet. Listen now. I am not leaving here until tomorrow. You can have tonight with your child to make your parting. But when we leave, he cannot come with us."

She turned away, and left the courtyard with the master and his retinue. No longer wanted, the women started to disperse again. Nepheret stood, unable to move even when some of the others nudged her, took her hand, spoke with her. Finally, when she was nearly alone, she shook her head and ran towards the room where Makty was waiting for her. She felt dry now, just as she had said to the strange woman, completely dry in soul as well as body.

—⁓⁓ 𓊽 𓎡 𓊽 𓎡 𓊽 𓎡 𓊽 ⁓⁓—

Dawn was beginning to brighten the sky, and although she could not see the land from where she lay, Nepheret knew that the fields and the wetlands beyond would be awakening as well. She had not slept at all, but had laid beside Makty-Rasut watching him, trying to find prayers that would carry some weight for his future. He had dozed fitfully, stirring every so often as though to check that she was still there. From today, she would not be. To her right, Moset-en-Tepi also stirred, opened her eyes, and saw Nepheret looking at her.

"What is it?"

"Tepi, please, when I am gone will you see to Makty when he needs it? He is still so young."

Tepi shook herself awake and sat up on her bedroll. "I will do what I can, but you know how it is. I cannot be with him for most of the day. He must learn to fend for himself. Anyway, when he is a little older, they will take him away from the women's room and put him with the other boys. Who knows how often I will see him after that?"

"There is a junior scribe that might help. Samut. He has given me some help before."

Tepi chuckled. "I know that man, for sure, and the kind of help he looks for."

Nepheret looked down briefly. "Yes, but he's good at heart, I think. He looks for more than just some pleasure for himself. He even taught me the signs that make my name one night."

"To be sure he has no real malice in him. But I don't know he can do much about your Makty."

"Will you do something for me? Please try to keep him here in the household where he knows some people. I can't bear the thought of him being sent away. However would I find him again?"

"How do you imagine you will ever get back? They say that Gedjet is ever such a long way away, in a different land which the Great King had to subdue with all his army. Do you really think they will allow you out? And how will you know the journey if they let you go? Nepheret, you must not pretend to yourself. Do you really think that you will ever see him again?"

Nepheret was silent for a while. Around them, the other women were starting to wake and prepare for the day.

"Please, Tepi."

"Look, I'll do what I can. But we both know that it may count for nothing. I can't sway the mind of the housekeeper if she is set on something, let alone the honoured master's family. And I won't put myself in trouble on a fool's task. What I can do, I will, but it will be less than you hope. If they decide to send him away, my voice will not be heard."

"I know, I know."

There was another short silence.

"Could you at least do this for me, then, please. I am going to leave now, before he is awake. They told me to be at the outer court when the sun was up, but I don't want him to see me go. Will you lie with him a bit longer so he wakes up with someone. Just until your own day begins? For today, at least?"

Moset-en-Tepi reached out to touch Nepheret, then held her in a long embrace before settling beside Makty and letting him nuzzle in to her warmth. Nepheret stood up, took a last long look at her son, then walked out of the room without looking back.

11. Present – A New Life

THE SWEETEST OF sisters fills up my heart,
  reviving my body at dawn and at dusk.
She is fairer than flowers,
  more lovely than birds.
We kiss in the meadows,
  soar up to the heights.

MAKTY-RASUT STOOD IN HIS PLACE in the morning circle. The whole team used Kinahny to speak in, all day, whatever their land of birth, and Makty's command of the language was now quite secure. Djedy-ab-Baal, the team leader, had just finished his preamble about how much work needed to be done in the small amount of remaining time. To Makty's mind, he was a fussy, over-anxious leader, who had insufficient trust in his team to just let them get on and work.

It slightly galled Makty to be working under his supervision, since both of them were aware that Makty was the more talented of the two. But Djedy-ab-Baal was older and, more to the point, had established for himself a secure position with the temple officials here in Gedjet. He was locally born, which gave him a considerable advantage. His name showed his origins, a half-and-half affair mixing proper name elements with Kinahny ones. Presumably his parentage was equally mixed.

Makty pulled his thoughts back from their daydream as the man to his left finished speaking. He had not been listening, and had no idea what his fellow-workers had done yesterday. Now it was his turn.

"Yesterday I finished the outlines for the scene at the back wall of the master's eternal house. They are ready for the base colour wash now that the dusty work is finished down at that end. Today –" He paused. He was not sure what task Djedy-ab-Baal had in mind for him now that the outlining was complete. He looked across at the older man.

"Today I want you to start laying out some writing that the honoured official gave me yesterday afternoon when I went to see him to report on our progress."

Makty nodded. "Today, then, I shall start laying out this writing in whatever places you direct."

He stopped listening again as the remaining three men spoke in their turn.

He had come down to Gedjet almost two months ago. His original intentions, in the shock of hearing Shunaya's news, had been very confused. He certainly intended to redeem the bulk of his resources at one of the holy houses. They would readily honour the commitments of their more senior counterparts in the Beloved Land, after keeping some proportion back for themselves. After that, he had no firm plans. Perhaps he could find a house on the outskirts of the city.

At some stage, when he had become established, perhaps he would let Shunaya know where he was. Or perhaps he would travel back up River to Waset and speak with Senenptah about the successful completion of his quest. Could Shunaya wait a little longer?

He supposed that she was just over half way through the pregnancy now, so there might just about be time for the journey to and fro before the baby was due. Some days he was acutely aware of her absence, and some nights he woke suddenly, confused by the lack of her body alongside his. Those were times when he remembered Senenptah's word spoken through her, but he forced himself to think of other things. He could never remember any of his dreams, and he missed the way they used to infiltrate his thoughts.

As soon as the temple steward had heard of his particular skills, he had told him about this piece of work. It was a short job, a quick tomb to be prepared for one of the regional governor's staff who had unexpectedly fallen sick. He still lived, but his state of health was fragile and he might not survive. It was impossible for him to travel home. Three months, start to end, was all that was allowed, and the team was being put together in haste that very day. He could stay in one of the back rooms of the temple while the job was done.

Makty had wavered, but the steward took him to see the room, talking constantly as though Makty's involvement was a foregone conclusion. He found himself surrendering with no clear moment of decision. His new quarters were comfortable, and better than many places he had lived in. But it was basic, and quite lonely, and at the day's end he missed Shunaya. His days and nights were indeed empty of purpose.

On that first day Makty had gone to the appointed place,

carried out a few tasks under the eye of Djedy-ab-Baal to prove his competence, and been signed on. The test was absurdly simple, almost insultingly so, and he presumed that reflected the general lack of scribal talent out here in the province. This job was unexpected, but it put him back in a place of daily, unchallenging labour. It dulled the nagging question of what Shunaya thought of his absence.

Every morning and evening he tried to speak of her in his devotions to Seshat, but the goddess seemed very remote and his prayers futile. Despite this, the rhythm of familiar work had spoken louder than the idea of going up into the hill country again to see her. Perhaps he would make the journey after this job was complete. He was aware that his knowledge of her circumstances was becoming steadily more and more vague, and he had very little idea of how pregnancy was changing her.

The circle broke up and the men scattered in little clumps to their various tasks. He went over to Djedy-ab-Baal, who spread out a sheet of papyrus. It had already been used at least twice before, and then scraped roughly clean for new text. Some parts were quite damaged, but the writing was clear and, to his relief, well executed. He had expected a barely literate scrawl that would need a great deal of effort simply to read.

"So here it is. This has to be spread between two places. This part to the left side after the cross-passage, and this part just opposite it, on the right."

"Above the drawings? Or beside them towards the far end? I'm not sure there will be room above if they are to stay neat."

They both glanced towards the entrance shaft, though the places in question were completely out of sight in the shadowed interior.

"Put as much as you can above it. The honoured official wants a number of boxes to be placed down at the far end, and the writing must not be hidden. The boxes will take at least half the height. Arrange the signs so they will all still be showing. Do you want my help to lay it out?"

Makty looked at him, trying not to let his irritation show. "I am sure I can manage, thank you."

"And just flat writing onto the wall. There is no time for any of that fancy relief work here."

Makty nodded, and was about to speak when Djedy-ab-Baal continued.

"And the honoured official wants us to use the modern quick writing style, not the proper signs. No matter what might be done in Mitsriy tombs where you've been before."

He looked up, obviously expecting Makty to voice some objection.

Instead, Makty simply nodded again.

"As he wishes. I expect that more people who might see the tomb would know the quick signs. I will start straight away."

He glanced down at the text, not reading it but roughly counting how many signs and groups there were. "I might finish tomorrow. Or it might spread into the next day. There are quite a number of the larger signs here. Also, I don't know whether the team doing the colour wash on the right will finish on time. Or whether they will splash the upper part as they work."

"I will talk to them and make sure they know how important it is not to slow this down. We only have a few weeks left now."

He strode off towards the two men responsible for the colour wash on the right. They were busy stirring the creamy-white powder into a large basin, and he started talking to them while they kept thickening the foamy mix. He had left the papyrus with Makty, who took out some of his own tools and started off down the narrow passageway.

The passageway smelled of damp plaster now instead of dust. He suspected that it would remain damp for a long time, out here in this province and away from the dry heat of the Beloved Land. He had serious doubts as to how long the painted decorations would survive, but that was hardly his problem to worry about.

The tomb was a fair imitation of others he had known, but with rough and ready compromises to allow for the different stone found here. The walls on the left had been thickly coated with a base layer to cover the irregular rock surface, well past the place where the main shaft was intersected by a very short cross-corridor. The two men on the left were busy on the last section before the end wall; their shadows waved and danced jerkily in the uneven light of the oil lamps. The team on the right were lagging several sections behind.

Makty looked at the blank area above the design he had outlined on the left. He wished now that he had known about this writing earlier, as it would have been easier to lay the whole lot out together. He glanced at the papyrus. Only about half of the text for the left would fit above, and he would curl the remainder around the tree and seated figure that completed the design. That meant that the right hand text would need to be split similarly. He frowned. Hopefully the writing would divide up in a sensible manner that would yield a pleasing appearance as well as making sense.

He held the papyrus up in the uncertain light, reading the text properly for the first time. As the official would look out from his eternal house after death, he would be reading this on his right hand side.

"And I was always faithful and loving to the wife of my youth, Merit-Iset, true of voice. I ensured that she was honoured both in the public place and within her own home. She walked at my side in every place that I went. I did not neglect her needs even for a single day, even while I fulfilled every one of my duties for my lord."

He stopped reading, fumbled with the papyrus, and almost dropped it. The written words stared bleakly, accusingly at him. The thought of Shunaya, presumably still living up at Kephrath, gnawed at him. The words of this official spoke out to him from the papyrus like the ominous decision of a judge. Would others say that he had neglected her? Grimacing, he turned around in order to think about the text for the right hand side.

"My four children bless my name every day and will always conduct the rituals and offerings with dedication, their hearts full of love for me. I was a good father to them, and they heard my voice with pleasure both evening and morning. I did everything that a father ought to do for his children."

Makty looked at the tools in his hands. Somewhere up in the hill country to the east was an unborn child of his own, nestling inside Shunaya's womb. Together they had brought this life into being, but every day that passed meant that he or she would only hear Shunaya's voice, not his own. How could the child ever learn to bless his name? Or have a heart filled with love for a man whose voice was never heard? Had he ever learned to bless the name of his own unknown father?

He closed his eyes briefly. Technically there were no problems. The texts were simple enough to craft, and they could easily be divided into portions that would settle neatly in the available space. The problem was not in the skill of his hands: he was very familiar with that and full of confidence. The problem lay in the poverty of his heart, which had been all too suddenly and deftly exposed.

He turned again to the left side and read the text again, looked at each wall in turn. Ahead and behind, the two teams working on the colour wash looked curiously at his indecision, nudged each other, grinned. He ignored them, facing the wall but not seeing it. He had been pierced to the heart by the simple words of the official, languishing near death somewhere in the town. Then he turned towards the shaft entrance and pushed past the two men standing there, shaking his head when they asked him what was wrong.

Djedy-ab-Baal was working his way down a list of items scratched on a piece of broken pottery. He had marked well over half of them as finished, and looked up as Makty approached.

"Is something wrong? I thought you had started on those

two texts? Is there a problem? Is the surface bad?"

Makty shook his head. He had no expectation that the older man would understand. "The surface is fine. There is plenty of space for the signs. But I am not the man who will be writing them."

"Well, I don't have anyone else who is anything like so good with signs as you. I have no time for false modesty now. Just go back in there and make a start."

Makty put the papyrus sheet down beside him, shaking his head. "Then do it yourself. Or find another scribe. I cannot do this. I have to go. Today. Now. I have been neglectful of other duties."

"But you cannot leave. Not now, not with so little time re-maining." Djedy-ab-Baal's face was blank with incomprehen-sion, then suddenly a look of scorn filled it. "If this is your way to try to get a bigger share, I'll not have it. You agreed what you agreed and I'll not change that now. This is not an extra task I am giving you, it's just a regular part of your duties. Maybe they behave like this down in the Mitsriy lands, but we don't work like that here. I'm not going to give you a scrap of silver more than our agreement. I'll not let you hold me to ransom like this."

The other men had appeared at the entrance, having heard their leader's raised voice. Makty shook his head.

"It's not that. Not at all. I'm not trying to cheat you. I don't want more share. I'm not even going to ask for any part of the share for the work I have done these last two months. But I cannot stay and write this for you. I have to go. Write the words yourself, or find someone else to do it. I am leaving."

"If you go now, you'll never get another piece of work here in Gedjet. I'll make sure everyone knows what you're like. Don't think you can just come crawling back to me now you've let me down like this. I'll make sure everybody knows what your name means. Everyone, do you hear? Makty-Rasut means unreliable. He won't finish a job that he's started. Makty-Rasut means can't-be-trusted."

Makty was already walking away, his tool bag under his arm. His face was closed and angry, but he refused to turn around. He made no reply as Djedy-ab-Baal continued to shout after him, his enraged voice carrying across the cemetery area. Makty kept walking all the way to the temple steward, collected his few remaining possessions and the weight of silver that represented his worldly wealth, and was gone through the city gate just before noon.

〰〰 ⟨ ꙮ ⟨ ꙮ ⟨ ꙮ ⟨ 〰〰

Three nights had passed since then, and Makty was struggling through undergrowth which was filling in the gaps below fair-sized trees. It had started drizzling earlier in the afternoon. At first, this had been a pleasant experience for someone who had hardly ever known showers or rainfall. He had entertained himself for a while by recalling former scribes who had spoken of other nations having their River falling from the sky. But the gentle start had deteriorated into a prolonged and rather relentless downpour, and the novelty had long since worn off.

He had remembered that the path up to Kephrath swept in a big curve after Ayaluna, and he had thought to shorten the journey by cutting straight across. The choice had made good sense at the time, and the track he had chosen initially angled confidently uphill. He had every expectation of emerging near the meagre village where he had asked for directions with Shunaya.

But then the path had branched several times, and had dwindled into something only used by wild animals. The folds in the land had become irregular, and the vegetation was much more of an obstacle than he had imagined. The sun was completely obscured by the rainclouds, and he had no idea if he was following a true line any more. He had a feeling that he should have encountered the main track again by now.

Worse still, the light was fading fast. He was quite thoroughly wet, and becoming quite thoroughly miserable. It was, he thought, overdue time when he should stop somewhere. But for some time there had been nowhere obvious to make any sort of camp, and he doubted his ability to make a fire with only wet wood in among the curtains of rain. He struggled on a little longer, reaching the top of a small ridge. To carry on at this stage was ridiculous, and quite possibly dangerous.

He pulled himself to the highest point of the ridge, ducking under the branches of a low tree. It was poor shelter, and likely to make him wetter still with drips from the drooping leaves, but perhaps it was better than nothing. Then, some distance away to his right, he saw the sudden glow of a flame, followed by a more steady light. Somebody had managed to set fire, and keep it alive.

He worked his way across and up to the lure of the flames. The distance was further away than he had first imagined, across several little folds in the land. When he finally approached, he saw that the fire was situated under the shelter of some kind of tree with much denser upper branches. The little camp was backed against the lee side of a tall bank. The ground underfoot was quite dry. It all made good sense when he saw the arrangement, but he was sure he would not have thought of it.

A man glanced up as he stumbled into the circle of firelight. He was wearing one of the Kinahny kefs, pushed back from his forehead to show grey hair in a casual manner, and his arms were marked with several old scars. A large dog lifted its head and growled.

"Peace, Aymar, don't you recognise a friend when you see him?"

He made a flat sweeping gesture of his hand, repeated, "Peace, Aymar," and the dog subsided, beating its tail a couple of times on the leafy ground, its tongue lolling out in a rather apologetic gesture. Makty looked at the man.

"Might I share your fire for the night, sir? I have some food that I can offer in return."

"That would be pleasant, though not necessary. I would be happy to share the camp with you even if you had brought nothing, Makty-Rasut."

Makty stared at him, perplexed. "Do I know you, sir?" He stepped a little closer, and suddenly realisation came to him. "I remember now. You're the huntsman and trapper up at Kephrath. I do apologise for not knowing you at once, sir."

"Kothar son of Tamar, that's right. And nothing to forgive, you only saw me the once and my guess is that Damari had already filled your head with half the village." He grinned, with an easy familiarity that Makty liked. This Kothar had a similar quality to his old workmate Hobniy, though the two looked nothing like one another. He moved close in to the fire, letting the heat start to warm his body, wondering absently whether Kothar would have made a good tomb worker if he had been born in the Beloved Land.

"So what were you doing out here? This is hardly the best route to come from Gedjet. You're lucky to have come across me and Aymar. Or maybe Damari knew something he wasn't telling me."

"Did he send you to look for me? How can that be? How could he know?"

"No, nothing like that. He just told me to keep a lookout for you when he knew I was going out, and he said I might have more luck this time setting traps down the hill instead of along the ridge. Until now I hadn't snared much, and I thought he was just plain wrong. But it's an odd way for you to come from Gedjet."

Makty looked across in the direction that he thought Gedjet lay. Kothar shook his head, pointed off at a different angle. "Gedjet is that way. And Ayaluna over there. I think you got turned around a bit in these woods. There's a reason the track goes the way it does."

"I thought I would come out at that half-ruined village. Beth something."

"Bayth Horon. I can see why you'd think so, but the shape of the land doesn't favour that journey. I'll take you a better way, but another time just keep to the road until you know how to find the paths out here. I can take you straight back up to Kephrath unless you particularly want to see Horon?"

Makty shook his head. "I particularly want to go straight to Kephrath. How far away is it now?"

"We can be there before noon tomorrow." The two fell silent as Kothar cooked some food over the steady fire. Makty opened his bag to retrieve some slightly damp bread and a soft cheese, still wrapped in fresh leaves. As they ate, the rain eased back again to a persistent drizzle. Kothar threw the scraps to the dog and settled back after banking up the fire. Makty sighed.

"I remember your house now. It's towards the end of the ridge, looking north."

"Shaharti's house. But yes it is."

Makty looked blank. Kothar continued. "It's Shaharti's house, not mine. We count lineage and the household through the woman's line, not the man's." He grinned. "I'm there by her sufferance. We do things differently up here in the four towns. But if you're going back to live in Gedjet you might not be worried about that."

"I won't be going back to Gedjet any more."

"No?"

"Not as a worker. I walked out on the job unfinished, just left the team without fore-notice. My name is nothing there now. Worse than nothing. They won't ever have me back there. I've never done that before in my life, you know. Not even once. I've always been dependable, always finished what-ever job I signed up to, no matter what it was like."

Kothar nodded. "They tell me that's a good thing when you're working for another man. I wouldn't know, I've only ever done things for myself. But that's what I hear."

Makty laughed. "Well, if I was leading a team I wouldn't sign myself on just now. Not worth the risk. And a man's name spreads around a town, whether for good or ill."

"That I do know. Up at Kephrath I had a name like that with the women when I was younger. When my Shaharti took a chance with me they all thought she was a fool. She told me later, how one girl after another came up to her at the time and said how I was just going to take her for a night or two's satisfaction and then drop her again. But she took the risk, went off with me, then invited me into her house a season or two later, and now look at me. That's a lot of years ago, mind."

Makty hesitated, thinking.

"And you have two children? Have I remembered right?"

"Three that are still on this side. You met two, our daughter who brought a husband in to Shaharti's house, and our son who hasn't moved out yet. He wants to move on up to Sychem to join with the Ibriym fighting men. Then there's another lad who settled with a girl in Giybon. You never met him. But as well as those three there have been two more we lost at different times, one before ever he came near to the birth, years ago now, and one who died the very day she opened her eyes."

"Oh. I am so sorry to awaken your grief."

Kothar grunted and nodded. After a pause, he went on, "That lady of yours, Milashuniyet, she looks very fine just now, if you don't mind me saying. She's carrying herself very well. It will do your heart good to see her. She's quite glowing with that child of yours."

Makty was silent again. "Kothar, I am completely covered in shame about Shunaya. I should never have left her."

Kothar leaned forward, stirred a log so that the firelight strengthened around them both. The bright eyes of the dog reflected the sudden flames. Kothar looked quizzically at Makty but said nothing.

"Worse still, it was not seeing sense in my own heart that brought me back, but something scribbled by a dying man down in Gedjet. I was supposed to write it out on his tomb walls. But when I read what he said it cut me right through. I just walked out then to come back and see Shunaya up at your Kephrath. Do you think she'll take me back? I don't know what I was thinking when I left her and went down the hill to Gedjet like that."

"You should talk to Damari about that. I would if I was in your place."

"Your priest? I don't know him. Not really, not except that day or two when we arrived. And I'm not from your village; why would he show care for me? It's different for you, you're close to him."

Kothar laughed. "That's not always a good thing. We've known each other since we were both children. We both know each other's faults far too well. I've seen him when he's been very low, just as he's seen me, and we've had our share of disagreements. Sometimes we've said some cruel things to one other. But for all I could say about that, I know when I need to go to him and hear his word on a matter. Maybe it's hard for you because of Nepheret being your mother? Wondering what she thinks of you?"

Makty shook his head. "I can't speak of her like that yet. I don't know what to think about her. All that long journey I made looking for her, and I don't know who I found yet. Do you know the story?" He paused and considered. "Well, another day, perhaps. You know, there's nobody in the whole of the Beloved Land that knows me in the way you've just said. I've never lived in the same place more than a handful of years."

"Or with the same woman, from what I hear?"

"As for that, hardly ever for more than a handful of weeks."

To his surprise, Kothar chuckled. "I wish my Shaharti had known about you in the early days. It would have made me seem like a safe wager after all." Between them, the fire crackled and chattered. The burning wood smelled sweet. Kothar glanced across, to see Makty's head hanging in shame.

"Don't mind my turn of phrase, lad. I never could use words right. Ask Damari one day when you feel up to it. For now, just go back to Milashuniyet and see what she says. I don't know if you heard, but she went to stay in Damari's sister's house. Sosanneth she's called, Sannah for short. Your lady's been helping out with the weaving Sannah does there. Go to Sannah's house and see what Milashuniyet has to say. That'll mean more than what I say, or Damari, or anyone."

"Kothar, I walked away from her all the way to Gedjet when I heard she was with child. She'd said nothing about that baby before, though she must have known. Surely she knew. I had nowhere to put myself. This never happened to me before. I thought women knew when to go with a man and when not to."

He gestured vaguely. Kothar nodded.

"She might have known and gone with you anyway. Not for me to say. But maybe she just made a choice. I'm thinking she wants you to make a choice too."

Makty fell silent, remembering again the words of the official down in Gedjet. He wished now that he had brought the sheet of papyrus away with him. He knew, though, that Djedy-ab-Baal would have forbidden it, and rightly so, since the team would need the text. The sky continued to darken. He thought about getting Seshat out of his pack to perform his evening devotions, but felt uncertain about doing so in front of Kothar. What would the little statue mean to him? He compromised by closing his eyes for a time and inwardly reciting a series of prayers.

After that they talked a little more, off and on about unimportant matters. Finally they settled for the night, with Aymar lying on the outside, nearest the embers of the fire and nearest to anything that might try to come near in the darkness. Makty listened to his reassuring canine breathing for a while before drifting off to sleep.

―――〰〰〰

Makty walked up towards the house that Kothar had indicated to him before heading towards Shaharti's house. It was in a narrow lane between several others, on the southern edge of the town, and the branches of a mimosa tree curved up and around the door. It had an irregular appearance, with a whole room on one side added quite recently, and several other places where it had been patched. It seemed to have grown by pressure from within. There were voices inside, and he paused. A young boy ran down the street towards him, carefully holding the lid on a pottery jug. He stopped at the house door, and then looked curiously at Makty.

"A bright day to you, sir. You're the Mitsriy man who was here before, aren't you? Have you come to ask grandma for some weaving?"

Makty was about to reply, when the door opened from the inside. A woman was there, holding a spindle. He remembered her when he saw her: Damariel's sister, Sosanneth.

"Where's that paste for the dye, Amar-Shaddai?" She took the jug from the boy. Then she saw Makty, put her head to one side in surprise, and held the door open. "And the day's blessings to you as well, Makty-Rasut. You'd better come in. There's someone here who will want to know that you're back."

Makty stepped in. The room seemed to have a great many people in it, and he looked around, slightly bewildered. An elderly couple sat near a fire in the hearth, another man was smoothing some timber in a corner beside a half-made stool, a young woman of around Makty's age had a baby at her breast. The boy he had seen in the street pushed past him and ran over to the young mother. Sosanneth closed the door behind him.

There, seated in front of a loom, sat Shunaya. She was just getting to her feet. Her face was fuller than he remembered, and her body was rounded, fruitful. Her hair, where he could see it beneath the Kinahny kef she was wearing, had become a little darker. Kothar was right, he thought, as she looked at him; pregnancy had made her all the more lovely.

Nobody spoke. Even the nursing baby had stopped. He swallowed, took several steps closer to her. She waited for him to say something. He reached out, took her hand, took a deep breath.

"Shunaya, I am so sorry. I did wrong to go down to Gedjet and leave you here. I have neglected you and failed to honour you as I should, both in the house and in the public place. I have not loved you as I should." He knelt down, rested his forehead against the bulge below her ribs. "And I have left you without a voice to hear when the sun rises and again when it sets. I have not been a good father to you." He stood up again and looked into Shunaya's face, ignoring the other people in the room, waiting to hear what she would say.

"And what now? Will you go away again to Gedjet once you have seen me today?"

He shook his head. "Gedjet is closed to me. I will not go down there again to work."

There was another pause. She was still studying him.

"I want to know you can be different with me than the way you have been with other women in the past."

He nodded, remembering the journey on the River.

"I walked away from an unfinished job when I finally re-alised what I had done to you, and to the little one you carry in your body. It is the first time I have ever failed to complete a piece of work in my whole life. Now I have no name any more in Gedjet. They chiselled out my name there on the day I left the job undone and came back to see you. I want my name to be bound up with yours now."

She blinked, nodding slowly, digesting this. He spoke again, this time in his own language which of all the people in the room, only the two of them knew.

"Shunaya, I went back around from the house of Waters, all in a circle and back again to here. But that is done now. I have passed safely by that and I am here with you. I just lost some time. Lost all of us some time. Forgive me for that. It was every bit as futile and empty as you told me in the message you carried from Senenptah."

She looked at him, softening visibly, and replied in the

same language. "And is this now the home place for us?"

He thought about it, and switched back to Kinahny so the whole room could understand. "I don't think this is our home yet. Not quite yet. Our journey is not quite over. But we are close to home now, I feel sure."

"I can live with that thought. But I will stay here among the friends I have made until our baby is born. I will not move again and have to pass through labour with strangers. If we move on, it will be after this birth is behind us."

She stepped forward, let him put his arms around her, let him feel the roundness of her new shape against his body. Then she looked up into his face with a familiar sharp humour, the mood that he had missed during the empty time working in Gedjet. "But leave me one more time like that without saying when you will be back, and you will be chasing dung and ashes in circles for the rest of your life."

Then she looked down again, and her face clouded. "I cannot tell you how frightened I have been. There were seven of us women with child in Kephrath. Then Birketh-Taliy came to her time just over a week ago. She went into her house one day when the birth pangs came on her, but she never came out again. The baby never turned properly. Now there are only six of us. She was lost, and her baby as well. The six of us who were left all stayed together that night, all of us in the same house to comfort one another."

She paused, remembering, tears in her eyes.

"Now, you could walk away from that job in Gedjet, and I am more than glad that you did. But I cannot walk away from this. One day my labour pains will start, and I shall go into a room with Sannah here, and the lady Nepheret, and Sophireth too, if she is willing. Who can say if I will come out to you again? I was full of fear. I am glad that you have come back, because I was very lonely and we should pass through this together, but I will not face it in another strange town where I know nobody. I will face it with these friends beside me."

11. Present – A New Life

Makty closed his eyes and held her against him, trying to remember the name of the serving maid who had chided him for casual humour about childbirth. Had anything in his life prepared him for this? He held her for a long moment, then looked around at the others in the room. Voices started up again around them, questions, the sound of food being prepared.

_____ 𓅱 𓏏 𓅱 𓏏 𓅱 𓏏 𓅱 _____

Makty strode along the last section of the hilltop trackway. He had already passed by the turn-off for Woodlands, which was also called Jarrar's Town – he was still not used to the way that everyone and everything seemed to have several names rather than a single one – and was almost in sight of the rooftops of Kephrath. He was returning from Shalem. Yissi, Damariel's apprentice, had walked there with him as guide, introduced him to several people and then left him to his own devices. The journey was only a morning's walk, and an easy one at that.

Shunaya was scant weeks from the time of birth, so far as they could tell, and he had taken the opportunity to take the trip to the nearby town. Before he had left, he had asked her if she wanted him to take an oath in front of witnesses to return again to her. She had stood up, rather stiff with back-pain, opened the door, and said that if at this point he could not find the inner motive to return, then no oath in the land would be of any use. They had kissed one another properly on parting that morning, while Yissi stood waiting patiently outside, and then she had closed the door again behind him.

He turned under the stone lintel of the town gate, nodded happily to two of the village women drawing water from the large cistern nearby, and walked over to the seers' house beside the high place. Inside, he could hear Nepheret singing. He knocked, and then, remembering the custom here, called out from the doorway. After a short pause, she opened the door.

"Blessings of the day to you, my son. How happy is my heart to see you."

He kissed her on both cheeks. "And a morning of light to you, mother." He had decided that the best way to become used to this woman as his mother was to keep using the title. For the first week or so the effort had been forced, stilted, but over time he felt that he was speaking the word more easily.

"Will you come in? Take some refreshment? How was your journey?"

"Thank you, but I have no need. My two weeks in Shalem were very successful, and I would like to tell you and Damariel everything about it later. But for now I must go on down to see Shunaya. She is well?"

"She grows larger every day. And more restless for the birth to happen. But the baby has not dropped yet, so there is some time yet. She is in good health and good spirits. Damariel has been at Giybon since yesterday. When he gets back, we will both come down to see you."

Makty headed on down towards the house he and Shunaya were using. It had been provided by Tarpashai, the woman Damariel had mentioned before. She had inherited the extra house after the early death of a relative, but with only one very young daughter had no immediate need of it herself.

The negotiations that had taken place to compensate the family for its use had been a pivotal moment for Makty, since this was a part of Kinahny culture in which he felt completely at home. The long sessions, conducted politely but with systematic care, reminded him vividly of all the many times when he had made arrangements for temporary housing while he worked on a job in the Beloved Land.

When he reached their home, he found that Sophireth and her baby were just leaving, and Shunaya was at the door. Nepheret had been right; even in the few days that he had been away she had grown larger. After a fond reunion, they sat together in the large room, from which the main door opened out onto the street. He had asked all about how she had fared during his absence, and finally started telling her about the journey.

"And this Shalem is interesting. It has an air of self-importance. Of tradition, if you like. For a good many years now they have had kings, ambitious kings who made alliances with other rulers up and down this land. They correspond with the regional governor down in Gedjet. And so, properly speaking, with the great king all the way back in the Beloved Land. I first learned the name Shalem as an apprentice reciting the route along the great ridgeway track, but while so many of the other places have fallen into ruin, or vanished quite away, this one is still there."

"But is it any size? Does it offer what you wanted?"

"Well, there are not actually that many more people than Giybon. Not even than Kephrath. But it feels more important, and its name carries more weight. I suppose like everywhere else up here in these hills it has declined in size. Its best days were most likely a lot of generations ago. But it is a place that could recover if the time was right."

She persevered, patiently. "But is there anyone there you can work with?"

Just then Damariel and Nepheret could be heard outside, calling their names. Makty went over to the door and opened it to them. There was a confusion of greeting and affection, until they were all sitting again with mint tea and almonds to hand.

"Yes, Shunaya, there are still a few scribes there in the town. Some of them moved with the Hathor shrine ladies when they left a few years ago. That was somewhere just south of the town itself." He looked at Damariel, who nodded.

"It was at Ramoth Hurriy. Most of the Kinahny novice sisters moved just down the way to Bayth Horon, but the chantress and the other Mitsriy women returned to the great river, along with a handful of soldiers and household servants."

"So anyway, there's half a dozen scribes still there, mostly just doing piece work for whoever will give them a meal. They are thoroughly demoralised now." He paused, frowning, thinking back around the people he had met and their various talents. "None of them are very experienced - I think the really good ones went down to the lowlands. And not one of them knows all of the proper signs, they mostly use a mixture of the Kinahny letters and the quick scribal brush-marks. But between them all we could make something."

Damariel leaned forward. "It won't be the same as the life you have been used to. You won't be making eternal houses for the dead like they do in Waset."

There was a little silence. All eyes were on Makty. "That's very true. I thought of that all the way along the track as I walked back. But it would be starting something new up here. A new life, if you like." He looked appreciatively at Shunaya, who was rubbing her hand across the swell of her womb. "I think we could start more than one kind of new life in these hills."

"So long as the one there in Shalem doesn't kick as much as this one. Or keep me awake at night so much."

They laughed. Makty turned back to Damariel. "I think this could work. I can make it work. I know I can. We will not be making tombs for the nobility here, but we will be doing something for the living. Just now these people are aimless. They undercut each other's prices, their standard of work is very uneven, they don't help each other with their different aptitudes. They have no discipline, no pride in their work. They are like geese running about without a herdsman."

"And you can change that?"

"I can, mother. I can change that." He had become genuinely excited at the prospect. "I can teach them to work as a team. The man who is good at artwork can help the man who can write, or the one who knows how much building material will be required for a job. Right now they compete against each other, and spoil each other's chances of being hired, and in the end not one of them does a good job. They are the mockery of the town and the subject of jokes."

"But do they have talent?"

"I think they do, yes. At least, they have good ideas and skill in their hands, although they have not been trained to use these properly. There is a man there who is good with layout. A couple who can write reasonably well. One who can work with stone. One who is writing songs to the gods that sound like the petitions you might make to a superior officer."

He paused and thought briefly before continuing.

"I can help them to work alongside each other, each man doing what he does best. We will hire ourselves out to the rulers and the nobles at fair rates, make promises of good work and then live up to them, share out the work amongst us all fairly, teach one another so that all of us work towards the same level of skill. I can make something of these people that will last. I can make a name that will be remembered. That has to be a good thing, surely? Whether in the Beloved Land or up here?"

"Indeed it is. It is a great task, and with the Mitsriy withdrawing from here year by year, one which is greatly needed."

"And you, my love? What do you think?"

Milashuniyet nodded. "It is good. At least, I think it is good. And I think the lord priest in Waset would be pleased and satisfied by your choice. Whether he still lives now or has finally travelled across the Sea of Reeds. I should like it that we please him one more time. But it is as I said before. I will not move to Shalem or anywhere else before this baby of ours is born. I want to go into the birthing house with my friends who are in Kephrath. With the lady Nepheret here, with Sannah, with Sophireth. I want them with me when the hour comes. And if by ill chance that should be my last hour, I should like to spend it here in Kephrath, where they have taken us in on the journey and showed us love."

Makty glanced across the room quickly to Seshat, whose statue stood on a little pedestal in the corner. "I do not like us to talk in this way."

"I know that. But we must speak of it. We lay with one another in Waset and began a journey in my body as well as along the great river. But who can say if that journey leads to life or death? Do any of your lists tell us? So far the road along the river has led us up to Kephrath, to your own mother and to a people who have become my friends. Now I want to share this part of my body's journey with these people. Then after that, all being well, we can move to Shalem and begin another new life."

"Shalem is not far away from Kephrath. We can leave there of a morning and be here before midday."

"So I have heard. Sannah's husband Qeren told me all about it while you were away, told me about the paths you would be walking and the sights you would be seeing. But before we think too much that, I need to live through these next few weeks, and give all my thought to this child."

Makty-Rasut stood by the window of the seers' house. He could not see Tarpashai's house, his home, from where he stood, as it was hidden by other houses and the curve of the ridge, but he kept trying. Damariel and Kothar were with him. They had given him small beakers of the local wine, but just now he missed the taste of the beer he had known beside the River.

Shunaya had begun serious labour in the dark hours before dawn, having had lesser pangs in the latter part of the previous day. She had woken suddenly, overwhelmed by a much stronger contraction, and held his arm with a grip like a crocodile's bite as her body clenched and finally relaxed again. He had run first to Sosanneth's house to wake her and Sophireth, and then back up to the high place to rouse Damariel and Nepheret.

After that he had been unceremoniously sent away from the little house. The time of labour was not a time when his presence was wanted. He had expected that, knowing that back down beside the River the women would have retired to one of the birthing houses on their own. However, expecting it, and being able to manage the enforced separation when it happened, were two very different things.

Most of the morning had passed since that first awakening, and the sun was close to the zenith. Damariel and Kothar watched him pace to and fro. They themselves sat waiting, clearly anticipating a long vigil. He turned to them.

"What will be happening now?"

Kothar laughed. "Most likely your lady will be cursing your name and vowing never to let you touch her ever again." Makty sat again on the bench, disconsolate. "But in my experience that will pass. I'm sure you will be sharing a bed again before too long."

The morning passed, and the first part of the afternoon followed it. From time to time one or other of the townspeople came up to the house to say some words to him. He had never been greeted by so many of the occupants on the same day. He suspected that a considerable number were within earshot of their house, and wondered how much more of the birth's progress they were hearing than he could. From time to time one or other of the men found some food for him, or heated up some mint tea, but it was all tasteless. He felt that the time being taken was too long, but they assured him that it was not at all unusual.

Finally, Nepheret opened the door. She was still wearing a very old smock that he had seen her carrying into the house in the early dawn. It had some new bloodstains on top of a patchwork of older ones. She was clearly tired. But she nodded to Makty, and he felt that his heart would burst with relief.

"Makty-Rasut, you and Milashuniyet have a baby girl." She smiled wearily. "If you were one of my people here I would say to you that your household now has a new daughter to carry it into the future. And that you should be with Milashuniyet as she names her baby. But you must choose your own customs here, since neither of you are native-born."

"But they are well?"

"Mother and baby are safe and well. The time was long, but all has gone well during the birth and afterwards."

Makty closed his eyes, his thoughts brimming with half-formed prayers of gratitude. The anxiety that Shunaya had voiced about the birth in previous months had lodged itself around his own heart, and he realised that he could hardly believe that the event had passed without loss. Damariel, Kothar, Nepheret were around him, touching him with affection, saying words that he was unable to comprehend in the enormous relief that had overcome him. Finally he opened his eyes again, took a deep breath.

"Can I see her now? Is it allowed?" He paused, thinking. "Does she want that?"

"Yes, yes indeed to all three of those questions. Go now to her, go on."

Makty ran off through the westering sun along the narrow lanes between the houses, past other people who called out to him as he ran. The news had spread rapidly. He stopped at the door and listened to Sosanneth's voice in the house. There was a new voice as well, one that made short wordless breathy calls for attention for a few heartbeats before falling quiet again. He opened the door very carefully and went into the main room, gloomy where drapes had been left in place across the windows.

He looked around. The room, the house they lived in, smelt of life and death all mixed together. Sophireth had just finished gathering a bundle of wet and bloody sheets into a pile and was rinsing her hands. Sosanneth sat on a stool to one side, shaking her hair out of a tight bunch and starting to tie her kef into place again. Like Nepheret, her outer smock had new smears of blood. They were both quiet, wordless at the end of the long day's labour.

But Shunaya was lying on a bundle of clean bedding, with the new infant wrapped in fresh strips of cloth against her breast. He wondered if she would ever recover from the birth. Her face was flushed and lined with fatigue, and her hair damp with the sweat of her exertion. Her body, where he could see it, was limp, worn out, and seemed somehow to have fallen back into itself now that the baby had been born. She looked at him as though coming back from a very long journey, exhausted but content. She reached out her spare hand to him. He crossed the room, knelt beside her and kissed her very carefully.

She took his hand and laid it gently on the baby's head. The tiny face was red and slightly misshapen, with eyes tightly shut even in the dim light. Every so often she would make a little whimpering sound and then press herself into Shunaya.

"Bless our baby for us, Makty, bless her now, and then we will name her so that Sannah and Sophireth can be our witnesses before they go back to their home."

Makty blinked and settled back onto his heels. He prayed every day to Seshat, and less frequently to some of the other gods. But he had hardly ever presumed to offer a blessing, still less make one up that he had not learned elsewhere. Blessing was not quite like prayer. It was weightier somehow, a step into deeper spiritual waters, and he was not sure that he was ready for that.

It crossed his mind that he should ask Damariel to do this, since he was the village priest, but then decided that Shunaya would not have asked him unless she wanted it. He pondered for a moment what to say. He was familiar with Seshat, comfortable with her, even if she had less to do with birth and infancy than some of the others. He squeezed Shunaya's hand and very delicately traced the wisps of damp dark hair on their daughter's head.

"I bless you, our child, in the name of Seshat, Lady of scribes.

May you have bread and beer and all the other good things of this world in your store-house every day.

May the days of your life be plentiful and sweet in your heart as you live in this land and grow up with us."

He felt that his blessing was entirely inadequate to the task, swallowed up in the vastness of the new child's life. But the acceptance of responsibility felt good.

As Shunaya nodded and held on to his hand as she drifted away towards sleep, he thought back on his life as a scribe along the River. He had only ever worked on the interior of eternal houses for men. Even during that first job in Waset the lady's direction had been for the courtyard, not the actual tomb.

Women were present in many of the scenes, of course, as companions or wives, slaves or family members. They might preside in the temple or conduct their own business, as well as take pleasure at the feast or in the marshes. They participated in the scenes to support, to affirm, sometimes to challenge, but only from the edges. Men's lives, clear-cut and well-defined, had always been central to the scenes he had drawn.

He looked around again at the women in the room. Sosanneth and Sophireth were quietly going about the business of cleaning up after the labour. Shunaya was stretched out with fatigue. As for the new infant, she was still finding out what it meant to live outside the womb.

He pieced together in his mind, from the pattern of movement and rest within the room, from all the things that remained unsaid between the women, something of the hours of today that had passed in birth. How would it ever be possible to prepare an eternal house that would portray this? How should the scenes of women's lives be shown?

Shunaya's eyes opened again as she pulled herself back into wakefulness.

"We should name our child."

He nodded, and smiled at her, a broad happy smile that gathered together past and future.

"Yes, we should."

Coda

O YOU WHO pass by this place, speak out a voice offering to the gods in bread and beer, papyrus and turquoise, and in everything good and pure for the life of Makty-Rasut, true of voice, and for his beloved Milashuniyet, true of voice.

MAKTY-RASUT CLOSED THE DOOR of the house in Shalem that he now shared with Shunaya. He put his tool bag, together with the extra bag he carried that evening, in the corner below the shelf where Seshat stood. It was the end of another working day, and he was content. They had been living here for the better part of a year now, having moved from Kephrath a few months after the birth of Izi-Mefkat. The little group of scribes were growing in skill almost daily as he organised them, and now offered scribal work of real quality to the elite families in and around Shalem.

Before another year was out he fully expected to receive instructions from the city ruler, a man whose predecessors had called themselves kings for many years. Knowing as he did the weight of tradition and history down in the Beloved Land, this title had seemed rather laughable to him at first. But, as he kept hearing, the great king by the River had withdrawn most of his officials and soldiers from the hill country, leaving an uneasy assortment of traders, land-owners and craftsmen behind. Meanwhile, these little rulers and city mayors were thriving, and it seemed all too likely that their dynasties would continue.

Shunaya stood up from her loom, stretched, then crossed over the room to hug him. He glanced across into the adjacent alcove; Izi-Mefkat was asleep, so he took the opportunity to share a longer kiss. The last remnants of former gratitude gifts had been spent on the loom and a selection of good quality raw materials, and Shunaya had used these to gain inroads into the wealthier parts of the town. They would find in the evenings that while Makty had been dealing with the town's noblemen in one way, Shunaya had been negotiating in the women's quarters of the same houses.

They settled themselves at the table and talked about the day. Makty was very excited but kept himself quiet as he listened first to Shunaya. He heard who she had met earlier in the day, how the conversations had gone, and how Shunaya now needed to find an assistant to work at the loom while she was out. Then it was his turn.

"Well, Shunaya, I have finished our final resting place. The last inscription and the last bit of painting. All complete."

She laughed, and squeezed his hand. "Well done. Though I hope neither of us will be living in it for a long time to come."

"Indeed yes. Many years from now. We are in no hurry."

"And so this means that our home is truly here, both in this world and the next."

He nodded. They sat together for a while, thinking about it. Makty had, as an act of faith, found a suitable piece of land almost as soon as they had moved. It had a short craggy bluff along the western edge, and although it was not much like the hillsides he had worked at back in the Beloved Land, it suited his purposes.

The tomb he had created had only a short run back into the rock. It lacked any sort of transverse corridor and had only a small pit for their bodies rather than a true vertical shaft. But it was good enough, and he had enjoyed working on the interior decorations in between other jobs over the months. The design was not quite traditional in appearance, not very conventional in subject matter, and was his attempt to capture something of their recent journeys.

"Of course it won't last in this climate the way it would back in Waset. Too damp, really. But it will do nicely for us."

"So what was in the extra bag you brought home?"

He grinned, retrieved the bag from the corner and started to open it.

"Periel, the wood-worker, made it for us. He said he has earned more silver this last half year than in the five years before that, and he wanted to show his gratitude."

He pulled a little box from the bag, unfastened the clasp, and opened it up. The inside of the lid was painted in the alternating colours of a Senet board, and a small cloth bag held the pieces. He took out a few of the cones and spools, placed them randomly on some of the squares. She laughed, picked up two of the pieces and set them down on the House of Life.

"It is beautiful. And very suitable. You must thank Periel from me tomorrow."

He took her hand where it still rested on the playing piece.

"You were right, Shunaya. All the pieces did come home in the end."

Notes

About the author

Richard Abbott has visited some of the places that feature in this story and others set in broadly the same region. As well as fictional accounts of the period, he also participates in the lively academic debate surrounding it.

Richard now lives in London, England. When not writing he works on the development and testing of computer and internet applications, and also creates mobile and tablet apps with a focus on the ancient world. One of these is the game of Senet. He enjoys spending time with family, walking and wildlife – ideally combining all three of those pursuits at the same time.

Look out for his other works, which include the following.

Fiction – full-length novels

- *In a Milk and Honeyed Land*, available from most online retailers, and general booksellers in

    - soft-cover (ISBN 978-1-4669-2166-5),
    - hard-cover (ISBN 978-1-4669-2167-2), and
    - ebook format (ISBN 978-1-4669-2165-8).

In case of difficulty please check the website http://www.kephrath.com for purchasing options. Feedback for this novel includes:

"the author is an authority on the subject, and it shows through the captivating descriptions of the ancient rituals, songs, village life, and even a battle scene... the story grabs hold of the imagination... satisfies as a love story, coming-of-age tale, and historical narrative. . . " (Blue Ink Review)

". . . The lives of these ordinary people are brought to life on the page in a way that's absorbing and credible. The changes that are going to take place in this area are quite incredible... a wonderous land that seems both alien and yet somehow familiar. . . " (Historical Novel Society UK Review)

Fiction – short stories

- *The Man in the Cistern*, a short story of Kephrath, published in ebook format by Matteh Publications and available at online retailers, ISBN 978-0-9545-5351-7 (kindle) or 978-0-9545-5354-8 (epub).

- *The Lady of the Lions*, a short story of Kephrath, published in ebook format by Matteh Publications and available at online retailers, ISBN 978-0-9545-5353-1 (kindle) or 978-0-9545-5355-5 (epub).

Non-fiction

- *Triumphal Accounts in Hebrew and Egyptian*, published in ebook format by Matteh Publications and available at online retailers, ISBN 978-0-9545-5352-4 (kindle) or 978-0-9545-5356-2 (epub).

About Matteh Publications

Matteh Publications is a small publisher based in north London offering a small range of specialised books, mostly in ebook form only. For information concerning current or forthcoming titles please see
http://mattehpublications.datascenesdev.com/.

Background and Glossary

Specific glossary for this story

There are only a few words and phrases that might seem unusual to a modern reader. It is, however, worth taking time to highlight some of the names that are used. To Egyptians, the Nile was simply "The River", though occasionally other descriptive words might be added, indicating the divine providence thought to be behind the Nile's bounty. Other rivers were seen as inferior imitations of the Nile, just as other countries were inferior as places to live.

Several names might be used for Egypt herself. The most common general name was *Kemet*, with a literal meaning of "The Black Land", referring to the fertile soil lavishly provided by the River. In contrast, the land either side of the Nile valley was "The Red Land" – *Desheret*, from *desher*, meaning red. The same word, with a slightly different visual representation, is used for the flamingo. These negative and uncouth associations of *Desheret* are why Makty-Rasut realises he cannot address Milashuniyet in this way if he is to keep her favour.

During the New Kingdom, the name which perhaps best captures the Egyptian attachment to their country was *Ta Meri* – "The Beloved Land". In many of the official texts and poems, this phrase is used to signal a nation that was strong, divinely favoured, and supremely worthy of loyalty. It is not just a simple alternative that could be exchanged directly for *Kemet*, but a term which carried a great many emotional overtones.

Ta Mefkat, where Milashuniyet was born, is part of what we now call the Sinai Peninsula. The name means "Land of Turquoise", and refers to the main commodity that Egypt extracted from this region. The best known source is at Serabit al-Khadim, which not only provided considerable quantities of turquoise for Egypt but has also given us a rich source of early alphabetic writing for scholars to study. The mining areas here, and at other similar places in the Sinai, were occupied by Egypt over a very wide span of years.

Within the Waset area, "The Place of Truth" is what we now call the Valley of the Kings, and "The Holiest Valley" is Deir el Bahri, with Hatshepsut's mortuary temple rising up against the rock face at its end. In Makty-Rasut's day this temple was a little over 250 years old.

The difficulty that Makty-Rasut has with Milashuniyet's name is with the -l- sound. Like a number of other languages, Egyptian does not distinguish visually between -l- and -r- signs. We do not actually know for sure that Egyptians had difficulty pronouncing these sounds as different, but the same sign is often used when foreign names with both sounds are written in Egyptian. The story presumes that Makty would struggle to say "Mila" rather than "Mira": to avoid the problem he comes up with a name that he can easily pronounce. The languages used in the province of Canaan, including biblical Hebrew as it developed a little later, did not have this difficulty, and have separate signs for both letters.

Town names are based on the ancient Egyptian ones, rather than modern ones derived from Greek or Arabic. *Waset* is modern Luxor, *Abedju* is Abydos, and *Min-Nefer* is Memphis, a little south of modern Cairo. *Per Bastet* is Bubastis. Further afield, *Djahy* is one of several names used by Egyptians for the Levant region, and usually indicates the area around Phoenicia, including the cities of Tyre and Sidon. *Ikaret* is known today as Ugarit.

Many of the personal names are taken from New Kingdom Egyptian texts. Others are made up, using many of the same patterns used in real names.

Senet

Senet, which plays a major part in this book both in actual and symbolic terms, is a real game. We have two main sources of information about the game: pictures in tombs, and actual boards or playing tokens found in archaeological digs. These locations inevitably pick out elite preoccupation with this game. The story supposes that the game was enjoyed much more extensively in other levels of society, rather like board games such as backgammon are today in many countries around the Mediterranean Sea. This is possible, but if so the fact is hidden from us.

At an elite level, the game had religious and spiritual overtones as well as providing direct entertainment. Tomb pictures sometimes show the deceased playing against one or other god. However, these pictures are not interpreted for us in context, and it is quite possible that the intent was simply to show how the justified individual – true of voice in Egyptian phraseology – had direct intimate communion with the gods. One suggestion is that Senet was also used as a form of divination, in the way that packs of playing cards are sometimes used for this purpose today.

Reny-Seneb, who Mentep and Makty talk about, was a real person whose tomb is located at Deir el-Bahri. This valley is best known today for Hatshepsut's temple, but Reny-Seneb dates from the 12th dynasty, several centuries before Hatshepsut reigned. His tomb contains various items of game paraphernalia. It is probable, though not certain, that he wrote about Senet as well as playing it. There are several copies of religiously inspired texts based on Senet from later years: these may well derive from a body of older material.

It is quite easy to get hold of Senet games today, as both physical sets and for electronic devices. DataScenes Development distributes a version for Android and Apple mobile phones and tablets which can be downloaded from the appropriate app stores.

The background

During what we call the New Kingdom – during which some of the best known pharaohs such as Thutmose III or Ramesses II reigned – Egypt controlled large parts of the Levant area. Their method of rule was unusual, but very effective. Most of their personnel and resources were concentrated in a few key locations, such as Gaza (*Gedjet*), and also at defensive points along the strategically important coastal road. Hardly anyone was stationed in the hill country or other outlying areas, though from time to time small garrisons of soldiers might be dispatched for particular purposes. Even more rarely, full-scale military campaigns were carried out.

Regional governors then imposed obedience and extracted revenue from other towns. Local rulers were allowed to keep their position, so long as they remained loyal and did not attempt to build up wider alliances with other rulers – they were strongly encouraged to stay independent of each other. In practice, this meant that the rulers became highly competitive, frequently accusing one another of disloyalty to the Egyptian authorities. In this way, the region was kept under control with relatively little expenditure. Indeed, official records show that the inflow of raw materials, people and luxury goods from these Asiatic provinces provided a considerable source of wealth for Egypt.

At one time scholars thought that this system collapsed extremely quickly, within a few decades after 1200 BCE or so, leaving essentially no Egyptian presence in Canaan. More recent careful investigation has shown that the actual situation was more complex. Egyptian rule in any direct sense was certainly over, and standing garrisons of troops were recalled. However, Egyptian influence remained considerably longer in the form of buildings, styles of pottery, and writing.

This author's main interest is in the written word, and here we find several fascinating issues. Firstly, the style of Egyptian writing we now call hieratic survived in the former province of Canaan for a long time, especially for technical information like weights and measures. In Egypt herself, writing style evolved from hieratic to demotic, but the older form remained in use in the province. The obvious conclusion is that the style was learned during the period of occupation, and stayed in use after that had ceased – it is like a fossil relic of this earlier time.

Now, learning hieratic is a process that needs good teachers and a scribal tradition. We do not have direct evidence for schools of this kind in the form of buildings or monuments. However, these little marks of numbers and letters, scratched on the surface of various everyday artefacts, show that scribes trained in the Egyptian manner were still carrying out their trade in Canaan. The novel uses phrases such as "quick scribal signs" for this writing style. This is in contrast to what Makty-Rasut considers "proper writing" – hieroglyphic – which would be used in Egypt for official or ceremonial purposes.

Next we have evidence from the biblical psalms, which date from rather later. Several critics have noticed that one group of these, those which are petitionary pleas for help in time of trouble, bear strong resemblance to earlier letters written by subordinates to their political superiors. A writing style originally used in the secular sphere for addressing someone of higher rank, was adopted for religious use addressing gods. This would seem quite an obvious idea for someone who has been trained in official protocol and is then asked to create spiritual songs.

However, the resemblance is stronger than that. Specific kinds of phrasing, and specific kinds of appeal for help, turn up in political letters from around 1350 BCE, and also in the earliest psalms from around 1000 BCE or so. Moreover, they do so in the same geographical location – Jerusalem (*Shalem*). This again suggests that there was a continuity of tradition that spanned those years.

In *Scenes from a Life* it is suggested that this link was set in place by an Egyptian scribe who found reasons of his own to move out to the province. Scribal teams in Egypt were well coordinated, with clear specialisation of skills, and it is easy to imagine that such a person would be able to organise and motivate a group of people in Jerusalem, whether Egyptian or native-born.

Jerusalem is mentioned in a number of New Kingdom Egyptian texts of approximately this era. However, archaeological finds recalling the period of Egyptian control are rare. One group of items was found in the area around the so-called "Garden Tomb" location, outside the old city walls to the north of the Damascus Gate. The finds are evidently Egyptian in nature, but establishing a date for them has been difficult. One view holds that they come from the reign of Ramesses II (a little earlier than this story) but other scholars argue for a later point in time. This debate continues without a clear sign of reaching a conclusion.

Egyptian dream interpretation

Egyptian dream interpretation appears entirely random if you see the texts just in translation, but in the original language it makes far more sense. It was largely based on ideas of wordplay – if you dreamed of one thing then the interpreter would think about other objects or situations that sounded similar or had similar word roots.

There was also, as with dream theory in other cultures, a strong emphasis on identifying whether the situation would turn out to be favourable or unfavourable for the dreamer. This second strand of interpretation has been largely ignored in *Scenes from a Life*, but in reality the priest Senenptah would routinely try to ascertain from Makty's dream accounts when an action should be taken or avoided to achieve a good outcome.

Now, interestingly, similar ideas are used in some modern schools of dream interpretation, especially those having a Jungian influence. In these, the unconscious processes active in dream sleep may well use word plays or visual puns to transfer meaning and significance to the conscious mind. So, hypothetically, dreaming of falling over – taking a trip – might suggest a journey, or even a drug experience. Of course, there are many other aspects to modern dream interpretation; this simply illustrates a point of contact across the years.

Returning to Makty-Rasut, the connection that Senenptah makes between white sandals and a journey is based on an actual dream text we have, specifically papyrus Chester Beatty III. This dates from less than a century before Makty's time, and was discovered at the royal workmen's village at Deir al-Medina, on the west bank of the Nile opposite Luxor and so quite close to Makty's home. It is currently in the British Museum. It contains a large number of single line interpretations, each of the form "If a man sees himself in a dream in [some situation] then: [interpretation]". Each interpretation has a brief summary as either GOOD or BAD, followed by a brief explanation. The words GOOD or BAD are picked out in red ink rather than the normal black.

The relevant line of this text is "If a man sees himself in a dream shod with white sandals, BAD; it means roaming the earth". Normally in Egyptian culture, roaming the earth would be perceived as BAD as it would mean being uprooted from the social network in which the person was embedded – family, friends, work, ancestral burials and so on. A journey would especially be seen as BAD if it involved travelling out of the Beloved Land, as it carried the risk of having to be buried outside the land's borders.

Anxiety about journeying outside the Beloved Land is one of the several themes of the Egyptian poem *The Tale of Sinuhe*. Sinuhe feels compelled to flee into exile, but dreads the thought of burial in a remote and rather uncivilised place. Others who hear of his situation urge him to find reconciliation while time remains. One of the great motifs of his eventual return to Egypt is the promise that a proper burial would again be possible. *The Tale of Sinuhe* was composed several centuries before the setting of this story, but remained popular for many years, and copies from the late New Kingdom have been found near Luxor, in particular at Deir al-Medina.

Senenptah feels able to offset the negative aspects of the sandals because of the fact that Makty-Rasut finds himself immediately after this in the river. Another line of the dream text reads "If a man sees himself plunging in the river, GOOD; it means absolution from all ills".

For those interested, Gardiner's 1935 translation of this dream text is freely available online at the Research Archives of the Oriental Institute, University of Chicago. A picture can be found on the British Museum web site.

The other word associations Senenptah makes for Makty are invented, but credible given the nature of the scheme of interpretation. Perhaps in time archaeologists will uncover an Egyptian text which confirms them! When Senenptah asks Makty if he has seen a royal sceptre, or a large dish, the words used sound like (and are spelled very similarly to) words for Asiatic and north respectively. For example, both north and dish sound something like *makhat*, though the signs used to draw the two words are a little different. These sorts of clues would suggest to the priest that Makty was being directed by his dreams to travel north into the Asiatic province, here called the Kinahny lands.

Many of the other details that are picked out in the dreams have a similar basis; others are just regular dream imagery that readers can enjoy deciphering for themselves.

Poetry and tomb writing

Tomb inscriptions are one of our main windows into Egyptian life at royal and elite levels. Tourists to Egypt, and visitors to museums all around the world, still look at these today. Here in London, the New Kingdom Egyptian galleries in the British

Museum provide excellent background material to this story, as well as being well worth a visit on their own account.

As Makty-Rasut comments to his friend Sanedjem-Keni, the royal tombs are focused almost entirely on formal religious themes. These are often individually expressed in different tombs, but display broadly the same ideas and images. This is because of the specific role that the ruler was expected to fulfil in the afterlife. A great deal depended on him carrying out the right actions in the right way, so the tomb decorations revolved around ensuring that he would be armed with accurate information for the task at hand.

The tombs of elite individuals lower down the social ladder – priests, high-ranking soldiers, city officials, and so on – are very much more varied. Some scenes are popular and appear often, such as a hunting scene of a married couple on a boat in marsh-lands. Others, however, are unique, and capture for us something of the particular life of an individual. If the person had carried out any sort of official duty then we expect to find something of this in the tomb record. In addition, lively and inventive images can pop up in surprising places. We learn far more about life in Egypt from these tombs than from those in the Valley of the Kings.

An important part of the tomb was the autobiography. This was not intended to be a dispassionate or balanced account of the person's life. Rather, it served as a kind of CV justifying to the gods why that individual should be allowed to enjoy the delights of the afterlife. These autobiographies therefore seem to us to be grossly self-congratulatory. In the early days of Egyptology, they were treated with great suspicion, or dismissed as having no historical merit. Nowadays they are regarded with more sympathy, and sifted for nuggets of value in amongst the generally up-beat expressions.

In *Scenes From a Life*, the snippets at the start of each even-numbered chapter are an invented but credible tomb autobiography for Makty-Rasut. Each one speculates how he might have presented for eternity the events described in that chapter. In contrast, the poems at the start of the odd-numbered chapters are taken from, or adapted from, one or other of the love poems which have been found in Egypt. Many of these were discovered near Luxor, in particular among the workmen's houses or nearby tombs at Deir al-Medina.

When reading translations of ancient Egyptian material, it is always worth remembering that the plain text version we read is only part of the whole. It is loosely similar to hearing the dialogue from a film soundtrack without seeing the pictures, since our written form is almost completely divorced from any underlying visual content. It does not really matter to us, and is largely overlooked, that the letter "A" originally derived from the head and horns of an ox. Today we routinely separate out writing from illustrations.

But with Egyptian writing, the visual and textual parts of an inscription were a unified whole. Since most letter signs still clearly showed their origins as pictures of real-world objects, it is easy to integrate the two. There are many places where one sign in the written text is placed so as to also form part of a composite pictorial scene. In other places, design elements in the picture can be read as words or suggestive puns.

The "hunting in the marsh" scenes mentioned above are loaded with such elements, indicating that the picture is not really about catching ducks or fish. The main message told by the visual metaphors is one of love, passion and fertility. A scribe such as Makty-Rasut would show his skill by weaving in such "hidden" stories in amongst a more simple surface-level picture.

A brief regional history

Egypt's New Kingdom lasted from around 1550 BCE to around 1050 BCE, and was generally characterised by strong and warlike pharaohs. At the start of this period Egypt conducted a successful campaign against Asiatic kings who had built their own capital in the Delta region and dominated the Nile Valley from there. Successive Egyptian rulers then pushed the borders of the region under their rule further north, and consolidated control over the territory gained. The province of Canaan became an important source of raw materials which were lacking in Egypt herself, and also of personnel. Canaanites were regularly taken into Egypt as slaves or hostages, but once there many of them integrated fully into society and, on occasion, ended up with high rank.

To the north, the Hittite empire was expanding from central Anatolia at the same time, and the two powers collided on several occasions. Perhaps the best known is the Battle of Qadesh, between Ramesses II and Muwatallis II. Although both sides claimed this as a victory – Ramesses in particular ordered multiple versions of the victory inscription to be carved at locations up and down Egypt – it seems clear that it was inconclusive. The most likely reconstruction is that the personal courage and charisma of Ramesses turned what could easily have been a major defeat into a draw. The two empires subsequently agreed a peace treaty a few years later, complete with diplomatic marriages, and remained on good terms thereafter.

However, times were changing. The Late Bronze Age, in which the Levant region was divided into independent city states, each serving as vassal to a major regional power such as Egypt, was drawing to an end. Critics dispute as to what caused the enormous political and social transformation between the Late Bronze and early Iron ages: all agree that it happened. Proposed causes have included climate change, large-scale migration of formerly settled tribes, and new military technology.

At the time of writing, researchers have investigated pollen counts in the mud below the Sea of Galilee to deduce that there was a series of poor harvests caused by drought. This in turn led to widespread hardship and forced migration of refugee groups. The Hittite Empire collapsed first, along with wealthy trading cities such as Ugarit along the Levant coast. The Egyptians survived, but only by withdrawing almost completely within their own borders. The province of Canaan was left to its own devices.

This power vacuum was filled by several competing kingdoms, each trying to seize land from each other. Some of these – Edom, Moab, Ammon – were east of the Jordan river. Others, including the Philistines and the newly emerging Israelites, were to the west. The sibling struggle between groups who were ethnically very similar to one another continued for many years, until finally, during the ninth and eighth centuries BCE, the Assyrian empire spread across from the east to swallow them all up.

In terms of the historical timeline suggested within the Hebrew Bible, the time of Egyptian withdrawal and the rise of new small-scale nations corresponds to the book of Judges, leading up to the reigns of the first kings. It is a confusing period, in which it is difficult to get a clear sense of how events meshed together. Alliances that seemed reliable might suddenly dissolve. The Egyptians had never maintained a strong presence in the hill country, so it is unsurprising that only scattered references can be found to Egypt in this biblical book. In the early Israelite monarchy, a few individual Egyptians are named, but for many years their once-strong nation appears only as a rather distant memory. Only later on do particular pharaohs emerge again from their borders for brief campaigns of conquest.

Although Egypt's actual presence in Canaan is remembered only indistinctly, the signs of the Beloved Land can still be traced through some of the written forms chosen for biblical poetry and prose, and letters traced out on archaeological finds.

Extract from *In a Milk and Honeyed Land*

There were four children of the god that year. I remember hearing that, many times over, through all my growing years, though it was a long time before I understood what it meant. That year was a unique year, a unique time to be alive. There were more of us then than any other year, before or since. Perhaps such a year will never come again, not now the hill country is changing and the new houses are leaping up in little clearings everywhere. Indeed the whole land is changing. Had I wanted, they would have built for me one of these houses in whatever village I chose, as a reward for all my efforts. Some would once have said that this would have been the reward for betrayal rather than the wages of labour.

But even these newcomers could see that my place was in the great house beside the high place of Kephrath, among the families of my birth. The place where I lived and laboured, loved and learned loss. So, whether through gratitude or pity, here I live still. I am at home among my people to be sure, but I am also a stranger in the eyes of these strangers. They even tie their kefs differently to us, bundled oddly around their head. I have not troubled to learn their style. I am strange here to them, though I have lived here my whole life, and the land is becoming strange to me, though I know every hill and valley in it. They still need us to uphold the new alliances, but the need sits uncomfortably with some of them.

I feel, however, some kinship with them. They have had something of an uncertain, shifting childhood, and have chosen to be here, to live here in this place that is beautiful but not overflowing with wealth. They have been brought up singing one song, and then have tried to learn another. They have found themselves willing to unite with people who they had not planned to meet, and who they came upon by chance. Though their customs are odd, their yearning is not. They feel, like me and like my own people, the hunger that comes with displacement, and the thirst that impels one to find a home.

This story tells of we three who lived past infancy, and the things that we did and said in those days. Although there were four of us born, Mahur was a sickly boy who died before the year of his birth had turned. Then there were three, for a little while. Then there were only two. We were the linen sashes that tied up all the leather-bundled tales of our village life. I remember those bundles that were carried on the backs of the Mitsriy scribes. They still travel the roads down near the coast, still with their escort of bowmen, but they have not come up this way now for many years. The traders who brought little caravans of donkeys up and down the great ridgeway road, or across the rough hillside tracks still come to us, but less often now, and at erratic intervals instead of every season.

I have been seer to my people, and sung the songs of the great cycle around the stones of the high place. Now I tell tales. I have watched over the threshold that divides the living and the dead, and although I am still doorkeeper in my own house, it is becoming a different house, a different life.

There were four children of the god that year. We were reckoned as once-orphaned, living each in the house of our mothers, brought up as foster child by their husbands, with half-brothers and half-sisters according to the overflow of life in that family. We did not understand what it was to be a child of the god for many years—the words that had meant so much to empty wombs passed us by in the silent air. The words meant nothing, but some of us grew familiar with estrangement as we grew up, looks of darkness and rejection from unwilling surrogate fathers, a sense of displacement amongst our peers, mixed pride and disdain. Others found happy acceptance. We still clung to each other. This is our story.

The Man in the Cistern – a short story of Kephrath

The Man in
the Cistern

A Short Story of Kephrath
~ Richard Abbott ~

Set about ten years after the conclusion of the full-length novel *In a Milk and Honeyed Land*, this short story follows Damariel and Nepheret as they tackle a new challenge to the four towns. A group of migrants has set up an encampment just down the trackway towards Shalem. What are their intentions? Do they come in peace or war?

The Lady of the Lions – a short story of Kephrath

The Lady of the Lions

A Short Story of Kephrath
~ Richard Abbott ~

Set about one hundred and fifty years before the full-length novel *In a Milk and Honeyed Land*, this short story is based on two historical letters written by a Canaanite woman to the great king in Egypt. The people of the four towns are being threatened by a band of rebels disdainful of the provincial ruler. Kephrath and her sister towns are outmatched by the raiders - can they secure help before their deadline runs out?

Triumphal Accounts in Hebrew and Egyptian

Triumphal Accounts in
Hebrew and Egyptian

~ Richard Abbott ~

This ebook contains the text approved by the external and internal PhD examiners for a thesis carried out under the supervision of Dr John Bimson at Trinity College, Bristol, England. It will be of interest to those who wish to explore cross-cultural connections between early Israel and New Kingdom Egypt, as expressed in triumphal literature. The thesis looks at issues to do with the creation of poetry in each of those cultures, and the links between them, as well as investigating when appropriate cross-cultural contacts might have happened to forge common links between them.